"It may be hard for some to accept that the same writer who recently snuck into the American canon as a visionary and paranoid pop surrealist also penned a half dozen or more proletarian-realist novels set in the California of the '50s and early '60s, the best of which occupy a region demarcated by Richard Yates on one side and Charles Willeford on another. But accept it."
—Jonathan Lethem

FURTHER PRAISE FOR PHILIP K. DICK

"A curious, oddly compelling book . . . Turning each page . . . the reader feels an odd suspense and a reluctance to abandon these four unpredictable but somehow endearing people."
—*Booklist* on *Puttering About in a Small Land*

"[Dick is a] dystopian master."
—*Publishers Weekly* on *In Milton Lumky Territory*

"Like Al Miller in his more realistic moments . . . Dick the novelist was loath to surrender to the convenience of a comforting consensus. However isolated his views left him, whatever pessimistic conclusions they seemed to yield, he was determined to write stories that gave an honest account of the world he inhabited." —*The New York Review of Science Fiction* on *Humpty Dumpty in Oakland*

"Remarkable . . . echoes of Dick's contemporaries such as Ralph Ellison, Richard Yates, Rod Serling, Raymond Chandler, and early Kurt Vonnegut, Jr., resonate, and a bonus exists in Dick's impeccable eye for detail. . . . Dick fans will be in rapture." —*Publishers Weekly* on *Voices From the Street*

"Despite its period context, *Voices* is surprisingly relevant to today. . . . Dick predicted the moral landscape of the future, if not its outward technology, with frightening accuracy. Highly recommended."
—*Starlog* on *Voices From the Street*

PHILIP K. DICK

THE MAN
WHOSE TEETH WERE ALL
EXACTLY ALIKE

A TOM DOHERTY ASSOCIATES BOOK   NEW YORK   TOR®

This is a work of fiction. All of the characters, organizations, and events portrayed in this novel are either products of the author's imagination or are used fictitiously.

THE MAN WHOSE TEETH WERE ALL EXACTLY ALIKE

A Tor Book
Published by Tom Doherty Associates, LLC
175 Fifth Avenue
New York, NY 10010

www.tor-forge.com

Tor® is a registered trademark of Tom Doherty Associates, LLC.

ISBN 978-0-7653-2306-4 (hc)
ISBN 978-0-7653-1693-6 (tp)

First Hardcover Edition: February 2009
First Trade Paperback Edition: March 2010

Printed in the United States of America

0 9 8 7 6 5 4 3 2 1

for Vincent F. Evans

THE MAN
WHOSE TEETH WERE ALL
EXACTLY ALIKE

1

The West Marin Water Company repairman kicked among the rocks and leaves, finding the pipe and the break in it. A county truck had backed over the pipe and broken it by its weight. The truck had come to trim the trees along the road; a crew had been up in the cypresses for the last week, clipping branches. It was the crew who called the water company, phoning from the fire station down to Carquinez where the water company kept its offices.

Although this break had caused him to make a twenty-mile trip, he did not feel sore at the truck. The water pipes were old and brittle. A break appeared at least once a week; sometimes a cow put her foot into a pipe, or sometimes a root forced a pipe open.

The repairman had said many times to customers along the line that the pipes should be replaced. He made no secret about his feelings. He said, too, that the man who owned the water company should put on a booster pump in summer when the water pressure got low. And he had told the owner that. The water company did not give a profit to its owner; the man lost money each year, and would have liked to sell it. He put as little as possible into the upkeep.

Now the repairman climbed a ridge. He had found the break; a dark stain of water had spread out over the ground between two cypresses. But he took his time.

Voices carried to him through the trees, the sound of children. He saw a man leading a group of youngsters, pointing and talking; the repairman recognized him as Mr. Wharton, the fourth-grade teacher. An excursion by the fourth grade. On the shoulder of the road a station wagon had been parked, not far from the water company truck. Mr. Wharton and his children came along the same path that the repairman had followed, and presently the two men stood face to face.

"Another break," the repairman said.

"Yes, I'm not surprised," Mr. Wharton said.

"You on your way to the lime pits?" The pits were a quarter mile in from the road, along the path. Each year, as the repairman knew, Mr. Wharton took his fourth grade to view them.

"It's that time again," Mr. Wharton said, smiling. His round red young face was flushed from walking, and his forehead shone.

The repairman said, "Don't let them kids tramp on the pipe."

They both laughed at that, the idea that the rotten old cast-iron pipe would break under the feet of schoolchildren. But perhaps it was not so funny. They both became serious, while the children roamed around among the trees pelting each other with pine cones, yelling and chattering.

"What do you think of Bob Morse saying that the water is contaminated?" Mr. Wharton said.

"No doubt," the repairman said. "No doubt it is."

Seeing that the repairman had not become angry, Mr. Wharton continued, "It's sometimes so muddy you can't see to the bottom of the bowl. It stains the toilets."

"That's mostly rust from the pipes," the repairman said. "I don't doubt there's nothing to worry about that." He scratched at the dirt with his toe. Both men gazed down at the ground. "What bothers me more," the repairman said, "is seepage into the pipes from people's septic tanks. There isn't an uncontaminated well around here, and don't let nobody tell you different."

Mr. Wharton nodded.

"Don't never sink a well in this area," the repairman said. "I know a lot of people, displeased with the company water being all sludgy with rust, put down wells, and got nice clean pure-looking water. But that water's ten times contaminated. The only contamination you could get in company water — I don't care how bad it looks; looks ain't what counts — what contaminates it is seepage, and that takes a lot of time even through these god damn rotten old pipes." He had begun getting worked up about it, and his voice rose.

"I see," Mr. Wharton said in agreement.

They walked along a distance, the children following.

"Nice day, with no wind," Mr. Wharton said.

"Cooler here," the repairman said. "Nearer the coast. I come out from San Rafael. It's really hot there."

"Wow, I can't stand that dry valley heat," Mr. Wharton said.

Both men were used to saying such things again and again, with almost everyone they met during the course of the day. Sometimes they discussed what medicines Dr. Terance, the M.D. of the area, prescribed, and also what medicines the pharmacist at Carquinez gave people who couldn't afford Dr. Terance. The doctor was a young man, very busy, who drove a new Chrysler and was never in the area on weekends. If there was an auto accident on the weekends, the injured were out of luck. They had to be taken across Mount Tamalpais, all the way to Mill Valley.

"Well," Mr. Wharton said, "we're off to the graveyard."

"Pardon?" the repairman said.

"Next stop is the graveyard. Didn't you know there was a little old graveyard near here? I always take my class to visit it. There are stones dating back a hundred and fifty years."

To Wharton, the history of this area justified living here. All the ranchers had collections of arrowheads, awls, hand axes, made by the Indians. He himself had a great collection of obsidian arrow and spearheads, shiny black and very hard. Labeled and mounted, his collection, under glass, was kept at the grammar school, in the outer lobby, for visiting parents to see.

In many respects Wharton was the authority in the area on Indian artifacts. He subscribed to *Scientific American*, kept snakes at his house — in his work room, along with his rock and fossil collections, his moon snail shells and worm castings, shark eggs. Of all his possessions, his trilobite fossil ranked in his mind as the finest. But for demonstration, either in his classroom or to visitors in his home, his radioactive rocks took the prize: in ultraviolet light (he owned a lamp with such a bulb) the rocks glowed various colors. When anyone found an odd rock or plant or bird egg or what seemed to be a fossil or Indian artifact, they brought it to him. Almost always he could tell if the find was important.

The little old graveyard, mostly abandoned, known only to a few adults in the community, certainly was historic; members of the original families to settle in the area were buried there. The old Swiss and Italian names. Some of the stones had fallen over. Gophers had made the ground uneven and had killed every plant except the wild rosebushes that overgrew the higher part of land. The oldest graves were marked with wooden crosses, carved amateurishly by hand; some of these had disappeared down into the grass and oats.

Now and then people — from outside the area, evidently — came and left flowers on the graves. Each year when he took his class here he found mayonnaise jars and glasses scattered about with dried stalks and blossoms sticking up from them or hanging over the sides.

As Wharton and his class made their way along the path in

the direction of the graveyard, one of the little girls came up beside the teacher and began talking. After rambling on several topics she came at last to ask, in a halting manner, if he believed in ghosts. Each year, on this trip, at least one member of the class became apprehensive; he was accustomed to it, and had his answers.

Speaking to all of them, Wharton recalled to them that in Sunday school — every child in the area went to Sunday school — they were taught about heaven. If the souls of the dead went up to heaven, how could there be ghosts haunting the earth? He pointed out that the soul had come from God — at least, so the children had been taught — and naturally went back. It was as silly to worry about the souls of the dead as the souls of the not yet born, of the generations to come.

And, stopping, he pointed out something more, a fact more along his own vocational lines.

Look, he told them, indicating the trees and brush around them, the soil itself. Don't consider merely the departed humans; consider all life, millions of years of living forms that had come and gone. Where had they gone? Back into the ground. In fact, that was what the ground was — a dense, rich layer from which new life came, lived out its span, and then sank back. All of it was natural and regular. The dead had merged. From bacteria to plants to small animals to man: all lay beneath their feet. The past. And how good it was; what a fine system. Halting, he showed them a compost pile, the moldering leaves piled at the base of a madrone tree. And the white chalky fungus. Sliding his fingers into the mixture, half soil, half rotting plant fibers, he showed the class what fertile, moist stuff it was; he had them smell it, touch it. Man was no different. This process involved our own ancestors, too. His insight, as in past years, calmed the children. Their apprehension, the rapid, jerky talking and giggling, ceased.

This was why he had brought them here: to acquaint them with this satisfying situation, the cycle of growing things that included them, too. Don't be afraid of nature, he told them. And remember — everything that happens is natural. There's nothing outside of nature. And so, in his own way, without denying anything that the children had been taught in catechism and Sunday school, he diminished their superstitions.

Being a grammar school teacher in a small rural town had made him tactful. He dealt with parents who were farm people, fundamentalists in religion as well as in politics and all social ideas. In his class he had great lumpy twelve-year-old boys from the ranches, near morons who could barely be taught to read. They would eventually go back to the ranch and become milkers; their lives were mapped out. And also, in his class, he had bright children from families who had moved out from the city. And ambitious children whose fathers were small retailers, dentists, or nearby professional men. There were even a few children from very wealthy families that owned houses with beach frontage.

Ahead, the granite tops of monuments could be seen, the largest of the markers. The most ornate.

But Mr. Wharton and his fourth graders were not interested in the lofty crypt and statues at the center of the graveyard; they had come to poke around for the oldest graves. Those at the edges, some of them even beyond the wooden fence that surrounded the graveyard. Had those tiny ancient markers slid down the slope, from the graveyard proper to the cow pasture of the McRae ranch? Or, when the fence was put up a dozen or so years ago, had the builders failed to see such meager graves and had ignored them?

A few cows watched the class as Mr. Wharton opened the gate. The cows could not come in the graveyard.

Already some of the boys had scampered to the first grave and were shouting out the date on the headstone. "1884!" they yelled, pointing. "Look, Mr. Wharton!"

In his car, the area Realtor, Leo Runcible, drove an elderly couple along the mesa road. Both old people murmured complainingly about the wind and the damp; they did not think that it would be so healthy, here, as inland. Too many ferns, the old man had said as they walked up to inspect a house. From his senility he had emerged for a moment to make that acute observation; where there were ferns there was always constant dampness.

"Well," Runcibile said, "there's no problem, and I'll tell you why. For the simple reason that I can find you several homes in excellent shape, in your price range, in dry open farm country." And now they were going to see those homes.

But of course those were farm homes, not at all fashionable, as had been the ones on the east side of the Bolinas Ridge, which he had just shown them. And they were not in good shape; Runcible knew that, and he knew that to this old couple, the farm houses would appear no more than shacks, ill-kept and dirty. The houses had been built by mill workers and county road workers. Very low-class. On mud sills. He did not like showing them; he avoided taking the listings. For god's sake, he thought. Are you going to stand out in the yard at sunset, getting in the fog and wind? Or are you going to be indoors, in your living room, where you can heat it up? He phrased that notion in his mind as he drove, knowing that these old people would not buy one of the farm shacks. If he sold them anything, it would be back at the Ridge, on the hillside, a stucco or shingle house. Not a white clapboard shack.

The old man said, "Will these places you're going to show us have a lot of land?"

"No," Runcible said. "And if you're wise, you won't *want* a lot of land." Both old people listened obediently, held by the strength of his tone. "When a man gets to his mellow years he wants to start enjoying himself. Not slave to ten acres of weeds that the county requires him to keep cleared every year because of fire hazard. I'll tell you something; there's a list of over forty weeds that the county forbids you to allow to grow on your land. You have to know what each weed looks like, and by golly, they better not catch you with those weeds, or it's quite a fine."

The old woman said, "Why does the county care?"

"Danger to cattle," Runcible said. "You'll see the list posted in the post office. Noxious weeds. They spread."

The houses he would soon be showing them were jumbled along several county roads, each house visible to the next. In the yards of several, rusting car bodies had been piled; he noticed that with anger each time he drove by here. But now there was a state law . . . he reflected that perhaps he should write to the highway patrol or to somebody in San Rafael, giving the names of the offenders in the area. Ruins property value, he thought. What do such *zwepps* care about their neighbors?

"What line of work are you in, Mr. Diters?" he asked the old man.

"I'm retired now," the old man said. "I was in the banking business. With the American Trust Company for many years and before that with Crocker."

The old couple had specified that their house cost not more than nine thousand. But Runcible judged that they could be bumped up to ten or even ten-five. He felt cheerful, because he had several houses in that price range. And the weather was nice. It was easier to show, in summer; the ground was not muddy, the air not cold.

To their right, brown fields passed. A bridge over reeds and water.

"What about utilities in this area?" Mrs. Diters said. "There is no natural gas, is there?"

"No, this is a butane area," Runcible said. "There's electricity from the PG&E. Water comes from the West Marin Water Company, over at Carquinez."

"Garbage pick up?" the old man asked.

"Every week. And septic tank service."

"That's right," the old woman said. "No sewers out here."

"This is the country," Runcible said. "But remember: no city taxes to pay. And you've got a good fire department located at Carquinez, plus a deputy sheriff, a doctor, dentist, grocery stores, drug stores, post office — everything you'll need. Do you want to be able to walk into town, or drive?" They had showed up at Runcible Realty driving an old black Packard, very well kept up.

"We might drive in to San Rafael to shop once a week," Mr. Diters said. "I think it would be cheaper than shopping locally."

"Just a minute," Runcible said. "Would it be cheaper?" This was something he had never liked, this taking of business out of the area, away from the local merchants. These are your neighbors, he thought. Or will be. And there's the cost of gasoline. Plus the time taken in going over Mount Tamalpais. An all day trip. "You'll find the services you need here," he said. "And reasonable. And I'll tell you one thing; if you've never lived in a small community before, you're going to discover something wonderful. The merchants here stand back of what they sell. They have to. They know they'll be seeing you again; maybe your child goes to Bluebirds with their child. And even if you don't have children, you probably know everybody in the community, and if you're badly treated in a local store, it's going to get around. Bear that in mind. There's no impersonal service; it's like the good old days. All done on a man-to-man business."

As he talked, he drove from the county road up onto a dirt drive. Ahead, behind bamboo, was the Peterson shack; grubby children played among the overflow from a trash barrel.

"Of course," he said in a lower voice, "this section here isn't part of the better community. Most of the men down here are part-time laborers. But they're good honest people." Stopping the car, he opened the door. Mrs. Peterson had stepped out on the porch of the one-story four room house; she waved to him and he waved back. A dog appeared, barking.

Not getting from the car, Mr. Diters said, "I don't think this would be the place for us."

"No," his wife agreed. Clearly, they did not want to look at it; they wanted to leave.

"It's reasonably priced," Runcible said, enjoying the situation. It was your idea to come here, he said to himself. When I'm finished showing you around Poor Man's Hollow, you'll be glad to buy a house up on the Ridge.

"It's so barren," Mrs. Diters said.

With a touch of compassion, he said to them, "It is a little lonely out here, at first. But you get accustomed to it. People are friendly. They'll always give you a helping hand. Nobody locks their doors." He started up the car and drove on.

In gratitude, the two old people bobbed their heads.

Runcible himself had come to this area as a stranger. He had lived in Los Angeles before World War Two. In 1940 he had gone into the Navy, and by 1944 he had gotten command of a sub chaser operating off the coast of Australia. His greatest glory had come in that year; as he told it, he was the "only Jew in the world to sink a Jap sub on Yom Kippur." After the war he had gone into real estate with a partner in San Francisco. In 1955 he had bought a summer cabin in Carquinez; he wanted to be near the water, and he had at once organized a yacht club — actually, revived an older yacht club that had fallen into disuse. In 1957, three years ago, he had moved his office to Carquinez. His competition was a slow, flabby local named Thomas, who had sold real estate and insurance in Carquinez unopposed for thirty-five years and was due (according to Runcible) to die. Thomas still handled the sale of houses by the older inhabitants to other older inhabitants, but Runcible Realty got all the new people coming into the area, young and old.

His ads in the San Rafael newspapers had attracted many homebuyers who otherwise would never have heard of Carquinez, which was slightly north of Bolinas on the ocean coast, cut off from the rest of Marin County by Mount Tamalpais. At one time, no one would have thought of trying to live on the west side of the mountain while working in San Francisco or the flat part of the county. But roads were improving. And so were cars. And more and more people were moving into Marin County each month. The large towns had already become overcrowded, and property prices were going up.

"Such nice trees," Mrs. Diters said. Now they had driven back into the woods once more. "The shade is nice, after the sun."

Along the road a group of children walked, following a man whom Runcible recognized. His own child was in this group, his nine-year-old son Jerome. The teacher, Mr. Wharton, carefully waved his group back, away from the passing car; the children halted on the grassy shoulder, and some of them, recognizing the Studebaker, waved. He saw his son's face light up, and then Jerome's arm whipped up and down.

"Out for a hike," Runcible said to the Diterses. "The fourth grade from our grammar school." He felt pride, a relaxed pleasure, at the sight of the hands waving at him, his son's smile, and then, as Mr. Wharton recognized him, the teacher's nod of greeting.

When you've lived here a while, Runcible thought, they will wave at you, too. That would please you, you two fragile lonely old city people, at the end of your life, yearning for a place in which to belong, to be safe and comfortable and wanted.

What a favor I would be doing you, he thought. To locate you here in the area. Where everyone knows everyone else. He waved long and soberly at the fourth grade of the Carquinez Grammar School, and the Diterses fixed their eyes on him. What hunger there. The envy.

He knew for certain that he would sell them a house. Perhaps on this trip. It was in the bag.

2

At the door of the ground-floor workshop, Walter Dombrosio set down the two cans of enamel. To the men at the lathe he said, "You got the game on? Willy fell down just now."

The clean-up boy, standing with his pan full of wood shavings, said, "Anyhow, the Giants scored."

"That new second baseman is really hot," one of the workmen said. They had started up the lathe; its whine put an end to the talk. Both Dombrosio and the clean-up boy waited, and then when the noise ceased, the conversation resumed.

"Boy, I'll tell you," Dombrosio said. "It'd kill me to fall down in front of forty thousand fans." He did not actually care about baseball, but he felt required to mention the game when he came downstairs here, to the shop; he showed them that he, too, followed the game. That in spite of the fact that he worked upstairs and wore a suit and tie he was no different from them. "He's trying too hard," Dombrosio said. "It proves there's such a thing as trying too hard."

The workman nodded, but once more the lathe started up. They did not care about his opinions; feeling his face redden, Dombrosio picked up his cans of enamel and moved toward the stairs. Smarting somewhat, he passed on back upstairs.

Here, on the main floor with its ceiling lost in the rafters, fluorescents on stems did the trick; no sunlight up here, as in the workshop. Cool and dim in the corners . . . the cellotex kept sounds from echoing and gave the premises that modern quality, that taste. An outfit that conceived new packages for rice and beer could certainly dress itself properly. Even here, in a warehouse on the San Francisco waterfront. The bare wooden beams; it all fitted in. At the front, the receptionist's desk. And the display of samples: *their* commodities.

He himself had installed the cellotex and done the painting. Oddly, the cellotex had so diffused the sound of the receptionist's electric typewriter that no one could guess how large the place was. The sound appeared to recede. But actually Lausch Company was small. Doors that might have opened into labs actually opened onto storage closets. Now, with the enamel, he entered the secret area where the new containers were designed. But even this, the principal area, was no larger than the ground area of a ladies' tea shop. And the desks filled it. The designers, all three of them, with their easels.

At the first desk sat a designer looking as if he had renounced his responsibilities; on the work-table before him Lucky Lager beer cans hid him. Being upright, the cans appeared full. And the shiny metal tops had not been punctured.

"Hi, Walt," Bob Fox said, smiling up at him. Lifting a beer can he offered it to Dombrosio. "Join me."

The cans, of course, were cement. Dombrosio accepted one; it felt heavy and inert, unconvincing to the touch. Only visually did it succeed, but that was enough. In a photograph, or on the shelf of their simulated grocery store, it would appear genuine; agents from the Lucky Lager Company could use it as a basis of decision when the time came either to accept or reject this new container design.

Holding the beer can as if drinking from it, Dombrosio

joined Fox in the ritual customary with the two of them, the fanciful consumption of the nonexistent contents of their containers. Some days it was beer; other days they ate invisible cereal, ice cream, frozen vegetables, smoked pretend cigarettes — once, even presented the receptionist with a pair of nylon stockings that she could not see. Land of make-believe . . .

"Not too warm for you, is it?" Fox said, indicating the beer cans. "There's some in the refrigerator, if you prefer."

"No," he said. "This is fine."

Taking the beer can he absently walked through the room, toward his own bench.

"My artifact," Fox said, following him to retrieve the can.

Dombrosio returned it, seating himself at his desk and once more picking up his own work where he had left off.

"What's that you're doing?" Fox said. He reached down and picked up a break-mold made of plaster; expertly, he studied it. "I'm not familiar with this project. This isn't the bumper-guard for that little French car, is it?"

"No," Dombrosio said, taking the mold back. "It's something I'm doing on my own time." He explained, "It's a gag."

"Ah," Fox said, nodding knowingly. "Another of your practical jokes." Another designer, Pete Quinn, had stopped momentarily, and Fox said to him, "Remember this guy and his gag about Henry Ford?" He went on, then, to repeat Dombrosio's tale of madcap college escapades.

In those days, back in the 1940s, Walt Dombrosio had known a number of men slightly older than himself who had gone to work at Dearborn for the Ford Motor Company. At that time he had had a workshop in his garage, at home, and he had made himself a costume. First, a rubber mask that gave him a greenish cadaverous face, with protruding teeth, sunken cheeks, hair like moss dribbled across his forehead. Then a faded frock coat, a cane, spats, black oxfords. Groping along, he had invaded the houses of the several Ford designers, looking to them, in the first horrified moment, like the Old Man himself come back from the grave.

A hobby, then. But a business now.

"I'd like to have seen those guys' faces," Fox finished. "When Walt came in, tapping at the door and drooling and mumbling, poking around sort of blindly." He laughed, and so did Quinn.

"What other gags did you pull?" Quinn asked. He was the newest of the designers, having come to work only a month or so ago.

"Hell," Dombrosio said, "I pulled so many I can't remember them all. That Ford gag was nothing. I'll tell you one that was really one."

This gag had been a cruel one, and he knew it. When he told it, he altered it so that it became much more original and much funnier; he made it, in the telling, become jolly. The two men, listening now, put on appreciative smiles, and that goaded him into even further ornamentation. He found himself gesturing, painting in the air the shape of the gag; it became three-dimensional for all of them.

When he had finished, and Fox and Quinn had gone off, he sat at his desk alone, feeling let down.

First of all, he felt shame at having embellished the story. While talking he could let the excitement carry him away, but afterward, left by himself as he was now, he had no emotion, no involvement, to protect him. For one thing — from the practical standpoint alone — he faced the prospect of becoming known as a bullshitter. Perhaps, among the others at Lausch Company, he had already gotten that reputation; the men went off laughing at his story, but as soon as they were out of his sight they winked at each other and said what he had heard said of others: that they could not be trusted. And of course it was important to be trusted. In matters of veracity especially.

A man who did not narrate the truth perhaps could not distinguish the truth, he reflected. So their minds might work, when applied to him and his tales. And in his work, being able to tell fact from fiction had grave economic significance — at least by extension.

Sitting at his desk, he tried — as he often did — to put himself in their places; he tried to imagine how he looked to them. Tall, no doubt, with a bulging forehead, hair beginning to thin. Glasses too dark and heavy, giving him that "double-domed" appearance, as his wife put it. Somewhat of a scholarly manner, the intense, worried expression.

Sliding his chair back from his desk, he glanced to see if he was unobserved. He was. So, cautiously, he put his hand down and reached inside his trousers. Many times, over the months, he had done this. Examining his groin, his attention attracted there by a jolt of pain. While carrying the cans of paints he had felt that pain again, and now he had to see; he could not resist.

No, there was no protrusion at his groin. No puffy, doughlike swelling off to one side. He caressed the familiar region, disliking his own flesh. How little he enjoyed doing this, but how necessary it was. Suppose, one day, after a pain, he did find that swelling once more, as he had, years ago? What then? An operation, at last?

The hernia was probably gone. But not absolutely. And, even if it was healed, it might return. Overexertion could bring it back; he might lift cartons too heavy, or reach up to screw in a lightbulb . . . and the dreadful tearing would once more occur — followed by more years of belt-wearing, or — the long-postponed operation.

And the risk, the terrible risk of the operation, was that it might make him sterile. He, with no children, yet; sterile before he had even begun.

As he sat indecisively rubbing his groin, a flash of motion from the corner of his eye caught his attention; someone was coming to his desk. He jerked his hand from beneath his trousers, but at the same moment the person appeared at the desk, halting before him as his hand came out. Knowing that he had been seen he felt terrible guilt, a sense of childhood shame . . . the person, a woman, too. His face flushing, he glanced away, catching only the sight of a woman's coat, purse, the smartly-dressed short-haired woman — and then he realized that it was his wife. Sherry had come by the office; here she was. Now he looked up and found her staring at him. His guilt grew worse; he knew that it showed on his face.

"What were you doing?" she said.

He said, "Nothing."

"Is that what you men do down here during the day?"

Head down, he sat clasping and unclasping his hands.

"I came by to get a check cashed," Sherry said merrily. "I'm going to get my hair cut and have some lunch."

"How'd you get into town?" He had of course brought the car in, to get to his job. And right now it was in the garage being worked on; it wasn't even running.

"Dolly Fergesson drove me." Seating herself, she opened her purse, got out her pen and checkbook, and began writing a check.

"You came all the way in just to get your hair cut?"

"That's right." She passed the check to him and began putting her pen and checkbook away in her purse.

"Don't give it to me," he said. "Take it to the business office. I have work to do."

"You weren't working when I came in," his wife said. "Look, I'm in a hurry." She faced him coolly and levelly. At last he reached out and accepted the check. "Thanks," she said.

A few minutes later he stood in the business office, waiting for the bookkeeper to bring the money. He could, from here, still see Sherry. She was moving among the desks, chatting with the designers. Everybody in the place knew her, of course; they smiled at her. Presently she was peering to see the different works-in-progress.

If they knew what she's really like, he thought, they'd keep their work to themselves.

She'll steal your ideas. Just what you're always worried about, a spy getting in. She'll peddle them down the street.

How happy his wife and the designers looked. How easily they mingled, Sherry seated on the edge of a desk, so stylish with her sandals and handmade earrings. So competent in her brown wool suit.

Returning as rapidly as possible, he came up beside his wife and Quinn; they were both inspecting a drawing that Quinn had made, and neither of them noticed him. Evidently Sherry had picked out some detail; Quinn was frowning. She'll tell you what's wrong, he thought.

Aloud, he said, "She'll improve it." He said it in a bantering tone, and both Sherry and Quinn smiled. But Quinn continued to study his drawing.

"Sherry took a year of art in college," Dombrosio said.

"Three years," Sherry said calmly.

"Oh," he said, with extravagance. "I'm sorry."

"And," she said, "you're forgetting my work."

"Your what?" he said.

"My mobiles."

To Quinn, he said, "Driftwood."

Sherry said, "And my leather work. And my jewelry-making. Which I've managed to keep up, in spite of everything."

"In spite of being home all day with nothing to do?" he said. "With all the time in the world on your hands?"

"Wait'll you have kids," Quinn murmured.

"That'll be the day," Sherry said.

Trying to catch Quinn with a wink, he said, "I'd like to see her working away with a power lathe. You know what she'd do? I'll tell you; get her hand drilled through." He reached out and took hold of his wife's right hand. But she very forcefully drew it away; he saw her smooth fingers with the green-tinted nails slide away from him. "Green," he said. To Quinn, he said, "Didn't we do a display with some woman with green nails and — what was it? Metallic silver hair." He laughed. "She looked about eighty."

"That's quite acceptable now," Sherry said. Rising, she took the money from him. "Thanks for cashing my check. I'll see you tonight."

She walked toward the door, and he followed.

"By the way," she said, pausing thoughtfully. "There's something I wanted to ask you. You know the field back of the house, where the septic tank is? Past that, where the patio is. Does it mean anything if there's water seeping up? I noticed a pool this morning, about the size of—" She made a vague motion. "Not very big. There's green grass growing, so it must have been there for at least a week. That's where the leaching lines are, isn't it? It must be seeping up from the leaching lines."

"Yes," he said. "Overflow."

"Should we worry?"

He said, "No. It's supposed to do that."

"Are you positive?"

"Yes," he said.

"Oh my," she said. Her alert gray-blue eyes fixed themselves on him. "We should be wary of being positive in this world."

Irritably, he said, "When liquid pours into the lines, like for instance when you take a bath or use the washer—"

"I thought the washer recirculated its water."

"Eventually it gets into the lines. That water you see seeping up to the surface — that's evidently a low spot. It's probably done that from the start, but you just now noticed it."

"In winter it's going to get worse."

"Sure," he said, being patient. "Because the ground won't absorb much water."

"Should I call John Flores?"

That was the local septic tank man. "No," he said.

"Anybody, then?"

"No." From a nearby desk he took a scratch pad. With his pen he sketched. "Don't you understand how the leach lines work? Stuff goes into the septic tank and there the solids sink down and bacteria go to work on them. The liquids drain right on through and out of the tank."

Watching his sketching, Sherry said, "Very profound. But I called Arbarth. The contractor who built the house."

Taken aback, he stared at her. He could think of nothing to say. "What do you mean?" he said finally. "When did you call him? Why didn't you discuss it with me first?"

She shrugged. "You were driving in to work."

"What did he say?"

"He said the lines shouldn't be doing this at this time. It's a terribly bad sign. He's coming over tomorrow morning as soon as possible to look at it. We may need a hundred more feet of line." On her face, now, was a faint, mocking smile.

"If you called him," he said, having trouble speaking, "why did you ask me if it was serious? If you already knew? And how much did he quote? Or did you bother to ask?"

"It runs about two dollars a foot," Sherry said.

After a moment he said, "Two hundred dollars, then."

"It's a lot," she said. "But I think it'll probably have to be done, from what Arbarth said." She seemed perfectly composed.

As steadily as possible he said, "We — haven't got two hundred dollars to spend on leach lines."

"I discussed that frankly with Arbarth. We can pay in four payments. Assuming we go ahead. But I also called Flores. I believe we should get as many estimates as possible."

"You should have discussed it with me," he said thickly. "You should have told me and then I would have called Arbarth; it's up to me, not you. I'm not going to shell out that much money — I'll hire some high school kids from around there and get the pipe from Grandi's and the gravel from over in Tocaloma — I'll rent a dump truck!"

"Arbarth said," his wife said, "that probably it's giving trouble because it wasn't done right in the first place. It has to be done right." Glancing at her watch she abruptly turned and hurried off. He caught a glimpse of Dolly Fergesson standing in the hall; she, too, was dressed up. Both of them anticipating the all-day shopping, the restaurant.

As he stood staring after her, Quinn came up beside him, carrying his drawing. "I can't see what she means," he said, holding the drawing up, frowning.

"Got your goat, did she?" Dombrosio said. "Don't let her get you down — she's a frustrated amateur painter. You know how they are. Housewives with nothing to do all day — they get bored." But then, in a flash, he felt guilty at saying anything against his wife. "She's got a lot on the ball," he murmured. "You should see some of her stuff. She had an exhibit once at one of those supper houses down in Sausalito." She could really have had a career, he thought. "But she decided to get married," he said. "Instead. Like a lot of women."

Still in a daze, he returned to his desk; seating himself, he prepared to resume work. Two hundred dollars . . .

He found himself unable to work for quite some time.

At five-thirty that afternoon he stood in the cold garage, gazing up at his red Alfa Romeo on the rack.

What if this costs a lot? he asked himself. In addition to the leach lines. The mechanic had gone off; he had not had a chance to tell Dombrosio what the Alfa had had done to it, or what it still needed.

What if Charley can't get it done by six? he asked himself. He wandered across the plank floor, hands in his pockets. Good god, suppose there's some part he has to order? How'm I going to handle all this? How am I even going to get back *home*?

This was not the first time that he had stood here in this empty cold barn, at the end of the working day, shivering and staring at his car, wondering how much it would cost — and then hoping only to get it back, forgetting the cost and merely praying that it would be back on the road.

From the washroom the mechanic appeared, the tall, lean Negro who had worked on Dombrosio's cars for so many years. Wordlessly, Dombrosio gazed at him.

"It's done," Chuck Halpin said.

Inside him, Dombrosio felt the burden slide away. "I'll be damned," he said. "That's fine. What did you find?"

"Nothing but dirty points," Chuck said, drying his hands on a rag. He knelt down by the jack and began lowering the car to the floor.

"I sure count on you," Dombrosio said.

Chuck said, "Someday I'll give you a set of torsion wrenches and you can go into business for yourself." But he was clearly pleased to hear Dombrosio say that. "I always get your car ready for you," he said. "Almost always, anyhow."

Another mechanic came over. He said, "Charley had to drive to South San Francisco to get your points for you." He indicated the '49 Cadillac which Chuck Halpin owned; it was parked on the upramp, in gear. "He just got back a little while ago," the other mechanic said.

Chuck Halpin said, "We could have had them ship the points by jitney, but they probably wouldn't have gotten here until tomorrow." As Dombrosio started to speak, he interrupted, "It's on the bill; don't worry." With his pencil he began making out the bill.

After a moment Dombrosio said, "Listen. I want you to do me a favor. Okay?"

Chuck Halpin regarded him.

"How about coming out to the house for dinner?" Dombrosio said. A rush of emotion in him made him go on, "I'll drive you both ways. You can drive the Alfa, if you want. Remember the last time I was in? You said something about wanting to take it out for a spin, sometime."

Slowly, Halpin said, "I've driven it."

"Around the block, maybe."

Halpin scratched aimlessly with his pencil. "What would your wife say? You're married, aren't you?"

"I'll call her," he answered. Going past Halpin he opened the door to the garage's office. "Okay? Is it a deal?"

Halpin, in a low voice, said, "If — you're sure it's okay."

"Fine," Dombrosio said. Closing the door after him, he sat down at the phone, lifted the receiver, and dialed.

Of course Sherry was not home, yet; she was on her way back with Dolly. But that did not matter. At least, it did not matter to him at this moment. In fact, in the back of his mind, he relished her surprise. Too bad, he thought, if she doesn't like it. She can lump it. Do her good, he thought. Should learn to handle social situations like this. The proper hostess ought to be able to meet anybody socially.

As he came out of the office, Halpin stood deep in thought. He now raised his head and said, "Listen, Walt. Are there any Negroes out in that town where you live?"

"I don't know," he said. But he did know. There were none.

Halpin said, "I don't want to lower property values." He smiled, and Dombrosio smiled back. "Of course, it's dark," he said. "We won't get there until after dark."

Dombrosio slapped him on the back; he felt the slim back wince under his hand. "You got to not be sensitive," he said. "All that stuff, it's in the past. I mean, look at ball clubs, for instance; look at the Giants, with Willy Mays and that new first baseman, and Sam Jones, and the rest."

The mechanic did not ask if Dombrosio had gotten hold of his wife; apparently he assumed that he had. Now he began removing his work uniform, getting ready to leave the garage. His movements were retarded and fumbling; it took him a long time to get the buttons of his uniform undone. Dombrosio went over and sat patiently in the Alfa, waiting.

3

From the kitchen drifted a sound that Leo Runcible knew well. A pan on the burner, unattended, had begun to go dry. Soon the contents would boil off and the expensive steel pan with its copper bottom, part of a set, would be ruined. Janet had already ruined the new tea kettle; she had the habit of filling it, turning the knob to high, and then going into the bathroom and taking a long meditative bath, during which she read a book. Sometimes she drove down to town and shopped, leaving a pan of eggs hard-boiling on the stove; and once she had even left the electric oven, mounted in the wall, on broil. He had gotten home to find the house filled with the reek of burning wood; the wall itself had begun to char.

He set down his newspaper. Where had his wife gone? A tinkle. She was fixing a drink. Getting up, he walked through the living room and looked into the dining room. There, at the sideboard, she was deeply intent on the mixing of sugar and water and bitters. From where he stood he could tell that the Old Fashioned would be too sweet; grains of sugar coated the inside of the glass. Without saying anything to her he continued on into the kitchen.

There, a small sauce pan bubbled; a layer of paste in the very bottom puffed like lava, showing the blackened bottom of the pan. Yes, the burner had been left at high. He took the pan off. The coils glowed a dangerous red, and he shut the burner off. Other pots and pans had been pushed from the burners, covered; the table was set, and evidently dinner was ready. As usual, Janet wanted one more drink before they sat down to eat. She would delay dinner, not telling him that it was ready, so that she could drink a little more. And if he said anything to her, told her how hungry he was, she would simply bring the drink to the table and have it with her meal. Instead of coffee or water.

"What's this sauce?" he said, re-entering the dining room.

"That's for the cauliflower," Janet said. Now she poured from the bottle of Cyrus Noble, the cheap bourbon that she brought home from the market. She smiled at him. "I'm making that cheese sauce that you like." On the sideboard, in the puddle from the ice cubes, lay the open cook book which Janet used.

The house stirred with things done wrong and not done at all. For instance, he could hear the hose running outdoors; she had left it, forgotten it. The wastebasket in the living room brimmed over with the envelopes of bills; she hadn't emptied it in a whole week. What did she do during the day? Played Scrabble with her several friends, no doubt; he had found the Scrabble board still on the coffee table when he had gotten home at five.

"Anything I can do to help?" he asked.

"If you—" She seemed to have trouble thinking. "Maybe cut me some cheese." She passed him on her way back into the kitchen. The sight of the sauce pan pulled from the burner did not interest her; she gave no sign of recognizing that he had removed it for her. "Are you anxious to eat right away?" she said.

"The Wilbys are coming over," he said.

"Had you told me?"

He did not answer. Standing in the kitchen, he looked here and there for something to do, some way to speed things up. But at the same time he did not want to put pressure on her.

If he did, if he made her tense, she would become even more inefficient. She would break things. And when she tried to clean up the mess, the broken glass and ooze, she would become cross; without any warning her nervousness would switch over and become resentment at him. All at once she would accuse him of picking on her. And from then on she would refuse to do anything; she might even throw down the broom or the rag, whatever she held, go to the closet, put on her coat, and leave the house. If it was after dark she would invariably drive off. And so he would find himself in a littered kitchen with the meal half done, his wife gone, the job left for him to do. He would have to do it all.

But what constituted pressure on her? When she had had a couple of drinks her perception became vague; she might fall to calling anything "pressure." She might mistake the actual words said, or put totally unintended meanings on them. Even now, his standing here in the kitchen; suppose he shut off this burner or put that one on? He had taken the sauce off; even that might do it. He could not tell how much she had drunk, and that was important.

Now, reflecting on this, he felt irritable himself. He felt illused. Why did he have to pussyfoot about in his own home? Especially when people of some consequence were coming? By rights, he should be thinking about his old friends, the Wilbys; he should not have to fritter his attention away on this problem, this perennial sensitivity of his wife when she had had something to drink.

"What are you so quiet about?" Janet said, from behind him.

"I want to make this a nice evening for Paul and Phyllis," he answered. "A nice relaxed evening where we can sit and talk, and not have any friction. I don't want you going off on any of your long rambling accounts about whatever happens to enter your mind at the moment."

She said, with no apparent ill-humor, "Dear, you don't get it. When I've had something to drink—" She smiled at him, standing over by the doorway, and, it seemed to him, swaying slightly. "All the material is there, but I can't seem quite to organize it."

"Well, you better organize it tonight," he said. "I'm tired, and it's a long drive out here for Paul." He added, "And as you know, if things go okay, eventually I hope they'll be moving out here."

His wife opened her eyes wide. "Really?"

"I told you that. I told you they were interested in the McGuffey house." He lapsed into silence, turning back to the stove and fretting at the knobs.

His wife came slowly toward him. "I won't mess things up," she said, in a soft, intense voice. "I know how much it would mean to you." He saw that her eyes shone wetly, and her hand, touching his shoulder, trembled. Nothing like a sentimental drunk, he thought. To be your burden in life.

"Let's just get dinner," he said. "Okay?"

Later, after they had eaten and were clearing the table, she asked if she could excuse herself as soon as the Wilbys came. She wanted to go lie down in the bedroom and either read or watch TV. Everything was prepared; she had water boiling for coffee, she had her wool robe, her glasses, her cigarettes, her lighter, ashtray, the heat in the bedroom was on, she had the box of Kleenex, and of course her book. It had come yesterday from their book club.

He said, "They drive all the way out here from Tiberon, and you go to bed and read. Don't you grasp how completely you've failed to give me the support I need? How can I do my work?"

At that she blanched. Once, for half a year, she had worked down at the office, doing typing, answering the phone, giving out keys to clients. She had saved him the cost of a secretary. But the strain had been too much; at nights she had not slept, and it was during this period that her drinking had first gotten out of hand. Before that she had drunk as he did: only socially, with perhaps a martini or two before dinner, an Old Fashioned afterward, and of course more at parties. But in the last year or so she had begun drinking alone, while he was at work. When he came home at six, he usually found her well on the way. The responsibility of helping him at his work had been too much for her, but he could not make out why. He had never asked anything more than minor office help from her, the paperwork, the phoning. In no sense had she had responsibilities. But even in the giving out of the keys she had become apprehensive. As if she was convinced that she would do something wrong.

Perhaps, too, she did not want to help him; he felt that all along. She resented being asked to contribute her time and help, but she did not recognize it consciously. On the surface she thought she wanted to help him. And yet she did not help him. He reasoned, if she really wanted to, then why couldn't she? There had to be a reason why she fouled everything up. Incompetence in an intelligent person did not make sense unless there was motive. He saw motive, there. The desire to thwart him, possibly out of a sense of jealousy. She resented his drive and ability. Or, like most women, she resented men in general. The whole masculine world, in which she had no part.

And if she did have no part, whose fault was that? Who kept her from accomplishing anything? Suppose she was no more than a housewife and mother. When she was offered a chance to participate, she shrank back; she muffed it. Here, he thought, is an example; she can't even go through the motions of social politeness and stay up on her feet to greet Paul and Phyllis. Old friends and possible clients, too.

He said, "God damn it — you know what it would mean to me if they located here."

"Yes," she said readily. "You'd finally have somebody you could talk to. You wouldn't be so lonely."

"I'm not lonely," he said.

"You and Paul could talk about boats."

Paul Wilby had for years been an amateur sailor. He owned a star class sailing boat, and entered it in races. In fact Runcible had met him at the Carquinez Yacht Club. But that was not it. He did not need to import anyone to discuss boats; this whole area was full of people who owned sloops and skiffs and yawls. Beach property, little summer and weekend cabins, littered the shore. The grocery store sold fishing licenses, bait and tackle. The post office put up notices of quarantined mussels. Even the local cars had hitches for pulling boat trailers.

"The hell with boats," he said.

For years Paul Wilby had been a successful contractor in Southern Marin County. He had worked with some of the top architects in the area, built fine forty-thousand-dollar homes up in the hills, and, in addition, he had gotten in with the subdividers. A number of the tracts along Highway 101 had been put together by his firm.

"I want to go into business with Paul," Runcible said. "There's lots of cheap land around here, still, but it's in big hunks. Two and three hundred acres." All the smaller lots had been sold off. And no subdividers had come in, yet. None had crossed the mountain. Sooner or later it would happen; the well-to-do ranchers who had land to sell would make their deals. Right now, he knew, old Bob Hanson had begun nosing around for a buyer for his Bear Mesa Ranch. In fact Hanson had bulldozed out ten or twenty acres of reasonably flat land along both sides of a county-maintained road, in order to attract subdividers. During the day the sound of the 'dozer could be heard in town, and everybody who cared had already figured out what was up.

Hanson's land, however, was not cheap. He seemed to want in the neighborhood of six hundred an acre. So that meant his buyer would need roughly twenty thousand dollars cash in hand. That was a lot of glue, and that covered only buying the land; in order to subdivide, the buyer had — according to county law — to put in roads. And that cost a fortune. And that still left the actual building undone; roads had to go in simply to break up the parcel of land into, say, hundred by sixty lots. Each lot had to be accessible by road, and a good deal of the land was hilly. The buyer, to make anything, had to have his own machines; if he hired the job out, he would probably lose. It might take years to sell off a hundred acres in the form of lots. And to attract people it would be necessary to provide a model home and an account of building costs. But now take Jancuzzi's property, for instance . . .

Janet said, "Isn't it true that—" She hesitated. "You never ought to go into business with friends, I've heard."

"Why?" he said.

"Because business destroys the friendship."

"Why?"

Haltingly, she said, "Because — isn't there a conflict? The same thing applies when a man and wife try to operate a business together. Look what happened to us in '57." That had been the year in which she had tried to work down at Runcible Realty. "It's the same when a husband tries to teach his wife to drive." Her voice trailed off and she smiled at him hopefully.

"Why are you really going to bed?" he said, in a tone of voice that insisted on a truthful and complete answer.

Janet said, "You know it always makes me feel dreadful to sit in the same room with Paul and Phyllis after what happened that time." Her voice was so low that he could barely hear her; he had to lean toward her, as if, he thought, he were some deaf old farmer. "That horrible game," she said. "That charades."

How like his wife to dwell on that. A few months ago the four of them had been at a party in San Anselmo together, at the home of a business contact. Janet had drunk too much, and when it came time for her to act out her book title, she had stood foolish and mute, flapping her arms, appealing to her team in an embarrassing, senseless fashion until finally time had run out and she had slunk to her chair.

"Nobody remembers that but you," he said.

Janet said, "I still ask myself. Even if I was sober, even if I had weeks to prepare — I still wonder how you act out *Roget's Thesaurus.*" She gazed at him helplessly.

"You row," he said. "Then you indicate the letter J."

"But what then?"

"I don't know," he said. "But I can tell you this. If you go to bed, if you aren't here to greet the Wilbys, I'll make it tough for you the rest of your life."

There was a silence, then.

Hanging her head she murmured, "I'll stay up for a while. But I really honest to god don't feel well. I think I'm getting that flu again. There's the same pain here that I had before." She ran her hand over her waist.

Seeing her expression, the concern in her eyes, he knew that she would stay up. She was afraid to desert him. As much as she yearned to go to bed, to lie covered up and warm, reading her book and eating an artichoke with lemon and butter sauce, she would remain in the living room, chatting, being an appropriate wife and hostess.

"You can discuss your book with Phyllis," he said.

Drawing herself up she said, "Phyllis Wilby reads nothing but confession magazines in beauty shops. There isn't anybody any more who reads good books but me." For a moment she faced him defiantly. Then, by degrees, she resumed the clearing of the table.

Pathetic, he thought. She calls that pornographic rubbish from the book club "good books." It's really the dregs, lying in bed eating boiled artichoke and reading about old men screwing little girls. And it's women like her who keep those book clubs in business, he thought. Getting their kicks secondhand, out of books.

Going to the living room window, he stationed himself with his hands in his pockets, looking down the hillside toward the road. A light here and there permitted him to locate other houses in the darkness. When they turned off the highway and up the driveway their headlights would light up the living room; the angle was quite steep. And Paul always took a long time parking, so that he could be sure of being able to get out again. Sometimes when he left he was too tight to do much backing and filling.

"Can they afford the McGuffey house?" Janet asked, from the kitchen.

"Listen," he said, "Paul can afford anything."

"But it would be so large. And just the two of them, no children . . . and all those bedrooms. Three floors!"

"The McGuffey house," he said, "is the finest house in the area. At any price."

"Oh," she said, "what about Marston's place?"

"Are you going to say that when Paul and Phyllis come?"

"I think you better wait and see what they say after they see the house," Janet said. "I know they'll say it's too large."

"They have seen it," he said. "And it's not too large. They need room for guests."

She came from the kitchen. "When did you show it to them?"

"Last month."

"How much did you quote them?"

"Thirty-two."

"But," she said, "you told me McGuffey wants forty-two."

"I don't care what that old fart wants."

Janet said, "You're his broker. You agreed to—"

Interrupting, he said, "I agreed to get the best price for his place possible. Well, he can't get forty-two. He's too damn greedy. He has no idea what the market will bear. That's my job to know."

"How long have you had the listing?"

He conceded, "A month."

"And you're already coming down ten thousand?" She came around to face him. "Would you quote that price to someone who wasn't a friend of yours? Just — someone who showed up and wanted to see the property?"

He shrugged.

"That's wrong," she said. "You have an exclusive on that, for three months."

"Four."

"McGuffey can't sell except through you. And you're going to sell it to a friend of yours for far less than—"

"Do I tell you how to make sauce?" he said, with difficulty. "Do I tell you what kind of soap powder to buy?"

"You shit," she said. "You wicked shit."

"Why?" he said, taken aback.

Without answering, she returned to the kitchen. Dishes clattered. He heard her speaking sharply to Jerome, who was in his room watching TV.

Ten minutes later, headlights flashed up at him. The Wilbys had arrived. He switched on the porch light and went to open the door.

As big Paul Wilby came up the steps, guiding his wife, Runcible saw that the man was frowning. Both Paul and Phyllis seemed withdrawn, hardly noticing him. They murmured together.

"Greetings," Runcible said.

"Hi, Leo," Paul said, extending his strong hand. They shook, while Phyllis, greeted by Janet, passed on inside the house.

"What's the matter, Paul?" Runcible said.

Wilby shut the door after him. He walked toward his wife,

took her coat, and then carried it to the closet. "Nothing," he said. And then, turning his head, he said, "Leo, are there any colored people living up here?"

"No," Runcible said. "None."

"You sure?" Paul said.

Beside him, Phyllis said, "Could any have moved in recently, Leo? That you wouldn't know about?"

"No," he said. "Tell me why you ask."

Paul seated himself on the couch and placed his hands on his knees. "Driving up your hill," he said, "you know that house on the right with the lattice work and the trees?"

Janet said, "That would be the Dombrosio house."

"I know," Runcible said. "I know what house that is. Well? So?"

Continuing, Paul said, "The porch light was on, and we saw a colored fellow on the porch."

"There was no doubt about it," Phyllis said. "We went very slow to be sure."

"What then?" Runcible said.

"He went in," Phyllis said. "Then we drove on."

"One of those moon-faced boys," Paul said. "You know what I mean — real coal black and shiny."

"The Dombrosios couldn't have sold their house," Janet said. "Could they?" To her husband she said, "You'd know right away." To Paul and Phyllis she said, "Leo always knows those things."

Runcible started to speak. But something seemed to be wrong with his tongue. It had become thick; it filled his mouth. He cleared his throat and rubbed his hands together, instead. The three of them were looking at him, his wife and the Wilbys.

"I can tell you," he said, and his voice came out hoarse and phlegm-filled, "that on my word of honor there are no Negroes living here in the area."

"Was he visiting the Dombrosios?" Janet said.

"Possibly," Runcible said, nodding. "Possibly he was a repairman of some sort. Possibly he was a friend of theirs visiting."

"I doubt that," Janet said. "They wouldn't have a Negro visit them."

Runcible saw only her; he saw neither the Wilbys nor the room with the things in it, his living room. "You doubt that?" he said. "I want to know why you doubt that. Don't tell me." He raised his hand at her. "I don't want to know. Paul," he said to Wilby, "I can swear to you that this is a really good place to bring up your kids. Nobody here would have Negroes visiting them and if anybody sold to Negroes, then—" He broke off, winded. His heart labored. "The same goes for Jews," he said. "You won't find any Jews here to dirty up your streets. I'll tell you what. Why don't you move here?"

They stared at him speechlessly.

"Are you a Nazi?" Runcible said. "You want to start up Dachau again, or something?"

They looked at him as if he had gone mad, as if he were foaming at the mouth. Involuntarily, he put his hand up, the back of his hand, and rubbed his lower lip.

"Say," Paul Wilby said. His face gradually flushed. "Don't you get up on your high horse with me. I've just driven forty miles, but I'll be happy to turn around and drive back if that's what you want."

"You can't stay here anyhow," Runcible said. "In the house of a Jew."

"Jew, smew," Phyllis said. "Get off it, Leo."

Janet said, "Dear—"

"I suppose you're not interested in the McGuffey place," Runcible said to the Wilbys, "now that you caught sight of a dark face."

"Oh hell," Paul said loudly. "I just asked if there were any colored in town. Isn't that what I asked? Is that so out of line? And like always, you're right up there on your god damn soap box—"

"I'm not up on a soap box," Runcible said.

"The hell you aren't."

Runcible said, "I wouldn't sell you the McGuffey place, and I'll tell you why. I'll be glad to tell you why. I've had all I can take of Fascism; I fought it and practically gave my life for it; I mean, in the cause to wipe it from the earth." He felt his ears glow and burn. Phyllis laughed a little short high-pitched laugh. Now his voice rose in volume; he was shouting at them. "While you were making big money from the war I was out giving my life. Well, I'll tell you what you can do with your money. Yes, I will tell you."

Her voice sharp, Phyllis Wilby said, "How dare you speak to my husband like that."

"In World War Two I was fighting in France," Wilby said, his face dark, his mouth trembling.

"Let's go," Phyllis said, going toward the door.

"Don't forget your coat," Runcible said, going toward the closet. "Here." He held out their two coats in a lump.

To Janet, Phyllis said, "Has he been drinking?"

Janet said, "My husband has not been drinking." She took one of the coats, gave it to Phyllis, and the other to Paul. "I wish you would leave," she said.

"You, too?" Paul said, dumbfounded in his slow way. "My god, not one of them but *two* of them." He shook his head. "We came all the way out here to be insulted by a couple of nuts."

Phyllis Wilby had already opened the door and gone out onto the porch. She waited, her back to the house, for her husband to follow, calling, "Come on — it's a waste of our time. A complete waste."

"Good night," Janet said, in a frozen, formal voice. She

guided Paul Wilby to the door; he protested, trying to remain in the room, but she forcibly placed him outside, on the porch, and pulled the door in, blocking him off. "Good night," she repeated, in an almost merry tone. Smiling, she shut the door. Then she turned to Runcible. He saw the stark, determined expression on her face. In the same merry tone she said, "Well, that was a surprise. What a surprise."

"Yes," he said, nodding.

They stood silently. After a moment they heard Paul Wilby's footsteps as he went down the porch stairs, and then the sound of car doors, and finally a motor starting up. The car drove off down the driveway, and then there was no sound at all. Nothing but the refrigerator in the kitchen.

"Wow," Runcible said. "You never know what the next moment is going to bring."

His wife's expression faded and became dull. The tenacity had gone. It had endured for the situation only. He saw timidity in its place, awareness of what the consequences might be. Consequences . . . the loss of a sale, loss of a long-time friend . . .

"Here I go reaming you out about treating them politely when they come," he said, "and then look what I go and do."

Janet said, "Do you think they really did see a Negro?"

"Sure," he said. "It would be just like that horse's ass Dombrosio to throw an interracial party at his place."

"But I know Sherry very well," Janet said, "and we've talked about Marin City and the Negroes, and the influx into Marin County, and I know how she feels; I know she wouldn't let something like that happen. She'd be too conscious of the feelings of the other people up here."

"I'm going to give him a call," Runcible said. Going into the bedroom he seated himself on the bed and got out the Marin County phone book.

"What are you going to say?" Janet said, appearing.

"I'm going to tell him what he did," Runcible said. "By bringing a Negro up here. He not only cost me a sale but he ruined a
deeply desirable ten-year friendship. I'll tell him; he ought to
know."

He began to dial.

4

Along the early-morning road Sherry Dombrosio walked, her hands in the pockets of her blue suede leather jacket. Since she had on sandals she avoided kicking stones. The slightly chilly wind riffled her skirt, the long dark one with the hand-printed pattern done by an artist-friend in Sausalito. The sandals, too, were handmade; she had made them herself several years ago. She still had leather-working tools, and at Christmas turned out a few belts and purses and wallets as gifts for their most personal friends.

To her right, pasture land fell away into a canyon of trees. A young calf grazed, dun-colored, square, his pink wet nose shining as it coasted over the grass. She saw, far overhead, a hawk or a buzzard; she could not tell which, not until the sun shone through its wings and she caught the characteristic red of the hawk's feathers. Now and then, in the past, she had seen a blue heron sometimes in the early morning, but today she did not; the oak in which it lived held only the sloppy nest, nothing more. The heron had flapped up to the Bolinas lagoon to spend the day.

At the turn of the road she stepped from the gravel pavement to let a pickup truck pass on its way to town.

It would have given her a lift, she reflected, if she had made any sign. Mr. Grimaldi had been at the wheel, a retired mining engineer who lived up at the end of their road. He was very circumspect about offering her rides; on rainy days, if she was slogging down the road to town in her yellow slicker and rain hat and boots, he always stopped whether she waved or not, but on sunny days like this he knew that she enjoyed walking. On the trip back up, however, when she was loaded with groceries, she liked a ride, in any sort of weather.

Her sandals crunched gravel as she returned to the road. At the right Mrs. Pestolesi's house with its pampas grass waving in front. Then the steep slope, and, at the bottom, the Chevron Station where this minor county road joined the state highway.

The wind stirred by her, causing the shaky-grass at the edge of the pavement to vibrate in its peculiar way. Stooping, she broke off a sprig of the grass; it continued to vibrate as she carried it. Like little wires, she thought. A toy plant from Hong Kong, but not too successful from the color standpoint. It occurred to her that she could dry the grass, dip it in a mayonnaise jar of water color, perhaps use a variety as decoration around the house . . . she had already experimented with the coloring of different local weeds; some came out novel and even stunning, their delicacy and intricacy impossible to duplicate artificially. The color brought out what was already there unnoticed.

If I had any sense, she thought, I'd set up my easel along this road; I'd paint that Chevron Station, the hill behind it, the rim of the lagoon. But if I did — like any other landscape by a Sunday painter. A Winston Churchill, and not even original.

If nature stirs you, she thought, you're not an artist; you're merely sentimental. So she strode on, long-legged, down the hill.

Carquinez put in its appearance below, eleven stores in a row, five on the left side of the highway, six on the right, the feed store dominating. And it was to the feed store that she intended to go; she had pet bantam chickens.

The sound of a car behind her caused her to step from the road once more. A gray sedan which she recognized as the Runcibles' passed her; she saw Janet Runcible behind the wheel, her eyes fixed straight ahead, sitting stiffly as always, like a little old lady. Gray car, gray person, Sherry thought. And it would never occur to either of them to give anybody a lift; Leo Runcible generally sailed by anyone on foot, aloof as a statue, barely even nodding.

But now the gray sedan slowed and stopped.

For me? Sherry thought. She continued at the same pace, not acknowledging the car, until at last she came up to the front seat and the driver. The window was rolled down, and Janet Runcible now turned her head and leaned out. But she did not open the door.

"I saw you walking along," Janet said. Her drab face was unusually drawn this morning, and Sherry decided that this constituted a morning after. "You know, being the only Realtor in the area, Leo has to think and act from two standpoints. As an individual person and as the town. He has to represent them."

"And last night when he called us," Sherry said, "he was what?"

Janet said, "He was rightly amazed and upset that considering the way most people here feel — rightly or wrongly — that you would have a colored person up to your house as overnight guest without consulting anyone else or how they might feel. He couldn't understand how since we all know each other and live on the same road and have our children in the same school—" She gestured. "It did cost him a very important sale, as he told your husband. You can't blame him for being upset. After all, it didn't cost you anything. You don't have to make your living in this community; your husband works outside. It's pretty easy for you to take this lightly. I can see it doesn't affect you a bit; I might as well save my breath." And, putting the car into gear, she shot off, leaving Sherry standing there.

They're really mad, Sherry thought. Presently she resumed walking.

One of the difficulties of living in a small community soon proved itself. As she entered Carleton's Feed Store she found herself once more facing Janet Runcible. Mrs. Runcible stood at the counter while the man weighed out dry dog food. Seeing Sherry, she at once turned her back.

This is going to be the situation from now on, Sherry thought. So she went up to the counter. "I don't intend to be badly treated by you or anybody else in this town," she said to Janet, when the man had gone off to get change. "Let's get this over and done with."

The man returned, gave Janet Runcible her change, and then went away to unload feed sacks from a dolly. Evidently he assumed that the two women were together.

"There's nothing to get over," Janet said. "At no cost to yourself you brought a serious financial misfortune to us, and of course it doesn't bother you a bit. Why should it? You're not a part of this community; it's just a residential suburb to you. But I should think that you'd care enough about the value of your own property to—"

"Nuts to you," Sherry said. "What Walter said last night to your husband goes double for me. We've got nothing to apologize for. If we had to do it over again, we'd do it over again. I agree with Walt one hundred percent; nobody has the right to tell us who we can and who we can't have in our home."

"Leo says—" Janet began.

"I don't care what Leo says," Sherry said. "Listen, there're a lot of people in this town who as far as they're concerned your husband is after the almighty dollar, and you know what I mean by that."

"You mean to infer about his race," Janet said. "I'm proud, and Leo is proud of a sacred heritage."

"Yes, well your husband is no Baruch Spinoza," Sherry said. "And it's pretty ludicrous him taking credit for that, for Mendelssohn and Einstein because they happen to belong to the same race; I might as well take credit for Franklin Roosevelt or Albert Schweitzer." Lowering her voice she said, "My husband and I have a lot more respect from other people in this community than someone coming in to speculate in real estate and try to make a fast buck by however it is he makes his living — no one seems to know for sure."

To that, Janet Runcible could find nothing to say. She started to speak, cleared her throat, picked up her sealed package of dry dog food. Her face had become colorless, heavy and not attractive. Her smile had long since gone. At last she shuddered, lowered her head, and pushed past Sherry and out of the feed store.

Going over to the clerk, Sherry said in a level voice, "Say, I want some chicken feed. About five pounds." It pleased her that she did not sound disturbed. Certainly, Janet was not now able to function. I'll bet she goes back home, Sherry thought. No more errands for her today; she couldn't stand running into me again, not after that.

What a forlorn little spinster-type-of-woman, she thought as she paid for the chicken feed. That nervous tic around her eyes, the strain showing, and of course the puffy lids from tying one on every night of the week. How little it had taken to shut her up. A few swift returns.

And they are wrong, she thought. They must know it. All that huffing and puffing, last night on the phone and now here . . . so much hocus pocus. To justify themselves. It's not us they're attacking; it's their own weak guilty consciences.

But then she thought, And look at me. Look at my line of talk. Now she felt guilty, thinking back. Bringing in Runcible's race.

That was bad, she decided.

And yet, they deserved it. It was justice. And their own sacred writing, the Old Testament, said, "An eye for an eye." They rejected the Christian "turn the other cheek," so why should she hold back? Their own code called for what she had done.

She stepped from the feed store, out onto the platform and then down the steps to the gravel parking lot. There was the Runcible sedan; Janet stood by it, holding her sack of dog food, waiting for her.

"What now?" Sherry said, jolted to find her.

Approaching her, Janet said, "I want to set you straight about something. We're not bigots. You have us so readily typed. Last night my husband threw a friend of ten years out of his house because that man, Paul Wilby, asked about that Negro friend of yours. He saw him on your porch and wondered if Negroes lived here in town."

"So?" Sherry said.

"My husband voluntarily gave up an important sale on which he would have made a great deal of money because he wouldn't tolerate anyone making racist remarks in his home. Leo is an idealist." Her red-rimmed eyes blazed up; her lips set violently. Sherry decided to make no move to get away or interrupt. "He almost gave his life in the cause of human liberty and equality. He fought in the war against Fascism not because he had to but because he believed in it. He's a noble, intelligent, sensitive man. If anybody in this community has done more to support good causes than Leo I want to know who that is. You tell me who. Who?"

Sherry said nothing. There's more, she realized. She groaned inwardly and held her package of chicken feed against her.

"If you had been at our home last night," Janet said, "you would have seen—"

"If your husband feels that way, then why did he call us?" Sherry broke in. "Why did he say what he said? If he's so idealistic, how come he was on the phone shouting about our 'ruining the community by our selfish actions,' and all that stuff? How do you explain that?"

Opening her car door, Janet paused and said, "Leo wanted you to know the consequences of your act. He wanted you to face the full import. Remember—" She seated herself behind the wheel and slammed the door after her. Starting up the motor she said in a calm, firm voice, "Your interracial party didn't cost you people anything. We paid the cost."

The Runcible sedan, with its gray woman inside, drove off.

Presently Sherry thought, Maybe there's something to that. I wonder. They're always so sensitive about racial slights, these Jews. Maybe Runcible took a remark directed toward Negroes as a personal insult. It would be just like him.

How well do we know Runcible? she asked herself. We see him go by in his car; we hear about deals he's pulled; we see his signs and his office. When we buy we pretty much have to buy through him, and the same applies when we sell. She thought, He's neatly-groomed, even good-looking. And he certainly holds grudges. He has feuds with half the people in town — or has had. It is a fact that he flares up at almost anything, goes off in a huff. And he does participate in all the civic business, school bonds and roads and right-of-ways.

He really must be quixotic, she thought. If he did that; if he told a client to go to hell because the client started muttering about seeing a Negro in town. And who would ever have thought of Leo Runcible as that?

Last night it had seemed so simple, so cut and dried. Her husband had come home with a Negro in the car, a mechanic whom he had known for years and liked and respected, and this was an all-white community, "lily-white," as it was called. Her first reaction had been, What will the neighbors think? And Charley himself had joked, during dinner, about property values going down. And sure enough, the local Realtor had phoned them that evening, very excited and upset and angry, and had bawled them out. Walt, standing there in the hall with the phone in his hand, had said exactly the right thing; he had told the Realtor to go peddle his papers, that this was a man's right, to invite anyone he wanted to his home, Negro, Jew, or Martian. Had Walter said *Jew?* She was not sure, now. In any case, he had gotten his attitude across. Beyond any doubt it had been a clash between human values and cynical property values, with Leo Runcible, hotshot promoter with a reputation for shady deals and fast profits, representing the latter.

But now . . . she could picture Runcible throwing the friend out of his house, making his speech and then, as soon as the man was gone, going to the phone, calling up her and Walt, and taking the exact opposite stand. They're nuts, she said to herself. Both of them, Leo and Janet; zanies. Real weirdos. And, she thought, they're really sore at us. If it cost them a lot of money — or if they have it in their mind that it did — they're not going to get over it right away. I know if it were I, a lot of time would go by before I stopped nursing a grudge over a lot of money.

If he were rational, she thought, he wouldn't blame us; he'd hold himself responsible. Did Walt and I make him sound off at his client? Did we force him to? But, she thought, people aren't rational; they're emotional.

Anyhow, she decided, there's nothing they can do to us except not wave or not give us lifts in wet weather. Runcible isn't of much importance in this community. Socially, he's a pariah. In fact, they have more to lose than we have, by their snubbing us.

What a laugh, she decided. The Runcibles snubbing us!

5

Ahead, Walt Dombrosio saw the red neon sign of a bar. A road-side tavern at the edge of Stinson Beach. Can I drive the rest of the way okay? he asked himself. If I have a couple of belts? I really feel lousy.

He coasted the Alfa from the road onto the gravel shoulder across from the bar. Stopping the car he shut off the lights and then the motor. Getting from the car he walked to the bar, his hands in his pockets.

The old story, he thought as he pushed open the door of the bar and entered. Troubles with my wife; the bartender must have heard from a million mouths the same tale. These red signs along the highway, inviting a man to stop off for a moment to suck at the tit, nurse away while spilling out the problems. And yet, he saw that the bartender, a brawny, hairy man smoking a cigar, was involved in his newspaper; he sat hunched over, smoking and reading, paying no attention to the three or four men drinking. He doesn't care, Dombrosio thought. He's not going to hear my troubles; he's busy.

Jews, he thought. I could complain about the Jews. Bar talk. Pole-axing me and at the same time beating the breast and sobbing how ill-used his race has been. Who can tell me? he asked himself. If I did right. Said right to that harangue.

So who do you go to? he asked himself as he sat down on a stool. Minister? Psychoanalyst? Sherry went to a psychoanalyst in San Francisco, now and then. But that was for women, and in addition it cost too much. The minister, he thought. What a joke. There was a minister in Carquinez. If I did go to him, he thought, what would I say? What sort of spiritual problem do I have?

The bartender put down his paper, his cigar, and came over, resting his big flat hands on the counter and waited expectantly.

Dombrosio said, "What's your bar Scotch?"

"Crawford's," the bartender said, glancing behind him.

It was a label that he did not know. But he said, "Fine. Give me a Scotch and water, no ice."

"I also have Teacher's," the bartender said.

"No," he said. "Crawford's is okay." And he thought, What a gas bag I am; I pretend that I know what I'm talking about. And it costs me ten cents a drink more; I pay for being a gas bag, because I have gone and named a brand, even though I don't know the brand.

"In your opinion," he said, when the bartender brought the drink, "is Crawford's a pretty good Scotch?"

The bartender said, "I'm not a Scotch drinker."

"The best Scotch I know," Dombrosio said, "is Cutty Sark." He had never had it, but he had seen ads for it in magazines that his wife brought home.

"Well, I'll tell you," the bartender said as he rang up the amount on the register. "Guys come in here and specify a brand of Scotch, like Ballantine or what you said, Cutty Sark, or Old Grouse, and on the third drink I give them whatever I have closest, Teacher's or whatever, and they can't tell. It don't make no difference to them." He grinned as he tossed the change on the counter.

Dombrosio made himself grin back; he made his face respond. "I'll bet they couldn't tell the first drink," he said. "Even on the first one, if you switched."

The bartender went back to his newspaper. A little later, Dombrosio heard murmuring voices and saw, over his shoulder, the bartender bending close to two men at the bar. They laughed. Are they laughing at me? Dombrosio wondered. He sipped his drink and stared straight forward, feeling his neck and ears become hot and red and then cold. Because I paid more for a label of Scotch and possibly the bartender did switch on me, and I didn't notice . . . he waited to see if I said anything, and I didn't. Maybe I should say something. Say that the drink isn't too good.

He searched his mind for some broad way to put it, to cover the situation if it really wasn't Crawford's that he was drinking. And if it was, if the bartender hadn't switched, would still leave him okay. But he could not find a way.

Turning to the man at his left, not one of those who had been laughing, he said, "Hey, what are you drinking?"

At first it seemed as if the man was not going to answer; he did not make any sign that he had heard, and Dombrosio felt further horror. But then the man slowly lifted his head and said, "Burgie."

"Have one on me," Dombrosio said.

The man lifted his hand in a sign of acknowledgement. "Thanks," he said, nodding his head up and down.

The bartender came over, unasked, with a fresh bottle of beer and poured it for the man. Dombrosio paid him. Nobody said anything. The man began to drink his new round of beer, and Dombrosio returned to his Scotch.

What is wrong? he asked himself. If he would listen, what would I have to tell him?

Nobody is trying to hurt me. I am not sick or broke. I have a good job. My wife dresses well and has a great figure. But if nothing was wrong, he thought, I would not be here in this dump with these guys; I would be home by now. Home and sitting down to dinner.

Did that Realtor guy take away my home by phoning up? No, he thought. I felt like this before. My troubles are not with Runcible, even though he did make me as mad and upset as I've ever been. If my troubles exist at all, they are with —

He thought, With someone who crowds me. Who leans over my shoulder. And yet, I somehow can't catch her at it; she seems still to be waiting, holding back. The time is not ripe, maybe.

What does she want?

So polite to the guest. Of course. A liberal; she went to a good university, moved in good circles. She could no more insult Chuck Halpin than she could fly. But I know, he thought. Underneath. Her real thoughts, kept hidden. People in her class can't come out and say it, even if they feel it. They have to want to fraternize with Negroes; they have to detest Faubus, the South in general.

He thought, My god, suppose that upset him so bad he won't work on my car.

I wouldn't blame him. The dark, constrained face swam up, visible. Intuition about the call. Not having to ask who or what; knowing. Probably not unique in his experience. From then on saying nothing all evening. Nodding to everything. Agreeing, eating, drinking, but not there; mind far away. Detaching himself, he thought. From the embarrassment.

Then I'll have to take it elsewhere, he thought. Find another garage. Sooner or later anyhow. Always happens just when you think you have some guy you can count on.

She can start in on me now, he thought. First chance. Really make me pay for showing up with a Negro. She actually agrees with Runcible. But she's too smart to come out directly and say anything. I'll get it indirectly. If I was home now she'd be reaming me out in subtle ways, a dozen. Last night with him still there; she couldn't talk. Or this morning. But now. Now I'll get it as soon as I set foot. Hold off if possible; sit here as long.

Me, he thought. I know I genuinely feel it; I'm sincere. I invited him because I like him. I know my own motives. I treated him like I would any man, white or Negro, because with a person like me it comes natural. That's the difference between her and me.

His glass was empty, so he ordered another Scotch. This time he did not specify, and he did not pay attention to what the bartender charged him; he simply took the fresh drink and drank it.

Not her I'm not. Scared of her to go home. For? For the hell of it; I like to drink sometimes. For? He thought, For —

For Janet Runcible one happy time was the happiest of all.

She could at this time tell in advance what people were going to say.

They only had to open their mouths. At once she knew all the rest. And it delighted her. She got their thoughts at a glance!

And it was not just simple thoughts. She also got the most intellectual discussions. If the conversation at a party got onto David Riesman or West Germany or science she could participate; she threw in bits of ideas herself, sometimes not even needing to finish them. And the other people got her ideas right away, too.

Her drink in her hand, she sat in the deep yellow chair in the living room. The table was set; the dinner was in the oven, cooking. There was nothing to do.

At his desk, in the other room, Leo sat studying papers and making phone calls. He still had on his suit and tie; he had just gotten home. Now he wrote with his pen. His gray, slightly curly hair made her think of steel. How hard he is, she thought. Narrow, hard wrists. A neat, narrow, hard man.

"Does the suit make you narrow?" she said. "Or do you? The tie." She started to laugh. Even the stripes, now, had become narrow. All was up and down, especially the lapels. First, the women models in the ads . . . so thin, with black ravenous eyes. As if they had been after blood. Yes, so bloodless.

Leo grunted. Papers rustled as they turned.

"Guess who I saw today," Janet said. She knew, before he spoke, that he would turn and ask who. So she went on, "I had a little talk with a gal who wears sandals and wears her hair even shorter than I do. You once said you could go for her, but I think she's probably more interested in other women. She holds her cigarette like this." Reaching toward the ashtray on the coffee table, Janet picked up a long cigarette butt and put it into the corner of her mouth. But the cigarette toppled away; grabbing at it, she discovered that she had let her drink slop. She forgot about the cigarette and began quietly to mop the puddle with a Kleenex from her purse, hoping that Leo had not noticed.

However, he had. When she went to throw the soggy Kleenex in the wastebasket she realized that he had stopped working and was regarding her with that expressionless gaze.

"The cigarette was out," she said. "It didn't burn anything." She retrieved the butt from the floor, held it for a moment, and then put it back in the ashtray.

Suddenly she knew that he was going to say that he didn't care whether she saw Sherry Dombrosio and talked to her or not. And it was exactly right; he did say it, a fraction of a second later.

"You can keep your women's gossip," Leo said. "Keep it to yourself."

"You used to like to hear about her," she said. "I've heard you tell clients about her. What interesting, creative people there are in the area. A woman who makes her own shoes."

Turning his head, Leo said, "The conversation probably started with her saying something like, 'Why did that kike husband of yours dare phone up my husband, that yid real estate broker.' " He studied her without blinking or moving a muscle.

"Listen," she said, "you should have been there if you think that. No, I'll tell you. I started it. You think I just stood idly by while she insulted and abused you." She felt tears coming to her eyes. "What good does it do?" she said. "You have so little faith in me. You're a doomed man."

"Why?" he said.

"You have a wife who devotes herself to you without any reward. Do you know what I told Sherry Dombrosio?"

Leo said, "It's all over. I called him. I expressed my reaction. He told me to mind my own business."

"And he hung up on you," Janet said. "That unimportant little person. What does he do? Makes cartons for milk. He isn't fit to lick the ground you walk over." She got unsteadily up, balancing herself by means of the table, and walked toward the kitchen with her empty glass. Tears ran down her cheeks as she walked. The room swam. Leo, at his desk, seemed to expand, to blur and swell soundlessly. And her shoes made no sound against the floor. Looking down she saw that she did not have them on; she was in her stocking feet. The shoes were on the couch, along with her lighter and pack of Kools.

"Let's have dinner," Leo said, from his desk.

"I knew you'd say that," she said. "You want me to serve you. Can't I emerge as a person, into the light for once? That image you have of me — it's destructive to me. These pains and disorders I've had — you brought them on by your constant pushing me, pushing me. I never can please you; nothing is good enough for you. Fix your own god damn dinner." Entering the kitchen, she grabbed up the coffee pot and hurled it into the sink. The top flew from it, coffee and grounds spurted everywhere; she saw the drainboard, the wall stained, the dripping black coffee as it leaked to the floor. Part of the pot rolled up nearby, and she kicked it.

At the doorway, Leo stood watching.

"Leave me alone," she said, at once turning her back to him.

"Can I serve my own dinner?" he said. "To myself? Will you go off out of the way?"

"Sure," she said. Taking a pan of peas from the burner she removed the lid and dumped the peas onto the floor; they fell in a shower everywhere, rolling off, bouncing against her bare feet. "Help yourself," she said.

"I'll leave you alone," he said.

"Yes," she said. "Get away. I wish I could kill myself." Her voice, in her ears, rose higher and higher until she could barely stand it. "Go on," she shouted at him.

He said, "I'll be in the living room."

After he had gone, she stood for a moment, taking deep, slow breaths. And then she got the dust pan and broom and began sweeping up the peas. Her head ached violently. What'll we do about a vegetable? she wondered. What can I serve? Picking up the coffee pot she began to reassemble it. The handle was bent.

From the living room Leo called, "Look."

"What?" she said, holding the coffee pot.

"Come and look."

She came out. He stood by the window. When she reached him he pointed. "What is it?" she said. She saw nothing.

"That guy weaving along the highway."

"Leo," she said, "I told them what a wonderful and unique person you are. I love you so much. I think so much of you."

He glanced at her. Then he moved away, rubbing his forehead. "That guy really must be drunk," he murmured.

"You're one of the finest persons in the world," she said. "I wish the world could measure up to your ideals. You deserve to live in a better world. You should have better people around you. I try, but I can't. I can only blurt out how I feel."

He nodded, or seemed to nod; it was so slight that she could not be sure.

"There's really a good dinner tonight," she said. "With or without peas. I got a leg of lamb. No wonder you're champing at the bit. You can smell it. I think it's almost done."

"You better get another package of vegetables," he said.

"Yes," she said. "I will." As she started back to the kitchen she said, "Do you want to come in and keep me company?"

"All right," he said, following after her. Presently he said, "Do I really put that much pressure on you?"

She sat at the kitchen table, tearing open a package of frozen string beans. "It's that your standards are so high. Nobody can meet them but you. You can't expect the rest of us to, Leo."

"I can't see what you mean," he said. "What standards?"

"You work so hard. You're so intense. You get carried away by what you do; you become so completely involved. Everything is a cause for you." She smiled at him, but he did not smile back. His face remained dark and serious, his forehead wrinkled.

They heard a sound, then. A roaring motor sound from outside. Both of them started.

Leo got up and went to the front door. She saw the door open; he went outside and the door shut. The noise of the car died away somewhat, but she could still hear it. She put the beans into the boiling water and then she followed her husband outside onto the porch.

"It's that same guy," Leo said, in the darkness beside her. Below, from the road, they could see headlights shining up. The car roared.

"Are you sure?" she said.

"Yes, he turned up from the highway. At the gas station." He listened. In the darkness she heard him swear to himself in that determined, terrible way he had.

"What's he doing?" she said. "Did he go off the road? Maybe he backed into a drainage ditch." The noise seemed to stay in one spot. The headlights did not move; they gleamed unalterably up.

Leo said, "I think the son of a bitch hit some car. Some parked car."

"Should we do anything?" she asked.

"Yes," he said. He turned and went back inside the house.

When she followed after him she found him at the telephone. He held it aside for a moment. "I'm calling the highway patrol," he said. "I'm going to report the son of a bitch."

"Oh," she said nervously. "Why don't you wait? We ought to go down and see what it is — maybe he didn't hit a car; he may be stuck and trying to get his car back on the road."

"A drunk," he said, staring at her. "A drunken god damn maniac. You saw him racing down the middle of the highway, weaving back—" He broke off. His voice lowered and became dark, controlled. His customary phone voice, the one for emergencies; for him a phone call always meant an emergency. "I want to report a drunk driver," he said. "This is Leo Runcible, in Carquinez. On White Star Road." He paused.

Oh god, she thought. I know it's one of our neighbors; I know it's someone we know. She could not bear to hear; turning, she ran out of the house and back onto the porch. The noise, the scream of tires and motor, still went on. Now it ceased and she thought she heard voices, men's voices from below. And — flashlights?

He's stuck in the drainage ditch, she thought. It goes all along the road, all the way down to the bottom. And the road's so narrow and it twists, and at night even people who live along it have a hard time seeing their way. If he came up even a little too fast, he could get into the ditch so easily.

Once she had done it herself. What an awful feeling. The poor man or woman. Even if he is drunk. And how does Leo know he's drunk? Oh, she thought; that's right — we saw him weaving along the highway. But suppose it's a different person?

New headlights, additional lights, came on. She saw, in them, the outline of trees below. And then shiny metal. The side of a car. That's the stuck car, she thought. "Leo!" she called. "Come here; he *is* stuck. And they're pulling him out."

The car shuddered as its motor screamed again. She could now see that it had no top. Wrecked? she wondered, pressing her arms around herself to keep warm. No, it was a sports car. Then it must be Walt Dombrosio's car, she thought.

"Leo!" she shrieked, running back into the house. He was still on the phone; he waved her away and then slammed the bedroom door. "It's Walt's car," she shouted, opening the door. At the phone, her husband nodded, his face blank as he listened to the phone.

Did he know? Had he recognized it? By the sound of the motor, perhaps? He has such a keen ear . . .

Her husband hung up the phone. "I reported him," he said.

"Do you know whose car it is?" she said, gasping.

"Yes," he said.

"Did you know before you called?"

Wooden-faced, he said, "It doesn't matter whose car it is."

"I'll bet you recognized the motor," she said. "I remember — you told me one night when some car woke you up. You said you could tell a sports car."

Leo said, "Cars go by the office all day long."

"What does that mean? Why do you say that?"

"I've seen a lot of accidents. Most of them are caused by drunks."

"No," she said. "You started to say something else." That you have learned to recognize most of the cars in this area by their sound, she thought. From inside your office. Like a boy's game.

"He should be reported," Leo said. "He's always hot-rodding

around turns in that damn red thing." Going into the dining room he seated himself at the table. In a tired, grating voice he said, "Can we eat? Or are you going down the hill and tell Dombrosio that I phoned the highway patrol about him?"

She stood where she was.

"Come on," Leo said.

At last she came.

6

The Carquinez Dads' and Boys' Donkey Baseball Club owned a huge old white clapboard building, with turrets and fire escapes, in the center of town. Two palm trees grew in front of it, one on each side of the entrance with its balcony and porch and railing. Several of the rear windows had been broken. In winter the basement filled with water. A discarded rusty red Coca Cola machine lay among weeds to one side. The flagpole, which jutted out from the center of the roof, had been snapped off during a windstorm. The building was ninety-two years old and not worth much. Now and then the CDBDBC rented the building out to local groups for dances or barbecues or raffles. And once the piano teacher from the grammar school had rented it to give a recital of American songs.

The CDBDBC occasionally used Donkey Hall themselves. Once a year, in July, they sponsored a livestock show, after which they held bingo and sold hot dogs and pop in the building's basement. In December the men of the club cooked a dinner for their wives, twenty or so men, all wearing fancy chef's caps and gowns, carrying silver trays. Crepe paper hung from the rafters of the hall. Tables, borrowed from the school, were decorated with original drawings, mostly humorous. Most notable of all, on May tenth, came the club's Project Day. Getting together, they discussed what worthwhile civic move could be undertaken without too much cost. One year they had bought paint and entirely repainted the post office and other public buildings of the town.

For several years the President of the CDBDBC had been the butcher at the Carquinez Grocery, Jack E. Vepp. His personal hobby was deer hunting, and in 1958 the Club Project, at his suggestion, was a mass deer hunt. Herds of starving deer had, for some time, come down into farmland from the hills in search of food and water; they ate valuable hay, left fleas behind them, got in the path of autos. Home owners complained that deer ate apples off their trees. The deer-hunting project received a lot of popular support, and Jack E. Vepp was re-elected the next year.

Most of the men in town had been asked, at one time or another, to join the club. An exception to this was a man living on Bass Pool Road who was suspected of being a Communist. The other exception was Leo Runcible.

In the evening twilight of the Chevron Station, Runcible stood smoking his pipe while he waited for the attendant to finish with his car. For the first time in months the lights of Donkey Hall had been turned on, and the colors glowed out above the streetlights of the town. Cars had begun appearing, parking in front of the Hall. The time was seven-thirty. Looking at his wristwatch, Runcible thought, The meeting is about to begin.

"Big doings," he said to the service station attendant. He did not know the boy's name; he knew that he lived somewhere in the area and that he was taking courses in business administration.

"Yes sir," the boy said. He lay partly beneath Runcible's '55 Studebaker, still working to cinch up the new radiator hose that he had put on.

"Do you know what they're up to?" Runcible asked.

"Must be the night they organize to pick up all the newspapers in town," the boy said.

"That was last month," Runcible said. "And they do that in the afternoon."

Two cars from town turned past the station on their way to the Hall. He watched them go. The town handyman Bill Conley. Then, in the Ford, Keith Asmason, who owned a dairy ranch a few miles north of the town.

"I'll have this hose on in a minute, Mr. Runcible," the boy said. "Sorry to keep you."

Runcible thought, That's all right. I'm not going anywhere tonight. He continued to watch the cars parking at the Hall. A main social event for the area, he thought. If they asked me, would I go? Would I join? Not for a million dollars, he thought.

The next car was a small red sports car. That's right, he said to himself. Dombrosio is a member; not only that, an official. He would be. Prove you're a man by joining all the men's clubs . . . be a regular fellow. The sports car turned the corner. He saw, inside it, not one person but two. Sherry Dombrosio was driving; Walt rode beside her.

"Do they now have women members?" he said to the station attendant.

The sports car halted at the Hall. The door opened and Walt got out. He shut the door after him; Sherry turned the car around and drove away. Soon she passed the Chevron Station and started to climb back up the road to the Dombrosio house.

Crouching down, Runcible said, "How come Mrs. Dombrosio drives him to the Hall?"

The attendant said, "You didn't read in the paper about his license?"

"No," Runcible said. He was barely on speaking terms with the couple who ran the Carquinez *News;* he had long ago ceased reading it. To him the little four page newspaper was a place to put ads, and nothing more.

The boy slid out from beneath the car and sat up. "Did you

know they got Mr. Dombrosio on a drunk driving charge the
month before last? Right here in town?"

"Yes," Runcible said. "I heard about it."

"The Motor Vehicles Department revoked his license."

"No!" he said.

The boy nodded.

"They can do that?"

"Sure," the boy said. "It's part of their crackdown program on
drunk drivers. They suspended his license for six months. So he
has to be driven around by his wife."

Runcible said, "But the guy works in San Francisco."

"That don't mean nothing to the Motor Vehicles Department.
They're really tough."

"How does he get to work?"

"She's been driving him," the boy said.

"Does she make two trips a day?" It did not seem possible.

"No," the boy said, scrambling to his feet. "She stays in the
city. Your car's ready; I got the hose on okay."

"That's sure lousy luck," Runcible said, as the boy made out the
tag. "Losing his license when he has to commute to San Francisco."

"Really tough," the boy said. "But mostly on his wife. In a way
he's got it soft; he gets a chauffeur."

"But anywhere he wants to go, she has to take him."

"That's right," the boy said. "Unless he wants to break the law.
And if he should get caught, they'd never give him a license again
the rest of his life."

"It wouldn't be worth it," Runcible said.

"No," the boy said. "I guess not."

And I'll bet he blames me, Runcible thought as he drove up the
hill toward his home. But perhaps Dombrosio had never found
out who had called the highway patrol. But he must know that
normally police cars are never in the area except on weekends.

Am I supposed to feel guilty? he asked himself. Ashamed because the slob didn't have any better sense than to drink and drive? My god, they yell at you every time you turn on the radio: if you drink don't drive, and if you drive don't drink. He's got nobody to blame but himself; he has to take the responsibility for his own actions.

But as he drove he became more and more disturbed. That's a dreadful thing to happen to a man, he thought. Losing his license and having to be ferried around by his wife, like a cripple. I didn't know the buggers did that; I thought they only fined drunk drivers.

That's a hardship case, he thought. A man who commutes. They must be a bunch of sadists up there in Sacramento. What's the matter with them? Practically Nazis, he thought. The guy's living depends on it. His home. His family.

It's really lousy, he thought. A dirty lousy stunt, with no concern for a human being and his needs. So the guy steps out of line once — so what? Is it so terrible? Did he hurt anybody? Hell, he thought. All the guy did was get his ass-end down in a ditch; he got his paint job scratched up, and he made a damn fool of himself. Maybe I ought to phone or write somebody in Sacramento, he thought. See what I can do. Put on a little pressure; get a fire lit.

But what do I owe Walt Dombrosio? he asked himself. A guy who wouldn't think twice before spitting in my eye. Did he buy that house of his through me? No, he went to that old worn out rustic Thomas. He started right out by costing me money; by now he must have cost me close to three thousand dollars directly, and no telling how much indirectly by turning people against me. People in the city who might want to move out here — after all, he's in the city all day. And now that handy-craft wife of his is in the city all day, too, with nothing to do. They can spread all kinds of bad advertising for Runcible Realty.

It doesn't pay to have people down on you, he thought. And

yet, that's the price for speaking out. By being blunt, being honest, I run up against the crumbs of the world. The bleeding hearts like Walt Dombrosio who have the starry-eyed idealism to invite a colored boy to their house but don't have to foot the bill.

When he got home, and had parked the car, he hurried up the stairs and into the living room. He found Janet in the bedroom watching TV with Jerome.

"Come here a minute," he said to her, leading her from the bedroom. "Did you know Walt Dombrosio lost his license because of that drunk driving charge?"

His wife hesitated. She had been sober now for several days; she had once again decided to go on the wagon. Her face, pinched and colorless, began to wrinkle with unease. "Well, yes," she said at last. "I heard that some time ago."

"Why the hell didn't you tell me?" he demanded.

"You — said you didn't want to hear town gossip." She faced him with defiance. "And I didn't want to worry you."

"Why should it worry me?" he said. "I'm not worried about Walt Dombrosio. So they haven't spoken to us for two months; what do we lose? Are we any worse off? I wouldn't be speaking to them anyhow — I had my say on the phone that night."

Janet said, "When you made that call did you know that they took people's licenses away for drunk driving? There's been a lot about it on the radio. Some judges claim it isn't legal." She followed him as he went to a closet with his coat. "It's part of a statewide safety program. The Governor is behind it."

"I wonder if I ought to call Dombrosio," Runcible said.

"Why?" she said, at once alert.

"Tell him I'm sorry."

With great firmness, as if she had thought it all out long ago, Janet said, "Then he would know it was you."

"No," Runcible said. "I'd just say I heard, and how sorry I was. It is a lousy deal, a man who commutes. Being driven everywhere by his wife. And that gal's a harpy. A real pusher. I wouldn't want to be in a position to have her put me down."

"Don't call him," Janet said. "Please don't. I have never told anyone that it was you who called the police that night."

"Are you sure?" He himself could not believe; he did not trust her. Perhaps she imagined that she had not told anyone. Possibly she did not intend — had not intended — to tell anybody. But when she had been drinking her tongue wagged, and he knew that sometimes in the afternoon she had a few drinks with the other wives in the area, at their homes, at his home, or down at one of the two Carquinez bars.

"If he knew it was you," Janet said, "he probably would have let you know by now."

But he was not listening to her. Restless and ill-at-ease, he wandered about the house. "What are they saying?" he said. "What's the general opinion about Dombrosio?"

"You mean," Janet said, "do they think he was treated fairly?"

"I mean, are they sympathetic toward him? My god, he might have run down one of our children — they have no children of their own, the Dombrosios. What do they care? That's another thing about them; they have no children so they have no interest in the school problems, the bonds and the tax rates. A lot of people around here are indignant about those foreign cars anyhow. He takes it into San Francisco for service; he doesn't go to the local garage because it's a foreign car. And he probably doesn't buy his gas here either. Do they shop at the Carquinez Grocery, or do they shop in the city?"

By now he had gone so far away from Janet that he could not hear her answer.

At the living room window he looked down at the lights of Donkey Hall, the parked cars. The activity. Their idea of civic improvement, he thought. Judging kids' costumes on Halloween to keep them out of mischief. What would I do? he asked himself.

All his proposals were known; in the old days, when he had first moved to Carquinez, he had published them in the *News* and he had paid to have them circulated in the form of petitions. Two or three new classrooms to the grammar school — the classes were growing larger each year. Even a new building with an auditorium and a hot lunch program. A nursery school. More streetlights. The town library open more than four hours a week, and more magazines than the *National Geographic.* A better road into town; that would have to be taken up with both the county and the state. A higher tax rate would have to come about, to support all this, and he wanted that, too. And the bank would have to lend more.

But the main thing: better water and cheaper power. Unless some kind of small industry moved in, there would never be enough capital to support the area, to supply the money to make the improvements. The ranchers would never fork anything over; they had made their money by being stingy, by hiring their sons and daughters to do all the work. Only a mill at Olema, the RCA station out on the Point, the small retail stores . . . and of course men employed by the county to work on the roads during winter, to clip the trees and haul off broken limbs. Some day it would have to come. All the improvements he wanted would eventually take place. But he wanted them in his lifetime.

And, he thought, if we don't do it ourselves, it'll be done by outsiders. Money from outside, subdividers who we don't know. This won't be a dairy farm area forever.

Below him, in the darkness, the lights of Donkey Hall winked. I hope you can raise the five dollars for prize money, he thought. It will really put a strain on you, you anti-Semitic jackass town planners with your appropriate name. And then, on to the annual weenie roast. If I did join, he thought, I could run the mustard concession or have the dart-throwing booth. We might make twenty dollars to put up for the livestock judging.

Raising his right hand, he made an obscene gesture through the living room window; at Donkey Hall below. Anyone in Carquinez who happened to glance up at that moment would have seen him; with the drapes back he was fully outlined by the living room light. But he did not care. I should print it on my office stationery, he thought. Runcible Realty, and then the finger. To all a good night.

In one of the third floor rooms at Donkey Hall, heated by a portable electric heater, four of the Advisors of the CDBDBC sat at a table, deep in work. Downstairs, in the main hall, the members of the club watched slides on VD prevention that one of the members, a retired Army major, had procured from the Armed Forces.

The four Advisors comprised Jack E. Vepp, the President of the club, Earl Timmons, the Vice President and a truck driver, Walt Dombrosio, Club Manager and commercial designer, and Michael Wharton, Club Treasurer and fourth grade teacher at the grammar school. In the past several years it had been Walt Dombrosio who had been the most help at Halloween; he had supplied materials for costumes, helped the kids, showed the judges what to look for in the way of original ideas. This year, however, he did not want to participate.

"Let them make their own costumes," he said. "They ought to know how by now."

Wharton said, "If left alone, most of them will simply wear the plastic costumes sold by dime stores. It'll be a choice among prepared costumes, and the parents who spend the most money will secure the prize for their child."

"Some of the ranchers' wives are going to sew," Vepp said. "So there's going to be some original costumes."

"Why don't you want to participate this year?" Wharton asked Dombrosio.

"It's hard for me to get around," he said. "You know I lost my driver's license."

They all nodded at that. "That's really bad," Timmons said. "Yes," Vepp said. "That's one hell of a break. That Motor Vehicles outfit has no legal right to do that." Wharton added, "You're still appealing that, aren't you, Walt?"

"I'm appealing," he said shortly.

"Somebody maybe could drive you," Vepp said.

"How about your wife?" Timmons said.

"She's probably sick of driving him," Vepp said. "I see her driving him all over the place."

"She's not sick of it," Dombrosio said. "But—" He shrugged. "I'm not free like I was. To come and go."

"Well," Vepp said, "we really count on you."

"Remember that April Fool gag we did," Timmons said. "That was really something — remember, you dreamed that up."

Dombrosio remembered.

"You made up all those cow suits," Vepp said. "And you used that new plastic — what's it called?"

"Polyethylene," Dombrosio said. "It's actually a hardened wax. An enormously long carbon molecule."

"I'll never forget that," Vepp said. "That was the funniest gag I ever saw or even heard of. We really had them fooled; we fooled everybody in town."

"That was quite successful," Wharton said.

In their cow suits, which Dombrosio had created in the workshop at Lausch Company, six Advisors of the club had joined a herd of cows at the Fairchild ranch. They had allowed themselves to be herded into the milking barn, and then, when the milkers came to hook them up, they had begun to argue and insult the milkers. It was all a good gag, a lot of harmless fun, and they had gone on then to the next ranch. And when that part of the gag was over they had gone into town, and even out onto the highway to stop cars. The suits had absolute fidelity of detail. It was Dombrosio's work at its best. One of the suits still existed down in the basement of Donkey Hall, part of the permanent historic display.

"Say, Walter," Vepp said. "There's an idea that came to me; it has nothing to do with the club, but it's along your line. You know the way quail come along in a bunch, about twenty or thirty of them all together? You know, even if you shoot a blast of buckshot in the middle of them, all you get is maybe four or five, and the rest get away."

"The quail are really fat this time of year," Timmons said.

"So anyhow," Vepp said, "what I got to thinking was, isn't there some sort of electric trap you could rig up for me? A bunch of wires that after the whole flock gets on, they get electrocuted but not burned up so their flesh is ruined. Some resistance wire, maybe. A guy like you, with your ability, could do that."

The grammar school teacher said, "It's too bad to put Walter to work like that. Doesn't he have enough troubles? Anyhow it's illegal to trap quail that way."

"No it's not," Vepp said. "What do you mean, 'work like that'? Walt don't have nothing against some nice fat quail for breakfast." He laughed, showing his gold-crowned teeth.

"I'm in enough legal trouble already," Dombrosio said. "All I need is to pay some huge fine for illegal trapping. I don't even think this is quail season."

Vepp said, "You can always shoot quail on your own property, any time of the year. You can say it was to protect your crop; they eat grain and stuff. Vegetables from your garden. Like crows or jays."

"I could rig it up," Dombrosio said. "But I don't think I want to. I'm not much interested."

The four of them were silent, for a time.

"It's hard to think of something to do," Vepp said finally.

"We could go bird-watching," Timmons said. "Along with the fourth grade." He nodded toward the grammar school teacher.

"Pick up rocks, too," Vepp said. "Maybe find some rare fossils. Or some of those arrowheads, those Indian things." He grinned, but Wharton said nothing. The grammar school teacher stared off into space as if he did not hear him. "How's your arrowhead collection?" Vepp said to him, still persisting.

"Fine," Wharton said.

"And your rock collection?"

Wharton nodded distantly.

Vepp said, "What about your milk bottle top collection?"

"I think he gave that up," Timmons said.

"That's the best," Vepp protested. "Those milk bottle tops. Real California history in them. I mean, look at those old dairies around here."

"Old Indian dairies," Timmons said. He giggled. "Old Indian twin dairies." He made a motion, indicated female breasts. "How about a collection of them? Stuffed and mounted under glass. That ought to go over big for the fourth graders." Both he and Vepp laughed, and Walt Dombrosio could not help smiling, too.

"Listen," Dombrosio said. "Hey listen, Wharton. You know those granite awls you have, those Indian awls? They're tools, right? You know what they look to me to be?" Already, Vepp and Timmons saw the gag and were laughing. "Say, I'll bet those are stone tools all right."

"Petrified tools," Timmons choked. "Indian petrified tools. What a terrific collection. They're about ten inches long — those must have been real masculine Indians. How could they have died out, since they had such big tools?"

Wharton said nothing. After a while Timmons and Vepp became tired of baiting him. Nothing had come from the meeting of Advisors; they had not been able to persuade Dombrosio to participate this year, and so there was no point in going on.

"I'm going downstairs and look at the VD films," Timmons said, rising. "Want to come along, Jack?"

Both he and Vepp departed, leaving Dombrosio and the fourth grade teacher.

Presently Wharton said, "It's too bad."

"What is?" Dombrosio said, now feeling a little guilty at having kidded the man. With Vepp and Timmons gone, he did not feel quite so jolly about it.

"You have a good deal of creative ability. It seems to me it could go into more important things than building traps so that Jack Vepp can slaughter quail."

"Well, you're a nature-lover," Dombrosio said. "You're an observer, a scientist. You have to see his point of view. There's nothing wrong with hunting; you eat lamb and beef, don't you? And it doesn't bother you."

Wharton said, "I don't mean that."

From the start, Wharton had made no bones about it; he had joined the CDBDBC to assist in the civic programs that the club did on occasion promote, but he did not approve of the high jinks so dear to the others. His dislike of Vepp was common knowledge. But if there were no public-spirited people in the club, he had pointed out, people like Vepp would turn the organization into nothing more than a — what was it Dombrosio had heard the grammar school teacher say, once? Into an excuse for renting dirty movies. Owning a hall to show dirty films. For stag parties; that was it. Men's smoker. Wharton could not stay out of the club because he feared it more without his presence than with. He could not rest comfortably in his house up on State Farm Road, in his den with his specimens of newts and snakes.

"How much do you make as a teacher?" Dombrosio asked him, all at once.

"Five thousand two hundred a year," Wharton said.

"Take home?"

"No," Wharton said. "That's before deductions."

"How do you manage to live on that?"

Wharton said, "Sometimes I consider weaving my own baskets out of reeds and making pots and pans out of clay, and chewing acorns. Like the Indians used to."

"They hunted and fished, too."

"I have no objection to that," Wharton said. "If it's for food, it's a good and perfectly natural thing. I don't like Vepp because he relishes it."

"In other words, it's bad if you enjoy it," Dombrosio said. "But it's fine if you do it cold-bloodedly."

Suddenly turning toward him, Wharton said, "You know what I wish you'd do? I wish you'd get hold of some high frequency generators for the school. And maybe an FM tuner. I think I asked you about building us an oscillator, last year or so. What ever became of that?"

Guiltily, Dombrosio said, "I got started on it. It's in my workshop at home. Half-finished."

"I'll tell you something else I wish you'd do."

"You know I'm always willing to help the school."

Wharton studied him soberly, said, "I'd like you to come and show the fourth grade how to use certain materials."

"You mean, work directly with the children? Like a teacher?" He did not feel favorably inclined; he felt nervous, self-conscious. "What materials?"

"Some of those new plastics. The boys buy those model boat and airplane kits, but they're nothing but prefabricated sections; all they have to do is glue them together. In the old days a kit consisted of balsa wood, tissue paper — we had to do all the work of cutting and shaping the parts. We actually made the models out of the wood. Now the model is made for them, but not assembled."

"True," Dombrosio said. "But consider this; look at the wealth of detail they can get into the new plastics. Tiny detail, like the engine cylinders and exhausts."

"You have some molds here in the Hall," Wharton said. "I noticed them in the storeroom where you work."

"Those are plaster of paris, not any of the new plastics."

"Tell me what you're doing. They look interesting."

"Just fooling around," Dombrosio said. He always had several pet projects going. And now, since the hearing at which he had lost his license, he had spent even more time puttering around.

"Did I see some of your masks? Rigid entire head masks, like those Martian invaders that you made? I always considered that to be a real innovation. You showed genuine genius in that."

"Thanks," Dombrosio said. It warmed him, to recall that.

Up near Drake's Landing there was a flying saucer group, composed mostly of middle-aged women and retired people. Last year, as a club stunt, he had made invaders from outer space masks and costumes, and even a dummy flying saucer which Timmons had hauled up to Drake's Landing in a flatbed truck. Late at night they had unloaded their tin and plastic flying saucer in the middle of a sheep pasture. Putting on their costumes and masks, and carrying toy rocket pistols bought at the drugstore, they, a group of four of them, had marched up the steps of the house in which the saucer group met. No meeting was in progress, but the woman who ran the group was there, in bed; they had gotten her up by making metallic whining noises with a vibrator that Dombrosio had salvaged from the junk pile at Lausch Company.

"You approve of that?" he asked Wharton. It had always seemed to him that Wharton disliked their stunts; he felt practical jokes to be cruel and not funny. "You told me, I remember, that most hoaxes were infantile. What did you call it? Sadism?"

"But I have nothing but contempt for that flying saucer group," Wharton said. "They deserved it."

"So that's an exception." He felt that here, for the first time that he could remember, the grammar school teacher had shown a seamy side of his nature. "It's okay to play tricks on people you don't like."

Wharton considered. "Their credulity — they wouldn't have fallen for the hoax if they had had normal common sense. You tested their ability to judge reality. Their scientific — or lack of any scientific — orientation."

Before the teacher could get off any further on his favorite topic, the value of science in training the mind, Dombrosio interrupted, "Let me ask you — have there been any hoaxes in science?"

"I suppose you could consider the whole geocentric cosmology as a form of hoax. You mean deliberate? Where there was knowledge that the idea was untrue?" Wharton frowned. "I've heard that some Soviet scientists deliberately created spurious data to make their genetics theories seem plausible. Wax apples—"

"What about the Piltdown Man?"

Wharton grimaced. "Yes. Certainly."

"I'm interested in that," Dombrosio said. "They don't even know who did it, do they?"

"If you look up the Piltdown skull in the *Brittanica*," Wharton said, "you'll find that most authorities were in doubt about it. For one thing, it never fitted into any system. Even when it was not known to be a forgery it was an anomaly. A brain like that of a modern person but the jaw of a chimpanzee."

"Isn't that actually what it was?"

"Yes. Whoever concocted it put the two together knowing that they had no relationship. It was a conscious job of deception, involving real skill and knowledge of the subject. As you know, it wasn't until the new carbon dating test that they could demonstrate that it was a fake."

"So a scientist must have done it. Maybe the one who found the skull."

"Maybe."

Dombrosio said, "But what would the motive be?"

"Search me."

"Did he probably eventually intend to make it public that it was a fake? If nobody ever found out, I don't see what satisfaction he would get. Maybe he intended to tell, but died."

"He may have gotten tired of searching for authentic stone age remains. My theory—" Wharton gestured. "Of course, by now everyone knows my anti-religious bias. I wouldn't be surprised if we find out someday that the Piltdown Skull was fabricated by a clerical person, bent on proving that all fossil remains were spurious. He hoped to get the Piltdown Skull accepted by the eminent scientific authorities of his day, and then he'd spring it on the world that he had put it together in his attic."

"But why didn't he expose it, then?"

"I have no theory about that," Wharton said. "Possibly he continued to wait because not all authorities did accept the thing; he was waiting for a more universal assent, and it never came. He delayed too long."

"Could other early human skulls be fakes? Like the Neanderthals and the other missing links?"

"There are too many of them by now," Wharton said. "Hundreds have been found. A tremendous variety since the war, in Africa and Israel and Asia. Mixed types. New types. Sub types. Apes more advanced in some respects than men. If you're interested, I have a few articles in *Scientific American* I'd be happy to lend you."

"I recall reading about some lake in Africa where they found a true dawn man."

"That was Leakey," Wharton said. "The oldest skull found of tool-making man. Between six hundred thousand and a million years old. A well-developed ape or poorly developed man." He walked over to Dombrosio, his forefinger extended. "There's a very interesting thing. They used to think that the near-men, such as Neanderthal and Heidelberg and the rest came *before* Homo sapiens."

"Didn't they?" Dombrosio said.

"Now they have found true human skulls that go back as far as any of the so-called dawn men."

"Then human beings existed side by side with the others."

"Human beings did not evolve out of the dawn men. Homo sapiens was one of a variety of types. We're not descended from Neanderthal or any of the others. They were variants, with whom our ancestors possibly intermingled."

"Then there could be Neanderthal blood in human beings today."

"Possibly."

"Then Neanderthals weren't a race," Dombrosio said. "They were more like a stock of — could you say degenerate men?"

"That means little or nothing. In any case, they ceased to exist, very suddenly. And they evidently lived over a wide area, from Africa to Asia to Europe. But not in the New World, evidently. In any case, no skulls have been found in either North or South America."

"Interesting," Dombrosio said.

From downstairs they heard voices and the scraping of chairs. The slides on VD had all been shown; the meeting was breaking up. Dombrosio heard cars starting outside the Hall.

"Want a ride?" Wharton said. "I can take you home."

"No," he said. "Sherry is coming back for me."

"Does it put much of a burden on her? She has to spend five days a week in the City, doesn't she? What does she do?"

Dombrosio, as he put his coat on, said, "She visits people she knows there. She gets along fine — she's satisfied. It's a good deal for her. She shops. Goes to a movie. Attends a few classes in commercial art. That used to be her ambition, to be a professional artist."

"Possibly she could help with the Halloween costumes," Wharton said hopefully.

7

On the first long grade up the side of Mount Tamalpais his wife carefully shifted into the proper gear, her eye on the Alfa's tachometer. Behind them, far below the hillside and rocks, the ocean could be seen. Gazing up, he took in the sight of the forest, the dense groves of redwoods and firs, the firewatcher's tower at the highest peak. In the cold misty light of 6:30 A.M. the tower looked like a little damp metal gun turret, far off. And they do have a Nike missile base up here, Dombrosio thought. Maybe that isn't a firewatcher's tower. Maybe it's a radar installation.

Since he did not have to drive he could examine the scenery. He could relax somewhat and look from side to side, even back over his shoulder at the descending curves of road and the ocean. It made him dizzy to do so.

"Don't take the turns too fast," he said.

Sherry said, "I don't hear any tire squeal."

"You never can tell what you're going to meet," he said. "These are blind curves." He had said such things many times, during the drives in and back. It still made him nervous to be driven. His wife's driving did not satisfy him, but he could not pin down what was wrong with it; she watched the tach, she did not over-rev the engine, and as she said, there was no tire squeal.

She slowed the car on the downgrade with the gears and not the brakes. I just don't like to be driven, he decided. And, without the steering wheel to grasp, he felt himself thrown around by each turn of the car. His stomach had bothered him from the first day that Sherry had taken the wheel.

I suppose I should be grateful, he thought. That she's willing to do it at all. From the very start, in fact, from the day of the hearing, she had driven him without outward sign of complaint; she had undertaken it as a job, and had stuck to it.

"What are you going to do, today?" he asked.

Sherry said, "Why do you ask?"

"You seem a little more dressed up than usual." He had noticed that she had on one of her best suits, the dark blue one. In his mind he had the idea that she only wore it on special occasions; the last time, as he remembered, she had worn it at a meeting with their attorney.

Matter-of-factly, Sherry said, "I'm going job-hunting."

He felt cold. Cold and faint. "What do you mean?"

"Job-hunting. I've thought it over and as long as I have to go into the City every day and be there all day I might as well apply for a job." She kept her eyes on the road. Her voice was moderate.

"What kind of job?"

"We'll see."

He said, "There's just four more months of this crap of you having to drive me. By the time you find a job, half of that will be over with. You can't get a job for two months."

"I think I can get a job sooner than that," she said.

"Have you been looking?" He had a full, absolute intimation; of course she had been looking. And she had not said anything to him until now. Now, she probably had a good prospect. Or perhaps she actually had the job. Naturally she would wait. Why should she tell him? His attitude did not matter to her.

"Yes, I looked," Sherry said.

"Why didn't you say anything about it?" He made himself be calm. He kept his feelings out of his voice, so that it got into it the same reasonable quality as hers. "I think it would have been a good idea to discuss it with me."

To that, she said nothing.

Unable to keep silent, he said, "Suppose I don't like the idea."

"We can use the money," she said. "With house taxes coming up. And we're going to owe a great deal of money for the leaching lines. And we haven't paid all of the attorney fees — I held up that check. Did I tell you?"

"Will you quit at the end, when I have my license back?"

Sherry said, "It seems to me that that should depend on how well the job works out."

"On principle," he said, "I don't like a wife of mine to work."

"Well," she said, "I intend to get a job anyway. I think you're being domineering and aggressive, and I don't like your tone of voice."

"I won't let you," he said.

Turning her head she studied him for an instant with her cold, intense eyes. Then she swung her head away, to face the road. In a distinct voice she said, "I won't drive you in anymore."

His emotions became too great, then, for expression. He stared out at the trees, the massive redwoods. Ahead of them a car appeared and passed, its tires squealing on the curve. Its driver glanced at them to see what sort of car theirs was.

"It's a wonder an American car will get around these turns," Dombrosio said.

"I gave him plenty of room," his wife said.

"You're really putting the pressure on," he said. "What do you want? I can't figure it out. What's it mean to you, to get a job? Is it like being a man?"

She said nothing.

"You're determined to wear the pants," he said.

"Why do you make so much of this?" she said. "Why does it worry you so? You must be terribly insecure about your masculinity, if my getting a temporary job threatens you so. You must feel that you're failing in some basic, vital way."

"If I were dead," he said, "would you get a job?"

That baffled her. "How — strange."

"You wouldn't," he told her. "Because if I were dead, it wouldn't be necessary for you to defeat and destroy me."

At that, she laughed sharply and her face flushed. "My god," she said. "You really are out of your head. This whole business about your license has driven you really mad."

"What would you do?" he persisted. "If you weren't married to me? You wouldn't get a job; you wouldn't care a god damn thing about a job. It'd be the last thing you'd care about; you'd sit home — you'd get a studio — and paint fine art. Great art, like Picasso."

"Thanks," she said.

"You'd go back to living off your family," he said. "You've never had a job. You've never worked in your life. When I met you, you were living off your family; if you want to work so bad, why weren't you working, then?"

She said, "How could I have worked, then? I was going to school."

"Lots of people work while they're going to school." He sprang at her; he had her, and he savored it. "*I* was working, then, when I met you. I was going to school and working; I didn't have a rich family to support me." His voice rose to a shout, but he did not care. "I know the real reason why you have no respect for me!"

"Why?"

"Because I'll never in a million years be able to earn as much money as you're used to. As that family of yours. You think I ought to be able to do as well as your stepfather. You're comparing me to a — financial wizard."

She laughed bitterly. "Willis, a 'financial wizard.'"

"Yes," he said. "That's exactly what he is. You think it's perfectly normal for a man to own a string of businesses that bring in a fifty percent return, year after year — my good god, when you're up in that bracket, money doesn't mean the same thing as it means to us. It isn't a means of buying things; it's power, sheer power. You expect me to compete with that? Remember — he didn't start out from where I am. That whole family, his father and his grandfather, were investors. I wasn't even alive when they made their money, their first money."

She said, "You always dredge this up."

Not listening, he went on, "Willis is so far up there that he's in a bracket where you can't even tell what's legal and what's not legal. They make the laws. They buy little town lawyers and judges. Except for that income tax suit, where he had to settle with the Government — except for that, he can do anything he wants. And I'm supposed to measure up to him. If I don't I'm a failure as a man. My god, when they feel like seeing us, they hop on a plane and fly out here, from New York. Any time they feel like it. And rent a suite at the Mark Hopkins. And they have lawyers all over the country."

"You should have used one of Willis' lawyers," Sherry said. "If you had, you wouldn't have lost your license."

"And you hold that against me, too."

"I hold it against you that you're so childish that when he phoned and wanted you to use Adamson and Rogers, you said you didn't need to. And you went out and got some boy just starting out, with no contacts of any importance."

"That's it," he said. "It's who you know."

"As far as the law goes," she said.

"What a world," he said.

"You have to adapt to it," Sherry said. "Reality is reality. You nurse your infantile pride . . . it's what's destroying you, if anything is. You can't stand anybody achieving something you can't; you envy them. You can't stand Willis because he's been financially successful and you haven't." She added, "Or rather, you haven't done as well as he." She glanced at him to see his reaction.

Yes, he thought. I did hear. *You haven't.* Aloud, he said, "My infantile madness is such that it gets you to say it out loud. That you do consider me a failure as a man."

With caution, she said, "I consider that you have no aptitude in the world of business, if that constitutes being a failure as a man."

"It does in this society," he said. "The man is the hunter; the man brings home the food. And that means the paycheck."

"So if I get a job," Sherry said, "that means I'm in competition with you as a man. That would make me the man."

"Yes," he said.

"And you think that's what I want. What I'm after."

"Yes," he said.

"Does it occur to you," she said, in a hard, small voice, "that it's all a projection on your part? That it's in your own mind?"

But he was deaf to that; he had heard it too many times, during their marriage.

Her argument, he realized, is merely that. Merely to say that it's in my mind. To assert that I do not know. No evidence is offered, of the kind that a man or a rational person, a scientist, would permit. What does my wife say to me? That I'm powerless to discover any reality except myself. And how can I answer that?

With fright, he realized that he could not. He could never be sure if what she said might not be true.

What a bad, unscrupulous, woman's argument, he thought. What a cruelty to perpetrate on me. Unless she is right. Oh god, he thought. All she has to do is say it. She undermines me; she ends the discussion. How can I go on? The more I say, the angrier I get — it only proves that she is right. What is so awful about a wife working? Lots of wives do it. Husbands stay home; some of them feed the baby, wash the dishes. If it destroys me, it does so only because I believe it does.

Such a little thing, he thought. She wants to get a job; she has to come into the City anyhow, and we do need the money.

But I knew this would happen, he said to himself. I anticipated this. So there must be something to my fears, some reality.

And, with panic, he thought, I know the next step. The next step is for her to work and me to stay home. I know it; it will come about, and nothing can stop it. I am so close to that already. This is what she's been aiming at for so long, since the beginning; the loss of my driver's license made me helpless, delivered me over to her.

He said, "Would you really do that?"

"Do what?"

"Refuse to drive me to work? If I didn't let you get a job?"

After pondering, Sherry said, "It might be a way of making you realize the need of both giving and taking in this world."

Flailing at her with fury he shouted, "What does that mean, for god's sake? What is that?"

Keeping herself calm, she said, "You can't expect me to be the only one who gives, Walt. I give and give. And I don't keep track; I don't have a little black book of all the good deeds I do. I've never complained about having to drive you in every morning and spend the whole day in San Francisco. But I think you're mature enough, adult enough, to face the fact that you have to be capable of giving back to me, as well as receiving from me. Do you know what it is, if you can't give back? It's the child all over again; the child with his parents. In a marriage, there are only equals."

He said, "That fucking analyst really equipped you with a language."

"Do you want me to stop the car?" she said. And, seeing a broad dirt shoulder on the curve ahead, she shifted gears and took the Alfa from the road, slowing it to a stop on the dirt. "I can stay here," she said, "all morning. There's a book under the seat. I can read about color-fast dyes." Bending down, she reached for the book. As she brought it out he saw it, a massive red-backed textbook.

The incongruity of it, this textbook on dyes out here in the middle of Tamalpais State Park, with the car parked on the shoulder of the road at six forty-five in the morning, was too much for him. He began to laugh, and, after a moment, Sherry, too, smiled.

"Why do we fight?" she said. She put the book back down. "We really love each other. Don't we?"

Certainly, he felt some kind of deep emotion toward her. In her blue suit, with her face fresh and smooth, her eyelashes and brows darkened with makeup, she looked attractive in the extreme. Nobody could deny that. His hands, his body, had touched her so often in the past that now merely to look at her was enough to arouse tactile sensations; the palms of his hands, his fingers and shoulders, all his surface area itched in yearning to come into contact with her. His physical system had been bred to it by enormous and persistent experience. Among the various realities, it was in some respects the most persuasive that he had ever known.

"No love-making here," she said, as he moved closer to her, as close as their two safety belts permitted. "Keep your belt fastened." That was a joke between them, a risqué joke that they had invented; it was not shared with anyone else on earth.

"Later?" he said. He bent to kiss her on the cheek.

"Well," she said, "if you're interested in making love to a

woman whose sole interest is supplanting you and becoming a man."

Hearing that, he felt his heart harden again. But he kept the tenderness in his voice; he kept the news from her.

I'm going to do everything I can, he said to himself. To keep you where you belong: at home, as my wife. I'll fight all the way, to the very end. Looking down at her nice legs and ankles, he thought, In all areas. I'll fight wherever I have a chance to win.

"Let's get back on the road," he said. He touched her gently behind her knee, a delicate, tender spot of her anatomy; she trembled, and her leg drew back involuntarily.

"You sound so pleased," she said. "You certainly perked up in a hurry." Smiling at him, she put the car in gear; in a moment she had started out onto the road once more.

That night, at home, he heard her in the bedroom phoning. She had shut the door before going in, but there was no mistaking the sound of her voice when she was on the telephone; it got an even firmer, more inflexible quality. It did not become louder or slower. It became more authoritative, as if the person on the other end, whoever it might be, was in the category of the plumber, the dentist: someone whom she had called, whom she wanted for something. She made the calls, he reflected. They did not call her.

Whatever it is, he thought, it is something that by rights I should be doing. Like that call to Arbarth, the contractor, which I should have made. She is beating me to something, again.

When she came out he said, "Who was that?"

Sherry said, "My stepfather." In her hand she had a pencil and pad of paper; seating herself on the arm of the couch she crossed her legs, smoothed down her skirt, and considered what she had written on the pad.

"Are they well?" he said finally. "I presume your mother's over the detached retina."

"Almost over," Sherry said. "It takes a long time to recover."

"How's your brother?" he said.

"They're fine. The children are fine. They wondered why we hadn't written."

"Good," he said.

"Willis asked after you. I told him you were down the street; I knew you wouldn't want to talk to him."

"That's true," he said. "Although I could hardly have . . . since you didn't tell me you were going to phone. Do you know, by any chance, what the call cost?"

"No," she said steadily.

"Why did you call him?"

Sherry said, "I wanted to find out who he knows in the Bay Area. That might have a job I'd be interested in."

"And what did Willis say?"

"He said he knew three or four firms. He's going to look them up and then call me back, probably tomorrow or the next day."

"It never occurred to you to simply go to an employment agency on your own. And not work through your stepfather."

"No," she said. "It was your idea, anyhow."

"Mine?"

She said, "You pointed out that I ought to get it right away, or it wouldn't be worth it. So I called him." Rising, she passed from the living room, back to the bedroom. The door shut after her, and soon he heard the sound of her voice; she was phoning again.

This time he got up and went to the door to listen. For a long time the intermittent phrases made no sense; he strained to hear, and at last he realized, with chagrin, that she was talking to some local person. He heard her dial, and on their phones they could only dial Carquinez and Stinson Beach. She was finding out about the next meeting of the Carquinez Garden Association, through which she and several other women purchased shrubs and flowers.

Feeling baffled and depressed, he returned to the living room and the TV set, with its noise and motion, its distraction.

Watching the TV he could forget his problems for a time. It did not enlighten him or improve him, teach him or even entertain him. But, like a warm bath, it relaxed him. And that was good enough. That was all, at the end of the day, that he wanted. It was a means of preparing him for full sleep: a halfway point between life and bed.

Toward the end of the week, his boss Norm Lausch asked him to come into his office.

Dombrosio stood by his desk, removing his coveralls, delaying as long as was feasible. In his several years with Lausch Company he had had few dealings with Norm himself; the man owned other businesses and he divided his time among them. His favorite seemed to be his house trailer outlet. He had, years ago, designed a terrific new interior for house trailers, and one of the largest manufacturers had taken him up on it. His own firm built the interiors, the special tables and shelves and cupboards; in fact, everything but the shell, the trailer itself. Most of his early money had been made in that business.

The man had a mild voice, difficult to hear, not high-pitched but in a sort of neutral middle range. He smoked a particular type of black ropelike cigarette, as long as a cigar, that he had brought in from the Philippines. Every time Dombrosio saw him Lausch had on a suit the color of Indian pottery, a reddish brown clay color, and heavy, like felt. He had attractive, pale hands; his nails were manicured, and he wore a big gold wedding band. His face was tanned — he used an infrared lamp at home — and his eyes had a pleasant light quality.

It had always been hard for Dombrosio, the few times he had gotten into a discussion with Lausch, to pin the man down. He had an affable, deceptive manner; he seemed to agree, to suggest, but always to elude. And yet he did run the company. He ran it through other men, with whom Dombrosio and the other designers and workmen dealt: Lausch himself was in and out. It was always hard to catch him; he apparently wanted it that way.

So why does he want me? Dombrosio wondered as he walked along the corridor with its ceiling and walls of cellotex, its rows of closed doors marked DO NOT ENTER. A natural reluctance had come over him; he did not need a specific reason, a well-defined anxiety. The situation itself generated the anxiety. Any employee, he realized, whose sole means of support is derived through the good-will of another person, his boss, has to feel ill-at-ease when that boss asks for him.

At the door he paused to prepare himself; he got himself into as poised a frame of mind as possible. And then he opened the office door, passed the secretary's desk, and rapped on the translucent-glass inner door.

"Come in," Norm Lausch's voice sounded.

He opened the door and entered.

At his desk Lausch sat with one leg up, his black oxford resting on the surface of the desk. He had been combing the hairs of his ankle with a pocket comb, but now, seeing Dombrosio, he put the comb away in its leather case and returned it to his pocket. "Hi, Walt," he said. "Sit down, keed."

Dombrosio sat down in the chair facing the desk. He did not feel like joking, and he did not answer.

"How's Juan Fangio?" Lausch said, with a friendly chuckle.

"Not doing much racing these days," Dombrosio said.

"You could come in by boat. Sail out of that bay by your town, whatever the name is — Carquinez? Sail down the coast and through the Golden Gate and dock right here at the wharf.

At the San Francisco waterfront, one of the world's finest ports. Make it the rest of the way by taxi. How long would it take?"

"All day," he said.

"Yes, but no fuel. You could sail."

At that, Dombrosio had to laugh. They both laughed, the two men sitting facing each other in Lausch's office. It was a funny idea, a good gag; Dombrosio appreciated it, and the intention behind it. His boss sympathized with his situation. By gently kidding, he made Dombrosio aware that he knew about the suspension, that he did not censure him, that he wished him well. And all done without embarrassing him; in fact, he had at the same time put him at his ease.

"On stormy days," Dombrosio said, "I might get blown the other direction. Toward Japan."

"Well, we've got one of their designers. Lend-lease." Norm Lausch did not seem in a hurry to get down to business; time did not seem to be an issue.

Dombrosio said, "Say, I wonder if you saw that package Quinn and I put together for that outfit that makes cat-crap boxes."

"Oh yes. Katty Kloset. But you want to be careful you don't get over into what the Ex-M-Co has."

For a moment he could not identify them. Then he remembered; they put out Jonny Cat, an absorbent compound used in cat-crap boxes. Its carton had been an inspired job; both in the design and inscription it avoided any unpleasant connotations, and yet it made clear what it contained. As Bob Fox had said, when they first began studying the carton, "That cat they've got drawn there *couldn't* have an asshole." Another outfit, not theirs, had designed the carton, and Lausch Company had yet to come up with one as good for their client, Katty Kloset.

"Of course," Dombrosio said, "Katty Kloset makes the actual box, not the compound. So it's not in competition. In fact, the consumer would use Jonny Cat to fill his Katty Kloset."

"Or Kitty Litter," Lausch said. "My wife buys that."

"Why? Do you know?"

"She thinks the name 'Jonny Cat' is vulgar. She knows it's a play on the slang for toilet, 'john.'"

"Why does that seem vulgar to her?" It had been noticed that Ex-M-Co had even left the letter h out of the name, spelling it instead with two n's.

"She has a brother named John. She's always been sensitive to the use of the name slangwise."

Dombrosio said, "So her taste preference doesn't tell us anything."

"One thing about the absorbent compound," Lausch said. "It can be used for other things besides filling cat-crap boxes. Jonny Cat plays that up big on the carton. You can use it to soak up grease in the garage — what else? For mulching plants. For garbage pails. What else can the box be used for? Our carton should play that up."

Trying to recall the company's literature, Dombrosio said, "As I remember, since it's made out of rubber it could be used as a photographer's pan. For film and prints being developed."

"That's not much," Lausch said.

"Well, there must be a lot more that a big flat rubber pan could be used for. It's not flexible, so it won't spill if carried; it won't buckle or fold."

"You mean it would make a good photographer's pan if the photographer happened to want to pick up the pan and walk around the room with it." Lausch folded his hands in front of him and squeezed them together with enormous force. "Listen, old pal. Guess who came in here today, looking for a job."

"My wife," Dombrosio said. And his heart, for an instant, ceased to beat.

"Yes, your one and only wife." Reaching into his desk, Lausch brought out a file card which he dropped in front of Dombrosio.

In the attractive, legible handwriting that he knew so well the card had been carefully filled out. At the top it read:

DOMBROSIO, MRS. SHERRY R.

Sex _f_   age _31_   married _yes_

race _w_   religion _P_

Taking hold of the card, Dombrosio examined it without finding himself able to read beyond the first lines. The rest blurred, but he continued to hold it, pretending to read it through thoroughly, to the very end. Then he laid it down on the desk again.

"When was she first in?" he asked.

"Last week." With his thumb, Lausch showed him the date on which the card had been filled out.

"Was I here?"

"No," Lausch said. "She came in looking for you, toward the end of the day. I happened to run into her in the front office and we got to talking."

"Whose idea was it?" he said. "For her to apply for a job?"

"Both of ours," Lausch said. "She waited around for you — I don't know where you were. Maybe you were out getting something. That was Thursday."

"I don't remember now," he said.

"She started looking at the displays in the consumers' store. I talked to her a couple of times before, a few months ago. She has a degree in commercial art, doesn't she? And she's done work with metal and leather — she showed me some belts that she made. And earrings."

"She works with various materials," Dombrosio said.

"Does quite good."

"Very good."

Lausch said, "Would you like to know the kind of job I'm considering for her?"

Taking a deep breath he said as levelly as possible, "Sure."

"Again, it was partly her idea, partly mine. First of all, she hasn't got any real experience. Certainly nothing that would qualify her to do the kind of work you're doing. She's done nothing original even in her own line, which is a sort of handicraft thing. You don't mind if I talk this way, do you? Completely frankly."

"Go on."

"And she knows nothing about our business. Obviously, a lot of what she knows she's picked up from you. I told her that she probably had no real talent, at least not along the lines we can use. She was quite calm about it; she seemed to have no illusions. This isn't a case where some starry-eyed kid just out of commercial art school walks in and tried to get hired as an industrial designer. To be frank with you, old buddy, what we'd be hiring wouldn't be her talent in the artistic sense so much as her personality."

Dombrosio regarded him.

"Let me explain," Lausch said genially. "She's extremely personable." He put his arms out and clasped his hands behind his head; leaning back, he continued, "She's got a lot of class. Her clothes, the way she talks. She's Willis Sherman's stepdaughter, isn't she?"

"You know Willis Sherman?" he said.

"No," Lausch said. "I never heard of him, frankly, until she mentioned him. She showed me an article about him from some magazine. Apparently he's got quite a well-known house in that town where he lives — what is it?"

"Tenafly," Dombrosio said. "New Jersey. He's wealthy. The family has had money for several generations."

"This magazine had a three-page spread. Pictures of the inside of their house. The furniture."

Dombrosio said, "It isn't a magazine; it's the rotogravure section of a newspaper. I've seen it. It was published in 1953."

"Don't you think that's something? For a newspaper to give a guy's house a three-page spread?"

"That section had a regular Sunday feature showing the interiors of houses in the New York area."

"But not any houses."

"No," he said. "Only very special ones."

Lausch scratched thoughtfully at the calendar on his desk. "See, your wife can talk art; she can communicate with the designers, with us. She also comes from a well-to-do society family; hell, you know it. Anybody can see it. It isn't a question of her being especially attractive. We've got a receptionist with — you should excuse the expression — a nice pair of cans. Now, take our consumers' store. We produce the packages and stick them in the store. We get clients in here to judge consumer reaction. But we have to talk to the clients; we have to talk them into buying the package. We have to do a sales job. And we've been trying to do that ourselves. But we're not qualified to do that. On the other hand, we can't get salesmen in, because that's not what we want either."

Dombrosio said, "How much would you pay her?"

"Not much. It's in the nature of an experiment. Want to know how I got the idea? You know those quiz shows they had on TV, those big money shows like the *Sixty-four Thousand Dollar Question*? I read an article about the girls who used to work on them; you know, bringing out the contestants. Anyhow, this article told what's become of them now that the quizzes have folded. I got to thinking we needed something like that in our business. Somebody to lead the client in, so to speak. You get me?" He gestured. "You know, like the airlines have; like airline hostesses. But somebody who can discuss technical aspects, about dyes and costs; not just some fluffball, some dame with a nice pair of knockers, but one with sense." His calm, mellow voice rolled on; Dombrosio hardly heard him. "Am I making my point?" Lausch asked. "Do you see what I mean?"

"You discussed the job with her. You told her what she would be doing."

"Sure," Lausch said. "Naturally I did. Of course, she's more interested in the work; she wants to put on a smock and start designing milk cartons for Golden State. But you can't always have what you want in this world. Frankly, I don't think she's got what it takes to turn out original stuff, but maybe I'm wrong. You'd probably know better than me. You know her stuff. What do you think?"

He shrugged.

"Hard to talk about your own wife," Lausch agreed. "Well, I won't press you. Anyhow, I can't give her a job like that; all I can give her is the kind of work I outlined to you just now. Admittedly, it's not precisely what she wants. But she'd be around designers; she'd be around creative craftsmen. And she would get a chance to do some work. She could try a few sketches if she wanted."

Dombrosio said, "Did she say how I felt about her working? About her coming here?"

"She said that you and she had worked together on stuff at home. That you thought her work was good. She showed me some sketches that you and she did together, on your own time. Sketches for a fiberglass car body. I know you're both interested in sports cars; you have that Italian car, whatever it is, that you drive. Or drove."

For a time he could not figure out what fiberglass car body designs Lausch meant. Then he recalled that, years ago, when the Chevrolet Corvette had been introduced, he and Sherry had done some pen and ink sketches of a Corvette-like sports car. But only for fun. He had not even tried to keep the sketches; they were more in the nature of "dream car" stuff, done by every high school boy who ever took commercial art. The motor magazines published twenty of them a month, and gave away free magazine subscriptions as prizes.

"And that's all she showed you," he said. "That's all she had to show. In the way of sketches."

"Plus her belts. And sandals."

Dombrosio thought, No mobiles. I'm surprised she didn't bring in some of her driftwood mobiles.

What an incredible world, he thought. That a woman could sell a hardheaded businessman on something like this. Sell him with what she's accomplished . . . a few Christmas gifts, a few earrings and bric-a-brac. And of course a cultivated manner of speaking, expensive I. Magnin clothes, and a three-page spread in a seven-year-old newspaper showing the house of a wealthy man in Tenafly, New Jersey who is not in the same line of business as Lausch, whom Lausch has never heard of, and whom he will certainly never meet or have any business relations with. She really knows the password, he thought. She's got it, whatever it is. That makes them recognize her as on the in.

He thought, Sherry really impressed him. In his mind he saw it so clearly: his wife coming into the office, greeting Lausch, the designers . . . making sage comments on the work in progress. Roaming around with her coat over her arm, awing everyone in the place. And especially Norm Lausch, who smoked Philippine cigarettes and had made his money in house trailers.

Quality tells, he thought. Quality wins out.

"She's got good breeding," he said aloud.

Pleased, Norm Lausch nodded his head up and down.

When Sherry came to pick him up that evening he said to her, "So you want to work here." No one else was around; the other designers had already gone home. The building was deserted except for the janitor sweeping up. He stood facing her across his work bench.

"I'm not sure," Sherry said. "I thought about it. As long as I'm looking for a job I thought it would be a good idea to apply here." She did not seem disconcerted or nervous; she returned his gaze with absolute poise.

At the very least, he thought, she's got poise.

"Why didn't you tell me?" he said.

"I did tell you," she said. "On the way home."

"When?"

"The day I made out the application blank."

"No," he said. "You did not."

Sherry said, "I did; I know I did. I remember the discussion as we were crossing Van Ness to the place where I parked the car."

"What did I say?"

She shrugged. "You were noncommittal. You seemed to be more involved in mulling over some work you had been doing. Bob Fox was with us; he walked part of the way. You and he talked about a squirt can for moths. I even remember that. Don't you remember? Your memory must be even poorer than it used to be. Or possibly you remember only what you want to remember."

Now, he realized, she was going on the attack.

I'll never know what she did say, he thought. Possibly she did say something; or possibly it's a complete lie and she said nothing at all. In any case, she has managed to handle it successfully; whatever she said, I paid no attention. It didn't catch my ear. We were crossing a busy street; I had my mind on other things; somebody was with us; I was tired from the day's work. Probably there was a lot of noise, too.

But what does it matter?

"You may have fulfilled the letter of the law," he said with difficulty. "But not the spirit."

"What law?"

"The law," he said, "that governs the relationship between decent people."

Her eyebrows went up mockingly. Now she wore an expression of dislike for him. "And what sort of people is that?"

"People who act in good faith," he said.

Her scorn broke through; she said scathingly, "Oh, don't make me laugh. Really — don't make me laugh." Turning, she walked away from him, carrying the packages that she had temporarily put down on his workbench.

Running after her, he grabbed hold of her. He seized her by the shoulder and spun her around. One of her packages fell to the floor; it gave out a tinkle of breaking glass.

"God damn you," she said, her teeth close together, her eyes small. "You made me drop that and break it; I think it was a fifteen-dollar bottle of Chanel Number Five."

With a swipe of his hand he knocked the remaining packages from her hands; they bounced away in all directions, clattering and fluttering to the floor. Her eyes grew large, then even smaller than before. A dark, wild color rose into her cheeks. The flush of hate. He had seen it only once before, in her. So swiftly that he could not see it, her hand flashed up; she slapped him. He grabbed her by the wrist, digging his fingers into her flesh. As he did so, she kicked him; kicked with her sharp, hard toe, the toe of her I. Magnin shoes. It hurt him and he let her go. His fingers flew open of their own accord. At once she stepped back, composed, wary, studying him with tension but no strong emotion. The hatred was gone.

"You broke everything," she said in a placid voice. "All my packages. You can walk back to Carquinez. You're not riding with me; that's a cinch." Without a further word, she turned and strode out of the workroom. The door slammed after her, and, standing there gasping and panting, he heard the sound of her heels as she departed. He heard her reach the stairs, go down; and then the sound ceased.

I could catch her, he thought.

He ran after her. At the foot of the stairs, near the street entrance, the janitor was standing with her, fishing for his passkey. Seeing Dombrosio he said, "You want to be let out, too?"

"No," Dombrosio said. Sherry did not turn to look in his direction; she waited with her back to him until the janitor had unlocked the street door and was holding it aside for her, and then she walked on outside, onto the dark evening street. She disappeared off to the right. The janitor resumed his broom-pushing.

For a time he remained where he was. He watched the traffic go by, and at last he saw a red Alfa Romeo speed past and disappear. She was on her way home. Back to Marin County and Carquinez.

She really would do it, he realized. Strand me here.

Going back to the workroom he surveyed the litter of broken packages. Some had begun to ooze liquid, and now he could smell the perfume. The thick, heavy reek.

Getting rags and water, the dustpan and a bucket, he began to clean up the mess. Toward the end, the janitor came in, saw him and what he was doing, and helped him.

After the mess had been cleaned up and the janitor had gone, he sat alone at his workbench. In front of him the half-finished model of a deodorant container looked like some ruined castle with its top leaning, its walls falling into disrepair. He fooled with a shaving of metal, reflexively.

If she wants a job here, he thought, she will get it. Possibly I will never understand her reasons; I am right in some respects but no doubt wrong in others. In any case, she has not been honest with me. She knows that, too, somewhere down deep. That was why she got so mad. We both know it. And after she has worked here awhile, in the same shop with me, then what? Will she move by degrees to become a full designer?

Will she be content to work at a bench exactly like mine, doing the exact same work as I do? Or — must she have my desk? Must I be out of here?

He thought, And if so, then will she be happy?

At a coffee shop down the street he got into the phone booth and, dropping in a dime, dialed. While he waited he studied the shapes of glasses stacked up in the cupboards behind the counter.

An unfamiliar woman's voice answered. "Hello."

He said, "Is Charley Halpin there?" He tried to remember if Charley had said he was married; there had been something about it, a long time ago. Some joking mention about marital problems.

The woman said in a low voice, "Jus' a minute. I go get him."

"Thanks," he said.

After a time the phone clanked and then he heard Charley's voice, a slow, suspicious hello.

"This is Walt Dombrosio," he said.

Instantly the voice became friendly. "Hi. Say, did you know: your wife brought your little Alfa in just the other day. I adjusted the timing."

"Listen," Dombrosio said. "I'm stuck in town, here. I can't get back home tonight." He paused. "Any chance I could drop over to your place awhile?" There was nothing clear in his mind; he only wanted a place to go, to be with someone. "I could pick up something for dinner. Or maybe you already ate."

A long, long pause.

"Well, I'll tell you," Charley said. "I don't know if you'd want to come over." The friendly tone was still there, but with more formality, now. With caution. "We just got this little tiny place, you know. It's not like yours. It's just a couple of rooms. Over on Hayes."

"That's okay," he said. But he was being turned down; he knew it. There could be no mistaking it. Now what? he wondered. "How about just for a few minutes. For a drink."

As if not exactly listening to him, more as if the two of them were thinking and talking along parallel lines that did not quite meet, Charley said, "We haven't eaten, and naturally you can eat with us. But there's no place to put you up; we have the front room half painted." He went on, giving details. Dombrosio barely listened. Once more he studied the glasses stored behind the counter of the coffee shop. Outside the phone booth a woman in a cloth coat waited to get in.

"Anyhow," Dombrosio said, "I'll pick up a bottle and come on over. Is Jim Beam okay?"

"I'll pick you up," Charley said. "You tell me where you are and I'll come by. And don't buy nothing; we got everything." He paused. "There's some other people here, if you don't care. We were having a little party. Nothing much, just sitting around."

"Fine," Dombrosio said. He gave him the location and then he hung up and left the booth.

When he went outside the coffee shop onto the sidewalk he found himself facing a red Alfa Romeo parked at the curb. For a moment he stared stupidly at it, without understanding. Not until Sherry spoke to him did he make out what was happening.

"I thought it over," she said in a steady, dispassionate voice. "It didn't seem to be the moral thing to do, to leave you here. No matter how you treated me. I drove around the block a few times and then came back to Lausch Company." Reaching out, she opened the door on his side. "You had gone, but the janitor saw you go this way."

He said, "I just called Charley Halpin. He's going to come by here and pick me up."

"That's okay," Sherry said. "I'll wait here with you, and when he comes I'll explain that you thought I had missed connections

with you, but right after you called him I did show up. You
didn't go into any details with him, did you? About our fighting.

"No," he said.

She shut off the car's motor and lights. "I hope he isn't too
long," she said. "It'll get cold in here with the heater off." She had
put up the top, and now she made sure the side flaps were in
place. "I'll have to replace those things you broke," she said. "Did
you look at anything to see what wasn't ruined?"

"No," he said.

"You just tossed everything into the trash barrel."

He nodded.

"Well, you can count on about sixty-five dollars gone to
waste. Because you can't control yourself; because you're like a
baby and have to have a temper tantrum once in a while." Sitting
in the darkness beside him in the car she went on, delivering her
tirade in a rational, almost toneless voice. He said nothing. He
listened.

"I really don't know if I want to work around you," she
wound up. "I have no idea how you'd behave. They say a man
and wife should never try to work together. You'd probably re-
sent everything I'd suggest. Just because I suggested it."

I'm not going to give up, he said to himself. I'm going to keep
on trying. But I know it's hopeless.

Presently the lights of Charley's old Cadillac flashed at them
as he drew up to the curb.

"Want me to talk to him?" Sherry said. "I'll talk to him —
poor baby, you look so tired." Patting him on the arm she opened
her door and stepped out, businesslike and confident, her coat
over her shoulders. Without a look back or another word she
crossed over to the Cadillac. Dombrosio could not hear what either of them said; their voices were lost in the evening traffic.

The Cadillac, after a moment, drove off. He caught a glimpse
of the man behind the wheel, and, in the back, two more faces,

dark, friendly with interest — they all waved to him, and Charley blew the car horn.

His heart ached as he sat waiting for his wife to get back in the Alfa beside him.

8

At the crack of dawn Leo Runcible's phone rang. It was the title company in San Rafael, telling him that Mr. and Mrs. Diters had come in to put money down. Hearing that, he felt a thrill of joy, the pure sense of accomplishment that ennobled his business; he had made a sale. And the deposit, the title company informed him, was on the larger of the two houses that the Diterses had been considering.

Two yesterday! he thought as he hung up. And this — actually three in one day. Three deals closed, bam bam bam. Right like that.

His gross five percent . . . he began figuring, savoring each number as he added. Fine, he thought. It came to two thousand dollars. Not bad, he thought; not bad at all. Going back into the bedroom he awoke Janet. "Hey," he said. "I have some news."

Later, when they had gotten dressed and were fixing breakfast, Janet asked him what he was going to do with the money. They could put it into their own house, she told him. On new outside paint, new gutters, and — she had a lot of ideas.

"Listen," he interrupted. "This money is spoken for."

"But it isn't," she said. "You already said you didn't expect to take in anything like this."

"Sure," he said, with irritation. "Fix up this place — pour it in and make some contractor rich. Maybe we ought to get one of those siding salesmen up here and have a four-thousand-dollar job of aluminum siding done. The whole works." He glared at her and she shrank back, fooling with the sash of her robe and avoiding his glare. "Is that what you want to do?" he demanded. "*Spend* it? Hell, let's get one of those sports cars like Dombrosio has; let's really live it up."

In a faltering voice, she said, "Then what did you want to do with the money?"

"It's not what I want to do," he said. "It's what I have to do. When you get money — listen to this. Learn something." He seated himself at the table and put toast into the toaster. "You invest it. Do you follow me? The smart man puts his money to work. I've told you that. I'll tell you exactly what I'm going to buy into. With this two thousand I can go ahead and put down what it's going to take to handle that unimproved acreage up on the Ridge."

"Jancuzzi's land?" his wife asked.

"Yes," he said.

She said, "You're going to go ahead without Paul?"

"Who needs him?" Runcible said. "I don't have to subdivide right away; what's important is to get hold of the god damn land before some a-hole from outside steps in and makes a killing."

"How much do you have to put up?" she asked, with tension.

He shrugged. "Oh, around six-five. I can raise it. Don't kid yourself about that; I'm good for that kind of money, any time. With or without the sale to Diters." After all, the man could back out and forfeit his deposit. But he won't, Runcible decided. Not that guy.

Triumph filled him. Finally he could really buy into something big. And without Paul Wilby, he thought. Without anybody on earth helping him.

In his underpants Walter Dombrosio stood before the bathroom mirror, shaving. He moved the razor methodically, getting no pleasure from the task. The door was open and he could hear the din of Sherry hurrying to get the dishes cleared from the breakfast table.

"Are you almost finished?" she said, appearing in her robe and slippers. Her hair, up in metal curlers, clung tightly to her skull, giving her a priestly, ascetic appearance. Without makeup her face had a wan quality.

He said, "Almost. You want to hear the dream I had last night?" He had been thinking about it while shaving.

"Sure," she said. Ever since having psychoanalysis she had liked to hear people's dreams. She seemed to feel that she learned things about them that they did not know themselves.

"I was in the market for a car," he said. "An elderly man, well-dressed, came by with his 1946 Willys. It was pink."

"A pink Willys," she repeated, seated on the chair at the vanity table and beginning to remove the curlers from her hair.

"The upholstery was excellent quality," he said. "Like an old Cadillac that had been pampered."

Sherry said, "The Willys comes from my stepfather's name. I wonder why pink. Wouldn't a '46 Willys be an awfully old car? That would be — sixteen or seventeen years old."

"It showed four hundred thousand miles," he said. "But in the dream I thought it was a terrific car. Very high class." In the dream he had wanted it very much; he had gotten the elderly gentleman to drive him around the block again and again.

"Did you buy it?"

"No," he said. "The man wanted a hundred dollars for it." In the dream that had seemed too much.

"Did you actually dream that?" she said. She regarded him; he saw her reflection in the steamed-up mirror. "I wonder what it means. You didn't buy it. I imagine it's a wish-fulfillment dream. Unconsciously you yearn for quality but you're unwilling to pay the price. Pink. I wonder why pink."

"Like a pink jellybean," he said.

"Childhood," she said. "That's why the car was so old. And showed so many miles. You want to go back to a safer, more simple time, when you were a boy. When candy was important; the oral stage." The curlers were off, and she had started brushing her hair. "The old gentleman would be a father-figure."

"Four hundred thousand miles are a lot of miles," he said, as he washed the lather from his face.

Later, at nine-thirty that morning, he and his wife sat in Norm Lausch's office. Norm had not showed up. The two of them waited without speaking, both of them tense.

"Now I'm beginning to wonder if this is a good idea," Sherry said. She put her cigarette out in the ashtray on Norm Lausch's desk and, getting her pack from her purse, lit another. "It seemed like a good idea last night . . . to clear the air." Sitting stiffly, very straight in the chair, her legs crossed and her skirt smoothed in place, she blew jets of smoke from her nostrils.

"You look very nice," he said to her. And he did not mean it ironically or maliciously; she did look nice, even more so than usual.

"Thank you," she said, with a smile in his direction. She seemed, now, to relax a trifle. Reaching out her hand, she took hold of his fingers and squeezed. "We've moved so far apart," she said. "The last few weeks."

"Longer than that," he said.

"You make me so angry," she said. "Breaking those things. You really hate me sometimes, don't you? All your hostility comes out."

All, he thought. Is it all? He said, "Maybe there's more."

"More hostility?" She put her face close to his; he smelled her hair, the faint odor, familiar and fine.

Suddenly there stood Norm Lausch in the doorway of the office, in his pottery-colored suit, beaming down at them benevolently. "Hi, kids," he said.

Turning so that she faced him, Sherry said, "We were making up."

"So I see," Lausch said. "Everything smoothed over?" Then his smile departed; he became serious. "Listen, kids. I know you've been waiting a long time to see me—" He yanked back his sleeve to study his watch. "I have a lot of business I have to get to; I've got to leave the building and drive down to Menlo Park."

And then his expression became benevolent once more.

Reaching his pale, clean hand into his coat pocket he lifted out an envelope. He opened it. Dombrosio saw small colored cards.

With a grin, a sly, pleased, winking grin, Lausch waved a finger at Dombrosio. "Teekits," Lausch said.

"What kind of tickets?" Sherry said in a conversational voice. Clearly, she did not follow what was happening.

Dombrosio rose to his feet. "For tonight?" he said, holding out his hand. Lausch tapped his hand with the tickets and then let him look at them. They were for tonight, all right. And for box seats.

"Giants play Chicago," Lausch said. "Under the lights. Be my guests. Three box seats, right along the first base line. We can talk on the way down and back. Okay?" Leaving the tickets with Dombrosio he moved back out of the office. "Okay, keeds?"

"Fine," Dombrosio said, overcome with pleasure and surprise.

Before Sherry could speak, Norm Lausch had departed. She and Dombrosio were by themselves, as before; it had taken only a moment for Lausch to appear and disappear.

"That means we won't get home until two or three in the

morning," Sherry said, with aggravation in her voice. "Well, I guess since you accepted there's nothing we can do. But I don't see how you plan to get up tomorrow morning; and I'll have to get up, too, to get you in."

"We'll make it," he said. With satisfaction, he put the three tickets into his wallet, for safekeeping.

A respite, he thought. Almost an omen. As if some force from above had reached down, for a moment, to relieve him.

Maybe Norm Lausch sees how I feel, he said to himself.

"Nothing pleases a man more than a couple of baseball tickets," Sherry said. "It's interesting that when something important comes up, some difficult problem that has to be solved, you retreat from it and take refuge in a ballgame." Her exasperation and jumpiness came out clearly in her voice and made it ring. "Well, now I've got the problem of amusing myself until dinner time. I presume you and I will eat dinner together somewhere in town. When does the game start?"

He told her when the game started and when they would have to meet Norm Lausch to be sure of getting there in time to find a parking place. And then he left her and walked downstairs to the ground-floor workshop to begin work for the day. He did not bother to say good-bye to her; he left her and went about his own business.

"You're not even going to say good-bye?" she called after him. "You really are in a foul mood. Or is it that you're in a good mood and you can afford to be rude to me?"

Alone, Sherry Dombrosio wandered about the main floor of Lausch Company, her purse and coat in her arms. She felt like a little girl roaming through some toy store. Santa's workshop, she thought to herself with delight. The very air smelled of activity; she took a deep breath. She savored each sight she saw, each smell and sound.

The high ceiling with its massive rafters caught her eye. And in the corners curly shavings of wood still remained. Sawdust on tables. The place boomed with far-off noises, intimations of happenings that she could not see. She could only imagine. What do they do here? she asked herself. They make things. All kinds of things. Out of paint and plaster and wood and metal and plastic and glue; they use every sort of material.

Collecting her courage, she peeked through a half-open door marked No One Permitted Entry Without Written Authority. At worktables the designers . . . hard at their tasks. Cellini's workshop, she thought. Santa and Cellini. Silver salt shakers and candy canes.

"Good morning, Mrs. Dombrosio," one of the designers said.

She took in the sight of the easel at which he worked. Could she come in? Of course. Maybe I'll be working here, she thought. Like the rest of them.

"Can I peek?" she asked, entering the room.

In his white smock, the designer continued to work, his eyes on the paper tacked to the easel. Before him, in a row, he had conté crayons, brushes, turpentine, rags . . . she saw all sorts of paints and pigments, some in bottles, some in tubes. The scent of color filled her nose.

"I guess I'm not supposed to look," she said. But she did look. Quietly, with awe, she peeped past him. The designer was drawing a spray gun. Like a Flit gun, she thought. How fast his fingers moved as he rubbed a line. He gave the drawing depth; she marveled at his skill.

Of course, she thought, what Mr. Lausch wants me for is actually a public relations job. She had no illusions about that. I wouldn't be behind an easel. Not for a while.

Since the designer paid no attention to her she felt free to explore. This was a tiny private room that she had never been in before; she took her opportunity and inspected a row of sketches tacked up on a beaver board display. The sketches, she discovered, were photostats, not the originals; they were black and white, now. The colors had of course not been reproduced. Below, in an open leather binder, she saw photographs of models. Cans and cartons . . . she thumbed through, taking them in as fast as she could. Cigarette packages . . . one which was quite familiar to her. Had Lausch Company designed it? So it seemed. She came to a photograph not yet clipped in, still loose. A shallow box with large letters. KATTY KLOSET.

There, in the margin of the photograph, in pencil: the name *Dombrosio*. With a start she identified it as her husband's name. This was his work. For a moment she had thought it was hers; in her art classes in recent years she signed herself that way, too.

Aloud, she said, "Say, I have an idea."

The designer said nothing.

She said, "Instead of calling it Katty Kloset, why don't they call it Katty Korner?"

Still the designer said nothing.

"Like the game," she said.

After a time the designer said, "Nobody wants their cat to go to the toilet in the corner. That's the whole point of the box."

She felt her ears redden. "That's so," she said.

Raising his head, the designer looked at her over the top of his glasses. "Kloset for water closet," he said. "You get it?" His tone was dry, hard, even a little ironic. Suddenly she felt out of place, as if she had transgressed. Maybe I went too far, she thought. I shouldn't be here; it does say private on the door.

"I guess I'm bothering you," she said.

To that, the designer said nothing.

"Did you know," she said, "that I might start work here?"

The designer said, "Oh yes. You're the woman."

"What woman?"

"The one Teddy calls the *mingei-ya* woman."

"Who is Teddy?" Then she remembered; he was the Japanese artist they had hired. "What does mingei-ya mean?" she said.

After a pause, still working at his sketch, the designer said in an abstracted, slow voice, "It's a word they have for people like you."

She felt herself flush to the roots of her hair. "I'd like you to amplify that," she said, as matter-of-factly as possible. "There's an unpleasant implication in your remarks, don't you think? Or am I mistaken?"

"Nothing unpleasant," the designer said, absorbed in his work. He seemed only barely aware of her, and that maddened her; she had seen Walt this way, when he was involved in some project, either in his garage workshop or upstairs with his easel. Clearly, these men, this type of person, withdrew into some private realm when they were at work. "It's hard to translate it," the designer said.

"Try."

He said, presently, "It means folk art. What you do at home."

"I've had enough of what I do at home," she said. "I want to get away from that and do the kind of thing you people are doing. Something important, that matters. Something creative."

"Can't—" He mixed pigments, squeezing tubes and dabbing with a spatula. "Can't you be creative at home?"

"I'm not interested in bohemian artistic expression," she said. "I've had my fill of that, when I was in college."

The designer said, "Yes, I guess we all go through that. In our time. Sandals and beards. Turtleneck sweaters."

"I want to produce something—" She could not phrase it.

"Cans for flyspray," the designer said.

When he put it that way, it did not sound so exalted; she knew that. She did not deny that.

"You make a new package," the designer said, "to make some housewife, when she goes into the supermarket, reach up and take down that package of soap. That particular package. Not another."

"Yes," she said, with excitement.

"Do you shop?" the designer said. "You shop for your family."

"Yes," she said. "I know how it feels, going along the soap counter. The aisle. I always look for one on sale."

"That little handwritten piece of paper thumbtacked to the shelf. That says 'limit one to a customer.'"

She nodded. "I never pay more than fifty-nine cents for a box of detergent, if I can help it."

"You price buy. You don't impulse buy."

"Is that what you call it?"

The designer said, "It's supposed to be impulse buying. Color has a lot to do with it. Position on the shelf. Brand name, of course. Ads on TV that set up conditioned responses. Press the button and the housewife jumps. Salivates at the sight of Dreft. Fels-Naptha."

"That's what I mean," she said. Now she had found a way to put it. Seating herself in a chair opposite him she spread her coat and purse over her lap; opening her purse, she got out her cigarettes. "I read that book about persuasion, how the consumer is manipulated into buying things he doesn't want."

The designer eyed her with ironic curiosity.

"And that's why this is so exciting," she said, lighting her cigarette.

"Sweet Jesus," the designer said. "You want to be on the other end of it." He paused in his work of spraying his sketch.

She felt a rush of pleasure. A tingle that entered each part of her and made her shiver. Not looking directly at the designer she said, "What is that phrase? Hammer or anvil; you're one or the other. I can never remember which signifies what, but — isn't that the choice?" She laughed with delight. "It's a very exciting thing, even being here. I can feel it coming in through the pores of my body."

"You can feel what?"

"The—" She gestured. "The importance of it all."

For a time the designer stared at her. Then he returned to his spraying. His face had a dark, reddened quality, and he did not speak.

Suddenly she longed to tell him about Willis. She wanted to let this man know about her stepfather. But there was not the time, now; glancing at her watch she saw that she had to leave. At ten-forty she had to be across town for a class at California Arts and Crafts.

"I'll see you later," she said, sliding to her feet and putting out her cigarette. "I have an appointment."

As she left the room the designer raised his head. He watched her go; she was aware of his eyes fixed on her as she shut the door. Feeling light-headed, even a little giddy, she made her way down the corridor. Following the arrow marked EXIT she arrived at a flight of stairs. Descending, she came out in the ground floor workshop. The noise of lathes and saws filled the air as she passed through.

At the rear, by a worktable, stood her husband with Bob Fox; they were conferring over blueprints.

"I'm just leaving," she said merrily, pausing.

In a somber voice, Walt said, "I thought you were already gone."

"No," she said, "I stopped to talk." The conversation with the designer upstairs had buoyed her up; she went on quickly, "Am I dressed right for the game tonight? Is this what women are supposed to wear to the ballgame?"

To Fox, her husband said, "We're going to take in the Giants game tonight."

"Lucky guys," Fox said. "I envy you. Where are you sitting?"

"Box seats," Sherry said. "Mr. Lausch invited us; we're going with him."

At that, Fox opened his eyes wide. "Not bad," he said.

Going to her husband, she leaned up and kissed him good-bye. "I'll see you about six," she said. "Here — right?"

He nodded and touched her briefly on the shoulder, the merest return greeting. "You look nice," he said. "In your brown suit."

At that, she laughed. "My brown suit?" She touched the lapels of her suit. "Do you call this brown?"

"Sure," Walt said.

"Does it look *brown* to you?"

With a stir of resentment and suspicion he said, "Sure it does."

Now she could not contain her merriment. Putting her hand to her mouth she said chokingly, "Walt—"

"What?" he demanded. And, on his face, she saw fear.

"This isn't brown I'm wearing. This is gray. Look at the weave." She held her sleeve up close to his eyes; he backed away, scowling, apprehensive. "You are. You're a little color blind."

He stared at her, not at the suit but directly at her.

"What color are my eyes?" she said. "Are they brown, too?"

"No," he said slowly.

To Bob Fox she said, "Did you know Walt was a little color blind? I've always known it."

In a frighteningly loud voice her husband yelled, "God damn it, what do you mean? For christ's sake, answer me!"

Stunned by his animation she said, "Didn't you know it, Walt?"

Saying nothing, Bob Fox watched both of them intently.

"You never can tell gray from brown," she said. "That suit Mr. Lausch had on, that gray suit—"

His lips read *brown.*

Presently Fox spoke up. "I'd call Norm's suit gray, for the most part. If you mean that one he had on when he was down here talking about the Pabst poster."

"Can I go now?" Sherry said.

Her husband regarded her with an expression that she could not read. But she did not bother to try; she was late as it was.

"Good-bye," she said, turning and starting toward the door. "Wish me luck."

The expression was still on Walt's face as the door shut and locked after her.

The baseball game was a good one. Or at least, so everyone seemed to think. During the game neither Norm Lausch nor her husband paid any attention to her, although they sat on each side of her. They either cupped their hands and yelled at the pitcher, a tall thin man who spent most of the time fooling with a hand-ful of dirt or his cap, or they yelled at the vendors who came through the stands selling food. Both men drank a lot of beer. She herself had several cups of hot bouillon and a hot dog. To her, the ballpark was terribly cold and drafty; she sat with her coat wrapped around her, her arms folded, trying to keep warm.

But she enjoyed herself, despite the cold. Toward the end, a batter hit a ball directly toward their box. A player, running at tremendous speed while holding his glove out, crashed into the rail in front of them, half-fell onto them, and, with everybody screaming and jumping up and down, managed to snare the ball. The batter was out. For a long time she found herself unable to sit down; she could not remember when she had been so stirred.

"Wasn't it terrific?" she kept saying, as they moved slowly out of the park at the end of the game, along with countless other people all of whom seemed to be pushing and shoving against her. But she did not mind them; she was still elated. "That one play, where that player almost fell on top of us catching the ball."

Chewing his cigar, his hands in his pockets, Norm Lausch said, "Yep, that was a dilly." Walt said nothing.

When they had gotten out of the ballpark and onto the sidewalk, the two men decided that they wanted to stop at a bar. She did not particularly want to, but on the other hand she did not object. After all, it did seem as if they should celebrate. She certainly felt in the mood; she had been like that all day, and the game had added to it. Now she understood why baseball was so important in men's lives. It stimulated them; it pulled them out of their depression. It was very much, she thought, like having a hundred or so dollars and being able to spend it for anything she wanted at any of the shops along Geary and Sutter.

The bar, at a corner, was crowded with men who had been at the ballgame; she heard all of them talking loudly, with much animation, about various players. Norm, by wedging himself gradually forward, managed to get them a booth. Both men ordered drinks, but she only had beer. As she sat sipping her beer she thought, once again, that as yet they had not discussed the job. They had not gotten around to it on the way to the ballpark; there had been some technical business for Walt and Norm to settle. In that, she had not participated. And at the ballgame, of course, there was no opportunity for discussion.

But now, she thought, the time has come.

"Let's talk about the job," she said.

Holding his cigar between his teeth, Norm Lausch eyed her and drank from his glass. Her husband stared down sightlessly, his glass on the table. He seemed to be off in meditation.

"Isn't now the time?" she said.

Grinning, Norm reached out and patted her hand. "One more round," he said.

Both he and her husband had another drink. She stayed with her one beer. Her impatience had grown; she could hardly keep quiet. Why did they just sit, drinking and now and then saying

something banal? Once, Walt started talking about some building material — she could have murdered him. And, whenever
Norm started the conversation, it had to do with baseball. Before
they left the bar, her enthusiasm for baseball had gone the way it
had arrived.

"All set, kids?" Lausch said, at last. Getting to his feet he loos-
ened his belt, tossed down the last of his drink, and then moved
through the crowd of people, away from the booth. She rose and
started after him. Again, neither he nor Walt paid her any attention; she had to navigate her way out of the bar by herself.

When she reached the sidewalk she found them standing together. They had beaten her out.

"Let's see," Norm said leisurely. "Where's the car? Where is
the car?"

They had come in his enormous new Buick. There it was, up
on the dirt by a railroad track. Looking around, she saw that they
were in a deserted industrial section of San Francisco which she
had never seen before. To her, the City was a place of shops and
houses and restaurants and theaters and schools; she had never
been here, south of Market, in the warehouse district. The closest she had come was the trip to Lausch Company, which was
along the waterfront. But that was well-lit. Here, she saw almost
no lights. Miles of dark streets. No stores or people. Only great
opaque buildings, all of them apparently old.

After he had unlocked the car, Norm held the door open for
them; they all got into the front seat, and he walked around to
the far side and got in behind the wheel. He started up the motor
and soon they were driving slowly along one of the deserted
streets.

"So many railroad tracks," she said, as the car bumped over a
number of them together.

"Yes," Norm said. It did not seem to bother him. But the smell
of cigar smoke, plus the beer and cold air and eyestrain, and now

the bumping of the car over the train tracks, made her queasy and irritable.

"Could we talk about the job now?" she said. She was surprised at how cross she sounded; and impatient as well. "Remember, Walt and I have to make the trip up to Marin County and across Mount Tam — we won't be in bed until four a.m. as it is." It almost seemed to her as if Lausch was driving nowhere in particular; they seemed to be going along one empty street after another, not getting any closer to Lausch Company and their own car.

"Okay," Norm said.

"I'm anxious to get your decision," she said. She glanced at Walt, but he did not speak; he still stared down, preoccupied. What was he thinking about? Experimentally, she touched his hand. He did not respond, and so she gave up trying to reach him.

Removing his cigar, Norm put it on the lip of the dashboard ashtray. "What do you say, Walter? I'd like to have her."

Walt said, "I'd rather you didn't."

"You two didn't come to any agreement?"

"No," Walt said.

"There's no agreement required," Sherry said. "That I know of. I'm a free agent. I'm being hired on my merits, not on whose wife I am."

"There's a lot of difficulty in having a husband and wife working together," Norm said. "Especially if there's some conflict already."

"If you hire her," Walt said, "I'll quit."

Norm turned toward him. "You'll what? Quit?"

Sherry's husband nodded.

"Why, you're nuts," Norm said.

Walt shrugged.

"What do you figure?" Norm said. "I can't get along without you? You're so god-awful original and inventive?"

"That's right," Walt said.

"Oh come on, kid," Norm said.

"What do you mean, come on?" her husband said, in a slow, deadly voice. She had never heard such a quality in his voice before; she sat absolutely silent, keeping out of it. Her heart labored with fright, and she drew away from both men, making herself as small as possible and wishing she were sitting in the back seat. How had this gotten started? "This hostess pitch of yours," Walt said. "What's that got to do with the price of apples? You have got some bug up your ass and you think it would be cute to hire some doll to lead clients around and give them the treatment. The soothing, honeyed treatment. In a week you won't even remember you had the idea. You'll be on something else entirely. Like having us wear our names on our work-smocks. Stitched in red thread."

Norm said nothing. But she saw his face. It had swelled up so that his flesh protruded from his collar.

"The package you fell for," Walt said, "in spite of what you said to me, has a couple of cans in front and a nice flat fanny in back. And two long legs sticking out at the bottom. And a prestige voice. And prestige everything else. You're the biggest sucker in the world for class. You'd pay anything to buy some of it because you know god damn well you don't have any of it."

Without saying anything, Norm Lausch brought the car over to the curb. He stopped it, opened the door and got out onto the sidewalk. "Buddy," he said. "Step out." He threw his cigar into the gutter.

Opening the door on his side, Walt stepped out onto the curb. No one else was in sight; it was another deserted block of closed-up warehouses. Sitting in the car alone she watched the two men standing facing each other on the sidewalk. The darkness, and the angle from which she watched, made it almost impossible for her to tell what was happening; in panic, she scrambled around the huge car, peering up, trying to make out what was going on between them.

Lausch took off his coat and hung it over the hood of the car. Her husband did the same. Neither of them spoke. Suddenly her husband squared away; he drew his fists up, awkwardly, like some man in an old-time fight drawing. She saw him draw back. Norm Lausch also raised his arms and made fists, covering himself. Both men half-crouched, and then her husband punched Lausch on the shoulder. The sound of the blow was so loud that it startled her; she jumped and exclaimed.

Waving his fists in circles, Lausch also drew back. Swinging his arm in a wide curve he smacked Walt on the neck. Walt fell back, stumbled, lost his footing entirely, and sat down on the pavement. He remained there, resting his palms on the cement and getting his breath. Then he got back to his feet. Again the two men faced each other, standing very close, their bodies almost touching, their fists up.

"I'll knock the shit out of you," Lausch said.

"Yeah," Walt said.

"You dumb shit," Lausch said. "Get out of here and don't come back. I don't want you around."

"It's a pleasure," Walt said.

They remained for a time, neither moving very much, still glaring at each other and making menacing gestures with their fists. Then, by degrees, they lowered their arms. They moved away from each other, stood. Walt rubbed his neck. Finally Lausch walked over to the car and retrieved his coat. He put it on and presently Walt took his coat, too. Carrying it, he opened the car door and got in again. As he slid in beside her, she found that he was trembling. His whole body vibrated, and she saw that even his teeth were chattering.

Coming around to the driver's side, Lausch got in, slammed his door, and started up the motor. Without speaking, he drove the car off, out into the street, in the direction they had been going.

Finally, when they had gone all the way across Market to the north side, and neither man had said anything, Sherry said, "I never saw anything so childish in my life."

The men remained silent. By now Walt had stopped shaking. He had not, however, put his coat back on; he held it wadded up.

"Really childish," she said. In her ears her voice sounded thin and alarmed, jumpy with fright.

At last Lausch said, "It certainly was."

"I'll pick up my stuff later in the week," Walt said.

"Okay," Lausch said. "Any time you want."

"This is dreadful," she said.

"No it isn't," Walt said. "What's dreadful about it?" His voice was hoarse; he cleared his throat violently.

"You want to think it over?" Lausch said. "You can, as far as I'm concerned." But he said it so formally that even she knew that it was only a ritual.

"No thanks," Walt said.

When they had parked across from Lausch Company, behind the red Alfa, Sherry said to Lausch, "What about me?"

Lausch said, "What about you?"

"Because my husband loses his temper does that mean I'm required to carry the stigmata along with him? Whether I want to or not?"

"Suit yourself," Lausch said, without much emotion. "If you want to come to work you may, on a trial basis. The way we discussed."

"That's very decent of you," she said. "I admire you for it. For your fair behavior."

"Okay," Lausch said. "That's all, I guess. Happy driving across the mountain."

Walt had already gotten out and gone down the sidewalk to the Alfa. He sat in it now, his back to them.

"Then I'll call you," she said to Lausch. "Tomorrow."

Lausch nodded.

"Goodnight," she said. Getting out, she shut the door and followed her husband to the Alfa. She got in behind the wheel, opened her purse, and searched for the car keys.

The Buick passed them. Lausch did not look in their direction. Her husband did not stir; she started to wave and then changed her mind. Evidently it was not the thing to do.

"What an evening," she said, as she started up the Alfa.

Sunk down in his seat, Walt did not reply.

9

From her bathroom window, Janet Runcible could see down the hill and into the backyard of the Dombrosio home. She could see the patio, the three sling green-plastic and iron chairs, the portable barbecue, a cup and saucer that had been left out. A tree cut off her view of the door leading out onto the patio. Shrubs, growing on the hillside, made it impossible for her to see into the back part of the house itself. But she could see the garage, which was attached to the house, on the side, off the patio.

Through the window of the garage she could make out the sight of Walt Dombrosio. The time was eleven in the morning. The day, she discovered by checking with last night's newspaper, was Wednesday. He had been home the day before, too; she had watched him then.

Had he lost his job in San Francisco? Had he quit? Or was he ill? Or was this his vacation?

But the sports car still started out in the early morning; she still heard it going down the hill about five forty-five. And it came back up the hill in the evening. The same time as always.

So, Janet decided, Mrs. Dombrosio was going off by herself. And at exactly the same schedule that her husband had been on.

It had to be Sherry driving the sports car because there were only two people in the Dombrosio family. And she had not seen Sherry during the day, only her husband.

In the silence of midday the scraping noise of a saw lifted up and floated to Janet. He was sawing. Walt, in his workshop in his garage, was doing something with wood.

Puttering in his workshop in the middle of the day, she decided. He *must* be out of a job. Unless, she thought, there's some job they have him working on at home. But that did not seem likely.

However, it did not seem likely that he had lost his job and that his wife had gotten a job immediately, that took her into San Francisco at exactly the same time and brought her back at exactly the same time. The whole thing was perplexing.

Giving up, Janet left the bathroom and returned to the living room, where her cigarette had burned itself out in the ashtray on the coffee table.

Suppose, she thought as she seated herself on the couch, he lost his job because they took away his driver's license? But — good god. God in heaven. That would mean that Leo was responsible for him losing his job, because her husband was responsible for him losing his license.

Now she felt so distraught that she could not sit down. Rising, she paced about the living room, her hands pressed together until her nails dug into her palms. Oh dear god, she thought. I prayed this wouldn't happen but I knew it would. This is what I feared.

From far below, the sound of the saw reached her. I can hear him, she thought frantically. Here in my own living room I can hear him at work in his garage. What is he doing? She put her hands to her ears. Is that going to go on all day long? Will I be stuck here in the house, forced to listen to it? I'm not the one who called the police; it was Leo. But, she thought, Leo doesn't have to hear that sound. He's at his office. He's safe and sound and out of here, at Runcible Realty. Insulated, protected.

I'm the one, she thought, who has to pay for what Leo did. It's always that way. The guilty party never pays. It's the innocent. That's the real meaning of Christianity.

Going to the bookcase she got out the King James Bible and then, for good measure, Leo's Jewish bible. Opening both books at random she closed her eyes and picked a spot within each. The hell with this, she thought as she read lines of text which meant nothing to her; they could not conceivably apply. There must be some way to tell what to do, she said to herself. To know what is the right thing.

At the end table she knelt down, then seated herself on the rug. From the rack under the table she dragged out newspapers and began sorting through them until she found the copy of *This Week* magazine that had come with the *Chronicle* earlier in the month. There was an article in it that she remembered; at the time it had impressed her as profound, and now she needed it for what moral guidance it could give.

She did not find the article she wanted, but in another magazine she found an article she had not before noticed; it was by a young new disc jockey — his picture was included and he looked like a nice, honest, reliable person — and in it he gave advice to the perplexed world. His advice, of course, was aimed primarily at teenagers, but, reading it, she saw that it had a wider application. If a thing is true, she thought, if it's right for one person, it's right for everyone else. No matter what age.

For a long time she studied the young disc jockey's various pieces of advice, and in the end she still faced what she had known from the start. *A person's first loyalty is to their husband.* They have to stick by him, no matter what he does; he's still their husband. Leo had stuck by her when she had had her terrible crackup in 1958, after the period in which she had tried to work at the office. He had suffered as much as she had. And he had lost the help that she could have given him; he was married to a woman who couldn't pull her share of the weight, and yet he hadn't deserted her.

If I had done my share, she thought, he wouldn't be so tense and on edge. He wouldn't have said those things to Paul Wilby, and he wouldn't have telephoned Walt Dombrosio; at least, not without thinking it out more clearly. It's my fault. I'm to blame. Whatever Leo may have done wrong, if he did do something wrong, can be traced back to me.

And so, she realized, if Walt Dombrosio lost his job because he had no driver's license, then it's my fault.

She thought, If I hadn't let Leo down in 1958, if I had stayed on at the office and done my work, if I hadn't been so weak, then Walt Dombrosio would not have suffered what he's suffered. His terrible sufferings, his having to be arrested and post bail and go to court and watch them take away his license, and then whatever happened between him and his employers —

It was too much. She could not bear to think about it. Putting her hands to her ears again she ran into the kitchen and shut the door; holding her breath she stood silently, grimacing, feeling the tears well up in her eyes. I'm not fit to be alive on this planet, she said to herself. She said it out loud. "I ought to be dead," she told herself, and now the tears dripped down her cheeks and onto the front of her shirt. She saw the great dark stains spread out on the white fabric.

Oh god, she thought. What I'd give for a drink.

I'll have to change my shirt, she realized. So she went back to her bedroom. She pulled down the shade, shut the door, and then unbuttoned her shirt and took it off.

In the half-light of the bedroom she rummaged among the clothes in her dresser drawers. Finally she snapped on the lamp. Mounted in the base of the lamp, under a plastic cover, was a verse that she had clipped out of a magazine years ago. Now, seeing it, she halted and reread it; she had read it thousands of times in her life, and it always had given her a measure of calm.

> And when that one great scorer comes
> To score against your name;
> It won't be "Whether you won or lost,"
> But HOW YOU PLAYED THE GAME.

Yes, she thought. It's how you play the game. And how have I played it? Pretty lousily. Hurting everyone around me, letting them take the burden from me and carry it themselves because I'm too selfish and bad. First my family, then Leo, even my neighbors. It's spread to the community. Like that time I never showed up at the cake sale, and so there was no white cake with chocolate icing. And they said a lot of people asked for one. They could have sold it easily.

With another wife, she thought, one with drive and determination, and with ability, Leo might have been able to put into practice some of those fabulous ideals that are tearing him apart inside. That time when he wanted me to run for the school board . . . how could I have done that? But another woman might have. A better woman.

First of all, Leo should have had a companion, a woman who could have worked with him, side by side, like those women in Israel. Maybe if he had married a Jewish woman — she had let him down there, too. She had not been Jewish and she had not even become converted. She had clung to her old faith, not because she respected it but because she was afraid to change. She did not know what a new faith might entail.

Where he needs me, she decided, is not in his home but in his work. Where the battle is.

Once it gets around town that Leo caused Dombrosio to lose

his job, then people will think even worse of him. And, she thought, I know he worries anyhow. I can tell. It's another cancer eating away inside him. I wonder if he knows about the job, yet. It took him two months to find out about the license . . . maybe he won't notice that Dombrosio is home during the day. After all, we don't speak to the Dombrosios. And Leo is at his office during the day, except when he has to come back to the house for something he's forgotten.

How will he feel when he finds out? she asked herself. Will he be able to forgive himself? And then she thought, Maybe he could give Dombrosio a job. At the realty office. But the only job would be a typing job, answering phones and giving out keys. He had an elderly partly retired woman who did that, the wife of a rancher.

Sooner or later Leo is going to find out, she said to herself. I won't tell him, though; I didn't tell him about the license. But — maybe I'm doing the wrong thing, again. The weak thing.

Going into the kitchen she put the coffeepot on the stove to re-heat. And then she discovered that she did not have her shirt on; she had taken it off, started looking for another, and then forgotten what she was doing. She had gone off into a daydream, again, into her worries. So she returned at once to the bedroom, to the gloom and the one yellow lamp. This time she got out a sweater from the drawer and put it hurriedly on. In the bathroom she stopped long enough to arrange her hair; the sweater had mussed it.

I could use some makeup, she decided as she studied herself. How dry her skin looked. And under her eyes she saw crow's feet. She began dabbing powder on, and then eyebrow pencil; without coloring her eyebrows were so faint as to be almost invisible.

While she stood at the mirror doing that she heard a strange sound. For a time she continued putting on lipstick, and then with a surge of dismay she identified the sound; it was the coffee boiling. She had ruined it. Dropping the lipstick into the bowl she ran into the kitchen and snatched the coffeepot off. The odor of burned coffee filled the kitchen; she threw the coffee into the sink with disgust.

And, after the disgust, she felt weariness and a growing, all-absorbing despair. Sinking down at the table she put her head on her arms and shut her eyes. The despair, by and by, became depression, the most empty feeling of all.

Suppose, she thought, it had happened to my husband. Suppose Leo became sick or injured and couldn't work. I'm a failure even as a housewife; I can't even fix a pot of coffee in my own kitchen without ruining it. How could I possibly do what Sherry Dombrosio has done, go out into the world and take over the burden as it slides from her husband's shoulders?

What a contrast between her and me, she thought. As soon as he lost his license, Sherry got right in and began driving him to work. Every morning, without fail. And now, a job. A real equal; a companion to her husband, ready to share — capable of sharing.

That's the thing, she realized. Capability. I'd be willing to, but I couldn't. She felt panic now, even at the idea. Going and getting a job, driving into San Francisco each morning . . .

That woman, she thought, is so superior to me that it isn't even funny. Attractive, capable, alert — she dresses so well. Look at her clothes, and then look at mine. Look at the slop all down the front of me . . . see it. She raised her head and examined the sweater that she had put on. It's clean now, she thought. But in another hour . . . stains and mess, dribbling down my front like a baby or a toothless crone.

But if I had had Sherry's upbringing, she thought. And, she thought, if I had had her money, the money her family had. To put into me, the way they invested in her . . .

She's a product of well-to-do society, Janet Runcible said to herself. That woman did not create herself; she is not responsible for what she is. Nobody is. A person is a product of their society.

How could I be like her? I never had her opportunities.

They train women like that to be executives, she said to herself. That class she comes from: the men are the natural leaders of this country, the ivy-league set. Classmates, all from the same colleges. Harvard, like Franklin Roosevelt. It's in their language; they practically have an accent. And they go to each other. They're lawyers for each other, doctors, business acquaintances.

And you can't get in, if you're not born into it. You're either born into that or you're not. What can I do? Can I go and learn the speech and dress? It took an entire lifetime to make Sherry what she is. Expensive boarding schools. Even dentists. They have their teeth straightened and worked on as little children. You can tell what sort of background a person has by his teeth, she realized. Look at the farm kids growing up here. If their teeth are crooked, no one even notices, let alone decides to pay out thousands of dollars for teeth-straightening. They wouldn't even know that such things are done. So when the girl or boy grows up and leaves this rat hole of a farm area, when he or she gets out into the real world —

Like me, she thought. Cut off from any hope of success. Of being anything. Doomed to a miserable life on the outside, looking in. What a wicked unfair world, she thought. To start some people with all the advantages . . .

And then, as a terrible overwhelming new insight, it came to her that the moral part was not the really important part. It was not a moral issue. It was a practical issue. And as she realized that a wall of fear rose up in her and burst from her; she rocked back and forth, her hands pressed to her ears, squeaking with fright.

"What does it prove?" she said aloud, in a voice that filled the kitchen. "It proves that I have no chance at all." No matter how hard she tried, she would not succeed. No matter what the need. No matter how dreadful their financial situation she could not go out into the world and compete because it would take a lifetime to learn to compete; it took a lifetime to get equipped, and this did not so much prove that the world was an evil place but that she, Janet Runcible, would never never in a million years be able to survive in it. Survive economically against women like Sherry Dombrosio — because even if an organization did let down its rules and hire a woman it would not be she who would get hired but Sherry and all the other women of her class, with her looks and speech-mannerisms and clothes.

So someone like herself would never be safe; she would never be able to sit back in security. She was doomed all her life, until the grave came and got her.

Getting to her feet she wandered about the house, paying no attention to where she was; she went from one room to the next and back again, scarcely conscious of the furniture — once she stubbed her toe on the leg of the couch, and once she ran head-on into the half-closed bedroom door.

What has happened, she decided, is that the whole structure of the family has broken down, since World War Two. In World War Two women started welding in war plants. Like men. And Communism has done the same thing as the war. Sherry Dombrosio should not be out earning a living because that is the man's job. No wonder I'm so anxiety-ridden, she said to herself. I have been let down. Haven't I stayed home and done my job, by having a child? That's a woman's job. Not working side-by-side in a factory, like some big slob of a Russian peasant woman, calling everyone "Comrade." That's not the American way.

In some ways those Dombrosios are Communists, she realized. That Negro that they had visit them; consider that. Interracial marriage is a part of the Communist program for America.

Sherry should not be out working. She should not have to be. Her place is at home having babies; she's failed at her real job. And if her husband hadn't lost his job, she would be home. He let her down. He deprived her of the security of his income-earning capacity.

It's the man's job, she told herself as she wandered frantically around the house. He's the one who's supposed to be out facing the world, and if he fails, it's not up to the woman to take his place. It's not up to me to take Leo's place if he's unable to bring home the bacon, any more than it's up to Jerome. What a woman must do is face the fact that her husband is a failure. She should do everything she can to get him back on his feet. She should see to it that he is healed and once more restored to the battleground. Once more serving in the lines.

Why is Sherry out there? she said to herself. Now her mood had ceased to be one of depression; she had become angry, and her entire body vibrated with her agitation. Again and again she clasped her hands together, made fists. Her pace speeded up. A man like that, staying home — how is he different from a bum? How long does he plan to putter around there in his garage, building birdcages or whatever it is?

If I were his wife, she decided, I would not tolerate that; I would stand for it possibly for a day, and then I would see an end to it. I'd have him back at the job; I'd make him wish he were out of the house and working. I'd make him so glad to get back to work —

Now, all at once, her emotions turned to the wife, to Sherry; she ceased being angry, and a tide of warm, soft commiseration flowed up in her, almost choking her. Her eyes burned with tears and she said in a low, unsteady voice,

"That poor woman. That poor, poor woman."

I ought to go and support her, Janet thought. Tell her how I feel, how well I understand. He made me go and work; he tried to make me take over for him. But I wouldn't. No, I told him. It's up to you, Leo. It's your reponsibility. You can't expect me to run your real estate business, any more than I can expect you to bear babies if I fail you there.

That woman has been thoroughly, wholly let down by her

husband. As much as if he had run off with another woman. The sacred trust has been broken, and the irony of it is that when they do that to their wives they always have a convincing story. There's always some rationalization to make the wife feel bad, so she thinks it's her "duty" to do something. Like go and work as Sherry has done. If Leo had lost his job, he'd start putting the pressure on me the same way; he'd endeavor to make me feel bad. Yes, they create guilt. They have plenty of ways. What you have to do is fight back; you have to not acknowledge the guilt.

She thought, You have to throw it back to them, where it belongs. It's their world, their man's world. Let them compete in it and leave the wives to do what the good Lord intended them to do: stay home and bear babies.

Oh yes, she thought in anguish. I've been through all this. I know all this so well. How the pressure is put on, in a thousand tiny ways. Such skillful ways. Does she know? In the world she came from there probably wasn't such things. Everything was aboveboard. Does she recognize what has happened? I can see it so clearly; I can look down on their marriage — an outsider — and see.

If she doesn't know, Janet thought, she certainly should. And he should, too. He shouldn't be allowed to go on deceiving himself and her as to the true state of affairs.

Going to the cupboard in the kitchen she got up on the little step ladder and, reaching up to the top shelf, pushed aside large cans of apricots and tomato juice until she found the bottle of bad Tokay that they had put aside in disgust the month before. Here it was, bad as ever, but at least it was something.

With a tumbler from the sink she carried the Tokay bottle to the kitchen table and reseated herself. It was really terrible stuff; it tasted like cough syrup. And much too sweet. She knew it would make her sick; in all her life she had never gotten so sick as she had, one time, on bad Tokay. Taking her glass to the sink she diluted the wine with tap water. That made it better.

Now she found it drinkable. And an ice cube made it taste almost pleasant.

Sawing away in his workshop, Walter Dombrosio heard only the saw. All at once he sensed someone; he glanced up and jumped with surprise. In the doorway — evidently she had gone through the house, finding no one — stood Janet Runcible.

Her lips moved. Against the scream of the saw she was saying hello. But he could not hear her. He shut the saw off; the blade slowed and finally ceased turning.

On her face was a smile, a rigid widening of her mouth, as if she had kept that one expression throughout her journey down the hill and into his house, through each room, until now she had found him; now the smile came into use. She wore a red sweater and cotton pants; many times he had seen her dressed in exactly that way on her trips into town to shop. Her long colorless hair hung down, unbrushed. He could not help noticing how gaunt she was. How tall and fleshless; her arms showed tendons, and the skin had a flabby look. On the backs of her hands he saw freckles against the white skin.

"Hi," he said warily, not pleased to see her. He had been deeply involved in cutting off the bottom of a door.

Still smiling at him, Janet said, "I don't want to bother you." Her words came out separately, carefully spoken. As if, he thought, she was being very sure not to say the wrong thing.

"That's okay," he said, in a noncommital tone. He had had almost nothing to do with the Runcibles since the incident about Charley; in fact he had done his best to put them out of his mind. With everything else that he had had to worry about, he did not have any time in which to dwell on the Runcibles.

Her eyes, red-rimmed, fixed themselves on him. They contained a luster that he could not classify. It was not amusement. Some emotion was busy inside her; something shone out as she gazed at him.

"Well?" she said.

To that, he could think of nothing to say.

After a long pause she again started to speak. The alive element in her eyes had grown in brilliance. Was it vexation? "Well?" she repeated. "What about it?"

"What about what?" he said.

With great deliberateness she said, "How about a cup of coffee?"

"You want a cup of coffee?" he said.

The brilliance in her eyes danced at him. As if she were burning to tell him something; as if she could hardly keep it back. And yet she did not seem able to say it. The words did not come forth.

"I'd like one very much," Janet said.

With great reluctance he shut off his equipment. "Okay," he said. "But I have to get back to work." He did not even particularly care why she had dropped by; he was only interested in resuming his work. He tolerated her, and that was all; people did come by, and there was no getting out from the burden of entertaining them. "I hope there's a pot made," he said as he walked past her and up the three stairs into the house. I hope to god I don't have to stand around while a fresh pot gets made, he thought. He could so easily imagine her in the kitchen, with her cigarette going, her purse beside her, prepared to spend the entire day. Talking on and on about nothing.

Behind him, Janet Runcible said something that he could not catch, a low murmur. She followed him at a distance to the kitchen, and, as he plugged in the pot, she placed herself by the refrigerator. Folding her arms, she leaned against the refrigerator; she did not sit down, as he had expected her to.

"It's already made," he said, in what he knew to be a be-grudging tone.

But she did not seem to care what his tone was. She did not notice what he said; she continued to gaze at him fixedly. It made him nervous and irritable. So he did not sit down, either; he stationed himself opposite her and returned her gaze.

She said finally, "You're not working."

"No," he said.

"You're home."

"I quit my job," he said. His resentment grew until he could only by a great effort contain it. He willed himself to become calmer. Take it easy, he told himself. This is an ignorant bag from up the hill who has nothing to do but sit home all day, and who has a natural avid curiosity about everyone and everything in town. This is all she has, this prying into other people's troubles. These harpies feed on gossip and misery and scandal; they listen for it all day long. From here she'll go to the next house, and from there to the next.

I have to humor her, he told himself. Out of charity.

Janet Runcible said, "Are you building a bird house?"

"No," he said. "I am putting up a door."

"Where's your wife?"

"At work."

"In San Francisco?"

"Yes," he said.

"Did she get a nice job?"

"Yes," he said.

"How long is she going to be working?"

"I don't know," he said.

"She doesn't like to work, does she?"

"I don't know," he said. He shrugged, holding down his antipathy for this woman. He made his voice toneless.

"Has she ever worked before? During your marriage?"

"No," he said.

Janet Runcible said, "You shouldn't let her work."

Unable to keep the savagery out of his voice he said, "Is that so."

She did not appear to notice his tone. She did not seem to care. "It's wrong," she said, "for the husband to stay home and the wife work."

"I see," he said. He put enormous heavy irony into his voice; it staggered with sarcasm.

"You should try to get a job again as soon as possible."

"It's a little hard," he said. "With no car."

"You could take the Greyhound bus in."

He said, "I'll wait."

"What will you wait for?"

"I'll wait to get my license back."

Janet said, "Leo did not know you were really drunk. He only thought you were drunk."

As far as he was concerned, her husband's opinion of the matter was of no consequence to him.

But something had gone wrong. The woman's face had become absolutely white. She stared at him. He thought that she was having some kind of attack; the idea flashed through his mind that she was an epileptic or something. That would explain her disorganized walk, he thought. Her sloppy manner; it would explain that.

Her lips moved. "I have to go," she said almost inaudibly; she turned, her arms still folded, and bolted toward the door. Through the house she ran. He followed after her, astonished.

At the front door she halted, in a state of confusion; she fooled with the knob, unable to open the door. Now tears had begun to roll down her cheeks. "Oh god," she said, letting her head fall forward until it struck against the door.

"What is it?" he said, not coming too close to her; he had a physical aversion to touching her.

"I just realized," she said; her eyes, blind and flat, peered at him.

And at that he, too, realized. He understood what she had meant. He saw why she had reacted. Why it was so important.

"Your husband called the police on me?" he said. "That night?"

The blind, pale eyes continued to stare at him; now they stared past him. She was crying and mumbling, but he could not make out what she was trying to say.

"That bastard," he said. "That dirty fucking bastard."

Sliding upright, supporting herself against the door, Janet Runcible became calmer. With labored dignity she said, "My husband did what was right."

"Right," he echoed.

"You might have run over some child." Opening the door she went out onto the porch. With elaborate caution she took hold of the railing and started down step by step.

He said, "I wish I had run over you and your husband."

To that she said nothing. Her back to him, she continued on down the path to the road. Without looking his way she started up the hill once more, toward her own house. Soon she had gone.

So he did do it, Walt Dombrosio thought. I thought so, but I couldn't be sure. That stupid woman. That ugly sagging stupid woman.

Presently he returned to his workshop. He turned the saw back on and resumed his work. His hands were shaking so badly that he had to stop almost at once. So, instead of working, he stood doing nothing, his hands in his pockets. And gradually, by degrees, his fingers searched once more for the swelling at his groin. Testing its existence, its perpetual presence in his life.

10

The house which Mr. and Mrs. Diters had bought could not be occupied until the utilities had been turned on, and Leo Runcible knew that from experience. It would be three days until the butane truck showed up from San Rafael, but there was supposed to be an emergency tank of butane at the feed store in Carquinez. If someone could transport the tank by car to the Diterses' house, and could hook it up to their butane pipe, they would have both heat and hot water, but otherwise not. The Pacific Telephone and Telegraph at San Rafael took their name and promised to send out a man with a phone before very long. The PG&E turned on the electricity at once, and the West Marin Water Company had never turned the water off at all; it was not safe to operate the ancient, rusty valve.

After he had gotten the hurried call from the Diterses, Runcible drove leisurely over to the feed store for the butane tank. It weighed something like a hundred pounds and he was not certain if he could handle it. But, he decided, between himself and Diters they could get it out of the car and across the field to the pipe. As far as attaching it went, he did not expect trouble. He had done such things many times. All he needed was a crescent wrench, and he had that in the glove compartment of the car.

He found the Diterses in the front yard. The moving van had left off their personal and household goods, evidently; he saw a huge pile of cartons, wrapping paper, boxes and barrels to the side of the house. And the flowers growing along the walk had been trampled.

"How's it going?" he called as he got out of his car.

Both Mr. and Mrs. Diters seemed keyed-up but cheerful. "The moving men broke a step," Diters said. "Unless it was already broken."

"I think it happened when they carried the piano in," his wife said. "Do you know, before they unload the van they make you sign a paper saying all your goods are undamaged?"

Going indoors with them, Runcible found that although they had unpacked most of the cartons they had not tried to put anything away. They had only wanted to see what damage had taken place on the trip over the mountain. Dishes, books, chairs, rugs, clothing, had been put everywhere, in no order.

"Let's get this butane attached," he said to Diters. "I'll need you; I can't manage it alone."

As he and the old man dragged the cylinder from the car, Diters said, "I appreciate your kindness, Mr. Runcible. You didn't have to bring this over."

"I want you to have heat," Runcible said. "It gets cold up here at night."

While they were attaching the pipe to the cylinder, the old man leaned toward him and said, "You don't suppose that step was already broken, do you? On a nice little house like this, in such good shape."

Runcible, concentrating on the pipe, said, "I can assure you that the step was in absolutely perfect condition. Do you have any idea what a piano and four men weigh? Over a ton. There isn't a front step in the United States built to take weight like that. You could pay forty thousand — ninety thousand — for a house, a brand new house you had built yourself, and the same thing could happen. And I'll tell you something else." He paused in the job of tightening up the nut. "There's a man here in town, John Flores. He can repair that for a dollar or so."

The old man's face showed his relief. How small it seemed, now. No need to fuss, Runcible thought to himself.

"I'll give you his phone number," Runcible said, as he got the nut tight. "We all call on him when we need something done."

Later, as he drove home to change his clothes, he thought to himself, But you won't get hold of John Flores right away. Flores was busy.

The entire back field past the Dombrosios' house had been dug up by the gang of high school boys that Flores always hired when he got hold of a leaching line job. Pipe had already been brought in, unloaded and stacked up, along with an enormous pile of gravel.

Slowing his car almost to a stop, Runcible leaned out to see how the job was going. In addition to the high school boys he saw a gang of younger children, boys and girls from the grammar school; they stood together on a rise of ground, watching the digging. Among the group his own boy Jerome stood; he was so busy watching that he did not see his father.

I wonder how much it's costing, Runcible said to himself. And can they pay for it? Does she make as much as he did? Probably not. Women are generally paid less than men, even for the same work.

Tooting his horn, he managed to dislodge his son's attention from the digging. Jerome waved, and Runcible waved back. The trench extended from the patio of the Dombrosio house for a distance of sixty or so feet, he estimated. Then, at a distribution box, it branched in two directions. The box had already been built. He could see the redwood sections set down in the trench.

The work had been going on for several days now, and progress was slow. Flores had no power equipment; he depended on the shovels of the boys. It's a wonder, Runcible thought, that they didn't carry the gravel in on their backs. That picture amused him; the boys, like Chinese coolies, bent almost double, trudging in a line from the Joslin Gravel Works along the Petaluma Road and then down Highway One to Carquinez, up the hill to the Dombrosio house at the Chevron Station turn-off. They could roll the pipe part of the way, he decided.

From his living room, the view was not promising. Below, the dirt and pipes and gravel spread out prominently. And what is it, he asked himself, but a project to transfer crap from the Dombrosio house to the outside world? And we have to watch it going on; we have to look down at the pipes and gravel that will compensate the world for the fact that Walter and Sherry Dombrosio have to go, at intervals, to the can.

This sort of joking speculation was typical of the area, of course, whenever a new septic tank or leaching field was put in. But he did not feel in a joking mood; he did not get the same enjoyment from bucolic earthy humor that the rustics did. If I have to take it, he thought, I'll take it in Breugel pictures.

In his bedroom he removed his coat and shirt and tie. While lugging the butane cylinder with Diters he had gotten black gunk all over his front. And, he noticed now, the cuffs of his trousers had caked mud on them. When had that happened? Probably very early in the day, at the first open field he had come to. No one could walk about in the country without getting gunk and mud on him; it was a foolish man who wore a business suit, white shirt and tie . . . but what alternative did a Realtor have? I have to meet the public, he said to himself. And I have to get outdoors and poke around. So he had long ago resigned himself to having to change his clothes a couple of times a day.

You can move out here, he thought as he put on a clean shirt, a civilized, cultured man of the world, and shortly you are seated

154 · PHILIP K. DICK

on the same hole as the rest of them; you are crapping into a long
pipe and treading on the same stuff. If you scratch your hand on
a rusty nail you die, like an old sheep, of tetanus; you go gallop-
ing around the field having convulsions. Out here (he rehearsed a
kind of gloomy parody of his customary speech to prospects)
you don't die of arterial sclerosis or throat cancer; you get run
over by a mowing machine or thrashed to death or you get lung
worms. Or — and this was a fear that he could not lose — your
butane stove blows up and splashes you across the pasture that
you have invested your life savings in.

Having found his new trousers he finished dressing and then
left the bedroom.

At the window he paused to glance down at the digging.

Try and discuss art out here, he said to himself. While a gang
of grinning teenage rustic simps are digging leaching lines below
your window. Try to keep talking year after year about the cultural possibilities of this place, its pastoral beauties, its repose.
The news up here is that the man next door got his hand lopped
off while working part time at the mill. And that is all the news.
A cow, maybe, got run over by a bread truck. Or a bobcat came
down at night and ate someone's duck.

And at this moment, the news is that John Flores is digging
three hundred feet of leaching line, and everyone is talking about it;
all the kids are lined up, even my own kid, watching every bit they
can see. How much is it costing? That's the question. How much is
being dug? That's vital, too. And what symptoms were there?

He made a mental note: find out what per-foot rate Flores is
charging him.

Even me, he thought. I have to know, too. Because there's
nothing else to know. When you live small you think small.

I wonder what it would take to make them think big, he asked
himself. In fact, he thought, I wonder what big would be, out here.

Now he noticed, out in the yard, his wife gardening. She had on jeans and an oriental hat and old shoes. Kneeling, Janet weeded with a metal-pronged tool among her bed of strawberries.

Are the idiotic better off than we are? he asked himself.

Some people are happy in this little way. Scratching in the earth, hour by hour. My wife, he thought. The other wives, the farm women. Yes, Janet is content when she can be like them. When she can't be, then the torment begins.

He thought, That is why she likes it out here; there is no complexity. Nothing to strain her, to put what she calls "pressure" on her.

He walked to the front door, opened it and stepped out onto the porch.

Down the road something moved. A shape, in the road, and he could not identify it. Voices carried to him, shrill. He saw, at last, that three boys were doing something in the road. Gradually they toiled up the hill until he saw that they had a wagon.

What are they pushing? he wondered. The wheels of the wagon squeaked rustily. The boys shouted at one another. They put their weight against the wagon, pushing it on up. At a house they halted, braced the wagon; one boy went up the path and knocked on the door of the house. When the door opened, the boy showed something in his hands and also pointed at the wagon.

Selling something, Runcible realized. Once again. What is it this time? Wrong season for apples.

Should he wait? He lingered on the porch, not going to his car. Janet won't hear them, he decided; she is too far lost in her gardening. She had not even heard him.

His wife, weeding, absorbed in her work. The leachlines below did not annoy her. The work in progress. The noise. How insulated, he thought. Would I like to be her? Here come the boys toiling up the hill with a wagon of something to sell; I see them; I hear them; I am aware of them, and so I have to stay here until they arrive.

The price we pay, he thought. For noticing.

Now the boys spied him. Yes, he thought as he stood waiting. A customer. The boys yelled at each other and redoubled their efforts; the wagon groaned and increased its speed up the hill. What did he see? Dirt, it looked like. Brown soil spilling from the wagon, and stones among the dirt. It did not appear very promising. Already, before they had even reached him, he fished in his pockets to be sure he had change. Embarrassing if he didn't.

"Hey, Mr. Runcible!" one of the boys called. They were older than Jerome. Eighth or ninth graders.

He nodded to them.

Puffing, the boys arrived with their wagon, all of them grinning at him hopefully.

"What do you have?" he asked.

"Arrowheads," a boy said.

"Indian relics," another boy put in merrily. Together, the boys brought the wagon around to show him; he saw a confusion of dirt and objects. Now a boy held out some small objects in a handkerchief. Runcible, lifting the edge of the handkerchief aside, saw two black arrowheads. Obsidian, he realized. The best kind found in the area. Highly prized.

"How much?" he said.

The boy who held the arrowheads said, "A dollar."

"For both?" he said.

The boys gathered for hasty agreement. "Apiece," the first boy answered, presently.

Picking up the arrowheads he examined them carefully. In his years of living in the area, he had never found an arrowhead himself, although he had always wanted to; had, in fact, always hoped and expected to. Eventually he would find one, he had reasoned, and he had not been impatient. There was no pressing need to find one. And he had seen a number of them, in various homes. He had heard stories of men finding beautiful large obsidian arrowheads in plain sight, in the middle of the road, or visible near the shore of an inlet or estero. Was there any point in buying them? he asked himself. Was the pleasure entirely in the finding? These did look like good ones, he thought. And he could display them in his office.

That idea pleased him. "Okay," he said, getting out his wallet. As he paid over the two dollars he indicated the wagon and said, "What's all that?"

"Relics," one of the boys said. "All kinds."

"More arrowheads?" he asked.

They seemed uncertain. "No," one boy said finally; he rummaged about in the dirt and held up what appeared to be a granite chunk. "This is an Indian tool."

"Where did you find these?" Runcible said.

The boys at once became secretive. Obviously, they had argued it out and agreed not to tell anyone. But, by picking up a handful of the soil, he got his answer. This soil was familiar. They had found the arrowheads down the road, at the leaching line digging.

"Down there," he said, pointing at John Flores' crew.

The boys, reluctantly, nodded. One of them said loudly, "But nobody cares; we got permission."

"From who?" Runcible said.

"From Mr. Flores," a boy said.

"Okay," he said. He poked among the chunks in the wagon load of dirt. They had found some Indian tools; awls, evidently, and some bones that had been made into hooks or punches. But he did not care about these. "All right, boys," he said. "Thanks." Taking his arrowheads, he returned to the house and shut the door after him.

He seated himself by the phone, examined the arrowheads once again, and then began to dial.

After several rings, Wharton answered.

"This is Leo Runcible," Runcible said. "Listen, some boys just came by and sold me a couple of obsidian arrowheads."

"Where did they get them?" Wharton said.

"You know Walter Dombrosio."

"Yes," Wharton said. "From the leaching field? Where they're digging?" He sounded triumphant. "I told him to keep watch. Every time anybody digs, I want them to watch."

"There was a lot of junk besides arrowheads," Runcible said. "What looked like granite awls. And leather punching tools. They had a wagon load; they're peddling it door to door."

"All right, fine," Wharton said in a businesslike voice. "Now here's what I want you to do." He did not wait for Runcible to assent; he went on immediately, "You go down there to the digging. You understand? Tell Flores to stop digging. Don't let him do any more digging. I can't get over for an hour or so, but I'll be over. Maybe you had better stay down there until I get there. To see that none of the children take any more away. Is Dombrosio home?"

"I don't know," he said, nonplussed at being ordered around by the grammar school teacher.

"Some of the things are quite fragile," Wharton said. "So better leave any further digging to me. I'll bring tools. Let's see — we have about five hours of daylight. Fine. Good-bye." The phone clicked; Wharton had hung up.

For christ's sake, Runcible thought. I'm supposed to be back at the office; I can't fool around with this. He started to redial, but changed his mind and put the phone back on the hook. His curiosity had been awakened a little; not to the extent that Wharton's had . . . but still, he did feel some excitement. And Wharton's professional tone had made it grow even more. Maybe there's something in this, he said to himself. What's the most they've found? Spanish treasure? Buried cities? No, that's the Aztecs and Incas.

Further south. Nothing like that up here . . . only pottery and tools and arrowheads. But still —

He left the house and made his way down the road on foot, to the digging.

A man makes a good buy in arrowheads and look what he gets himself into, he thought as he walked. How long had it been since he had set foot on the Dombrosio property? And now, he thought, I have to go down there and beg to have the work stopped, and for what? For myself? Do I get anything out of this? I put myself in the position of having Walt Dombrosio say no to me, and I get nothing out of it.

But Wharton was right; the work should be stopped. Science, mankind itself, had a priority above them all. The interests of cultural research had to be served.

By the time he arrived at the digging he was breathless with excitement. As soon as he caught sight of John Flores he cupped his hands and yelled, "Stop digging!"

Heads turned.

"Stop digging," he panted, scrambling onto the field and hurrying toward Flores. Dirt flew up ahead of him; stones, kicked by his shoes, rolled away. "Did you people find some Indian relics?" he said, halting in front of Flores. "I talked to the West Marin School District—" His mind found the most impressive way to express his errand. "They advise that you halt work immediately."

The dark, wrinkled face of John Flores recalled to him the man's peculiar fame. He could neither read nor write, and yet he was one of the most respected, shrewd and able businessmen in the area; he sometimes bossed eight or nine persons and did a good deal of the heavy work for the ranchers and homeowners. Flores stood almost seven feet high. He wore a tan cloth jacket and jeans and boots, and fixed on his nose was his one pair of glasses, the round steel-rimmed glasses that had been fitted onto him when he was a child.

Formally, with his usual politeness, he nodded good day to Runcible. "How are you?" he said.

None of the boys were digging, now; they had halted to gape and listen. So there was no urgency. Getting his breath, Runcible paused. "I got down here as soon as I could," he said. "To inform you."

The problem with Flores was that the power of words was wasted on him; he slogged through to the meaning, and that was the best he could manage. To him, any sort of diction was as effective as any other. He looked only to see how his practical interests were affected. "Say," he said, "we got to get through. It's costing us money." He had no accent, although he was a Portuguese; he had a full voice, impressive in its depth, like that of a radio announcer. "Look, we got the job half done."

There was no answer to that; at least, nothing that Runcible could think of.

While he stood there, unable to combat Flores' ruthlessly practical position, he saw the door of the Dombrosio house open. Walt Dombrosio, in a sports shirt and slacks, stepped outside. He saw Runcible and Flores together and came toward them.

"You ask Mr. Dombrosio," Flores said.

"Right," Runcible said, bracing himself.

"What's going on?" Dombrosio said, when he reached the two of them. He had a dark expression, opaque and withdrawn. Obviously, he had no desire to see Runcible; this unexpected meeting did not make either of them happy. Runcible felt the man's hostility.

Runcible said, "I just now talked to Mr. Wharton at the school. You're a friend of his as I understand it."

"Yes," Dombrosio said.

"Did you know that some Indian remains were found here?"

He pointed to the long trench, in which several of the boys stood with their shovels. "Turned up by the digging," he said. "Wharton wants you to stop until he can get over."

"I don't care," Dombrosio said. "What sort of relics?"

Flores put in, "Mostly stone things. I looked at them. They weren't much of nothing. We threw them back. Some boys took them." He clearly did not like the idea of stopping work.

"Let's see," Dombrosio said.

"The boys took them," Flores said, gesturing toward the road. "To sell. Nothing to see; they got them all."

It did not seem wise to Runcible to say anything about his two arrowheads. Perhaps Dombrosio might claim them. After all, they had been found on his land; he would have a strong case.

"Do I have to pay for the time wasted?" Dombrosio said.

"It's your job we're on," Flores said. "I'm not going to take the loss — I'll tell you that."

"At least you ought to split it," Dombrosio said.

"No," Flores said. "It's your idea to quit. I wouldn't quit; I don't care nothing about no Indian relics. If you want me to stand around idle, you're going to have to pay me. I don't have my men stand around idle for nothing."

After a pause, Dombrosio said, "Maybe they can dig around for more relics, instead of just standing."

Runcible said, "Wharton asked me to have them do no digging at all. All I'm doing is repeating what he said; I have no involvement in this. I'm not getting anything out of it." He felt indignant that it should seem as if he were costing Dombrosio money.

"Maybe something valuable will turn up," Dombrosio said in a grim voice. "I'll be in the house." Turning, he walked off.

"I'll tell you," Flores said, when Dombrosio had gone back into the house. "That's not a very smart guy, to have us stop."

Runcible said, "It's his obligation to society and I admire him for it. He's absorbing the cost and that's admirable."

With a grunt, Flores wandered off and seated himself on the fender of his truck, to wait.

Following him, Runcible said, "Show me where they found the relics."

The man's large black hand came up; he pointed.

"Over here?" Runcible said, following the trench. The boys, with their foolish, grinning faces, gazed at him. "Here?" he said.

Flores nodded.

With care, Runcible jumped down into the trench. Dirt rained down the sides and covered his shoes; he saw mud on his trousers once more, on these fresh ones. Sure enough, bits of stone lay among the lumps of brown adobe soil at the bottom of the trench. Squatting, he picked a fragment up.

The most impressive Indian remains, he knew, were enormous mounds that had been dump heaps composed of every sort of thing considered worthless by the Indians, everything thrown away by them over a period of centuries. Strange, he thought as he scratched at the dirt. That we should pore over five-hundred-year-old garbage. Studying each bit. Seeking something valuable.

Could a mound be here, exposed by the digging? Most of them, if not all, had been found near the water. The Indians had lived on shellfish, clams and mussels and abalone, and the shells of those creatures had made up the bulk of the content of the mounds.

Already he had found additional granite tools; from the dirt he lifted out a heavy — what was it? An awl, possibly. A stone cylinder that tapered at one end, almost like a bowling pin. And bits of bone that had been clearly shaped by intention. God damn, he thought exultantly. He had never done anything like this; how exciting it was. But then he realized that everything belonged to Walt Dombrosio, and his triumph, his sense of discovery, vanished. I'm finding this stuff for him, he recalled. So, clambering back to his feet, he stopped.

Maybe I better get out of here, he thought, before they accuse me of stealing my two arrowheads.

But curiosity kept him. I think I'll hang around until Wharton gets here, he decided. I don't want to miss anything, if it does turn out to be important.

Less than an hour later the grammar school teacher showed up in old clothes, carrying pick, shovel, rock hammer, gunny sack, and a roll of wire mesh over his shoulder. He waved at Runcible as he tossed his load down.

"You have on the wrong clothes," Wharton said as he dropped down to the trench floor and began scooping up trowelfuls of earth and tossing them against the wire mesh. "You need work clothes, my friend."

"I know," Runcible said.

"Go back up to your house and change," Wharton said.

Feeling chagrined — after all, he had already stood idle for fifty minutes — Runcible trudged back up to his house. As rapidly as possible he changed to work clothes and then returned to the digging.

When he got back he found to his amazement that Wharton had ceased digging. He sat on the ground, his legs folded under him, deep in meditation.

"What's wrong?" Runcible said.

Wharton, holding a granite tool between his hands, said, "There's something wrong. These things aren't usually found in soil of this kind. I got all there are." He pointed to a heap, and Runcible realized that in the time it had taken him to change his clothes, Wharton had collected all these objects. And, he realized, there were no more. Or at least Wharton did not expect to find any more.

Approaching, Flores said, "Mr. Wharton, can we start work again? Are you through?"

Wharton said, "Wait a minute." Absorbed, frowning, he ignored both Runcible and Flores. Suddenly he hopped to his feet and returned to the trench, beckoning to Runcible. "Come here," he said.

Getting down beside Wharton, Runcible looked. The man was pointing at the surface of the ground, the untouched surface waist-high to them. "See the contour?" he said. "There's a wash, here. It's dug down."

"Water," Runcible said, pleased. "I had the idea that mounds usually were found near water."

Wharton said, "There's a run-off that spills down the hillside, here. It comes from above. It probably carried these artifacts down here over a long period of time. Possibly a few inches a year."

"I see," Runcible said.

With a wry smile, Wharton said, "This will make a fine leaching line. With spill coming down from above. They'll be lucky if the pipes and gravel don't carry the run-off up into their house."

"That's Flores' work," Runcible commented.

Still pondering, Wharton gazed in all directions. He studied the hillside above them, the trees, the several houses. "Whose land is that?" he said finally. "Where those eucalyptus trees are? Back about a thousand feet from the road, where all those boulders are."

Runcible, with a queer sensation in his stomach, said, "That's my land. Part of my property."

The grammar school teacher put his hand on Runcible's arm and forcibly turned him, pushed him down so that he faced in a certain direction at a certain angle. "See?" he said.

"No," Runcible said.

"It takes a zigzag course down the hillside. You see, in winter when the heavy run-off occurs, the grass, the weeds, are so high and so thick that unless it happens to spill over your driveway or between you and your butane tank you're not going to notice. The water's down almost in the ground. The adobe almost melts.

It seeps as well as spills. You've seen it, I'm sure. You just haven't paid any attention to it."

Runcible nodded.

"It carries a good deal of earth along," Wharton said. "See how the gouge runs. Very wide, but not deep. We'll have to go up the hill and take a look at each step until we find where it starts. Or where it's been picking up this stuff. Those boulders look interesting to me. Do you use that land for anything?"

"No," Runcible said. "Not back there."

"Then you won't object to it being dug up, if necessary."

"I'm not sure," he said, guardedly.

Wharton eyed him. "Oh, come on, Leo. You don't use that land. I want your permission. Do I have it?" He gripped Runcible friendlily but forcefully on the arm until at last Runcible nodded.

"I hate the way it looks," Runcible said. "When there's anybody digging. It comes from having had to watch street repair as a kid in the city. Where I lived, there were old sewers that always broke."

"Maybe you'll be famous," Wharton said.

"Pardon?" Runcible said, not following the man's reasoning; he seemed to skip along so rapidly.

"If we find something important. The University of California always sends out people to chart these things, if anything of value turns up. Who knows — maybe you'll wind up on television."

Runcible shrugged. But he felt his heart labor. And a great thrill of intimation sailed up inside him. So it isn't on your land after all, he said to himself. Mr. Dombrosio. It's on my land, only it happens to have washed down on yours by accident. I mean, a little bit has washed down.

Putting his hand into his pocket he felt for his two arrowheads. They were not there, and for an instant he felt horror and panic; his scalp crawled and sweat came up on his forehead.

"What's wrong?" Wharton said.

But now he remembered; he had changed his clothes, had left them in his other trousers. The arrowheads were safe. And, he thought, we may find a lot more. And other things besides. *And they are mine.*

11

At the office of the Carquinez *News,* Seth Faulk opened the envelope that Mrs. Runcible had handed him. While he read she remained at the counter, standing silent and — it seemed to him — tense in her long coat, with her purse between her hands. She kept her eyes on him; he could feel her.

"You want me to read this through now?" he said. "While you're here? It'll take a while." He preferred to put it aside until later; for an hour he had been working on an ad for the grocery store, and it had to be done by noon.

Janet Runcible said, "I'll wait."

Inwardly, Faulk sighed. He continued reading, skipping whole lines, getting the general sense only. From the start it was obvious that Leo Runcible had written this himself; not only had it been typed on the typewriter at the realty office (the same on which all the other Runcible proclamations had been typed) but it had in it the usual Runcible-isms. The throwing the gauntlet to everyone. As if Runcible could not stick to telling, or even educating, but had to incite. Faulk thought, The man must see the world as composed of either friends or enemies. Those who are for him are supposed to read this and flock to his defense. The others I suppose will behave as usual.

He glanced up at Mrs. Runcible, standing there so stiffly. Almost every day, through the windows of his newspaper office, he saw her going by, doing her shopping. Today she had on no makeup at all. His knowledge of her — a bit of his knowledge of everyone in the area — had in it the notion that she drank and that when she looked like this she was getting over a morning after. In one part of his mind he held news that might or might not be worth printing, and in the other he held an enormous conglomeration of gossip and fact that would never be printed, true or not, because it lay outside the purpose of his newspaper. The fact or theory that she drank was not important to him professionally. But she interested him anyhow. She had such a dried-out quality. Her hair was so stringy, so colorless. The coat, he thought, looked like a man's coat. And her hands. He saw that her fingers were drawn up, interlaced rigidly. As if, he thought, she might pop apart.

"What did Mr. Runcible say about this?" he said, holding out the typewritten page, back in her direction.

She winced at the question, clearly expecting it but nervous at having to hear it. "He'd like to have that included in the next issue," she said. She added, "of the *News*."

"As a news item."

"Oh yes, as a news item." Panic crossed her face and then disappeared; the tension once more set in.

"He really found all this stuff," Faulk asked, mostly to himself.

"He certainly did," she said in a bleak voice.

In his mind he consulted his experience. I don't want to be identified with any of Leo Runcible's promotion schemes, he said to himself. In the past, especially in the early days of Runcible Realty, he had been roped into printing as news items various attention-getting statements of Leo Runcible. Finally he had made a deal; he had forced Runcible Realty to run, in informal compensation, half-page ads. Runcible paid for the ads, and then the statements were put in as news. This had seemed to work at first. But, he had found, some people identified his paper with the bombastic tone and sense of the items. So now he had to put it carefully; he couldn't simply run what Runcible handed him.

It could go, he thought, possibly:

REPORT OF AN INDIAN FIND

But always Runcible seemed to like to see his name somewhere in the big type at the top of the column, not in the body of the article alone.

RUNCIBLE REPORTS INDIAN FIND

That might do it.

> In a statement to the *News,* today, Leo Runcible revealed the discovery of a possibly rich new find of Indian tools and remains that may be the largest found in this area in many years.

Surely, Faulk thought, that separated the paper from the item.

> According to Runcible, the find was made by chance on land owned by him hitherto not suspected by even the most expert authorities on Indian culture of yielding anything of worth. Details of the possibly sensational trove uncover the fact that it was Runcible himself who suspected the possibility and kept the find from once more being lost and depriving American science and universities of a rare opportunity. As he put it to the *News,* "I saw at once that we were on the track of something of inestimable importance," Runcible confided.

At the counter, Janet Runcible studied him as he sat leaning back in his chair, referring to the typed sheet and then closing his eyes as he worded the item which he would use.

But even as he put together the item in his mind he thought, I wonder if it's on the level. I'd better inquire before I print anything.

Does this mean that Runcible is going to give away an arrowhead with each lot? Is this a new way of promoting his various schemes? Will this bring people into the area, etc.?

Of course, it was good if people came into the area. That was the hope of all the little businesses, all of whom ran ads in the *News*. On this point, Seth Faulk agreed with Runcible Realty; they had an aim in common, and both of them knew it.

I wonder who this would bring, Faulk thought. Like that big shark they caught up on Tomales Bay . . . people did drive up to that shrimp shack to look at it; the picture in the S.F. *Chronicle* did bring about a thousand curious people. But what did they do, then? Buy a few pounds of shrimp? A few beers? Yes, he thought. Before they made that long drive back to town.

There had, in the past, been professors from universities come to the area to study Indian finds. There had been articles in the big metropolitan papers, the San Rafael and the S.F. papers, with pictures. Those had publicized the area quite well.

Of course, he realized, it depends on what the bastard finds. No amount of arrowheads will bring anyone unless he finds so many that he really *can* give them away. But just to look . . . no, no one will come to look, because they can look now; they can go up to the grammar school to Wharton's classroom and look at his collection. And no one does, except on evenings that the PTA meets in his room.

Aloud, he said, "This is very interesting."

Janet Runcible, with visible pride and relief, said, "I knew you would think so."

"I think I'll give Leo a call," Faulk said.

"He's down at the office," she said, at once.

"Yes," he said, putting the typewritten paper back in its envelope, "I'll phone him and get a few more details before I run an item." For one thing, Runcible probably didn't do it alone; there's no mention of anyone but Runcible, Runcible, Runcible in this paper, and we can't do that; we have to spread it around where it's due. Nothing brings down trouble faster than to leave people out.

Later, after Mrs. Runcible had left the office, he carried the envelope back to his wife and had her read it. Seated at the largest of their three presses, Mary opened the envelope and read the paper from beginning to end. Then she said,

"You'd have to completely rewrite it. He makes it sound as if it was absolutely certain. But it's just his idea, isn't it? That he's found something valuable."

"I called his office," Faulk said. "He's out with a client, but he'll call me when he gets back."

Mary Faulk said, "He gets so excited. You'd think it had to do with the Civil War or something really important."

"This would be important," Faulk said. "Indian remains can be important."

"Why?" his wife said. "All these Indians here ever did was eat raw oysters — I can see those Eastern Indians, those Cheyennes or Apaches, the ones who built wigwams and shot with bows and arrows. These California Indians were just — dirty."

At that Faulk laughed.

"They didn't even ride horses," Mary Faulk said.

Faulk said, "Listen, it's not your job to decide if they're important or not. It's what people think. Other people."

"There's no one in the world who gives a darn about our Indians," she said. "Except the University of California, and possibly the people at Sacramento. The California Historical Society and the Marin Historical Society. And they have to. It's their job. Like the pound has to take an interest in dead cats."

"You'd like an obsidian arrowhead to show visitors," Faulk pointed out.

"But that's not what he said he found anyhow. He says he found a burial mound or something."

"There's always junk in a burial mound," Faulk said. "Pots and baskets — they buried all the chief's possessions with him when he died. Or maybe that was the Egyptians."

"If Runcible wants space, let him pay for it."

Her lips pressed tight with determination, she resumed work. To her, there was no discussion; he knew her attitude toward Runcible.

But we have to play along, he realized. Not with the man but with his ideas. He's had a few good ones, like when he got them to vote on expanding the school. At least he's looking ahead to the future. And that's a darn sight more that the ranchers are doing.

And, he thought, Runcible does make news.

"He's brought business into this area," he said. "He's made it more prosperous."

His wife did not answer. She did not approve, and she never would; she shut Runcible out on principle, and no matter what the man did, he would never be acceptable to her. Mary had been born here, had grown up in the area; she had gone to the old River School and to Tomales High — she knew all the ranchers' wives personally, and when she wasn't setting type or proofreading she was on the phone talking to one of them after another, getting the news of what they had done, their little Sunday jaunts, their dinners, their birthday and social events. He himself handled the non-social news, such as robberies and deaths and car accidents and new tax rates, and of course the ads.

I wonder how it feels, he wondered, to be disliked by all the original people, here. To never be accepted, no matter how long you live here or have your realty office here. These original people went to Thomas, still, even though the old man was semi-retired, an invalid with a bum leg who got out of his house one day a week and who could not even get to some of the property he listed. He had to send his clients on with a shakily-drawn pencil map.

What'll they do when Thomas dies? he wondered. Stop selling their property entirely?

Once Runcible had had a sign made, at his own expense. A big sign, nicely painted and lettered, put up alongside the road coming into Carquinez; it read: YOU ARE ENTERING CARQUINEZ. DRIVE SLOWLY. LIVE HAPPILY. One weekend a carload of area farm kids had tied a chain to it, pulled it down, and burned it up.

Maybe it wasn't appropriate, Seth Faulk thought. After all, this is still a farm area, not a suburban town, zoned, with tree-lined streets and ivy-covered fire station. But the man meant well. And it cost him money. And when he found out they had torn the sign down he didn't try to put another one up; he did give up. And that had bothered Faulk; he had expected Runcible to go and commission another one.

And, Faulk thought, has the man ever done any harm?

Show me where he has done harm, he said to himself. He's gotten his clients a good price for their land when they wanted to sell; if anything, he's bumped up the prices too high. And he's worked his head off finding the right house for people wanting to enter the area. He works. He's always out of his office, driving around; he's never just sitting behind a desk . . . as, he thought, I am, or the insurance broker is, or the banker is, or, for that matter, the guys at the gas stations.

If there's one man in this town who earns his money, it's Leo Runcible.

It's been said, he remembered, that Runcible has vulgarized the area. Said by well-to-do retired people up in the Ridge area.

He thought, now, of a headline. His thoughts phrased themselves along professional lines.

RUNCIBLE DIRTY LITTLE JEW FROM OUTSIDE, IS ALLEGATION

Leo Runcible of Runcible Realty wears yellow shoes and a purple necktie, it was alleged today by residents of the Ridge area, according to reports reaching the *News*. Some residents reported having heard him remark "Bullshit!" at various times and Sheriff Christen is looking into these reports.

He found himself chuckling at this imaginary item; it would be on page one, of course, in the far-right column.

Then, of course, Leo Runcible would fire back at his detractors, and that, too, would get into the paper. How would the man reply? He would get his typewritten statement immediately to the press; there would be Janet Runcible, in her long shapeless coat, standing at the counter, waiting while he read the statement.

RUNCIBLE DEPLORES OLD FARTS IN FIERY STATEMENT

Today, in a speech calculated to cause great perturbation in certain ranchers of the area, Leo Runcible branded as "old farts" those who took the position in yesterday's discussion regarding Runcible's use of language and wearing apparel that Runcible might be a "dirty little Jew from outside," as it was put to the *News*.

There could be one of Mary's notes, too.

Wednesday, Leo Runcible and family motored to San Rafael late in the day and spent an hour with his attorney discussing a lawsuit.

From the back of the press, Mary Faulk appeared. "Say," she said. "Do you have any intention of going and looking at what he found?"

With chagrin he said, "No." It had never occurred to him; he had only taken up the problem of getting at the truth of who had made the find.

"Look at them and see if they're important," Mary said. "Don't take Runcible's word — look what you're doing; you're falling for his line of spiel, like everyone else, like those clients of his."

He felt his face redden.

"What a dreadful reporter you are," she said, and returned to setting up type. "All you care about is what people say," she said. "Words, words."

He shrugged. But he had no answer.

"Like legal notices," Mary said. "Just words."

To that he had a reply. The *News* printed many legal notices, and they were a major source of revenue. Without them — he started to say — the paper would not be solvent. But as he spoke he glanced out, through the front window at the street and cars and stores. Going along, past the post office, was a green Mercury which he recognized; he scrambled to his feet and peered.

The car, from the San Rafael *Journal*, showed up when there was real news, when there had been a robbery or a fatal accident. He hated the sight of it, the familiar dusty green fenders and hood, the card on the windshield, the two men inside wearing classy business suits. Now he himself in his Hawaiian sports shirt stepped quickly out onto the porch of the press building to watch the car as it traveled slowly along, until finally — as he knew it would — it parked in front of Runcible Realty.

"What is it?" Mary said, coming out after him. Now she, too, saw the San Rafael car parked before Runcible's office. Saying nothing she ducked back inside, back to her work. There was nothing to say. He remained where he was, on the porch, feeling shame, understanding how foolish he was.

"I guess I spent too much time thinking," he said to her, at last. "You were right. I should have gone to see those things he dug up." He shut the door as he came slowly back inside the office.

The dirt road climbed among bishop firs, so steeply that the large-animal vet slowed his truck almost to a stop. The vet, Tom Heyes, shifted into low gear. As the truck reached the ascent, various objects in the rear began to slide; he heard them slithering and bumping across the metal floor behind him. But he continued on up, hearing the roar of the engine. Stones flew up and clanked against the fenders and hood. The truck lurched as one wheel got down into a furrow.

The winter rains had carried away parts of the road, had left huge holes and mounds; he heard the bottom of the truck scrape as he turned a curve to the right. And still the road climbed. At one place a tree had fallen and, at some earlier time, blocked the road. But the tree had been dragged far enough off to let trucks and jeeps pass. And older cars, the vet thought. Those with high clearance.

In the fir forest there was little sunlight. The ground was damp. The vet saw ferns, huge and black, with leaves dripping. A constant drizzle of moisture from the trees . . . the ground was covered with bushes. A glade that extended up the sides of the ridge to the top, miles of first growth. It had never been logged, although back toward the highway there had been some bulldozing.

For a little time the truck crossed a flat field into which some sunlight got. Ferns and firs did not grow here; instead he saw dry grass, and several steer munching. And, at the edge, two deer without antlers grazed. They paid no attention to the truck. Ahead, the vet saw cattle on the road, some of them calves with huge brown heads.

The road divided. He took the left fork, and soon the truck again moved in the shadows between trees.

At the top of the ridge the fir forest ceased for the last time. Great boulders lay everywhere, among grass and dirt; the land had a smooth, flat quality, and the few trees had been bent and stunted by the ocean wind. He felt the wind, now; it snapped the windshield wipers back and forth and whistled into the cab of the truck.

Almost at once he found himself passing above an estero. The gray water stirred with the wind, and the reeds along the mud banks bent and swayed, releasing flights of grebes. On the water itself grebes like dots of black clay bobbed. The road kept close to the mesa overlooking the estero, on firm high ground, safely above the marsh. For that he was grateful; he did not want to get bogged down, out here.

Telegraph poles ahead caught his eye. Now he saw the rotting line of fence that marked the beginning of the oyster farm. The fence carried down to the water and out into the water, where it sagged at last and disappeared. To keep sharks and rays out, he reasoned. To protect the oysters. The barge was nowhere in sight. Probably beyond a bend of land. At the end of the estero the white clapboards of shacks caught the mid-morning sun. Almost there now, he thought.

How desolate it was. No cars. No voices. Now, not even cattle or deer. And the fir forest far behind him. The ground, on each side of the road, was mostly sand.

This collection of shacks and barns by the estero had once been connected to the world by sea. Boats had supplied it, the original town of Carquinez, back about 1900. No roads had crossed the ridge to link up with the towns inland; everything had come in and out by water. The few people who remained now made their living from oysters, which they brought over the ridge by truck. They had some livestock, too, a few sheep, cows, chickens. And they grew vegetables.

The vet had been out here to the old town only a few times. He did not like it, and the people had almost no money. But he felt that he had to come; there was no other vet in the area, and people as poor as this depended on their animals. He had been notified by a postcard. There were, he thought, no phones out here.

To his left he saw, as he always saw when he came out here, a large abandoned farm. Barns, the main house . . . all falling into ruins, without paint or wiring. Dark brown, destroyed by wind and water, the salt air. The wood eaten by rot and termites. A steer appeared from between the house and the barn and walked slowly away.

At the town itself he saw an ancient gas pump with a hand-crank. The pump, rusted and leaning to one side, had no glass top of any sort; it was only a column of tin with a chain and wheel visible inside. For their boats, he decided. He saw several old men, now, sitting on the long wharf and on the steps of the principal building of the town. It was used, still, for storage. Everywhere, in blue-gray mounds, the oyster shells were heaped. The road had turned from dirt to broken shells; they gleamed ahead, and he heard the tires crunching over them.

A man rose to his feet. He wore pale jeans, a wool jacket as dark as hide, and a hat. None of the other men stirred.

The vet pulled his truck up beside the men. "Hi," he said.

The man on his feet nodded.

"I got a postcard," the vet said. "You have a sick sheep?"

Turning, the man waved him to follow. The vet parked his truck, shut off the motor and got out. From the back he got his bag and followed the old man, down the oyster shell street, past what had once been a creamery building; he recognized the metal roof, the pipes of the refrigeration equipment.

At a corral he found the old man standing by an open gate, waiting. "How'd you know it was sick?" the vet said.

The old man pointed. On its side, in the dirt, lay a sheep. At first the vet thought it was dead. But as he walked up to it the sheep opened its eyes. It kicked its legs slightly.

"I been getting it up," the old man said. "But as soon as it lies down it can't get back up again."

Fifteen or twenty other sheep stood here and there, some of them watching. The old man squatted down beside the sick sheep, took hold of its fleece, and dragged it up. The sheep managed to get a purchase on the ground; it stumbled forward and then slowly tottered a few steps. It did not seem to see where it was going. Once, it fell forward onto its knees and then down on its face. But it managed to struggle back up.

The vet noticed that the sheep dragged its hindquarters. A spinal infection, he thought. The sheep wobbled about like a broken machine; its parts seemed to fly off in opposite directions until its rear dragged and its legs slid out from beneath it. The sheep sat down heavily and then tipped over and lay on its side once more, as he had first found it.

"I think you're going to have to destroy it," the vet said.

The old man said, "No, that's my best ewe. I get two lambs out of her every year. She's only six years old."

Opening his bag the vet got out his instruments. With a rectal thermometer he took the sheep's temperature, and then with his stethoscope he listened to its lungs. It did not have much of a fever, and its lungs sounded all right.

"No pneumonia," he said. "Not yet, anyhow."

Holding the sheep with his knee, he examined its rear legs and spine. Maybe it's tetanus, he thought. But more likely it's a cyst in the spine.

"I'll give it a shot of antibiotics," he said. He got out the bottles and needle, and presently he had done all he could do for the sheep. "You watch it," he said. "If it dies, better have an autopsy made to find out what it had. So it won't infect the rest of your flock. Give it about a week." He began putting his instruments away. The sheep lay where it was, its eyes open and staring; it made no move to get up.

"I think a dog got it," the old man said.

"No," the vet said. "There's no sign of an injury."

"Terrible black dog got in here last year," the old man said. "I mighta got him, but I didn't get my gun in time."

As he started to leave the corral, the vet heard a coughing noise. He picked out a ram standing with its head down, its front legs wide apart. The ram coughed, shook its head, stood breathing heavily.

The vet said, "That ram there. That could possibly be lung worm. I don't say it for sure, but it could be."

The old man said nothing.

"You don't want it to get into your pasture," the vet said. "In wet, it gets down in and can infect the whole flock."

"Don't worry about that ram," the old man said, walking with the vet from the corral and back down the road. "I got over three hundred sheep. That ram's just tired. He just bred all them ewes. He sneezes like that because he's tired."

"Lung worm is highly infectious," the vet said. Seated in his truck he wrote out a bill and handed it to the old man. The old man read it, reached into his jeans and got out a leather purse; from it he took three dollars and passed them up to the vet.

"Don't ever come back," the old man said.

The vet was astonished.

"My ram's okay," the old man said. "It was a courtesy, my calling you to come out here. I wanted to give you the business."

After a moment the vet found his voice and said, "Three dollars to drive twenty miles out here and give a shot of antibiotics — that isn't much business."

The old man said, "I don't need you to look at my ram. I didn't call you to look at my ram." He turned and walked away, back to the other old men seated along the wharf.

For a moment the vet sat without starting up the motor of his truck. He felt like yelling after the old man that he had lost money making this trip out here, and that he was giving him good advice, free advice, about his ram. That the ram might infect the man's whole flock, and that this might save the flock, this advice. But the old man did not want to hear that another sheep was sick; it was hard enough for him to accept that his best ewe was dying of a spinal cyst. He believed a dog had injured her and that she would get well with the aid of a shot from the vet. The old man was scared and angry, and it was the vet who had brought him the bad news, so it was the vet who was responsible.

I ought to know these old farmers by now, the vet thought as he started up the truck. They lead simple lives and anything that upsets them scares them.

Instead of being angry, he thought, I should feel sorry for him. But he could not. There had been so much of this; it always scared farmers to find out that they had not only sick animals but animals with highly contagious diseases. I always have to take the blame, he said to himself. No wonder the last vet left. No wonder Dr. Bryant couldn't make a go of it, here.

I should have stayed in Canon City, he said to himself. On my brother-in-law's ranch.

Look at those old men, he thought. Seated along the broken-down wharf, hands on their knees. Waiting for the oyster barge. What do they do? Open the oysters? Stare out across the water. Never fix or repair anything. Never paint their houses. Never go anywhere, except bring their oysters into town once or twice a week and pick up supplies. They might as well be dead and buried.

He drove up the road past the wharf and through the old town itself, past the abandoned grocery store with its broken windows stuffed with rags, past what had been a feed store, a barn that had been the blacksmith's place for the entire area. To his right he saw the old abandoned original Carquinez School.

The building, square and yellow, still had its flagpole. But no flag. The front steps had fallen away. The door hung open. Inside, he saw only darkness.

Now the road rose as it circled back. He passed shacks made of boards, tarpaper, without foundations, leaning and settling into the sand. A rusting auto body, upside down, lay in one yard and he saw two children playing nearby. Worse than Poor Man's Hollow, the vet said to himself. The children wore dirty rags and their hair hung down in strings, uncut, like the hair of animals. In a sense this was an extension of Poor Man's Hollow. Some of these people were itinerant farm workers, fruit pickers and mill workers . . . at least, he supposed they were. Actually, he did not know how they survived. They couldn't all live off the oyster farm.

As he drove on, the vet saw something that surprised him. From the top of a shack a television antenna stuck up, held by guy wires, a three-section mast at least fifty feet tall.

So they have TV sets out here, he thought.

On his drive back, up the ridge and among the fir groves, he took a moment to flip open his note pad to see what his next call was. His wife had taken the information and he read it for the first time. In her neat hand she had written, "Sheriff Christen. 11:30 to 12:00. At Mr. Runcible's house, not office."

There're no animals there, he thought. At least, none that I know of. And why the sheriff?

Sometimes Christen called him in when an animal had died and there was suspicion of poisoning. In the past, dogs and cats had gotten rat or gopher bait, and Christen had wanted to know if it looked deliberate. Maybe the Runcibles have a cat, he thought. There were plenty of cats in the area; all the farmers had them, to protect their feed.

I might get five dollars for that, he thought. So far today he had made nothing; the cost of medicine and gas had eaten up what he had taken in.

At the Runcible house he found ruddy-faced Sheriff Christen in his Sam Browne uniform, and Leo Runcible wearing a cloth cap, tennis shoes with holes in the toes, paint-stained trousers, and a heavy cotton sweater. This was the first time he had ever seen the Realtor in anything but a business suit and tie, and at first he did not recognize him. With them was a third man whom he had never seen before. There were several cars parked in front.

"You didn't see Dr. Terance, did you?" the sheriff asked him. "We're waiting for him, too."

The vet said, "What's going on?"

"We want you to look at some old bones," the sheriff said. To Runcible, he said, "You know the vet, Dr. Heyes."

"Yes," Runcible said, shaking hands with the vet. "Glad to see you, Doctor." The unfamiliar man held out his hand and Runcible said, "This is — what's the first name? Bill? Bill Baron from the San Rafael *Journal.*" Runcible's face had a glazed expression; his eyes gleamed. His voice, the vet noticed, was gruff, as if he was nervous or under pressure.

"I didn't see Doctor Terance," he said as he shook hands with Baron. "What kind of old bones?"

The three of them led him along the side of the house, into the back yard. A section of fence had been lifted aside, and the men took him into a field behind the yard. There, among boulders and piles of dirt, the vet saw an excavation. The hole had laid bare the base of two huge rocks. The dirt had spilled away naturally, he saw, and in addition there had been recent digging. Shovels lay around here and there, and in cardboard cartons he saw what looked like granite stones.

Spread out at the base of a eucalyptus tree were bones. Sheriff Christen led him to the bones, knelt down, and pointed.

"Looks like bear," the vet said. "Deer."

"How long ago killed, would you say?" the reporter said.

The vet picked a bone up. It felt dry and light; it had turned yellow, and the edges were jagged. Taking out his pocketknife he scraped at the end. The bone had become hollow; the marrow was long since gone. It had no moisture in it of any sort.

"Hard for me to say," he said. "Seems thoroughly weathered."

"Look at this one," Runcible said.

The vet accepted the bone and saw that it had become partly petrified. Almost like rock, he thought. He had seen whale bones like this. Fossilized. Thousands, perhaps millions of years old.

"I'd say this is quite old," he said.

"What's it from?" the reporter said.

The bone seemed to him to be a large joint, perhaps an old cow hip end. Ball and socket, once. But for a cow bone it seemed unusually massive.

"What do you want Terance for?" the vet said.

The three men glanced at each other. Then, at last, Sheriff Christen stepped down into the excavation. The vet followed him; together they made their way down the base of the rock. A kind of cave had been exposed. He saw the signs of water; the rock was worn smooth. Once, he decided, this had been the mouth of a stream.

Exposed, at the back of the cave, lay a skull. Someone had propped the dirt roof of the cave up with two-by-four sections. Around the skull he saw other bones, and shells, mostly oyster shells. And, he saw, there was a tapered granite tool of some kind.

"My god," the vet said. "Somebody got murdered?"

The other men grinned. Sheriff Christen said, "Well, maybe."

"A long time ago," the reporter said.

"Oh," the vet said, understanding. Now he bent down near the skull. "Can I pick it up?" he said. "Or is it too fragile?"

"Put your hands under it," Runcible said, in an authoritative voice. "So you're supporting its weight. Go ahead."

With care, the vet ran his hands down the sides of the skull until he had a grip on it. They had had it out before; he could tell that. Taken it out and put it back, he thought as he lifted the skull from the dirt.

At once he saw that there was something wrong with it. "Wow," he said. "It's deformed or something."

"Or something," Runcible said.

From behind them a voice called. They turned, and the vet saw a man running toward them through the eucalyptus trees, carrying an armload of books. As the man ran he yelled, "I was right! I have it here! You can tell by the teeth!"

A book fell from his arms and struck the ground, its leaves fluttering. The man started back, hesitated, then continued on toward them. The vet recognized him, now. The fourth grade teacher, his face aflame with excitement.

"The crown and root runs together!" Wharton yelled at them. Beside the vet the sheriff began to chuckle in a low voice. Runcible, tensely, watched the grammar school teacher approach. The reporter kept the same manner as before, one of interest mixed with reserve. "The teeth are fused," Wharton yelled, and arrived beside them, panting and holding out a book. "The teeth are all exactly alike!"

By its shape the vet recognized it as a textbook, with a library stamp on the spine. Wharton was showing them a photograph, and in a glance he saw that it was of a skull, first profile and then full-faced. Wharton held the photograph next to the skull which the vet held; the man's hands were shaking, and he continued to repeat himself.

The reporter said, "It's not possible."

"Why not?" Runcible said.

"They never have found one before," the reporter said.

"That's a fine reason," Runcible said loudly. "A great reason. What kind of a reason do you call that? I'll tell you what kind of reason I call that." His voice rose hoarsely, trembling. "That's a horse's ass reason; do you know that?" He stared at the reporter with anger. The reporter shrugged. "I suppose," Runcible said, "that airplanes won't fly and the Russians didn't reach the Moon."

The skull in the photograph was labeled *Neanderthal Man*. The vet thought, That's right; it isn't possible. They've never found any remains in the New World, of any dawn men or extinct men, or whatever they're called. Runcible stood with his face flushed, yelling into the face of the reporter. Beside him, Wharton continued to jabber on about the books; he kept trying to show Sheriff Christen something, but the sheriff stood off to one side, still chuckling to himself, grinning on and on.

Above the racket, the vet managed to think to himself. It must be one of Runcible's publicity gags, he thought. Like that sign, or when he had all the buildings painted. It must be a fake.

12

On Saturday morning Walt Dombrosio walked down to the post office before twelve, since at twelve the window closed and although he could get the mail from their box he could not get magazines or packages. In the box he might find a red card saying that there was mail too big for the box, and he might have to spend the rest of Saturday and all day Sunday wondering what it was.

This Saturday, when he opened the box, he found a slender dark brown small envelope from the bank; it had a transparent window, and his name and address were written in pen, not typed. He knew at once what it was. Several times in the past year or so he had gotten one of these. It was a notice that their checking account was overdrawn, and that the bank had handled the check anyhow, at a special rate.

As soon as he was outside the post office he tore open the envelope. He was right. The check, put through against "insufficient funds," was for only ten dollars, so that meant there was not even ten dollars in the account. Sherry had made out the check, he noticed. In his heart he felt wild fright; he began to walk back up the hill toward the house as rapidly as possible.

When he got back home he found his wife out on the patio,

seated in a wicker chair in her halter and yellow shorts, reading a book.

"Listen," he said, "we're overdrawn."

Sherry said, "No, we're not."

"What do you mean we're not?" he said. "Look at this notice." He waved it at her, and, at last, she put down her book and accepted it from him.

"They're wrong," she said presently.

"The bank is never wrong," he said. "When was the bank ever wrong?" Her lack of concern goaded him into a frenzy; he felt as if he were watching a world in slow-motion.

"I went over the check books just the other day," Sherry said. "We have about two hundred dollars in the account. I'll call the bank." She read the name of the teller. "I don't recognize this man," she said. "He probably doesn't know us; he probably put a check through to my old account, the one we closed when we opened our joint account."

"It's Saturday," he said. "The bank's closed."

That did not seem to bother her; she put down the notice and again picked up her book. "I'll call them Monday," she said. "Or you can go in. You'll be here; I'd have to call from the City. So maybe you should go in."

With as much control as possible, he said, "Maybe you better go inside and get the checkbooks and go over them again. Now."

"No," she said, with a hint of exasperation. "I just did."

"Where's the last statement?"

"In the drawer," she said. "I suppose."

He went inside the house and into the bedroom. For the last few months he had been letting her reconcile the checkbooks, since it was her paycheck that they were depositing, now, not his. She wanted to, and he could not stop her. And she wrote the checks for the bills.

Her attitude was one of competence; she always wrote out her checks neatly, filling in the number of the check — which he could never remember to do — and the stub. Her writing was precise and legible, and the bills got opened, examined, and paid before the tenth. And yet here they were; here was this overdraft notice.

The statement, he discovered, had not been opened. And it was almost two weeks old. Seated on the bed he tore the large bulky brown envelope open, spilled out the canceled checks, and studied the account sheet which the bank had made out. It showed a balance of only forty-five dollars.

He ran back outdoors, carrying the sheet and the checks. "Look," he cried with ferocity, holding them between her and her book. "Why didn't you open this? How could we have two hundred dollars balance? Two weeks ago we had only forty-five, and we haven't made a deposit since the third — have we?" She did not answer. "Have we?" he yelled down at her.

"You stop screaming at me," she said in her low, deadly tone, "or there's going to be a real fight."

More quietly, his voice shaking, he said, "Where are the checkbooks? I want all three. The big one and the two little ones."

"There's one in my purse," she said. "The big one is where it always is." Now she did lay her book aside; she closed it. "I don't like the way you're speaking to me," she said, standing up. "A decent husband doesn't address his wife like this."

He said, "A decent wife—"

"A decent wife," she said, interrupting calmly, "would expect her husband to support her."

This diversion, so unexpected, so unrelated to the subject at hand, almost unhinged him. He found himself unable to go on; all he could do was gape at her. What was happening? His wife stood facing him with her lips pressed together, indicating that she was angry, that she, too, was upset, but not as he was; not in the same way or to the same degree. According to her, he had done wrong. He could not turn her attention to their finances, now; she saw only a man who had mistreated a woman, evidently by his overly loud voice, and by his demanding tone. Her gentility, her heritage, was upset.

And what about the reality which we face? he thought as he turned and walked a short way off. It seemed to him that he was about to blow up and explode like a bottle overheated; he could sense himself, all his parts, flying off. His hands danced in the air and he clasped them together. They at once separated; he could not keep them clasped. His toes, in his shoes, writhed. His tongue crawled. As if, he thought, my body is breaking up.

This is what they mean by unbearable maze for the rats, he said to himself. No way to go. I can't talk to her but I have to. I have to stay here and try. And yet, it was too much. Behind him his wife waited with composure, but still simmering, still ready to castigate him. He turned, attempting to control himself and his speech, but immediately his words shot out foolishly, they escaped him.

"God damn you," he said, "you must be crazy or something. All I want to do is find out why." He waved the notice. "Why this thing!"

Sherry said, "And you know we agreed that reconciling the checkbooks is my responsibility. You abdicated when you couldn't make a go of it as the breadwinner of the family." Her voice was cool.

This isn't a conversation, he thought. It can't be. It's an attempt; I want to find out: *where are we?*

"We have to get money into the account," he said, panting at her. Gasping for breath.

"Listen," she said, "I warned you."

"You're crazy," he said. "All you have is being hurt, being a female with pride. What do I care?" What does it matter? he thought. What — now he could not even think, let alone talk; she had deprived him of the power of using words.

"I won't tolerate this," she said, her arms folded. "I don't want to be married to a man who can't control himself. You really must have some deep-seated childhood neurosis. And I can't be your analyst. All I can do is pick up the phone and call around and see if there is a good analyst that could take you."

With intolerable effort he managed to say, "Pay for my help?"

"Yes," she said. "I'll pay."

He said, "Can't you just — listen? You? Personally?"

"Not to your villifications of me," she said. "Your system that you've woven that makes me somehow responsible for your psychological state. Look at you."

He realized that — god forbid — he was crying. Yes, he saw. Tears were actually coming down his face. Springing forth. And she knew that he could not control them.

"There's no use trying to reason with you," she said. "You're too emotionally disturbed. When you get this way you're like some sort of animal."

"Don't you ever feel sorry for me?" he said.

"Should I?"

"Something," he said.

"Pity," she said. "I consider pity a degrading emotion. It degrades both of us."

He said, "What — about compassion."

"I don't see any difference."

"There is," he said. "Lots."

"You want me to hold your hand?" she said. "Let you put your head on my bosom?" Her tone was so flat, so matter of fact, that he could not tell if this were an authentic offer or the most terrible sarcasm; it was not worth looking to see what he felt in answer because he could not even decipher the question.

He said, "Honest to god, this is too much for me. I really think some blood vessel in my brain is going to burst. Look." He was able to seat himself facing her; seated, his elbows on his knees, he

192 · PHILIP K. DICK

felt more calm. The posture reassured him. "What do you want to do?" he said. "Why do you treat me like this?"

Her expression said, What kind of man are you, carrying on like this? She almost smiled; her lips moved toward it, enough to make known to him that message.

"You want me dead?" he said.

The smile pursed, stayed. Her eyes flashed as coldly as he had yet seen in her. She hated him for asking such a thing.

"Why can't I even ask?" he said, feeling as if he were going to die right now, on the spot. "Am I committing a crime by trying to find out? I mean, I ought to be able to find out." Is that too much to allot me? he thought.

"Nobody's persecuting you," she said.

"They are," he said. "You are."

With detestation she shook her head slowly. "You really are sick," she said, speaking the word sick as if she had found the final evil in him; she had seen it emerge. All his sins, his weaknesses and vices, came from this. And she was not surprised. It was what she would have expected.

"I'm leaving," he said, breathing through his mouth, requiring an enormous amount of air; he did not seem able to get enough air. Almost asthma, he thought. He wheezed.

"I wish you would," his wife said.

Panic made him leap to his feet. Yes, she did wish it; of that at least he felt convinced. Was she acting? It did not matter because if she was, if this was a way of handling him, of getting the response she wanted, she would be able to maintain it; she could keep it up, on and on, for as long as it suited her, perhaps even for years. So what did it matter if it were only a technique? From his standpoint there was no difference.

This is the dreadful thing she can do, he thought. She can make herself feel what she wants to feel. There is no natural feeling, only the most useful one. Once, when she was a child, they taught her what was the proper way to feel. They managed to train her, away from having feelings that simply occur. When she learned that, she had — what? The ability to deny. To shake off, like a pitcher shakes off a sign from his catcher. To select among her emotions, like he does, that skinny tall guy on the mound. That craftsman, with style . . . Johnny Antonelli. The best pitcher the Giants have, the one he liked best to watch. Fire one at me, he said to himself. I can't hit it; I am swinging in air. But my wife, he thought, she throws junk. What they call junk. Yet a junky pitcher, a hurky-jerk pitcher can make you fan out as big as life.

Ah, he thought. How my thoughts get away. He sighed, sat clasping his hands, admiring the smell of the mid-day summer air. The country air. While, across from him, Sherry regarded him with the same acuity. Her expression had not softened. Like mine has, he thought. She can outlast me. My energy is gone, but hers remains. And then all at once he had it; or thought he had it.

I know why she jumped on me, he thought. When I waved the bank notice at her. I know why she slapped me down!

She was waiting for this. She knew — oh god damn it, not that the bank account was overdrawn — but that sometime I'd stand up and yell at her. My god, he thought; she was ready — she had it mapped out. That's why what she says doesn't fit. It's geared for another situation; it's to answer what she's expected, not the issue.

She's answering questions in advance, questions I haven't asked. I have to listen to her answers, he thought excitedly. And figure out from them what's what, what the real situation is.

Finding himself beginning to laugh, he said, "You really get me. My god, you can get my goat."

"Do we have to go through this again?" she said, with weariness. "Every day? This bickering? You obviously feel it's a strain to live in the same house with me. I'll see that you're not saddled with a heavy alimony settlement. In fact, you can have the house. Even the car, if you want. I'll make it as easy on you as possible."

"Okay," he said, nodding reasonably.

"Let me know what you decide," she said. She reseated herself in her wicker chair, crossed her bare legs, lit a cigarette, and then picked up her book. Laying the open book across her stomach, she studied him and at last said, "I really think you should see an analyst."

"Fine," he said, rising. "Maybe I will."

"If we separate, you'd have to pay for it. The analysis. I can't support you indefinitely, but I'll help you at first."

Nodding, he walked away from her, toward the path.

"You didn't get my Kleenex when you were down in town," she said, her eyes on her book, now.

"No," he said. "When I saw the bank notice I forgot."

She said nothing; she read.

"Maybe I can get it later," he said. "I'm going down to Donkey Hall for a while."

Presently she said, "All right."

He went on, then, along the path to the road. His hands in his pockets he started down the hill once more, toward Donkey Hall. As he walked he realized, suddenly, that he had never gotten at the checks; he had never managed to find out exactly how they stood.

So she had done it after all.

His despair returned, then. She managed me once again, he said to himself, in a sort of daze; he found himself mumbling aloud and grinning, as if he had to hear it to believe it. God damn, he said in vague admiration. Should I go back?

Yes, he decided. Donkey Hall can wait.

When he got back he found that she had gone inside; she was no longer on the patio reading her book. Entering the house, he searched for her.

"Oh," she said, surprised to see him. She had gone into the

bedroom; seated on the bed, she was using a needle to get loose a splinter from her finger.

He said, "I really have to hand it to you."

"Why?" she said, engrossed in the splinter. "Look at this," she said. "I got it carrying in wood for the fireplace; it's one of those long soft splinters that breaks." With a gasp of pain she jerked the needle back. "It hurts," she said.

"Want me to do it?" he said.

"No," she said at once. "You'd hurt me more; you'd enjoy it." She continued fussing with her finger, her lower lip stuck out.

"Sissy," he said.

Raising her head she said in a quavering voice, "I can't get it." She held up her finger.

He took hold of it, then. At his touch she shivered. Beside him on the bed she yielded; he felt her tense, stiff body relax. Within his grip her hand was warm and slightly moist with perspiration. Her mood now was one of almost childish care. He thought, Pain isn't easy for her to endure. And, as he sat with her, holding her, he began to lose his sense of her as an enemy, a dangerous thing.

"You haven't held me for so long," she said. "Couldn't you put your arm around me?"

He did so. After a moment he drew his hand up and pressed it against the right cup of her halter. Beneath his fingers her breast stirred; he felt it rise to meet him. So he reached beneath the fabric and took hold of the breast itself.

"Mind what you're doing," she said. But she did not try to move his hand away. "How long has it been since we last made love?"

"A long time," he said, holding her nipple between his fingers. The nipple grew and became hard. She sighed, pressing against him.

"Is it wrong?" she said. "In the middle of the day?"

"No," he said. Now, with his other hand, he reached behind her and unfastened her halter. As soon as he lifted it from her she took it and laid it off to one side. He gripped both her breasts, one in each hand, letting her nipples protrude between his fingers so that he could look at them. She watched them, too; the sight seemed to arouse her.

"Go pull the drapes," she said, her eyes half shut.

"In a little while," he said. He pressed and squeezed.

"Somebody might see in," she said. "Somebody might drop by. Please." But she made no move herself; she remained in his grip. "I really wish you would, Walt. It makes me nervous."

Rising from the bed, he went from window to window. The room became much darker. "More like it," he said. "Gloomy."

When he came back to her he found her on her feet, unbuttoning her shorts. Standing on one foot, she slipped them off and put them with the halter. "Is it wrong for me to want to?" Her face had a slack, craving expression; her fingers flew and she breathed erratically. "Take off your clothes and I'll run and put my diaphragm on." For an instant she pressed against him, warm and naked and a little damp.

Swiftly, he gripped her and dropped her back onto the bed.

"Wait," she said, smiling up at him, trembling. "Not so fast."

With his left hand he separated her knees. Holding her with his body he became big enough and hard enough — he did not wait. In an instant he had his clothes undone. Her smile vanished; her body jerked.

"My diaphragm," she gasped, struggling, trying to push him out of her. "Walter — I can't have a child; I can't get pregnant." Her voice rose to a wail. "Let me go." Now she was crying. "Oh dear god, if I get pregnant — what about my job? Let me *go.*"

He clapped his palm against the inside of her thigh; he forced her open until, at last, he was able to get entirely in. And at once he felt his juices begin to spurt.

"Oh," she shrieked, writhing under him. "You're coming!" She got her right hand loose and pinched his shoulder. "Get it out of me! You insane lewd fool — let me go, you rapist! Rapist!" Screaming with fright she flung herself back and forth, pinching him and surging up at him, trying to bite him.

"I think a lot of you," he said, regaining his grip on her. And he did. "I love you," he said. He managed to kiss her to the right of her mouth; she snapped her head back and forth, avoiding him.

"It's all inside me," she gasped, her eyes blind. Her nails raked against his arms. "You did it; you came inside me. Let me go so I can wash it out — maybe I can wash it out."

But he kept her, enjoying it, knowing that he had her locked up tight, here, in the grip of his body. He was much bigger than she. And presently he began to move again; he started a second time inside her.

Later in the dank basement of Donkey Hall, under an overhead light, Walt Dombrosio worked while Jack E. Vepp and Earl Timmons watched. The air was filled with plaster dust and the biting fumes of quick-drying enamel, and now and then Timmons coughed. Both he and Vepp, despite the fumes, grinned unrelievedly.

He found it hard to work with the two men watching and grinning, and for a moment he put down his brush.

"Not through, are you?" Vepp said.

"No," he said. This was a most arduous part; he had always done this kind of job with painstaking care, giving it as much time as was needed. He did not like being rushed. Finally he resumed work. The yellowish cast, behind his brush, spread out.

"This'll make Sammy really run," Vepp said.

"What do you mean?" Dombrosio said.

"He means good old Leo," Timmons said, with a laugh. "That book about Jews. You know — it was on TV."

"Be quiet," Vepp said. "So he can work." Both he and Timmons peered in fascination.

Once, later on, there was a rattling at the knob of the door leading down from upstairs. The door, of course, was locked. But Vepp walked over and said close by it, "Beat it. Go on. We're busy; you know that." A muffled voice could be heard. Vepp repeated himself, and then they heard steps going away.

"I hope that wasn't our teacher friend," Timmons said.

"No," Vepp said.

"If he finds out," Timmons said, "he'll say something."

"I think he's resigned," Vepp said. "I think he's no longer an Advisor."

"He could still get down here," Timmons said. "If he saw what's here he'd figure it out."

"I'm the only one with a key," Vepp said. "I'm the only one entitled to a key; you know that."

Dombrosio said, "I can't work while you guys talk."

"Be quiet," Vepp said to Timmons.

They watched in silence, after that.

"He's got some guy coming down today," Vepp said suddenly; it startled Dombrosio and he swore. "Sorry," Vepp said.

"What guy?" Dombrosio said, pausing.

"Some professor or something. From Berkeley."

"The University?" Dombrosio said.

"I guess so. Wharton got hold of him. Some guy who's been up here before. In the past. That's what I heard in the market, anyhow. Lila Giambossi told me. She knows everything; she used to be a phone operator before they switched the exchange to San Rafael."

"You used to be able to find out from her where the doctor or the sheriff was," Timmons said.

"Any hour of the day or night," Vepp said. "All you had to do was pick up the phone and ask."

Dombrosio said, "Can I go on working? Will you shut up?"

"Sure," Vepp said apologetically.

They both looked contrite. But soon they would be talking again; their attention would wander and they would get restless.

"You don't have to watch," he said.

"Hell, I wouldn't miss this for the world," Vepp said. "I'll tell you — you know you're always saying what a tough New York gutter-rat scrapper he is? Our friend is?" He nudged Timmons.

"I never said that," Timmons said. "I said that he's always jumping into a controversy; he always has to get his two cents worth in. Like the school business."

"Anyhow," Vepp said, "when my boys pulled down that crappy sign, that 'live happy' sign, he didn't do nothing. He never opened his trap." He clapped Timmons on the back. "So when he finds out he's been had on this, he won't dare open his trap. He'll crawl around and shake our hands; he'll come sidling up to us — he has to. What choice has he got? Sure, maybe for a week or so he won't wave to us." Vepp laughed. "That'll really make me weep."

"I'll tell you what I think," Timmons said. "I think he'll move out of here. He'll be the laughing stock of the area, and don't think he'll like that. He's very sensitive. He can't stand to be laughed at. I tell you, he'd rather lose a sale, lose money, then be made a fool of. Remember that time Joe Tamino sold that piece of land direct, without a Realtor?" He went on to recount the whole business. Dombrosio waited, holding his brush.

I wonder what he'll do, he thought. When he finds out. He's sure hooked as of now. My god . . . the man must have run up two hundred dollars in long distance phone calls. If what people said was so. Runcible had evidently called every newspaper and educational institution in California. Strange cars had been parked in front of the man's house all day long, and Runcible was coming and going constantly. With that look on his face, Dombrosio thought. That busy, vital look.

"He'll really be sore," he said aloud.

"Of course he still won't know who did it," Timmons said.

"He'll guess," Dombrosio said. Or maybe not.

Dipping his brush, he resumed his careful, expert work.

13

Crossing the living room step by step, as if balancing herself on some fragile wire, Janet Runcible said, "Leo, could you get the phone? It's Mr. Freitas. He's down in town, at the Chevron Station. He wants to know how to get up here." Her words, passing through her dazed, alcoholic personality, came to him so slowly that he could hardly wait to the end. He got up from his desk before she had finished her sentence; striding by her, he picked up the phone.

"Hello, Tony," he said, with all the force and geniality he could create; he let it flow from him — it rolled out, pleasing him; his own joyfulness buoyed him up, swept him on. "How was the drive over our little hill?"

In a dry voice Anthony Freitas said, "Thank you, Runcible, it wasn't too bad. I know it fairly well."

Catching the man's formality, Runcible made a readjustment. "You're at the Chevron Station," he said in a businesslike manner. "All right. I'll be down there right away. Give me three minutes."

"Good enough," Freitas said. "You'll recognize my De Soto. It's black. On the order of two years old."

"Okay, then," Runcible said, and hung up.

As he put on his coat and started from the house, Janet came once again toward him. She had, for today, put on her tailored gray wool slacks, and although she looked fashionable enough, the slacks made her seem older. Really getting along, he thought as he stood at the door. Her face, lined. Too bad, he thought, as he opened the door.

"Later," he said, as she started to speak in her protracted, laborious fashion.

"Leo," she said, "I — want you to—" She studied the floor as she tried to find words. "Be grateful," she said. "To Mr. Freitas. For coming out here." She swallowed noisily.

"Grateful!" he said. "Are you out of your head? What have you been into, the kerosene?"

"Mr. Freitas—" she began.

"Doctor Freitas," he corrected, scathingly. "He's a fudnik; he has a Ph.D." Shutting the door after him he hurried down the steps to his car. A moment later he had shot off down the hill, as fast as he could go, toward the Chevron Station.

Twice in his life he had seen Dr. Freitas, once at a lecture Freitas had given at Marin Junior College and once at a party in Ross. He had shaken hands with the man after the party, and evidently Wharton, who knew Freitas very well, had been able to bring him to the man's mind. He's about the top person in anthropology in this country, Runcible said to himself as he drove. The realization filled him. He could have let out yells of glee. Hot dog! he shouted to himself. Hot hot dog!

But if the man thinks he's going to patronize me, he thought abruptly, he's mistaken.

Because, he thought, I know what I've got here.

When he pulled up into the gas station he saw standing by a black DeSoto a dapper small man wearing a gray suit and bow tie. The man had a top coat over his arm. How long has it been since I last saw one of those cotton top coats? Runcible asked himself. The man appeared to be in his late fifties. He had light hair, a squarish, sandy-colored face, and a wispy, tended-to mustache. When he raised his hand to greet Runcible, Runcible saw silver and jewel cufflinks.

"My stuff," Freitas said, "is in the car. Possibly you can give me a hand." His voice had a twang, but not a regional one. It was, Runcible decided, a university accent. I hope he's not a fairy, he thought; the accent did have a pansy quality. The man, too, smelled of talc and aftershave, and Runcible felt dismay. But what does it matter? he thought as he opened the trunk of the De Soto and, at Freitas' direction, lifted out a great metal and leather black case. It's who he is that counts, not what.

I don't care if he screws rats, he said to himself as he lugged the case to his own car. He's in a position to bring my find to the attention of the entire academic world.

Freitas, accompanying him, said, "Pleasant little village. I know it well. You have a species of beaver here that exists nowhere else in the country."

Half-hearing him, Runcible said, "And we're growing. We have land here for industry."

Freitas laughed.

His ears burning, Runcible said, "I'm sorry."

"Please don't be," Freitas said. "Any job well done is worthy of respect." He got into Runcible's car, on the right, and shut his door. Runcible got in behind the wheel, and soon they were going back up the hill, toward the house.

Gazing out, Freitas interested himself in the countryside. He did not speak, and Runcible found himself becoming more and more agitated.

"Did you look at the pictures?" he said finally.

Freitas turned his head. "No. Not that I know of."

"Photographs I sent on to you. Of the skull."

Gesturing, Freitas returned to his study of the scenery.

"What would it mean," Runcible said, unable to keep silent, "to find a Neanderthal skull in this area?"

Freitas said, "Oh, about what it would mean to find it anywhere in the continent."

"And what's that?" He felt his dander go up; the man rubbed him the wrong way, very much so.

"That Mousterian culture obtained in this region. As well as in Europe, Asia, and Africa."

"And that's a pretty important discovery," Runcible said.

The smaller man turned toward him and regarded him. "Is it?" he said.

"Isn't it?"

"I suppose." Freitas considered. "But you see — merely finding a skull and a few flint instruments . . . well—" He smiled slightly. "It's difficult to explain in a way that you would appreciate."

"Try," Runcible said.

"What do they say . . . 'one swallow does not a summer make . . . ' "

"There's more," Runcible said. "All you have to do is dig. I'm positive of it."

Freitas said, "I don't believe you understand. A particular stratum — actually, several strata — are associated with the Mousterian culture. Roughly, the mid-Pleistocene period. What is involved in this is glaciation. There are both warm and cold fauna associated with Neanderthal remains . . . we can date our finds as occurring at about the 40,000 year level, but no doubt both before and after what you'd call the ice age. He may go back into the Pliocene period. And of course he's replaced by Neanthropic man. By ourselves, in the form of Cro-Magnon types. What I'm trying to make clear to you is this. The finding of an isolate skull signifies very little. It could be, say, a genuine skull, found elsewhere — not even on this continent, but brought in from Europe or Asia. And deposited — how deep did you find it?"

"About eight feet down," Runcible said.

Freitas smiled.

"Water had washed through that land," Runcible said.

"I see."

"It probably was much deeper, earlier."

"Possibly. But you see — what does it prove? The stratum is absent. It's found at a level which we would have to date as perhaps a thousand years. An archeological level, so to speak. You've had Indian mounds at, say the four hundred year level. You understand that. What can we establish by means of your find, assuming it's a genuine one? Nothing that I can see."

There was silence.

"That's ridiculous," Runcible said.

"Why?" Doctor Freitas regarded him.

"It's of—" He gestured with one hand, holding the wheel with the other. "Incredible importance."

"But we can't *authenticate* its importance. We can't demonstrate that it has that importance. We can only make a supposition."

"I see that," Runcible said. "But my god, there ought to be as much interest stirred up by this as by any scientific discovery that—"

"Oh, if it's *publicity* you're thinking about," Freitas broke in, "you'll certainly get that. The Sunday supplements will be writing about it for a century. Assuming it's genuine."

After a while Runcible said, "What about the carbon test?"

"The 'carbon test,' as you put it, will tell us something. An age spread. But only of the skull — and if it's genuine, the age isn't in dispute anyhow. It's the *indigenous* element that concerns us. You see, suppose it was found in, say, the Near East." He eyed Runcible. "Say in Palestine. An actual Neanderthal skull, and there have been quite a few found, and showing, of course, an age of about, say, 100,000 years forward. By being brought here to California it doesn't lose the chemical characteristics collected by the so-called 'carbon test.' You see?" He added, "In fact, it will be the carbon-dating test which will be a central technique by which we'll date the skull."

"You can tell me," Runcible said, "if the skull is genuine or not. But that's all."

"Not quite all. Who told you it was a Neanderthal skull in the first place? Where did you get the idea?"

"Wharton."

"Well, he's a competent amateur. But—" Freitas shrugged.

"You think," Runcible said, "that this is a publicity stunt."

"That would be an ad hominem argument," Freitas said.

"Meaning what?"

"Meaning that we would be making an error in logic by consulting questions as to the motive or — employment of the finder than the actual qualities of the find. Of course, we'll avoid that."

"Even if I am a Realtor—"

"It could still be authentic. And you could genuinely believe it authentic and yet it might be not. And so on. What you believe or what you want are of no matter. You see?"

They had come to the house, now; Runcible reflexively parked and shut off the motor.

"Will I be able to persuade your wife to fix me some coffee?" Freitas said as he opened his door. "I see her there on the porch. At least, I presume she's your wife."

Runcible groaned; there stood Janet, supporting herself on the porch railing, gazing down at him and Freitas cloudily.

After he had had coffee, Doctor Freitas, evidently at his leisure, strolled through the back yard and out onto the wilder land and at last to the eucalyptus grove. Runcible followed, lugging the black case for him.

The skull, of course, was no longer outdoors; he had had it brought inside for safekeeping. But before he examined the skull,

Freitas wanted to see the site. He stood listening while Runcible explained the history of it, Dombrosio's leaching field, Wharton's calculations that had brought them up to the eucalyptus grove, the digging by Flores' high school boys with shovels.

"And everything was free," Freitas said. "I mean, in soil. Not in rock."

"In soil," he admitted. "But it had to be free; it was no doubt washed here from higher up. You'd probably find some in rock way up." He pointed up the hill, but Freitas did not notice. The man had put on a canvas worksuit that covered him from neck to ankles, plus boots over his shoes; squatting down, he now began scratching at the dirt with a pronged tool.

"Has this been screened?" he said. "The dirt shoveled through a wire screen?"

"No."

Freitas pondered. "Well, let's see the skull," he said, after a time. But he remained at the site. For almost an hour he poked and dug, collecting various samples into envelopes and bottles, making notes, saying nothing to Runcible. At last he rose. "The skull," he said.

They returned to the house. He had locked the skull in a closet, in a suitcase; he now carefully carried the suitcase out and laid it on the bed. When he opened it Freitas laughed. Pounds of cotton were wrapped around the skull, forming an enormous soft pale ball.

"I'll unwrap it," Freitas said, seating himself on the floor with the ball before him. Taking great care he unwrapped the cotton folds and laid them to one side.

Soon the skull was exposed. Grimy, dry, yellow . . . Runcible felt the same fear of it, and the same nervous curiosity, as before. As if it were some illicit thing, he thought as he watched Freitas. Dirty pictures. Forbidden and exciting, stimulating . . . he felt his pulse race as Freitas ran his hands over the pocked, encrusted jaw.

"The appearance," Freitas said finally, "is undoubtedly Neanderthaloid. See here? Look at these teeth. Possibly this creature could not manage to speak. He must have lived on a diet of vegetables. Uncooked seeds. Wheat grains. He ground his food. Possibly he had meat as a rare treat. This jaw must have made speech impossible. But we can't be sure. Still, he had the brain capacity for it. Odd. Really not like us at all." His voice trailed off; he had become absorbed.

"It's brittle, isn't it?" Runcible said.

Freitas grunted. "You know, we were coeval with this man. Leakey has shown that."

"Wharton was telling me," Runcible said.

"They used to dismiss finds of Homo sapiens skulls down at the old levels. Must have *dropped* there. The good old Darwin boys. The primitive, the crude, the inferior, had to come first. Higher and better had to evolve out of lower. Aristotle . . . right?" Freitas glanced up and back at him. "Consider." He tapped the skull with a metal instrument of some sort, tonged things, like pliers. "Actually, these poor things used up all their physical energies, their psychic and physical, merely to survive. That's the real difference. Not that we're smarter or more evolved. But we had an abundance. Time left over. I pity this." He touched the skull.

Runcible, feeling self-conscious, said, "Alas, poor Neanderthal."

"Yes," Freitas said. But he did not laugh. "Indeed, poor Neanderthal. God, they must have been repulsive. Very little, you know. Although I've heard — in pseudo-Freudian circles, mostly — that our myth about ogres may be a racial memory of these. I doubt it. Very much. Neanderthal was a bent-over vegetable-eating thing . . . he couldn't stand fully erect, you know. He did make tools, though. So if man is defined as a tool-making animal, this fellow was a man."

Both of them were silent.

"I'll tell you what it was more like," Freitas said. "No ogre that we feared. But a grubby timid creature . . . in my mind, I see them like terribly underprivileged factory workers in the nineteenth century, in England. Or medieval serfs. Incredibly limited, pushed aside, back off out of the way. Possibly allowed to carry wood. Build the fires, skin animals, chew the pelt. You know, it has occurred to me — maybe the reason our ancestors had time to paint those superb bulls on their cave walls . . . maybe they had slaves. This." He tapped the skull. "An inferior race to do the menial work for them, to free them."

"Why not?" Runcible said. "If they really did live side by side and not first Neanderthal and then Cro-Magnon."

"The crimes we've committed," Freitas said. "The crime of life, I suppose. Supplant the weak. Kill and enslave the inferior. The crime is to be weak; is that it? If you can be beaten you deserve to be beaten. Christ was a sinner par excellence, then." He glanced at Runcible with a wry grimace. "Excuse me. You already have your attitude on that dictated for you."

"How long will it take to make your tests?" Runcible said.

"Weeks. At least."

"You're going to take the skull with you?"

"I'd like to. But if you won't release it, I can get what I want from it here."

"It occurred to me," Runcible said, "that you might want to spend the night. There's plenty of room."

"Maybe so," Freitas said. "I'd like to look up Wharton while I'm here. Maybe we could get him over."

"Hell," Runcible said, "he's over here every day, as soon as school's out. Digging around like a prospector hot on the scent."

The time was two-thirty. "Fine," Freitas said. "Maybe I'll do some digging with him. He probably has tools — I didn't bring anything except a little spade."

"Down in the basement," Runcible said, "there's every kind of digging tool in existence. I drove up to Grandi's and bought all I could get my hands on. The works." He hesitated, and then he said, "You think it's genuine? The skull."

"I can't tell."

"I don't mean scientifically; I mean how you feel about it. Don't you get an intuition? I always do about clients. I can tell as soon as I see them if they're fakers, if they've got the glue to back up their talk or not."

Freitas said, "If I had found it I would have had the instantaneous emotional reaction that it was genuine."

A wave of dizziness rushed through Leo Runcible, a sense of power and joy and — god knew. He had never felt such things before; it swept him away.

"This must be how a stamp collector feels," he murmured.

"Better not get your hopes up too far," Freitas said drily. "Wait for the tests."

"Okay," Runcible said. But I know what they'll show, he said to himself. I know.

A week later, when he dropped into his office to pick up a key, the elderly woman who did his secretarial work rose from her typewriter and said,

"Mr. Runcible, there were two men looking for you. They said they'd be back. I think they went over to the coffee shop. One was that professor, Doctor Freitas."

Ten minutes later he saw them crossing the street, Freitas again wearing a gray-striped suit and bow tie, and with him a taller heavier man who looked like an insurance salesman. He had on a Stetson hat, a dark suit, bright green tie, and under his arm was a briefcase.

"Can we talk?" Freitas said, as soon as he and his companion had entered the office. "This is a colleague of mine, Jack Bowman. Also from the anthropology department."

The three of them retired to a side room that Runcible used as storage space. Seated on a wooden box, Freitas said,

"As far as we can tell, at this point—" He fixed his eyes on Runcible. "Your skull has no antiquity."

"Meaning what?" Runcible said. He felt his blood stop in his veins; his body processes halted.

"It could be fifty or a hundred or two hundred years old. It's contemporary, in other words."

To that, Runcible could say nothing. He heard, from the other room, the sound of the phone and the old woman answering it. Business, he thought. Going on.

"What now?" Runcible said.

Bowman said, "We'd like to take the skull and the artifacts with us. For further tests."

"Sure," he said, with a sensation of brine, terrible, scalding brine, in his mouth. "What can I lose?"

"You can lose your skull," Freitas said. "Or rather, we could possibly lose it or damage it. We'll be careful, naturally. Bowman is quite interested in it. So am I."

Bowman said, "Who else have you called to examine it? I've seen several newspaper articles on it, but I couldn't tell who has actually studied it thoroughly, and how qualified they are, and so on. All I could get was that you feel it to be authentic, and you have some authority to back you up, someone of professional status."

"You know Michael Wharton?" he said. "He feels it's the real thing. He looked it over pretty thoroughly."

Bowman glanced questioningly at Freitas.

"The local school teacher," Freitas said. "Fourth grade. Has a good lay knowledge." Both men smiled slightly; they exchanged what might have been a wink between them. Runcible went through the motions of lighting himself a cigarette. He did not look directly at them.

"And you," Bowman said. "For the record, you're a Realtor in this area. What is your background? Any academic training?"

"No," he said.

"Everyone here digs," Freitas said. "For arrowheads, anyhow."

"Let's have a look at the site," Bowman said.

Runcible drove them from the office up the hill to his house. Several curious persons stood around on the road; he had had a better fence put up around his property to keep unauthorized people out, and he had POSTED, NO TRESPASSING signs everywhere. Neither Freitas nor Bowman noticed the people; they passed on through the gate, and soon they were back in the eucalyptus grove with their tools and work clothes, preparing to scratch about.

"Have you been getting much noteriety?" Bowman asked once, when a group of people appeared on the hillside above Runcible's property. "You want to be sure that they can't get in here and start carting off everything as souvenirs. They'll strip you blind. Every rock and bone and shard."

Runcible said, "When I'm at work I have my wife watch. And at night there're so many dogs in the neighborhood nobody can get around on foot." He had seated himself on a eucalyptus log, near them.

"Listen," Freitas said. "We would have given a testicle apiece if it could have turned out to be mid-Pleistocene."

"I know," Runcible said.

He continued to sit and watch the two men dig. An hour or so passed, during which no one spoke to him, although the two men discussed various subjects between them. Once they stopped working to examine what looked to him like a pale, corroded domino; they did not bother to show it to him but put it away in a container.

"I better get back to my office," he said at last.

They scarcely noticed him.

Depressed and vaguely resentful, he left them, got into his

THE MAN WHOSE TEETH WERE ALL EXACTLY ALIKE • 213

car, and drove back to Runcible Realty. There, he picked up where he had left off; he got the house key from his old woman and carried it up onto the mesa to the party it belonged to.

That evening, as he was closing his office, Janet phoned him.

"Leo," she said, "Mr. Freitas and that other man asked me to call you. They're leaving now and they want to take the skull. They said I should check with you before letting them have it."

"They can take it," he said.

"They're using your portable," she said. "To type out some sort of receipt."

"Okay," he said, with irritation. "I don't care."

He got home to find them still there. They were in his study, seated across from each other, deep in discussion. When he entered the room Freitas said,

"We forgot about our car. It's down at the bottom of the hill. We'd walk, but we have too many things, including your skull."

"I'll drive you," he said.

Bowman said, "We found several things of interest." They had spread out a large light cloth on Runcible's desk, and on it Runcible saw a number of grimy objects, evidently some of bone, some of granite. And, on the floor, wrapped in newspapers, a large round object.

His heart picked up in its beat.

"Yes sir," Bowman said. "Another skull. Plus pelvis and thigh bones. This one seems to be a female."

"What's that mean?" Runcible demanded. "Isn't that a good sign?"

Freitas said, "Again, it's distinctly Neanderthaloid . . . no doubt of that. This really is puzzling. Except for the carbon dating test, your skull gave evidence of authenticity. And our first examination of this more complete group suggests — to us, anyhow — that we have the real thing." Behind his calm manner a tremor of excitement stirred; Runcible caught it, and he saw the same emotion on Bowman's face. The same tension.

This is how I must have looked, he thought. When I first got wind of this, of what it might be.

"The carbon dating test destroyed Piltdown," Bowman said. "It gave it the final push into oblivion. Out of the *Brittanica* and into the circus tent." He gestured toward the bundle on the floor. "Here, we've got the test from the start. There's no reason even to doubt. Your skull simply is not out of this period, and probably neither is this. Of course, we'll test." He paced around jumpily, rubbing his lower lip.

"What do you think?" Runcible said. "What does it mean?"

"It means we have to suspend judgment," Freitas said.

Glancing his way, Bowman said sharply, "This is really a mess. It really is." He had a worried, resentful look, now. "Suppose in some way these things failed to deteriorate — possibly they were placed in protracted contact with material that contaminated them in such a way that the carbon balance was perpetually maintained." He shrugged. "I give up; it's ridiculous in its own way."

"Hasn't the hydrogen bomb testing fouled up the carbon deposits in the world?" Runcible said.

Neither man answered him.

"I'll tell you what I think," Freitas said. "I think this is the Piltdown skull all over again. A thorough-going fake, with every detail skillfully manufactured, but no way of fooling the carbon dating test. That's why we use it, for christ's sake."

Bowman said, "You'd think anyone today, knowing about the carbon dating test, with the skill to do this good a job, and the motive to do it, would procure a sufficiently old skull. When a stamp forger wants to counterfeit a valuable old stamp he gets another issue of the same period, on the same paper, old paper. He only fakes the inked part. His paper stands up under the test."

"Is there any proof that it's a fake?" Runcible said.

"You mean indications that the skull has been worked on? By tools? Metal tools? Stained?" Bowman considered. "No, actually. We can't tell about the stuff we found today, as yet. But we'll see later on, when we get it all back to Berkeley."

It took the three of them several more hours to get the findings properly insulated and packed into Freitas' black De Soto. Evidently their activities had been noticed; two cars of reporters appeared, both from San Francisco papers, and the reporters hung around during the final part of their loading.

The next morning when Runcible bought his *Chronicle* he found on the first page, in the left-hand column, an article about him.

REALTOR'S SKULL PRONOUNCED HOAX
BY UNIVERSITY OF CAL SCIENTISTS

Seated in his car he read the article with numbed feelings.

University of California anthropologists, studying the recently unearthed alleged stone age skull found by Realtor Leon Runcible at Carquinez, in Marin County, have come to the tentative conclusion that the skull is either the work of a clever prankster or an accidental natural formation no older than three hundred years, it was learned exclusively by the *Chronicle* today. Ridges around the brow, the receding jaw and fused teeth, according to Jack Bowman of the University of California anthropology department, may indicate no more than that a deformed individual existed "who possessed by chance some of the physical characteristics" associated by anthropologists with the Neanderthal race, a long extinct "missing link" that existed hundreds of thousands of years ago in Europe and Asia but not in North or South America, according to most experts. Research on this skull, plus later finds, is still going on. The anthropologists involved in detection of the possible fraud or possible highly valuable scientific find now say that an entire skeleton may have been unearthed. It was three weeks ago that Leon Runcible of Carquinez claimed to have unearthed a genuine Neanderthal skull, and although his claim was not backed up by any scientific evidence, it was widely felt that such a find was within the realm of possibility. The Neanderthals, a sub-human race remarkable for their stooped posture, receding chins and ridged brows, once inhabited most of the world, it is believed. Numerous skeletal remains of Neanderthal types have been found in the past forty years. The Neanderthals made flint tools and may have had primitive religious rites. They are the best known of the so-called "missing link" races that existed before true men. The announcement of this possible hoax or possible invaluable scientific find brings to mind the recent exposé of the so-called Piltdown skull, for many decades universally accepted by scientists throughout the world as genuine. It was shown to be a hoax, compounded of a Homo sapiens skull and

Runcible did not turn to page six for the balance of the article. The hell with it, he said to himself, folding up the paper and placing it on the seat beside him. He drove to his office, and from there he telephoned the *Chronicle*.

"Listen," he said harshly, when he had gotten hold of someone higher up than the switchboard girl. "This is Leo Runcible. There's that article on page one of today's *Chronicle* about me and the skull which I found."

The man at the other end seemed to know about the article. So leaning back and holding the phone away from his mouth, he continued in a firm voice, the voice he used when he called someone to get something done. It was not the voice he used with clients nor the voice he used with friends.

"Here's what I have to say," he said. "I'll tell you what I think about that article, and you can print it. There's no hoax involved; you hear what I'm saying? Do you hear?" He spoke slowly; he did not let his pace speed up. He let them hear his controlled exasperation with them and their article. "This area here — do you know the area I'm talking about? I mean the Carquinez area of West Marin, one of the finest if not the finest area in Northern California — is known for its finds. Its historic and scientific finds. When was the last time you sent a man up into this area?"

The person at the *Chronicle* said that there had been several men up recently to cover the story about the skull.

"Well, then I wonder what kind of men they were," he said. "If they could come up to this area and not see what sort of place it is and what sort of people live here. Do you mean to infer that there are people up here who would play games with the public good? Let me tell you this. We have too much respect for the public good up here. We have too much respect for ourselves. If there's any hoax it's in your article." Now his voice did rise. "And you can quote me. If you're more interested in a sensational approach to science than getting at the real truth, then go ahead, and god help you. But don't count on me any more, for anything. I think the additional news coming out of this area can better go to some other periodical."

At the other end the man said something, but he did not listen.

"Good-bye," he said. And he hung up. For a time he sat at his desk, calming down, getting his voice under control. Then he dialed the operator and got the number of the University of California at Berkeley. Soon he was connected with the University switchboard, asking to speak to either Bowman or Freitas in the anthropology department.

It was Bowman that he managed to get hold of, at last.

"Listen," he said, "did you see today's *Chronicle*?"

"Yes," Bowman said. "We were going to call you, but Tony

hasn't come in yet. I was waiting for him; he ought to be here any time now. It's after nine."

Runcible said, "What did you tell the *Chronicle*? That the skull I found is a hoax, or what did you say?"

"We examined the more complete skeleton," Bowman said. "We found artificial varnishes and traces of bleaches and acids used to give the material the appearance of age. Evidently whoever made them didn't give this one the same care. He must have just done it. Some of the varnish wasn't fully dry. Particles of dirt were embedded in it."

"Then there's no doubt," he said, keeping his voice steady.

"Absolutely no doubt," Bowman said. "Somebody did it in a shop, using modern tools and substances." His voice had an aloof, unsympathetic ring; there was no friendliness there, at all. No breaking the news gently.

"Thank you very much," Runcible said, in as formal a voice as possible. "That answers my question." He hung up, then.

While he was sitting at his desk, meditating, the phone rang. He answered it, and again found himself connected with Bowman.

"I wanted to tell you," Bowman said, "but you rang off so abruptly. In no way are we accusing you, or do we necessarily think that you had anything to do with the manufacturing of these objects."

To that he said nothing.

"We're only reporting what we discovered," Bowman said. "Which is what you asked us to do."

"That's right," he said.

"We'll be happy to mail you or bring you all the findings. And of course we'll return the objects themselves."

"Okay," he said.

Bowman said, "The *Chronicle* article, by the way, is based on our earlier findings. On your first skull. We haven't said anything to anybody yet about what we found last night; we wanted to talk to you first and see what you said."

"Go ahead," he said.

"Fine," Bowman said. "There's no alternative, actually."

Runcible said, "I'd like to have them examined by someone else. Do you have any suggestions?"

That seemed to set the man back. "Well," he said, "I don't know. You could take them to another university. Almost any one that has lab facilities. I'll look into it, if you want. Stanford, I'm sure."

"I'll do that," he said. "Stanford. Thanks."

Bowman said, "But there's no doubt that the things were made in a workshop. There're even marks made by metal tools."

"Fine," he said.

"Don't you understand me?" Bowman said in a sharp tone of voice. "This isn't conjecture on our parts. There are even tiny bits, particles of metal detectable on microscopic and spectroscopic analysis. This is the sort of thing you can prove. We can even tell you who manufactured some of the resins. Du Pont, for one. It's theirs; they invented it."

Runcible hung up, then.

That's it, he said to himself. That's the whole business right there. Somebody faked it and planted it on my property.

But after a time he again dialed the operator. He asked her for the number of Stanford University in Palo Alto, and then, when he had the number, he began the task of getting hold of someone in their anthropology department.

14

Across from him, seated on the living room couch with the newspaper open on her lap, Sherry said,

"This is fascinating. This about Runcible and his Neanderthal skull."

Walter Dombrosio studied her. Had she guessed? She knew his ability and his experience and she knew about his hoaxes in the past. But she seemed not to tie the two together, the article in the newspaper and her husband.

"Yes," he said cautiously. "I saw that."

She continued, "It's been in and out of the paper for weeks, now."

"I know," he said.

"What do you think? Is it genuine?"

He said, "Don't the Cal scientists say it's a fake?"

"Yes," she said, reading intently. "They say it isn't old and that it's been worked on by some knowledgeable contemporary craftsman with a background in stone age objects and races. But it also quotes Runcible as saying that he's going to get Stanford to look at it."

"What does Stanford say to that?" Dombrosio said.

"They haven't said anything." She laid the paper aside, folding it up neatly and smoothing it. "They would, wouldn't they? Look at it. They could hardly refuse."

"I guess so," he said. He did not feel much like discussing it with her. In fact, he talked very little to her in the evenings; after dinner, when they had done the dishes, he usually went off by himself to read or work, while she read or watched TV. Tonight, however, she clearly wanted to talk.

"Don't you think," she said, "that Runcible had it made as a publicity stunt? Like that Realtor over in Sausalito who says Drake landed there and not in Drake's Bay, and that the plate of brass is a fake? It's a way of advertising the area. Runcible will get more people in here, possibly quite a few more."

He nodded.

"You can see his motives," she said. "Almost everyone I've talked to says that. That a man like that would do just this sort of thing. It's really pretty clever, don't you think? It has brought him a lot of publicity . . . but I wouldn't like that kind. Most of the papers hint that it's a promotion stunt. They don't say so, of course. Isn't that because of the libel laws?"

Dombrosio said, "Sure. If they said it, he'd sue them for libel, and he'd get his publicity that way."

"I really detest people like that," Sherry said. "Brash and pushy. Oh, I'm not supposed to say that. It's a shame he's Jewish."

"Yes," Dombrosio said. "He gives a bad name to his race."

"No, I mean we can't really criticize him publicly because if we do it looks like anti-Semitism. So that gives him carte blanche to go on doing this sort of thing. Stirring up this awful publicity."

"The kind of publicity he's getting isn't making him very happy."

"But he must have known they'd discover it to be a hoax. He must have known he'd get this bad publicity after a while. After some scientists came in and examined it. And—" She took up the newspaper once more. "He deliberately called them in. As soon as possible."

"Maybe any publicity will do," Dombrosio said. But now he had a twinge of uneasiness. Runcible had gone out on a limb — but was he suffering? Had he lost by it? "He's clinging to it," he said to his wife.

"Yes," Sherry said. "He's still trying to push it as genuine. With no scientific backing whatsoever."

"The simp," he said, with anger.

Sherry said, "He wants more publicity."

"No," he said. "He just can't admit he's been taken."

She stared at him. "*Taken?*" Her eyebrows, by degrees, rose. "You don't think he had it faked himself? You mean he genuinely thought it was real? He was taken in?" Her quick brain had caught his choice of words; she studied him long and silently.

"Possibly," he said, wishing now very much to drop the topic.

"Then someone else did it!" she said. "And poor Runcible is the victim. Oh, how fascinating." She contemplated that, and then she laughed. "What a peculiar theory. What does that tell me about you?"

He eyed her.

Sherry said, "Let's see. That possibly you can't admit to yourself that you're gullible. Do you see how you've projected your own problems onto Runcible? He's become a symbol for you."

At that point he managed to divert her; going into the kitchen he began searching in the refrigerator for something to eat, some dessert. She joined him, and together they got out a frozen pie.

Later, as they sat at the kitchen table eating, he thought over an idea that had been in his mind almost continually during the last week or so.

If he left Sherry, he could move into San Francisco, rent a room or apartment, and from there he could go to work without a car. He could get a job now, instead of having to wait the two months until he could get back his driver's license.

Across from him, Sherry ate her pie, holding her fork with delicate grace. How pretty she is, he thought. Her face had that sweet look that had always attracted him; her eyes, so large and gray blue, had an innocent quality. The perfect American face, he thought. Unspoiled. Unmarked. And yet she was not represented accurately by her looks; she was not unspoiled.

It does not show, he thought. There's no tip off. A well-bred and attractive woman who knows what she wants and pursues what she wants. She grew up calling the shots, he thought, and she doesn't intend to stop. Marriage never meant knuckling down to some man.

I'd be a lot better off, he decided. If I left her. There's no doubt of that. I could run my own life, again.

And yet —

He could not ignore the pride it gave him, the public pride of having a high-class wife. It raised him up a notch, too. She made him look better in the eyes of the world.

In his mind he saw, with anxiety, himself lacking Sherry; himself as an individual and not her husband. What would I be? Not more than now but less than now. Let's look at it rationally, he thought. I'd lose. For instance, she can work; she can contribute to our income. That's valuable, to have a wife who's economically able. What if I had lost my job, couldn't work, and she couldn't work either?

That terrified him; he felt it throughout his body. Stuck out here in the country. Suppose she couldn't drive the car. Really stuck, possibly to starve. There was no relief agency out here. No one to borrow from or complain to. No jobs, except that of a milker. Or a day laborer at the mill. And those required a car, too.

"Why are you looking at me that way?" Sherry said. "What are you thinking?"

He said, truthfully, "I'm thinking how nice it is to have a pretty wife."

Smiling, she said with terrible perceptiveness, "And one who can work."

That shocked him; he blinked rapidly and tried to recover. "Do you think I like this?" he demanded. "Christ, my pride. What do you think it does to me? It's destroying me."

"Oh," she said, "it's not so bad. It's not destroying you; you like to think it is."

"It is," he repeated.

"You suffer some discomfort," she said. "But it gives you time to mess around in your workshop. And you can go down to Donkey Hall and hang around in the evenings with the other donkeys. Remember, when you got home from Lausch Company, from the drive back from S.F. You were too tired to do anything but go to bed."

He said, "I'll be working again in two months."

"Maybe," she said.

With horror, he said, "You know I will be!"

"In two months, you'll have your license. But what then? I'll still need the car to get to my job. You'll go in with me . . ." She pointed her finger at him, triumphantly. "You could do that now. Go in and look for a job. But you're not. It'll be the same, then."

"You'll be quitting," he said feebly.

"No," she said. "I'll still be working. I like my job. I like Norm Lausch. He's a good man to work for; he leaves you alone to do your job. And I'm getting to do more creative work and less public relations work all the time."

He realized, then, that she told him almost nothing about her day at Lausch Company; she never discussed it, had not from the very start. And it had not even occurred to him to ask. The job was her sphere; she had taken it over, and he played no part in it, now. They had both accepted it; she had because she wanted it that way, and he — god knew. Why do I go along? he asked himself. What do I get out of it?

It came to him then that he had not gone along; that, in fact, she had compelled him. There was nothing voluntary about it. She had completely organized his feelings.

He said, "You'd have made a good executive in a big company."

"I am an executive," she said. "Am I barred because I'm a woman? Norm Lausch doesn't think so."

"You mean you're bossing people around, there?" he said. He could not help considering it amusing. It was so presumptuous of her, almost irrational. Like a daydream. "You know," he said, "I can tell you what your big defect is. Want to hear?"

"Oh god," she said. "Another of your five hour orations."

"You're impatient," he said. "You can't wait. It's like when you decide to rearrange all the things in the house; you have to do it then and there, right on the spot."

"If I wait," she said, "it might never get done."

And we're also objects, he thought. People are things which she moves around, rearranges to suit her. She drives out spontaneity in others because she can't wait for them to feel what she wants them to feel; that which should come voluntarily she forces.

And she really doesn't see the difference, he thought. It's not wickedness but blindness. Her vision is just not good enough for her to distinguish. Just as long as the outward appearance is the same. As long as the people do move, do get rearranged . . . she can dispense with the mythical interior: the soul.

I have to leave her, he decided. And, sitting eating his pie, he pondered, as before, on the best way of doing it.

At his desk in his study, Runcible read over the letter that he had just typed. Spread out on all sides of him, and on the floor, were photographs, great glossy positives. Into a large-size manila envelope he put the letter and two of the photographs, and then, after sealing the envelope, he addressed it to the anthropology department of the University of Chicago.

Then he put a new sheet of paper into his typewriter and began a new letter. This one was to the anthropology department at Yale.

He had, at his right, a stack of photostats made from newspaper articles dealing with him and his finds. And, beside them, photostats of reference paragraphs from various scientific books which he had been able to buy or borrow. The books themselves had been stacked up in the corner of the room. Each book had markers hanging from it; he wanted to be able to get at the citations without hindrance.

After he had finished the letter to Yale he once more brought out his most important letter; he had written it but not mailed it. The letter was to L.S.B. Leakey.

While he sat reading it over he heard a knock at his door, the knock that his wife made. "I'm busy," he said.

Through the door Janet said, "Michael Wharton is here."

"Okay," he said. He put the Leakey letter back in the drawer and turned his swivel chair around.

The door opened and the grammar school teacher appeared. He had a look on his face that was new to Runcible; his cheeks were puffy and his neck was bright red. His eyes seemed to be watering, and for an instant Runcible thought that the man must be undergoing an acute attack of hay fever.

Wharton, in a squeaky voice, said, "I've been talking to Doctor Freitas on the phone. About their discovery that it's a hoax."

Reaching out, Runcible took a cup of coffee from the window sill above his desk. He drank from it and said nothing.

"I know who did it," Wharton said.

At that Runcible glanced up.

"Where did we find the first artifacts?" Wharton said loudly. "The arrowheads? You tell me." He had taken on an almost hysterical manner; his adam's apple bobbed up and down and his eyes shone.

"Down the hill," Runcible said.

"On whose land?"

"Walter Dombrosio's."

Wharton said, "He did it. He can; he knows how. That's his job. We were talking about Neanderthals, at the Hall. I know it."

"I thought of that," Runcible said. It had occurred to him a day or so ago, after he had talked to Bowman on the phone. "Listen," he said to Wharton. "I want to find out something from you." Going to the heap of books he got one and carried it to the grammar school teacher; seating himself on a leather footstool he opened the book on his lap. "They make casts of skulls," he said. "I've been researching this. What they call break molds."

"Yes," Wharton said, staring at him.

"Did you ever do anything along those lines? And if not, who has?"

Wharton said, "I've made break molds."

"I have photographs," Runcible said. "But I want to mail some casts to universities back east and possibly some in Europe. And I'm going to get all the evidence possible to the university at Tel Aviv. That's Moshe Dyan's university. Interesting; did you know he was the supreme military commander of the Israeli forces in the war against Egypt, the Sinai Campaign? And he's one of the world's foremost archeologists." Closing the book he rose and carried it back to the stack. "There's an example," he said over his shoulder. "It's possible to combine an interest in science — interest, hell! Authoritative knowledge. Dyan is a professional. A scholar . . . teacher. In the best tradition of Jewish culture. The Jews have always revered learning."

"You have nothing to send to Tel Aviv University," Wharton

said. "Except some faked-up thing that Walter Dombrosio man-ufactured in the basement of Donkey Hall. He and Jack Vepp and Timmons. I wondered why they've been keeping me out of there."

Runcible said, "Listen." He pointed his finger at the grammar school teacher. "What would you do," he said, "if you had a heart condition. And you went to a doctor — admittedly a good doctor, a specialist. And he told you that there was no technique known that could save you."

To that, Wharton was silent.

"And he told you," Runcible said, "that, say, you had six months. What would you do?"

Wharton made a gesture.

"I'll tell you what you'd do," Runcible said. "Or at least what you'd do if you had any sense. You'd go to another specialist, and another, and another, until you found one who could save you. That's what you'd do."

Presently, Wharton said, "Hypochondria."

"Oh no," Runcible said. "Not hypochondria. Not at all. Self-preservation."

"Maybe so," Wharton said.

"Is science sacred?" Runcible said. "Science is, maybe. But not a particular galoot who's the employee of a particular university. Let me tell you something about that university."

"Cal, you mean," Wharton said.

"Yes. Cal." He leaned back in his chair. "That's the biggest university in the world."

Wharton nodded.

"The most richly endowed. In what departments? In physics. Teller works for them. Lawrence. All the physical sciences. Chem-istry. They have the Bevatron up there. Millions of dollars. It's part of the national economy. The national research program."

"Yes," Wharton said.

"It's a huge machine," Runcible said. "Do you know what it turns out? Not knowledge. Not scholars. I'll tell you what that place turns out. Technicians, with an eye on a fat paycheck at some big company, such as Westinghouse or General Dynamics. Do you think they give a damn about whether a bunch of stooped-over lunks roamed North America a hundred million years ago? Is that going to change the national economy? Is that going to provide cheap fuel for steamships, or possibly a new warhead on some missile to drop on Soviet Russia?"

Wharton said nothing.

"Maybe if I had sent them a box of some kind of dried algae," Runcible said, "and asked if it was full of protein and could it be grown in Joe Doak's bathtub, I might have gotten a decent answer and the courtesy of a thorough investigation."

"The University of California did the radiation dating work on Leakey's Oldowan skull," Wharton said.

"Yes," Runcible said. "But they know who Leakey is. He spent twenty-five years working in that gorge. Sure, they gave him the royal treatment. They know the difference between a skull coming to them from L.S.B. Leakey of Olduvai Gorge Tanganyika, and Leo Runcible of Runcible Realty, Carquinez, Marin County, U.S.A."

"Twenty-seven," Wharton murmured.

"Pardon me?" Runcible said.

"Leakey worked the gorge twenty-seven years, not twenty-five."

Runcible said, "When a man like Leakey sends in a skull, they have to look at it. When I send in a skull, they don't have to. It's as simple as that. A man doesn't do what he wants but what he has to do. They can get away with short-shitting me, but not with Leakey; if they did that, they'd get shafted by every scientific authority in the world, and they know it." He paused, and while he was thinking how to continue, Wharton said,

"How much money have you put into this, so far?"

"I don't know," he said.

"You have an idea."

Runcible said, "A few dollars."

"I'd say you've put in a hundred in phone calls alone."

"More like two," Runcible admitted.

"So you've probably put three hundred in all, including books, tools, phone calls, telegrams, photostating, and your time. How much time? All your time; you haven't been doing any real estate work in two weeks."

Runcible said nothing.

"You could bankrupt yourself with this," Wharton said.

After a time Runcible said, "It brings in business."

"Does it?"

"Eventually."

"You're not doing it to bring in business."

With amusement, Runcible said, "Dyan learned the military terrain of the Middle East by scratching around with a shovel, digging for old buried idols."

Wharton said, "You're deluding yourself if you think you're doing this for business purposes. That's a rationalization. You're exposing yourself to public ridicule."

To himself, Runcible thought, He was a nice Jewish boy, but he had too much ambition. Aloud, he said, "What a way to spend Easter."

"What?"

"You haven't heard the new crop of jokes." Standing, he put himself in the posture of Christ on the cross; he dangled his arms out and hung his head. "What a way to spend Easter," he said. "I'll tell you another." Reseating himself, he said, "Would you mind crossing your legs? We have only three nails."

Wharton, in spite of himself, laughed.

Sharing the man's upsurge, Runcible said, "Here's the one I like best. Drop that cross once more, and you're out of the parade."

At that, Wharton laughed until tears ran down his cheeks. He sank down in a chair and wiped at his face. Runcible, too, found himself unable to stop laughing; together, they laughed for a long time.

"Here's another," Runcible said, when he could speak again. "It's longer. Takes place in the stable. It's my Joseph joke. Do you know it?"

Wharton shook his head no.

"Mary's there," Runcible said. "In confinement. Joseph's carrying stuff around, bales of straw. All of a sudden his foot slips and he says, 'Jesus Christ!'" He paused, getting his joke ready. "And Mary says, 'Say. You know, I like that much better than Irving.'"

"That's a subtle one," Wharton said. "It affects you more mentally."

"I like that the best," Runcible said.

"Yes, it's the best. But it's hard to explain why."

"It's impossible to explain why," Runcible said.

"The best jokes can't be explained," Wharton said. "It's a form of art."

"Art," Runcible agreed. "A good joke is art." Turning back to his desk he picked up a letter. "I want you to read this. It's going to Duke University. I'd like your opinion. Actually, I should have had you over here all this time to read what I'm writing. I think I'll open up these envelopes and let you read everything over." He tore open the manila envelope addressed to Yale.

With obvious reluctance, Wharton took the letter. He glanced over it and then, without finishing it, said, "If you had Dombrosio tell you he faked it — if he admitted it — would you accept the situation, then?" He dropped the letter on the desk.

"That asshole, Dombrosio," Runcible said. "You want me to tell you something about him?"

"I want to know if you'd accept it then," Wharton repeated.

"Listen," Runcible said. "That jerk has it in for me. I wouldn't trust anything he says, not if it has to do with me. You want to know why he has it in for me? I'll tell you, but don't spread it around. You remember when the police picked him up when he was drunk and got his car stuck in the ditch. Well, I was the one who called the police. Naturally I didn't know it was him. Anyhow, they took away his license, something I didn't know they did, but that isn't important. And my god damn wife went down there in a gushy bucketful of remorse and poured the whole thing out to him, all about my calling." He was silent, then. "No," he said. "I wouldn't believe him if he said he faked it. It would be just like him."

"Well then that explains it," Wharton said.

"What explains what?"

"Why he'd do it."

Runcible said, "A guy like Dombrosio — let me tell you about him. That kind of fink. Yes, fink. I suppose I'm offending you."

"No," Wharton said.

"Dombrosio," Runcible said, "is a weak, mean fink. A grudge-holder. That wife of his gives it to him; she sticks it into him on the average of once a week. She wears the pants in that family, and not only the pants; she's got what you usually find in the pants. So what does he do? He can't take her on, because he's weaker than she is; she can throw him around like a dead cat. So he gets off in his workshop down there — hell, I see him; I can look out the window and see him — and he nurses that grudge, the impotent bastard. And then you know what he does? He finds a scapegoat. And I know about that. We know about that. We've had that for three thousand years."

"I see," Wharton murmured.

"No," Runcible said. "You don't see. Because the guy's practically a pal of yours."

"Take it easy," Wharton said. "Please."

Runcible said, "I'm sorry. So anyhow, he has to find someone he can do dirt to, someone other than his wife or his boss — when he had a boss. If he had a dog he could kick it. Christ, if he had a kid he could beat it. But he's got nothing. Only me. He's got me to kick and beat and spit on. And *this* is his way."

"What is his way?" Wharton listened alertly.

"To get your ear," Runcible said.

The grammar school teacher stared at him, once more red-faced.

"Sure," Runcible said. "Now, listen. Don't get sore. I'm not saying anything about you, just him. You're too pure; you haven't got a bad bone in your body — and don't think he doesn't know it. He knows it. He drops it in your ear that—" He gestured. "He has a workshop; he's got the skill, the know-how—"

Wharton said, "I'm surprised at you."

"How do you mean?"

Struggling with words, the grammar school teacher stammered, "All this elaborate theorizing. It's as plain as the nose on your face." Then his agitation increased. "No racial reference intended," he said.

"Hell," Runcible said. "I'm proud of my hook nose. My Shylock nose. I wouldn't get it fixed for anything in god's green earth."

There was silence for a long time. Wharton stood off to one side, picking at his sleeve. Runcible returned to studying his letters.

"I'll see you later on," Wharton said finally. He seemed to be worn-out, now. His animation had subsided. "I'm going to drop by Walt Dombrosio's place and talk to him face to face."

"Suit yourself," Runcible said, intently studying a letter and not looking up at the grammar school teacher. "If you want to pal around with that fink, that shithead, go ahead. It's a free country."

"Good-bye," Wharton said.

Runcible grunted and continued reading as the door shut after the teacher.

* * *

As he walked down the hill to the Dombrosio house, the grammar school teacher thought to himself that he could never shake Runcible's faith. Because it was not faith; it was an affirmation.

The man declared that the thing was true. It was his religion, his dogma. He had seized a position, like a bulldog on a mound, and he meant to chew up all comers and spit them out, large and small alike.

Even if there were proof — even if absolute evidence did arise to back up his claim — that would not affect him.

Wharton thought, Neither proof for nor proof against is meaningful to him and his position. And that's what I call true idealism. In the correct and best sense of the term.

Flashing his lantern ahead of him he picked out the path that led to Dombrosio's front porch.

I don't know why I'm going here, he thought. I know that Walter did it. And he certainly isn't going to write it out and notarize it. In fact, he thought, suppose I do get him to say it; I get him to admit it in public, say, to one of the newspapers. Won't that make Runcible seem even more ridiculous?

At the bottom porch step he stopped short. I'll just be piling on more evidence to the contrary, he realized. How strange this is. By getting Walt to confess publicly, I'll just make Runcible's plight a trifle worse — in fact, a good deal worse.

If he's determined to go on, then the worst that could happen would be to get Walt to come out and prove that he manufactured the skull.

They're both crazy, he said to himself. One of them sawing and painting away in his workshop, the other at his desk writing letters and gathering citations from reference books. Both of them ingesting all there is to know about Neanderthal Man. A race that existed forty thousand years ago. All the data, the minutiae. Abandoning their real work, he thought. Their workaday jobs. Runcible not at his realty office, Dombrosio not in town searching for and finding new employment.

At least, he thought, I can go in there and tell Walt Dombrosio what I think of him.

But he tarried. He did not go in. He considered. And at last he turned around and went away.

I have to face facts, he said to himself. It's fruitless to talk to either of them. I might as well bow out.

Otherwise, he said to himself, I'll be just like them.

Early the next morning Leo Runcible was awakened by the telephone. When he had gotten out of bed and gone into the hall to answer it he found himself hearing an unfamiliar voice.

"You don't know me," the man said. "My name is Dudley Sharp. I'm attached to the anthropology department at UC. This is Leo Runcible I'm talking to, isn't it?"

"Yes," he said, holding the phone with one hand and tying the sash of his bathrobe with the other.

"I hope I didn't wake you," Sharp said. "But I wanted to talk to you as soon as it's practicable. Bowman gave me an opportunity to examine your first skull and the later find, the more intact skeleton that he and Doctor Freitas turned up. Now, you understand — I *hope* you understand — that both finds have been thoroughly worked on by someone recently. In the past year or so, judging from the resins used. But you also understand, don't you, that they didn't start from scratch. That is, in both cases they worked on actual skeletal remains which they got hold of somewhere. They didn't build a skull or a skeleton. They used him, the way the Piltdown hoaxer rebuilt an actual very old human skull and a chimpanzee jaw."

"Yes," Runcible said, rubbing his eyes with his thumb and forefinger.

"I'm very much interested in the authentic remains which lie beneath the worked-over layers," Sharp said. "If you follow me. In other words, I've been briefly trying to reconstruct — I don't mean I've physically altered or harmed your finds; I mean I've mentally tried to picture what the individual or individuals who did the work had before them to start with. The two skulls — in fact the entire skeleton, the later find — are very peculiar."

"How?" Runcible said.

"The hoaxer has augmented in some cases, and in others evidently entirely reconstructed," Sharp said. "I'd better see you face to face; this is costing me too much. I'm paying for this myself. Can I drop over, say sometime later today or tomorrow?"

"Of course," Runcible said. "Or I could come there, to the university."

"That would be better," Sharp said. "It's hard for me to get away; I have classes until late afternoon."

"You think that there is a Neanderthal skull beneath the layers that were deliberately added?" Runcible said.

"Oh no." The man seemed to laugh. "Nothing like that. But the skulls are atypical. It may be that the hoaxer, once he had the notion of fabricating a Neanderthaloid skull, searched around for a skull that would serve as a good basis. He may have tried to procure an actual Mousterian skull and failed, so he did the next best thing; he got hold of a malformed skull — I don't know where or how — and off he went. You ask if it's a Neanderthal skull underneath, so to speak; but recall, the radioactive dating method has already established that it's only a few hundred years old at the most."

"True," Runcible said.

"I'll see you, then," Sharp said. "Glad to have talked to you. When you get over here I can go deeper into it with you. For one thing I want to inveigle you into letting me try to restore the skull and intact skeleton as they were. But I have a hunch that'll be hard to get your permission for."

Before Runcible could say anything the man had rung off.

After he had gotten dressed he returned to the phone. Janet was still in bed; she had not wakened up. He dialed the operator and gave the number of the *Chronicle*.

Presently he was talking to someone at the paper.

"Listen," he said, after he had identified himself. "You've had a good time running humorous articles about me, for purposes of circulation building. And that's all fine. Now I want you to do something. I want you to call the University of California, the anthropology department, and interview a professor there named Dudley Sharp. In fact, maybe you had better send a man over there."

The newspaper asked why.

Runcible said, "Through various tests — he can discuss them with you; I can't — I'm not a scientist — he's established a few things that indicate something a little different than the glib idea that's probably sold you people a lot of papers, that my finds are fakes. Hoaxes."

The newspaper agreed to follow up the lead, and Runcible hung up with a deep sense of satisfaction.

He ate breakfast with more gusto than he had in months.

15

In his workshop, sharpening a wood gouge, Walter Dombrosio looked up to see Michael Wharton standing in the doorway. With him was another man, tall, with dark-rimmed glasses and a crew cut, very young, smiling friendlily.

"We rapped on the front door," the young man said, "but nobody heard us, so we came on in. Mr. Wharton thought your wife might be home but then he remembered that she would be in town at work."

Wharton said, "This is Dudley Sharp from the University of California."

With wariness, his heart hammering, Dombrosio at last shook hands with Sharp. "I was busy," he said.

Wharton said, "He wants to find out where you got the skull and skeletal remains."

"Yes," Sharp said, still smiling, holding onto Dombrosio's hand. "This is all on an informal basis, of course. I can assure you that you won't put yourself in any jeopardy by telling me. I'm here as a private person, like Mr. Wharton, here, who I understand teaches at the local grammar school."

"Where I got what skull?" Dombrosio said. But he knew that they knew.

Wharton, naturally, had worked it out. He felt frightened, but after all, he had expected it. He had prepared what he would do and say.

"The remains that you planted on Runcible's property," Wharton said. His face had a pinched quality; he spoke brusquely, as if he wanted to say as little as possible. It was obvious to Dombrosio that the grammar school teacher had not wanted to come. He wanted to leave, now; he hung back near the door. All this was distasteful to him. It was Sharp who had gotten him to come here.

"What's the matter, Wharton?" Dombrosio said, feeling anger at the man. "If you don't like it here, take off."

His eyes twinkling, Sharp said, "I prevailed on Mr. Wharton. Let's you and I discuss this, and leave him out; all right? That would be fairer. You tell me where you obtained the skulls and that will be the end of it; we won't pursue the topic with you. Nothing related to what you did or why; we're not concerned with that."

He managed, after some argument and struggle, to get both of them out of the house; like door-to-door salesmen they hung on tenaciously, retreating step by step, Sharp talked pleasantly, rapidly, constantly, until finally he had shut the front door and locked it.

Still trembling, he threw himself down on the couch in the living room.

Well, it was known. What now? Was there a way they could get him? A law he had violated? Giving false information to the police? But he had given no information; he had simply buried the junk, first on his land and then on Runcible's. Trespassing, possibly.

The most serious involved the original bones and skulls themselves. There they might have him. If they could prove how he had gotten them. And that was exactly what they were interested in.

I have to deny it, he decided. No matter what happens. It's one thing for them to accuse me; after all, I could have done it — I have the skill and tools. I have the ability and I live in the area. But that won't prove I did it. Nobody who dislikes Runcible will be convinced; they'll take my side against him. So by god I'll deny it until I'm dead. Even if Timmons and Jack Vepp say I did it.

He had a brilliant idea, then. I'll say I got the idea of faking it *after* he found the skull, he decided. I decided to make additional skulls and skeletons *because* he found them; I decided to do it and plant them on my land, but I changed my mind and gave up. The work I did at Donkey Hall — *that had nothing to do with what Runcible found.*

Nobody can prove that the work I produced is the same work that Runcible dug up. I defy them to do it.

Let them come here and threaten me all they want, he said to himself. Like they did today. The hell with them.

Going back to his workshop he resumed the sharpening of the wood gouge, feeling in him a grim, powerful assurance. A certitude that he knew could not be broken by anything that happened. He was in some inner sense safe.

But then a moment later he thought, All they had to do is look over the possibilities. There's only one place I could get it at. If they think about it they'll realize that, and if they go there and dig around they'll be sure; they'll find the parts missing.

And, he thought, that's something Jack Vepp can tell them because he was along; it was his jeep we used that night and his map and shovels and Coleman gasoline lantern.

Christ, he thought dismally. I know there's a law against grave robbing. Even those old abandoned graves that nobody knows about hardly, with those wooden crosses, no descendents bringing flowers or keeping the grass cut, the whole place falling into ruins. Wharton would know about it; he knows all the old structures in this area. Worse, he may even know who's buried there; he can get hold of the families.

But even Wharton would not know that. The graves were too

old, too abandoned. There hadn't been a person buried there in sixty years. The most recent date that he and Vepp had made out on the crude wooden tombstones — or boards, actually — was 1899. And one of the names only had been at all familiar. The families did not now exist in the area. Of course, the glass jars lying around . . . he had thought that possibly they indicated that some relatives had been by with hand-picked flowers. Vepp thought no; he had argued that the jars had been left by fruit pickers who were winos, who had sneaked there to drink. Fruit pickers and mill workers and milkers who had used the place because no one came there.

That graveyard, he thought, belongs to us all; it's part of the historical background of this area, and no one was using the bones buried there — no one has lost anything. We have a right to them, just as we have a right to the Indian relics, the arrowheads and granite tools, left over from before that. The older bones.

We are the descendents, he decided. We've inherited all that stuff, there. Including the wooden headstones, if we want them.

Carrying a shovel, Sheriff Christen trudged on up the path ahead of the others. Behind him came the vet, Doctor Heyes, and then Dudley Sharp from the University of California, and then Wharton the fourth grade teacher, and finally Leo Runcible and Seth Faulk.

A barbed wire fence surrounded the graveyard. The hillside, overgrown with tall brown oats, was safe from cattle; a second fence, made of stakes and boards, had been put up outside the barbed wire. Brambles had heaped themselves up onto the second fence, and some had gotten as far as the barbed wire. The brambles were black and thick, and Runcible saw within them the burrows of gophers.

With surprise he saw several wooden crosses outside the barbed wire, outside the graveyard. Brambles and oats had almost covered the crosses, and he wondered if anyone had noticed them besides him.

Wharton said, "Whoever put the barbed wire up overlooked those." He, too, had seen them. "They may be the oldest graves, but there are no dates on them." As he climbed on up the dirt trail he said over his shoulder, "And there are no doubt totally unmarked graves."

In the center of the graveyard stood a single structure, made of what appeared to Runcible to be either marble or granite. The square of stone had become so dirty and weather-stained that he could not tell what it had originally looked like. Set in each side was a stained glass window, and as he got closer he discovered that the glass depicted a scene: an angel praying. On the side facing the trail a black iron door could be seen, locked with chain and padlock. On each side of the door was a stone vase with dry stalks of plants poking from it.

Lettered in brass across the top of the structure were the words: ANGELO BASTIONI, and then farther down on the sides, and smaller, were the words: THEA BASTIONI, TULIO BASTIONI, ANGELO BASTIONI JR., LUCIANO BASTIONI, MARIO BASTIONI, GIA BASTIONI.

Obviously, this had once been the burial place for this one well-to-do family. Other lesser dead had crept in furtively, perhaps when the surviving Bastionis were not looking. He did not recognize the name. As far as he knew, no one by that name lived in the area, now. In fact he had not encountered it before this.

Wharton said, "The Bastioni family owned tracts of land here, deeded to them from the Mexican government. Original tracts, very large. Embracing most of this area." He tossed his shovel down beside the trail and knelt down to retie his boot lace.

Ahead, Sheriff Christen had reached the gate of the barbed wire fence. He unhooked it and dragged it aside for the others to pass through and into the graveyard.

The vet said, "Over to the right. The weeds are trampled down."

To Runcible, Dudley Sharp said, "This is fascinating, this little old abandoned graveyard." He called to Wharton, "What is the oldest stone here, to your knowledge?"

"About 1800," Wharton answered. "I'll show it to you." He led the anthropologist and the vet along a gravel path overgrown with oats, up a slope to a terrace at the higher end of the graveyard. There, the huge, wild rosebush had put out its canes over a broad area; a number of marble headstones had become concealed by it.

Seth Faulk said, "I've seen roses from the road, this bush. I always wondered what was up here."

"You should have looked," Runcible said. He left Faulk and strode on up to join the others.

Following after him, Faulk said, "There's no news out here, not usually."

The sheriff had gone on by the rose bush; with his heavy boots he smashed down canes of the bush and got through to the far side. There, brambles joined the rose bush and formed a wall under which, Runcible saw, the barbed wire fence had tumbled down. Raising his shovel the sheriff hacked and cleared a way until he disappeared from sight, beyond the wall of thorny growth.

"They could put the dirt back," Wharton said. "But probably not the weeds. So look for bare earth."

The vet, Seth Faulk, and Wharton all went off together to the far right; it was not possible to see down the slope on that side because of the angle. Runcible and Sharp remained near the center of the graveyard, by the Bastioni crypt, each man holding his shovel.

"I should have come out to this area a long time ago," the anthropologist said. "What else is here?"

"Everything you could want," Runcible said, preoccupied. He had noticed exposed earth, and he started in that direction.

244 • PHILIP K. DICK

Beyond the Bastioni crypt he found an open grave. A mound of dirt had been flung up out of it, but tufts of weeds were growing in the mound and he realized that it had been there a long time. The grave was empty, and its sides were so regular, so square, that he knew that this was a formal grave, one dug but never used.

"I thought we had it," he said to Sharp, who had followed. From far off they heard the sheriff's voice.

"He wants us," Runcible said, and started in that direction. By taking the route through the brambles and rose canes that the sheriff had made he was able to get over the broken barbed wire. Under his shoes the rusted wire yielded and snapped; he tramped it down for the anthropologist, who followed, holding the canes aside gingerly with his hands. A smear of blood could be seen on his right wrist; either a barb from the fence or a rose thorn had cut him.

They found Sheriff Christen standing at the edge of a shallow trough, poking with the blade of his shovel. Bits of gray broken wood, termite-eaten, lay strewn here and there in the dirt. The weeds had been cleared back. Someone had dug here recently.

"This looks like it," Christen said. He pushed the blade of his shovel into the dirt and it sank down. The soil was loose.

On the far side of the rose bush Wharton appeared and called to them, "We found recent digging outside the fence."

"Here, too," Christen said. He continued to explore with the blade of his shovel. At last he gripped the shovel handle with both hands and, pushing the blade down with his heel, lifted dirt up and aside. "Want to help me?" he said to Runcible.

Together, the two men dug. Sharp had gone a little way off to investigate a wooden cross still standing. "I wonder if I should let this alone," he said to them. "It looks to me like it's been dug up and then put back." Kneeling, he tugged at the cross; after a moment it came up, free, and he set it aside. "They've been here, too," he said. "They probably opened a number of graves. Once they got started it wouldn't be hard. These little graves are closer together, probably touching."

The sheriff and Runcible had dug several feet down; it was not difficult because others had dug so recently. But now their shovels reached adobe. They found themselves slowed down; they had to cut the adobe with the sharp edges of their shovels, wiggling the blades back and forth and pressing down with their full weight.

"Maybe they started here and gave up," Runcible said.

They removed all the loose earth. No bones emerged. Either the grave robbers had taken all the remains from this spot or they had stopped short. There should be caskets, Runcible thought. That would be necessary in a burial; even in 1800 they didn't just dump the corpse into a hole. It's only Indian corpses that were treated that way. And these are not Indian corpses; these are the graves of the white farmers who came over Mount Tamalpais and settled here.

"It's interesting to see which graves they ransacked," Runcible said to the sheriff.

"Yes," the sheriff said. "The poorest graves. They probably figured those were fair game. No one would care. Or if they did, they couldn't do much. They were smart enough to stay out of the big crypt in the middle."

It did not seem as if they had anything where they were now digging, so they restored the dirt and returned to Heyes and Wharton and Faulk. The other three men had exposed a wooden casket; they had put down their shovels and were examining it.

Wharton said, "If it hasn't been opened, should we open it?"

"I think it has been opened," the vet said. He tugged at the top, and it lifted a crack. "Better set yourselves," he said. To the sheriff he said, "Do I have official permission to go ahead?"

"Go ahead," Christen said.

Together, Faulk and Heyes opened the casket. In it lay a

skeleton intact. On its left hand they saw a gold ring, evidently a wedding ring. And, in the casket, were the metal remains of shoes, a belt, snaps of clothing, a pile of what had been leather.

"May I see?" Sharp said, putting his hand on Runcible's shoulder. Runcible moved aside, and the anthropologist peered intently.

"Anything?" Faulk said.

"No," Sharp said. "As far as I'm concerned you can close it."

"But they did look in here," Runcible said.

"It's hard to tell," Wharton said. "This old casket has deteriorated quite a bit. It wasn't much to start with."

They dug further. By clearing the soil to their right they came onto a wooden cross buried and almost destroyed; they could not read the carving on it or make it stand. Evidently it had fallen over at some far-distant time in the past and become lost, probably during the winter rains.

A half hour later they found in the loose soil a jumble of bones.

"This seems to be where they got the skull," the vet said. No skull could be found, although all six men continued to dig.

Sharp laid the bones out on a canvas sheet. He paid no attention to the other men for a long time; absorbed in his work, he let them go on digging.

"What do you think?" Christen said.

"Well, the skull is gone," Sharp said. "I suppose this could have been a headless corpse tossed here. I'll tell you what I'd be more interested in finding." He rose to his feet and again picked up his shovel. "I'd like to see an intact skeleton that has deformations along the lines that I've run into. And one that hasn't been worked over in a machine shop. Especially the skull." He had a tense expression; his forehead had become wrinkled with concern.

"We'll have to root around in more caskets, then," Faulk said.

"Yes," Sharp said. "If we may. If it's permitted."

"You can go ahead," the sheriff said, after thinking about it.

For an hour they dug. Once they had gotten the hang of it

they found it possible to go from one casket to the next without having to lift the intervening dirt; they located the caskets quickly, got them open, and then went on. Sharp inspected each skeleton with care.

At three-thirty in the afternoon they came onto a casket that had fallen almost to bits. As they opened it the lid came apart in their hands; fragments of rotten wood, as soft as cloth, tore loose and rained down into the soil.

"Either very old," Christen said, "or badly built, or both."

Dirt covered the skeleton; dirt had seeped through the wood during the years. They blew and brushed the dirt away until the skull was visible. At once they all gasped; all of them saw the difference. The deformity that the anthropologist had been searching for.

"I guess our friends didn't see this one," Sharp said. "Or they would have used it." As he bent down he said, "It would have saved them a lot of effort."

The jaw of the skull seemed to Runcible enormous. And yet it had little or no chin to it. And the teeth. As if they were all molars, he thought. Massive and square, unlike anything he had ever seen, except in the skull that he and Wharton had dug up in his own eucalyptus grove.

All at once he said, "Listen. This could be a fake."

They glanced at him. "Of course," the vet said. "That would really be clever. They'd know we'd be coming here looking." He stood up, away from the open casket.

"No end to it," Wharton said in a jerky, hectic voice.

"We can tell," Sharp said, running his fingers over the cheek of the skull.

The brow, Runcible said to himself. Yes, he thought. It does look like a Neanderthal skull. And yet it is not. He had seen so many photographs of Neanderthal skulls, in the last weeks. This was different. Even though there were so many Neanderthal types, even mixtures of Neanderthal with true men, this could not be called one; he looked down at a deformity, not the manifestation of a special race. Glandular, he thought. Like that wrestler. What was it — thyroid? Iodine lacking in early life, or something like that.

"I wonder how he ate," Seth Faulk said.

"It does make you wonder," the vet said.

Sharp said, "I can tell you right now; this is a Homo sapiens skull. Don't get excited."

They all nodded.

"He was a short man," Sharp said. "Probably didn't walk quite upright. And the overhanging brow. And the jaw. His speech must have been affected."

Runcible said, "The Neanderthals are supposed to have mixed with true men."

"Yes," Sharp said. "At least, it appears as if that was so. From the remains we've found since the war." He inspected the leg bones. "You mean, possibly this could be an — offspring of miscegenation. Of Neanderthal and Homo sapiens stock." After a time he said, "None of you have ever seen anything like this before? In this area? Any people living here, born here? With this sort of deformity?"

They all said no.

Sharp said, "Who would the oldest people in the area be? Is there some backwoods part, here? The boondocks? A farm left over from the old days, up on the Ridge somewhere, maybe?"

"Let's see," Sheriff Christen said. "There's the old town."

"What old town?" Sharp said. His face lit up as if with fright.

Wharton said, "There was a previous town of Carquinez. Not where the present one is, but on the other side of the Ridge. On the ocean side."

The vet said, "On the estero."

Sharp said, "Does anybody live there now?"

"A few people," the vet said. "Very poor run-down people. It's almost in ruins, now."

"Abandoned," Runcible said. "Just shacks."

"They still live by oyster fishing," Wharton said. "The way the Indians did before them."

"Let's go out there," Sharp said. "They may have old paintings and daguerreotypes. Back country people usually have."

The vet said, "Yes, I've seen them, in one of the shacks I was in. On the mantel."

"Did you notice anything?" the anthropologist said.

"Just faces," the vet said. "Ugly old people wearing black clothing. Frowning. You know."

"Well, we'll see," Sharp said. "Maybe I don't know."

16

From his living room window Walter Dombrosio watched the caravan leaving Runcible's house. First came Sheriff Christen's car and then the vet and Seth Faulk in the vet's special truck, then Runcible in his well-known Studebaker, and finally Wharton and Sharp in the school teacher's station wagon. As the cars passed his house, Dombrosio saw the shovels and spades that were being carried along. The equipment with which to dig.

The procession seemed to him like some official party. He could never see the sheriff's car without having a reaction to the seal on the door and the special license plate and the radio antenna. And here the car led the others, off to the graveyard. There was no doubt in his mind; he knew where they were going. Stepping out onto his porch he watched them descend the hill to the Chevron Station. At the highway they turned right, in the proper direction.

Even the newspaper editor, he thought. Who doesn't even like Runcible; he's got him, too. He's got everyone who counts.

Along the highway the caravan of vehicles moved slowly until it disappeared out of sight beyond a grove of trees.

Hands in his pockets he went down the porch steps and out

into the road; soon he was going aimlessly down the hill, taking long strides.

I'm his idea man, he realized. He'll be famous forever. This area will be remembered because of his — *his!* — find, the way Heidelberg is known because of the skull found there.

This'll either be the Runcible Skull or the Carquinez Skull, he realized. In any case, he will have this place in the encyclopedias. And himself along, too. And I'll be like that chauffeur who found the Drake plaque. Nobody even remembers his name; he was just "the chauffeur who found the plaque." A guy looking for something to get the battery of his boss' car working.

And I can't even follow them. All I can do is walk along here by myself. And who has my car? he asked himself. Who stole it? My wife.

He continued on down the hill, walking slower and slower but still going on. How can I go back into that house? he asked himself. Back to the old drafting board. For what? What little project? Quail traps? Cow suits? How now, brown cow, he thought. Have to keep hands, fingers busy or get into trouble; get bawled out. Shame.

The banality of his thoughts horrified him, the dreadful emptiness. And at a time like this. No, he thought. Must be a hardworking breadwinner, producing away, like all other husbands. Keep family together. He jerked his hands from his pockets as he went on; he stared down at his hands, his feet, at the road — he did not look up.

A buzzing. Noise, across the valley. He did not look up. He listened. He shaded his eyes. He looked at his wristwatch. One-thirty in the afternoon.

It did sound like the Alfa. A red dot moved, far off, along the straight stretch of highway. She couldn't be coming home so early.

It's probably someone on his way up to Point Reyes, he thought. He saw the car reach the Chevron Station, and it did not turn up the hill. It continued on. So it was not Sherry; he was right.

As he watched, the Alfa slowed. It turned at the next road, Bluff Road, which led up onto a rise of land and a few houses. None of them have an Alfa, he thought. Someone from town visiting. But he had never seen or heard any other Alfa around except his own, and this one moved so confidently up the road, so rapidly, that he could not believe this was the driver's initial trip here. Strangers can't make it, he thought. Not fast on these narrow blind roads.

For a time he lost sight of it; a hill cut off his view. But he still heard it. And then, presently, the sound ceased. The Alfa had stopped at one of the houses.

Who do we know? he asked himself. Who lives there?

I can walk down to the highway and then up Bluff Road in half an hour, he said to himself. And I have nothing else to do, because she has left me nothing.

He thought, Dolly Fergesson lives there. And they are sure great buddies, the two of them.

Taking great deep breaths, he quickened his pace.

When he turned the curve on Bluff Road and caught his first glimpse of the Fergesson house, sure enough; the Alfa was parked in front of it. And now he read the license plate. It was his car. His wife was inside with Dolly. Something has happened, he said to himself. Or she wouldn't knock off in the middle of the day. Gasping, winded, he strode up the hill to the car.

In the car, lying on the front seat in plain sight, was Sherry's big leather purse. He stood for a moment, resting his hands on the door of the car and getting his breath.

Really in a hurry, he thought, to leave her purse in the car. I know what it is, he thought. I know. And all I have to do is open the purse, only catch sight of it, the little white card.

Bending, he opened the purse. Lying at the top was the card; he was right. He lifted it out. An appointment card, for today. For Dr. Gorme. The gynecologist that she went to. She's pregnant, all right. Naturally she rushed here to confer with Dolly.

He ran up the steps of the house. From beyond the front door, inside; he heard their voices. He opened the door. The two of them sat together on the couch, Dolly in old slacks, her hair tied up, his wife in suit, heels, dressed for the job. Standing at the door, he saw them jump; their faces froze and they ceased talking.

He said, "I hope it's a boy."

His wife's face lost all its color, but she said nothing. She did not answer or show any other reaction.

"Hi," he said to Dolly. She nodded a little.

Sherry said, "I'll tell you one thing." She laughed a short brisk laugh. "It won't be a boy."

"Why not?" he said. And then he saw the phonebook, the phone moved to the end of its cord and put down on the couch, the pencil and pad of paper, the unfolded note on his wife's lap. Going over to her he took hold of her by the arm and, with a tremendous pull, lifted her to her feet; she stared at him — her eyes flew open. "Come on," he said. "Okay?" He dragged her across the living room; he felt such hatred and fury at her that he grabbed her by the back of the neck, he dug his fingers into her neck and propelled her to the door.

"I won't be pushed," she snarled, at the door. Catching hold of the door with both hands she hung onto it. She grasped it and clung to it.

"We're going," he said, yanking her away from the door.

"You're going to accomplish it anyway," she panted as he tore her fingers loose and shoved her with his knee out onto the porch. "So what does it matter."

That was true, he realized. So he took her by the wrist only; he twisted her left arm until she sagged and gasped. And she came along. She kept up with him, along the short path to the car.

"I'm not going to drive," she said.

"I will," he said, pushing her down into the seat. Instantly he ran around and got behind the wheel. But she made no move to get out of the car; she stared ahead with a dead expression.

"Too bad," he said as he started up the car. "Really too bad. I really feel sorry for you."

"No you don't," she said.

He turned the car around in a driveway and drove back down the hill. For a time neither of them spoke.

"Aren't you afraid Sheriff Christen will see you driving?" his wife said at last, in a distant voice.

"No," he said.

She said, "What I do about the baby is my own business. Not yours."

"I'll be darned," he said. "It's not mine, then?"

"It's yours," she said in a quick, disconcerted way.

"Not Lausch's," he said.

"No, not Lausch's," she said.

"I don't really care," he said. "What I care about is you're pregnant; I don't care who by."

"God damn you," she said. "I know you mean it."

"Welcome home," he said.

"I'm not home," she said. "You can't keep me from getting my abortion. Dolly got an abortion a year ago when she was pregnant."

He said, "I'll keep you from getting it. You don't think I can? I'll drive you over to Sheriff Christen and have him arrest you for trying to commit a felony. For trying to murder my child."

"You liar," she said.

"I'll kill you," he said. "I'll beat the living hell out of you. And everybody'll be on my side because it's natural. Natural for a father to feel like that. With a wife like you, wanting to do a hideous un-natural act like that."

"It's just your word," she said. "I'll deny it. You know what I'll say? I'll say you got mad when you heard I was pregnant; you beat me up so I'd have a miscarriage."

"I'll have them get Dolly Fergesson on the stand, and she'll testify."

"She's a friend of mine," Sherry said. "Not yours."

"That doesn't matter. She still has to tell the truth."

"Do you think she's going to get up there and tell the truth? Admit that she had an abortion? Give out the name of her abor-tionist?"

"I know I can get some kind of court order," he said. "Restrain-ing you. It's my child as much as yours."

"You just want me pregnant so I can't work; this high and mighty talk — it's just rationalization."

"I don't hide it," he said. "I'm not rationalizing. All I care about is you can't work anymore. And he's not going to want you waddling around that place, I can tell you that. There's nothing more repulsive than a fat ugly-looking pregnant woman. Some public relations that would be." He felt glee, thinking of that, imagining her with her front bulging out, her body drooping un-der the weight. Her feet shuffling along, arches flattened by the load. "Too bad," he said, "about your figure. Maybe you'll never get it back. Even after."

"What an incredible terrible way for you to talk," she whis-pered, ashen-faced. "A husband talking to his wife like that."

"All the awful things you've said to me," he said. "In the past."

"I never attacked you so brutally as you're attacking me," she said, rallying. "You have no love for me. You never did; when you said you did you were only pretending."

"I love you," he said.

With tears in her eyes, she said in a quavering, shocked voice, "The only reason you love me is because you can hurt me."

"No," he said.

"When I need your help," she said, "you really lay it on. You would be happy if I lay down and died." She stared at him as he drove.

"No I wouldn't," he said.

"This is what I deserve," she said. "I'm a wicked selfish person and I'm getting paid back. I don't blame you. I don't see how you could ever have lived with me; I don't see how anyone could live with me or love me." From her purse she had taken her handkerchief; she pressed it to her mouth, so muffling her words that he could barely make them out. "I'm the bad one," she said. "What you're doing to me I've compelled you to do. You're just getting back. When you raped me that day — you were paying me back. I let down my guard for a minute, and you assaulted me, like some animal would. Like a male cat does to a female; he sneaks along after her, following her, and the first second she isn't watching, he jumps on her."

He said, "What a view of life. Of relations between men and women."

"But it's so," she said. "It was revenge on your part."

"Then," he said, "if you know, then don't complain. If you understand that it's revenge."

"Why?" she said. "Is revenge supposed to be a virtue?"

"An eye for an eye," he said. They had gotten back to their own house, now; he brought the Alfa to the side of the road and parked. He shut off the motor and opened the door on his side.

"I'm not going in," she said.

Grabbing her by the arm he lifted her up; he dragged her from the car.

"Let everyone see," she said. "I don't care; I want them to see you pushing me around. Like a low class drunk, which is what you are." As he propelled her up the path, she raised her voice. "You're nothing but a low class drunk who beats up his wife. You have bad taste. All you watch on TV are those low class programs like Fibber McGee and Molly. Let go of me!" At the porch she managed to tear her arm loose from his grip. Facing him, her eyes shining with defiance and rage, she said, "You unfit wop." Her mouth trembled. "You and your Negro friends." He saw her hesitate on the word; she could not bring herself, even at this time, to say nigger. She wanted to, but it would never be possible for her.

He said, "Nigger, you mean."

"I would never use that word," she said, with frenzy. "I wouldn't but you would."

Opening the door he pushed her into the house; he slammed the door after them.

Sherry said, "You couldn't beat up Lausch, so you beat up your wife instead; you beat up a helpless woman who's pregnant to boot."

"Lausch and I were good friends," he said. "Until you showed up. We got along fine."

"All right," Sherry said. "So it is me you hate." Retreating from him, she came onto the end table by the lamp. On the table were little model boats that he had built years ago when he had been in junior high; he had kept them all this time. Her eyes fixed on the boats, and he saw her hand dart down. He knew what she was going to do. "Do you think it bothers me to be disliked by a boy who never grew up?" she said, picking up one of the boats. "What do you do when you lock yourself in your workshop? Honest to god, I think you play with yourself. I think you *still* do." And she threw the model boat at him; it came sailing toward him.

He did not try to catch it. His hands reached for the chair nearby him, the white modern chair, upright; he lifted it and hurled it at his wife's head. She stood where she was, staring at the chair as it silently dropped onto her. The chair struck her, legs-first, in the chest; but he saw that only vaguely — even before it had hit her he was running across the room toward her, reaching out to take hold of her. To protect her. To salvage, to make repairs.

"Sweetheart," he said, trying to put his arms around her; she stood evidently stunned, her face blank. The chair lay at her feet. "I'm sorry," he said. "I love you. Let's stop this."

She said, "I wish either you were dead or I was dead." Her face squirmed with pain. "You could have killed me," she said in a chanting voice, a suffering voice.

"I know," he said. He still tried to take hold of her, but she slunk away; without even seeming to see him, she stepped back, and his hands could not grasp her. "Let me hold you," he said.

"Why?" she said. "To hurt me more?"

"No," he said. "I'm sorry."

"I'll never forgive you," she said. "For mistreating me. I'll make you suffer. As long as we're together. You better leave me, because it's going to be terrible for you."

"Maybe so," he said.

"I mean it," she said, more quietly. She had become calmer; she rubbed her chest. "There's this terrible thing in me," she said. "This ugly part of me. I want to do back to you twice what you do to me, every bad thing you do. You shouldn't stay. I'm sick. I know it. I'm a sick person. All this is my fault, all this awful fighting. I provoked you by this abortion business — you're right. You should beat me up for it; it's a sin. It's a crime. It's your child." Her voice dropped lower and lower; he could hardly hear her. "You have a right. If someone says they're going to murder your child. If I was any real mother I wouldn't even consider getting an abortion. That dreadful Dolly Fergesson . . . what an empty sterile life she leads. No kids, just going out for lunch, getting her hair fixed. Buying all sorts of clothes. She never does anything. I feel so sorry for her husband."

They were both silent, for a time. He did not try to touch her; he let her stand by herself, meditating and rubbing her chest.

She said, "I think you do love me."

"Yes," he said. "I do."

"The hate that you feel," she said, "isn't really for me. Do you know what it is? It's bottled-up hate you feel for Runcible, and you've turned it on me because he's out of reach and I'm here — I'm available. That's what I should be for. That's what a good wife does; she lets her husband take out his fears and aggressions on her. That's how she protects him from the world."

He said nothing.

"Isn't that so?" she said, in a halting voice.

"No," he said. "I really hate you."

"I don't believe it," she said. "You love me. You said so just now."

"I feel both," he said.

"That's not possible. You either feel one or the other. A man who loves his wife — really loves her — could never say that." She gazed at him with a hopeless, broken expression. "Won't you let me get an abortion?" she said.

"No," he said.

"You can't stop me," she said. "I'll do a lot of things like jumping down stairs — I'll induce a miscarriage. And then I'll go on working; I won't have to give up my job. I'm sorry. I know it's wrong. But I'm going to do it. I'm not going to be tied down here serving strained spinach to a snot-nosed sniffling child of yours, like some fat floozy of a housefrau."

"What I'll do," he said, "is sell the car."

"The — Alfa?"

"Yes," he said. He went to the telephone, took it and carried it to the couch.

"You need my consent," she said.

"The pink slip," he said, "says or. Either Sherry Dombrosio or Walter Dombrosio."

Sherry said, "If you sell it I'll buy another car."

"With what?"

"With the money we get for it."

"We won't get enough," he said. "I'll make sure about that."

"When you get your license back," she said, "you'll want to drive it. You'll regret it. We can't get by without it. We can't earn any money — we can't get into town. What about when it's time for the baby? How'll we get to the hospital?"

He said, "You can go in on the Greyhound bus."

"You'll kill me and economically ruin us — we'll probably lose the house."

"I don't care," he said.

"Why not?"

He said, "I just don't. Why should I?"

"All this," she said, "so I can't work?"

"More than that," he said.

"Could I go back to work after I have the baby?"

"We'll see," he said.

"You won't promise me?"

He shook his head.

"Promise me that," she said. "And I'll go ahead and have it."

"You'll have it," he said. "Anyhow."

"Please," she said.

He said nothing.

"Tell me, then," she said, "that you love me, and all that business about hating me was just your being mad."

"I love you," he said.

"Will you kiss me?"

"Sure," he said.

"Do you mean it?" She eyed him frantically.

"Yes," he said. And he did. He went to her and put his arms around her.

"You hurt me," she said. "You hit me right in the chest with that chair. Do you want to see the bruise?"

"Okay," he said.

"It probably hasn't formed yet," she said, in a small, childlike voice. "Why are you so rough? You don't realize how strong you are; you're really terribly strong. Do you know it? You could kill me. You would have. I think you were going to, for a minute."

He said, "It's a good thing you calmed us down."

"Yes," she said. "I kept you from doing something you would have felt dreadful about. Aren't you glad?" She peered at him hopefully. "I kept it from being a really awful fight, didn't I? That shows I'm a good wife, doesn't it?"

"Yes," he said, his arms around her. "You're a very good wife." He patted her. "Don't worry about that."

"I knew I was," she said, gazing past him at the wall, holding onto him determinedly, and then patting him back. "But I like to hear you say it," she said.

17

In Sheriff Christen's official car they drove out to the estero, to the old town. It was almost dark by the time they came out on the water. Two dim yellow lights could be seen on the far side. The lights were so close to the water that, to Runcible, it seemed as if the slight motion of the tide would extinguish them. As Christen drove, he watched the lights, wondering if they were still going to be there the next moment.

"How can they stand it out here?" Faulk said. "I'd go out of my mind. It's so uninhabited."

"Do you think they'll cooperate with us?" Sharp said.

The vet said, "I can't tell you. How are we going to put it? They wouldn't be able to understand why we'd want to see pictures of their parents and grandparents; we'll have to make up a story."

As they drove they considered a story. By the time they had reached the wharf they had decided to say that there was a sum of money, not very large, due on a piece of property. They did not know the name of the man to whom the money was supposed to go, but if they saw a picture of him they would recognize him.

It did not seem to any of them that it was much of a story, but probably it would do. The people would recognize Sheriff Christen and the vet, so they would know this was an official visit; that was probably more important than the story itself. Runcible, gazing out into the darkness and trying to pick out the tumbledown buildings, the shacks and abandoned stores, thought to himself that this was certainly a part of the area which he had shut from his mind. He had never taken anyone out here; in fact he could not remember ever having been here before. And yet, he thought, I must have been out here at least once.

What really are we here for? What are we trying to find out? We want to see old pictures, to see if any malformed jaw can be discovered. That was what Dudley Sharp wanted, anyhow. And what do the rest of us get out of it? he asked himself. What do I get?

We know already that malformed persons lived here once, he thought. We've seen their bones. All we could learn now is how they looked when alive. But anthropologists can reconstruct from the bones anyhow. In time we could trace the bones at the graveyard, find out who was buried where we dug. Who, for instance, the person was that Walter Dombrosio transported to my eucalyptus grove. Yes, he thought, I could find out the name of the person whose skull I found. It might even be a Bastioni. Even Angelo Bastioni himself. Born 1835, died 1895. In the sheep business, perhaps. Despite his unusual jaw.

A family, with a congenital malformation. Passed on from Angelo to Gia to Rudolfo to Petri. Well, he thought, we will be seeing some old pictures, and maybe that will end it. Then I can go back to my realty office, and Sharp can go back to Berkeley.

Or, he thought, was Angelo Bastioni possibly a Neanderthal, or partly Neanderthal? Mousterian blood, left over from the old days, from the cold winters? Angelo Bastioni, formerly a chipper of flint axes, more recently in the dairy business. Now deceased.

"Maybe we ought to forget this," he said aloud. "I don't see what we have to gain out here."

The vet said, "I tend to agree."

At the wheel the sheriff said, "It's up to you people. I'm doing this for you, not for myself." He slowed the car. "I've got plenty of other things to do."

"This is quite important," Wharton said. "Getting to the bottom of this."

"The bottom of what?" Runcible said. "It's been established that the skull was deformed from the start. Possibly we can find some trace of an hereditary taint of some kind." He felt tired and irritable; the digging at the graveyard had not been a pleasure to him. "What's the point of stirring up some old secret, that there's bad blood of some kind in some early family—" He gestured. "Whose present-day representatives live out here like Okie share-croppers. Or worse. Like something out of Steinbeck."

Sharp said, "Obviously we can't stop."

"Why not?" Runcible said.

"When the first Neanderthal skull was found," Sharp said, "years ago, it was thought to be merely a deformity."

At that, the sheriff drove on. Runcible lay back against the seat. What can I do? he asked himself. It is out of my hands. I can't stop this man, this nut from the university, from pursuing this. From digging around and dragging old crap up to the light of day.

And he thought, Nothing good is going to come to light in this lousy scummy area. Out of these chicken wire shacks and rotten old ex-stores that haven't been repaired or worked on in forty years.

There ought to be a county condemnation order made out against this dung heap, he thought. On sanitary grounds. On reasons of health. A pollution of our assets . . . our carefully maintained houses and farms are menaced. This could at least be zoned, he thought.

"Where do you want to stop?" Sheriff Christen asked.

Sharp said, "At that house with a light. Where you see a light."
I'm not going in, Runcible said to himself.

When the car had stopped, and the sheriff had turned off the motor, Runcible said, "I'm staying here. I'm not going into that pig pen and wallow around with people that dawn man wouldn't have had in his home." He found, to his amazement, that he was almost unable to speak. He felt terrible rage toward the other men in the car.

Seth Faulk, after a pause, said, "What is it, Runcible? Now that this has led into an undesirable real estate area, you're no longer interested." He, too, sounded angry. "You lost interest when you figured it might cost you some money."

"Money," Runcible said. "Listen, it's pride that would keep me from setting foot in there. I don't have any dealings with these oyster peddlers. Somebody ought to take a match and burn these shacks down. This whole business gripes me; really gripes me. We started out with something of importance, something scientific. Now what do we have? I'll tell you what we have. We're going to go to a lot of trouble to prove that there's nothing around this area — we can't dig up anything more important to humanity and mankind in general — than the degenerate ancestors of a bunch of degenerates. I'll tell you what I call that. I call that foolish. I call that moronic. And anybody interested in it is moronic. Listen, you think I sent all those telegrams and made all those phone calls and dealt with really important people in the university circles such as Bowman and Freitas — Freitas, who I understand is about the foremost authority in his field in the United States — to get out here in this place and find out that some subnebbish's grandfather had a club foot and a missing palate and talked like he had his elbow stuck in his gullet?"

His voice had risen, and the sound of it had evidently carried to the shack. The door opened, and a man appeared on the porch with a lantern. "Who's there?" he called in a stern, nervous voice.

266 · PHILIP K. DICK

The sheriff said, "This is Christen. Sheriff Christen. And the vet, Doc Heyes."

The man came cautiously toward them. "What's all the racket? You got a drunk man there?"

Ignoring the man and his lantern, Runcible said, "We have to keep this on a level that has meaning."

Sharp said, "It isn't possible to determine the meaning in advance."

"You have to wait," Wharton said. "We don't know what results we're going to get by the time we're through."

"That's how contemporary science operates," Sharp said as he got out of the car. To the man he said, "Sorry to bother you. We're looking for a particular person but we don't know his name."

In the light of the lantern, Runcible saw the man shaking hands with Dudley Sharp. Wharton, too, got out, and so did Seth Faulk. The sheriff remained behind the wheel. The vet hesitated, and then he, too, stepped from the car and came around beside Sharp and Wharton and the man with them.

"I guess I'd better go in with them," Sheriff Christen said to Runcible. "So that guy from the university doesn't go prying into any more than he has to. These people have rights; they live in this area, too. I'm supposed to look out for them." As he got out he leaned back and said in a hoarse whisper to Runcible, "I don't like that guy, that Sharp. He's always grinning; you know?" He tapped Runcible on the shoulder in a friendly manner, but Runcible did not stir. He showed no sign; he ignored the sheriff.

The door slammed. He was alone in the car. The six men moved together up the path, to the chicken wire and tar paper shack, the man's lantern lifting and falling in the darkness.

In all they visited three little old houses. Michael Wharton had been out here, before, and this half-abandoned town fascinated him. It had, to him, the ancient aura; it survived from the past, and it was the past that had always captured him. This trip was sheer delight.

But, he thought as he sat on the sofa in the third crowded tiny living room with its lamps and carpets and fringed mats and hooked rugs, this is no pleasure for Runcible. In each case the Realtor had remained in the car with an expression on his face of weariness and resentment.

They had seen a number of old pictures, now. The oyster farmers had been glad to trot out faded, crushed photograph albums tied up with yellow tassled cords; they had spread out one brownish picture after another and given complete accounts of the individuals shown. They were childishly glad to have someone come by and take some interest in them. How lonely this was out here, he realized. There was nothing for these people, now. Their chickens and sheep. Their oyster barge. And TV. In each cramped little living room a TV set sat on its table, and the members of the family had their chairs placed around it. That was why so few lights had shown. Reception was not good out here; the picture was blurred and grainy. But the people were glad to have it. And he could not blame them. In fact, as this elderly woman told them about another great aunt, and pointed again and again to the portrait photo, he found his eyes straying to the TV screen, which had been left on. Red Skelton was doing something with a bathtub, and in spite of himself he began to watch.

Sharp's voice broke him from the spell of the set. "Look," Sharp was saying to him and the vet and Seth Faulk and the sheriff. He did look, then.

On the sofa lay a group picture, showing four men. Three of the men appeared perfectly ordinary; the pictures had been taken, he guessed, about 1890. The mustaches indicated that. The men evidently were at a mountain cabin; he saw a chopping block, an ax, the clapboard side of the cabin, a dog. The men wore overalls. All had a stern, solemn expression. The fourth man, he saw, had a gigantic jaw. Even in this old picture the jaw was conspicuous. And, he thought, the man seemed stooped and smaller than the others.

The old woman droned on. Sharp pointed to the fourth man, and she continued on that topic, without a pause.

"Oh indeed," she said. "Yes, that's the chupper jaw."

"Was that his family name?" Sharp said.

The old woman — she wore a dark silk dress and black stockings, and her hair was hidden by a scarf — smiled and said, "No, not the family name at all." It seemed to amuse her and she laughed.

"Why, then?" Sharp said. "I never have heard that word."

To himself, Wharton thought, I have.

He said, "Chopper. Chipper." What was it exactly?

"Chupper," the old woman repeated.

"But it's from some other word," Wharton said.

"I never heard it pronounced anything but chupper," the old woman said.

"Where was that taken?" Sharp asked. "That picture."

"On the Ridge," the old woman said. She had told them all her name, but Wharton had not caught it. "On the east side, the other side. It was wilder in those days. Nobody living there hardly."

"They weren't farmers, were they?" Wharton said.

"No," the old woman said. "They operated the lime pits. That's how they got the name chuppers. Anybody who worked at the lime pits got called a chupper. They didn't like that; it always made them mad."

Sharp persisted, "But why the jaw?"

"Everyone who worked at the lime pits nearly always had the chupper jaw." She wanted to go on to the next picture; obviously there were more relatives to show. But Sharp stopped her.

"Did just men get it?" he said.

"No," she said. "Women too."

"Did women work at the pits?"

She stared at him in confusion. "No, of course not."

"Do you have any more pictures of the chupper jaw?" Wharton said. "I'd like to see more, if you don't mind."

Considering at length, the old woman said, "I believe I can lay my hands on another picture." Rising, she squeezed by them and out of the living room. They heard her rummaging in a drawer somewhere.

The old woman returned with a packet. Seating herself, she opened the packet by unwinding a red thread. On her lap she laid out more pictures, and from them she selected one.

This old photograph showed a young woman. Again they saw the jaw, and the heavy brows. The woman had a brutish expression, sullen and inert, as if some heavy force had settled over her; she gazed at the camera without comprehension or interest. Terrible, Wharton thought. What a terrible misfortune it was for them.

And, he thought, these people are now the bones back at the graveyard. Under the wooden crosses. Where Walt Dombrosio and Jack Vepp rooted around; they dug these people up and confronted us with them.

"It looks worse," he said to the old woman. Now he remembered the name she had called herself. "Mrs. Neeldo," he said.

Mrs. Neeldo said, "It is worse. This picture was taken—" She studied it, and then the group picture of the four men. "Taken twenty years later."

At once Sharp said, "The malformation worsened over the years?" He leaped up in agitation.

"Yes," the old woman said. "It finally got so bad they couldn't hardly eat or talk."

"What did they eat?"

Mrs. Neeldo said, "Oh, they ate a lot of porridge. Soft foods. They didn't have no teeth, some of them. They had them taken out."

"Why?" Sharp said.

"So they could talk better."

"What finally happened to them?" Sharp said. "There're no more chupper-jawed people, are there? Aren't they all dead?"

Mrs. Neeldo, reflecting, said, "I believe the last person with a chupper jaw died in 1923. Just a moment." She called into the next room, "Arthur, when did the last person you know of have the chupper jaw, and when did he die?"

A man's voice from the other room answered, "You were right; about 1923."

"But," the old woman said, "most of them moved away anyhow. Before then."

"Why?" Sharp said.

"Well," Mrs. Neeldo said, "it was so terrible; it was getting so much worse. All of them living on that side of the Ridge were getting it. We didn't get it over here." In the group picture she pointed out one of the men, not the man with the chupper jaw. "That was my great uncle. He worked cutting down trees with these others. That man with the jaw; his name was Ben Taber. When that picture was taken he wasn't working at the lime pits; he had quit. He came over the Ridge for a while and lived here, in Carquinez."

"They thought by moving away from the lime pits—" Wharton began.

"Yes," Mrs. Neeldo interrupted. "They had a settlement by the pits. Roads were so bad, then. Nothing but dirt."

"What caused the jaw?" Wharton said.

"The water on that side," Mrs. Neeldo said.

"The water," the vet said, after a time.

"Yes," she said. "It had some kind of salt in it that gave them a poison. They got it from their wells that they dug."

The vet said, "The lime pits aren't far from Poor Man's Hollow." He stared at Wharton. "Actually, not far from Carquinez."

"This is Carquinez," Mrs. Neeldo said. "Oh, you mean the new town. That's so. Well, we don't get over there very much."

"Where did they move to?" Sharp said.

"Up north," Mrs. Neeldo said. "Up into Oregon. Along the coast somewhere. I can find out the name of the town for you. As far as I know they're still up there. Those people."

"The lime pits," Seth Faulk said. "The water. We've always known our water supply was contaminated."

"Can I smoke?" Sheriff Christen said, reaching into his breast pocket. Wharton could not tell if he understood; his face showed nothing.

"Surely, Sheriff," Mrs. Neeldo said. "I'll get you an ashtray." She rose and hurriedly looked about the room.

When they had left the house and gotten back into the car, Leo Runcible glared at them without speaking. At last, when Christen had started up the car and was heading back toward the Ridge, Runcible said,

"What did it have to do with?"

Wharton said, "The water."

"I knew that damn water was going to give us a black eye some day," Runcible said. "That water company ought to be put under arrest. That repairman — he looks like some shambling cave man himself. He's worse than a Neanderthal; he's something on the level of the Peking man. The first time I saw him I knew there was some god damn thing wrong with the water; he must live in it. That stuff comes out of the pipe as black as sheep shit. My god, you go to fill a glass and it's swill; it's unfit for animals. You can see the bugs floating around in it."

Wharton said, "It's minerals in the soil or something." None of them felt like speaking.

Staring out of the car window, Leo Runcible thought, You morons. That's what you are; a bunch of morons. I told you so.

"Here's how I feel," he said, when none of the rest of them had said anything for a time. During his long stay alone in the car he had had time to do a good deal of meditating. "You're probably aware now what a moronic idea it was to go out to that godforsaken podunk, those oyster shacks and people with nothing to do all day but whittle on the pier. Isn't that right? I mean, let's be reasonable. Haven't you pushed the thing far enough as it is? We're all conscious of the foolishness that this has turned into; I mean, my god. Nobody wants this. I see no point in this. Do you?"

None of them answered.

"Well, I'll tell you," Runcible continued. "Let's just forget the whole thing. Let sleeping dogs lie. Isn't that right? Isn't that a grain of common sense in this whole foolish god damn mess? I say, if we have any sense — and I know we do — let's get the hell out of here. Are you with me? Do you follow me? Let's not rush out like a bunch of howling wolves and spill over our chins." To Seth Faulk he said, "That newspaper of yours; it won't be any bigger or better; it won't have done any better job of serving the community by printing a lot of inflammatory crap about the water supply and the boogie man that's going to get us. I mean, who benefits? There are ways and ways. And I'll tell you; the quiet way is the best way."

Presently Wharton said, "We only have the viewpoint of one old woman. We have no evidence that the water supply is — or was — involved."

"There you see," Runcible said, spreading his hands in the darkness of the car. "What the hell — some old crone in there gives out with her ten-dollar's worth of spiel — my god, she's probably been sitting in there for thirty-five years boning up that pitch. Do you call this science? I'll tell you what I call it; I call it old wives' tales. Isn't that so?" He addressed the five of them in the car with him.

The vet said, "There are some things for the good of the area that aren't worth making public."

"There, that's what I mean," Runcible said. "Let's face facts;

are we adults? Are we grown men? Or are we like those horses' asses at Donkey Hall, a bunch of overgrown boys playing pranks, goosing women by sticking electric shocks up their skirts? I know something that you know; there's been bubonic plague in California for years, now. And it's hushed up. You have to hush it up. We live in this area. We have our homes here. Our kids go to school here. Am I right?"

It had seemed such a reasonable statement to make, earlier, as he had sat alone in the car. We have our families and businesses, here, he was telling them; he spoke in his most powerful, mature manner, the one he used at the crucial moment in a sale, when the client was wavering on the now-or-never brink. Whether to sign or not.

"We have a responsibility," he said. "To the merchants here, to the families, the farmers. To the area itself." And then, in the darkness, he saw Sharp sitting there, outlined against the car window. And he thought, My god, that's right. That bastard does not live here. He's from outside the county.

Runcible said, "Sharp, what do you say."

The man said nothing.

"Come on," Runcible said. "Are you going to play some kind of big time game, or are you going to take into account the lives of living human beings who work here and live here?"

Sharp said, "This whole business has to be looked into."

"Why?" Runcible said.

"It could be vital new material for the field."

Runcible said, "You mean you might make your fugging reputation on it. Isn't that more what you mean?"

The man said nothing.

"Okay," Runcible said. "You go ahead and research this; you bring a bunch of ninnies like yourself in here and fart around and dig up what you can, and maybe you will dig up something; maybe you will finally find out that you've got a bunch of degenerates living around the turn of the century who got some bone disease by working in the lime pits. Miners get a disease. Factory workers get a disease. Maybe you can even prove the crap that did it to them is still in the water, only maybe not so much now because we have pipes instead of wells. And maybe you can even get people to stop moving out here because they don't want to wake up some morning and discover that their faces have swelled up and they're deformed and can't eat and talk and look like something out of the pages of the *Brittanica* that walked the earth forty million years ago. Or forty thousand. Whatever it is."

"There's a lot in what Runcible says," the sheriff said.

"True," Sharp said. "We can conduct a quiet study. We don't have to broadcast it."

"You think those fugging newspapers will let you keep it a quiet study?" Runcible said. "Those big time sensational yellow San Francisco newspapers?"

"We still have to go ahead," Sharp said.

"You turd," Runcible said.

"Easy, now," the vet said. "Take it easy."

Runcible thought, Yes, you're all turds. You're all of you on my turd list. And by god it'll be another forty million years before you get off. That goes for all five of you. Who needs you.

When they had gotten back across the Ridge and were getting near the highway, Runcible broke the silence and said,

"It wouldn't be any skin off my nose to leave this area. I've done every god damn thing in the world for this place. I'm tired. The hell with it. I've had all I can stand of hick farmers standing around up to their waists in sheep shit."

No one said anything to that for a time, and then Seth Faulk said, "Sure, you can move on and open a realty office somewhere else. You can always move on."

"Meaning what?"

"You weren't born here," Faulk said. "You don't have any real ties here. The only reason you're here is for the profit. The fast buck. Everybody in town knows that."

Wharton said, "That's untrue. There's no truth in that."

The sheriff, at the wheel, said, "Be quiet, Faulk."

"No," Runcible said. "I like to hear the jerk. Listen, Faulk. You know what I'm going to do? I'm going to stop advertising in that boring moronic once-a-week sheet of yours, and you know what's going to happen then? You'll go out of business."

"The hell I will," Faulk said.

Wharton said, "What really is the worst that can come of this?"

Runcible said, "Everybody will move out of here, and this will become an abandoned area."

"I doubt if it'll go that far," Christen said. "There'll be a scare for a while, but maybe we'll get a new water supply out of it."

"You're nuts," Runcible said. "Real grade A nuts."

When they got to Runcible Realty he opened the car door and stepped out without a backward look. The car drove off and he went on to his own car. As he got into it he realized that he still had on the old workclothes that he had worn for the digging. His trousers were caked with dirt.

Going to the office, he unlocked it and entered. In the back he had several suits hanging up in the closet; he took off the work clothes, put on a clean shirt, a tie, and then a pressed, fresh suit that was a favorite of his. Then he locked up the office and went to his car.

The hell with looking like that, he said to himself. Like a bum. Like one of those fruit pickers or oyster farmers.

The suit made him feel better, but not much better.

This is really lousy, he said to himself. This thing really has turned out bad. That moron Dombrosio. That grade A moron.

As soon as he had gotten home he went into his study and picked up the telephone book. To his wife he said, "Listen, what's the name of that guy who owns the water company. Do you remember?"

From the kitchen, Janet appeared. "I — forget," she said.

He managed to get hold of the water company repairman at his home. From him he got the name of the owner of the company. The owner, an elderly retired man, lived in Sonoma County, in Fountain Grove. Doesn't even live in Marin County, Runcible thought to himself as he sat by the phone while the operator made the connections.

Presently a gruff male voice said, "Hello."

"Mr. Neroni," Runcible said. "Sorry to interrupt your dinner."

"Who is this?" the old man demanded.

"My name is Leo Runcible," Runcible said. "Listen, sir, I have some business I want to talk to you about. Urgency in this matter is of the essence." He stared at the wall on the far side of the desk. "I'd like to see you tonight." Glancing at his wristwatch he said, "If you don't object I'll drop over to your place about eight this evening, and we can get this expedited. Is that satisfactory?"

The old man said, "We were going out to the movie."

"This can't wait," Runcible said. "It involves the net worth of your Carquinez Water Company. The West Marin Water Company," he corrected, glancing down at a water bill.

"I see," Neroni said. "Well, I'll tell you. That doggone water company. Want me to be frank?"

"Yes I do," Runcible said.

"I've been losing money in that company for ten years straight. I've never made any secret about that."

"Yes, that's my understanding," Runcible said.

"I wish somebody would take it off my hands. All it amounts to is a yearly tax write-off. Is that what you want to do? Bid for it? Put in an offer? I'll sell it to you; you don't even have to come over here, if that's what you want to find out. We can settle it right now on the phone, or I can give you the name of my broker and you can come to an agreement with him."

Tilting all the way back in his chair, Runcible said, "Frankly, sir, I doubt very much if the West Marin Water Company is worth buying."

"If you don't want to buy it, what do you want? What is this about?"

"I'll see you at eight," Runcible said. "Possibly we could work out some kind of transaction. I have highly valuable unimproved land I could make available. On the Bolinas Ridge. It could be subdivided, if roads were put in. Of course, that would take a businessman with real acumen and an ability to see the forces at work in the future."

They talked further, and then Runcible rang off. The man was definitely interested; no doubt of that. And well he might be.

Going from his study to the kitchen, Runcible said to his wife, "Who would you consider the most prominent rancher in the area?"

"I wouldn't want to say," she said tremulously. "Maybe Enrico over on the lagoon. Or Reilly."

"They're going to have to put up," Runcible said.

"For what?"

"For the Carquinez Water Improvement Association." He reported back to his study and shut himself in. First he called Bill Baron, the reporter on the San Rafael *Journal*, whom he had known off and on for years, and who had been giving him sympathetic coverage on the Neanderthal find. "Listen, Bill," Runcible said, as soon as he had hold of him. "You want something? You *really* want something? I'll give it to you. Get yourself set. It's the water."

"What's the water?" Baron said.

"That skull. That so-called Neanderthal skull. If I didn't respect you and think so much of you I wouldn't be sitting here now. I'd be out somewhere having a short and well-earned respite. So remember me. Will you?" He paused. Taking a deep breath he let out a long noisy sigh. "It isn't a hoax and it isn't a scientific discovery. It's a medical fact that has to be dealt with in a resolute and immediate manner. There's some kind of toxic substance in the soil that gets into the bones."

"I see," the reporter said, with interest.

"What we're doing," Runcible said, "you understand, there's been a long time since this bone ailment cropped up. But we have to take precautions. We're dealing here with the country. We have to recognize that. Otherwise, there'll be a lot of hysterical fat-assed people running around crying head for the hills." He stared up at the ceiling. "We've formed a group of public-spirited responsible people in the area and we're going to buy the water company. It's in outside hands right now, incidently. It needs work done. Lots of work. We're going to have a brand new water system, new pipes, new pumps, absolutely the best purifying system imaginable. Regular inspection — the works."

"And who's going to put up the money?"

"The prominent people in the area," Runcible said. "The men who count. The men who care about the future of this area. Don't worry about that part."

"You have their commitment already?"

Runcible said, "I don't need their commitment. I know them." He gave the reporter the whole story, all the details he could think of. And then he hung up and sat for a while.

It's now or never, he decided. Using the number on his desk list, he dialed George Enrico, at Red Dam Ranch.

When Enrico answered, Runcible said, "This is Leo Runcible, and you're going to be sorry you heard from me. I'll tell you why. Do you have a minute? You better have, George. Your cows' lives are involved in this, that's why. What do you use, incidently?

Well water or piped water or what?" He leaned back until he was comfortable in his chair. "Evidently the water around here is contaminated."

Enrico said, "Everybody knows that."

"We have to buy the damn water company and remake it," Runcible said. "There's no choice. I'll tell you why. You can listen; it's worth your valuable time."

After he had talked to Enrico he called Thomas Reilly and then, one after another, the other big ranchers in the area. He finished barely in time to get out of the house and into his car for the drive up to Fountain Grove.

As he started up his car, Janet came out of the house after him. "Your dinner," she said anxiously. "Can't you eat?"

"No," he said. "I can't."

I know they'll come through, he said to himself as he drove. They'll chip in; they have to. It's in their interest. Common sense, sheer practicality, will swing it.

And if they don't, he said to himself, then I'll have to. I wonder if I can. He thought, I wonder how much it will cost to rebuild the water company, from top to bottom. Forty thousand dollars? A hundred thousand? Five hundred thousand?

Jesus Christ, he thought. They just have to chip in.

And I know they will. My intuition tells me they will.

18

At their Christmas Eve party, Janet Runcible became drunk and talked to everyone about personal problems. To a new couple that had moved into the area she told the news that she and Leo were overdrawn at the Novato Bank to the tune of three thousand dollars.

"It's already been thirty days," she said, leaning past two men who were talking together. Painstakingly keeping the attention of the new couple, she continued, "And Harry — that's our banker — called and said that he thinks so much of us we can go another sixty days if we want. It's a form of loan. He has that much respect and confidence in Leo."

The new couple nodded and listened, but it seemed to Janet that they were not too interested.

"Excuse me," she said, then, and, getting to her feet, she walked carefully past them, into the kitchen with her empty glass.

Half of the new couple, the young wife, appeared in the doorway and asked if she could help. She was a short, rather heavy-set young woman, with a pretty face marred by makeup. Her husband had been transferred to this part of the country by the Federal Government; he did something connected with ocean surveys.

"Martha," Janet Runcible said. "You know, when you get to

know my husband better you'll understand what a wonderful fabulous person he is." She smiled at the younger woman, waiting to see on the girl's face an answering smile, one of sympathy and understanding.

As many people had showed up at the Christmas Eve party this year as any of the years before; the Runcible house was filled up with talk and people and motion. The front door opened and shut, as someone either arrived or left; she could not see which.

Martha Leghorn said, "I like your husband very much."

"But you don't know him." Janet said. A mood of deep sorrow overcame her as she stood at the sideboard pouring Djinn— their mainstay drink, these days; gin with angostura bitters— from the half-gallon jug into her glass.

"He seems to know about so many topics," Martha said, seating herself at the table. "I feel so ignorant. All I know to talk about is — well, I don't know. Somebody said something about Shakespeare, and I remember I read *Macbeth* in college."

"May I refill your glass?" Janet said.

"No thank you," Martha said. "Bob doesn't like me to drink too much." She lowered her voice. "He's always saying I drink too much when I'm out. He's very strict. He comes from the South, you know. From Atlanta. They're very straightlaced there."

"Where were you born?" Janet said.

"In Modesto," Martha said.

"Do you like it here? Isn't it beautiful here?" She felt, then, the beauty of the countryside, the Ridge, the fir forest, the ocean. "This is a paradise," she said. "You're so lucky you moved here. And when you get to know the people better you'll find they're just wonderful. So friendly. So helpful. There isn't a thing they wouldn't do for you."

"We like our house," Martha said. "Your husband saw to it that we got a good one. He went over the foundation himself."

Janet said, "To Leo nothing is more important than that the

people who come to him and depend on him are happy." Putting down her glass, she went over to the girl and took hold of her hands. "You must be happy. I want you to promise me. To us it's the most important thing in the world." And, as so many times before, tears sprang up to her eyes.

Standing at the window, Sherry Dombrosio gazed up the hill at the lights of the Runcible house. She saw all the cars parked; she heard the noise. "Quite a party this year," she said.

"Why not?" Walt said. "He serves good liquor. He knows how to get people to show up. But I'm not interested in getting people that way. By bribing them."

Sherry said, "I don't see how he can afford it. Isn't he supposed to be on the ropes? The girl at the grocery store told me that his bill is three months overdue. He hasn't paid them since last October."

"Sure he's on the ropes," Dombrosio said. "But he'll recoup. His whole life is like that. He'll borrow, or get hold of some land and speculate on it. That kind of person never gives up."

"Who would lend to him?" Sherry said. "He has no assets, now that he sold that land on the Ridge. At least that's what I hear. But of course you're always hearing so many rumours about him and no one can ever pin him down or get the truth out of him."

"He'll get some pal who's a banker to back him," Dombrosio said. "They all work together — they buy off one another."

"He couldn't use his water company as an asset, could he?"

"No," Dombrosio said. "It's too encumbered. You saw that article in the *News.*"

Turning from the window, Sherry wandered aimlessly about the living room. Her great stomach — she had been pregnant now for five months — swayed out ahead of her, and she at last sank down in a chair. The restless, fretful frown that he had seen so much of late had once again appeared on her face. In the end, she had not taken happily to quitting her job. But a pregnant woman could not make the drive into the City, let alone hold the kind of public relations position that Lausch had wanted her for. On her last day at work, that evening when she had gotten home, she had become hysterical. He had never seen her really so before that. For a week she had avoided him, lying in bed until almost noon, hurling dishes at him during meals, shutting herself in the bedroom as soon as dinner was over.

Too bad, he thought as he watched her. Tough luck. The biological heritage betrayed you, didn't it? Woman's weakness. They say smart employers are wary of that, of hiring women because of that. I don't blame them.

"God, I feel nauseated," Sherry said. "I should be over that by now, the sixth month. I'm so bloated — I'm nothing but a big bag of gas."

"Can I get you anything?" he asked.

"No," she said shortly.

"Some ginger ale." He went to the refrigerator and opened it. "What about a piece of pie?" he said.

"I can't eat starch. I'm supposed to lose four pounds by the end of the month. And it's almost the end and I still weigh one hundred and forty-five pounds." She stared down morosely as he walked past her with his piece of pie. "Do you have to eat that in here?" she demanded. "Couldn't you eat it somewhere else? You know I can't stand to see you eating when I can't. It's unfair."

He said, "It was your idea to get pregnant."

"No it wasn't. It was yours." Her eyes flashed in fury. "I didn't want to; I never wanted to at any time."

"Too late now," he said.

Too late, he thought, to wish you had your old figure back. And your job. It isn't natural for women to work anyhow, he said to himself. This is natural, this gigantic bulk, this pregnancy. It should have happened a long time ago; then there never would have been the trouble between us in the first place.

Now we are both where nature intended us to be, he said to himself. I have a job; you have your pregnancy. I go away from home at six in the morning and return at seven in the evening; you are here all day peeling potatoes and dusting. Too bad if you don't like it, because that is the way it is. Don't blame me.

With a tremor of irritability, Sherry said, "You can hear the racket all the way down here. What's the point of living out in the country? We might as well be living in a multiple-unit apartment in Oakland."

"I guess a lot of people felt they had to go," Dombrosio said. "Out of gratitude. For him fixing up the water."

"Well, I don't feel any gratitude," Sherry said. "Do you care to know how I feel? I think that man has jeopardized our lives and health and future."

Dombrosio said, "How do you mean?"

With her hands she indicated her distended womb. "I have to live in constant anxiety. We both do."

"There's nothing in that chupper jaw crap," Dombrosio said. And he had to laugh. It always amazed him to hear her, on this topic; he had never been able to accept the fact that a woman of her education, background and intelligence took it seriously.

Sherry said, "It happened once — it can happen again any time. Any child born in this area; you know that. I've been drinking that contaminated water for years and so have you. Isn't that so?" She paced about the room. "And there's no way we can tell until it's born; that's the dreadful part. We have no idea what's going to come out. God in heaven, I could be creating some dreadful freak inside me, keeping it growing." She shuddered.

"And it's Runcible's fault," Dombrosio said.

"Yes," she said.

"Why?"

She said with absolute conviction, "Because there wasn't any anxiety about it before he made an issue out of it."

Yes, Dombrosio thought. That's right; Runcible made an issue out of it. She's correct. No one worried about it before that.

So in her mind, Runcible is responsible — possibly even responsible for the fact that she is pregnant. And in that case, in her unreasonable system, Runcible would be responsible for her having had to give up her job.

"Did he cost you your job?" Dombrosio asked her.

She gave him a look of malice.

"Answer me," he said.

"The question is foolish," she said. But in her voice, and in her expression, she showed that on some deep level she did hold the man responsible for her fall, for her loss of position.

"It would be ironic," Dombrosio said. "If you did give birth to a child with the chupper jaw." Ironic, he thought, because it was I who dug that skull up and doctored it; it was I who brought the chupper jaw back into view for the first time in decades. My historic role.

"Why ironic?" Sherry said.

That's right, he thought. You don't know, even now. It has never come out and you have never guessed. Who does know? he asked himself. Wharton and that anthropologist, so I presume Leo Runcible.

He said, "Maybe we should drop up there for a few minutes. To the party."

"Why?" Sherry said.

"And shake hands. Wish him whatever it is you wish. Let bygones be bygones." He had seen, not long ago, Wharton go by in his car. And Wharton and Runcible had not been speaking for months. "This is the time of year," he said. "Doesn't Christmas affect you that way?"

"No," Sherry said. "And I'm not going up there."

Going to the window, Walt Dombrosio gazed up at the lights of the Runcible house; he listened to the noise and saw the motion and the parked cars, the open front door. Most of the guests were not from the area, he had noticed; the cars, by and large, were from out of town. We're not the ones who go up there, he realized. Not area people.

"I think I ought to go up," he said to his wife. "Have a drink with him and show I don't harbor any grudge against him, for what he did." This time of year did affect him, even if it did not move Sherry's hard heart. "That was a long time ago," he said, "when he called the police on me. I'm not one to hold grudges anyhow; you know that." He was thinking now that after all he had forgiven her for what she had done, for plotting and scheming to get a job at Lausch Company, for siding with Lausch against him, for the color-blindness business — for all the careful cruelties she had practiced against him.

Her eyes narrow, Sherry said, "I don't see how you could. I don't see how you can forgive a man like that. After what he's done to us. It would be a betrayal of me, if nothing else." She touched her stomach, grasping it, stroking it, an automatic gesture, now; she seemed always aware of it, in every situation. "Walt," she said, "if there is anything wrong with this baby, if there's any deformity — the other night I lay awake thinking about it. What would we do? How would we survive? Our first baby — suppose he *was* some kind of freak. Would we put him in a home, or what? Should we keep him? I just don't know." Anxiously, she regarded him. "At night when you're asleep — my god, you go right off to sleep — it seems so real. Of course, it doesn't seem so real right now. You know how nocturnal fears are."

"The baby will be okay," he said. "You're not being rational."

"Everyone who sees me," she said, "who lives here and knows I'm pregnant — they're thinking about the baby and wondering if it'll be normal. I can tell; it's true. Everybody is waiting to see."

Yes, they're waiting, he thought. It was true; it was not in his wife's mind. The penalty, he thought. For living in a rural area. The ancient superstitions. Maybe we ought to move out of here, he thought. But no. We're part of this area. We want our child born here.

"I guess I won't go up there," he said. "It would be sentimental. I'd regret it in a couple of days." Instead, he seated himself and picked up the evening paper. He began to read, and soon he had become involved in it, as he did every night at this time.

But by and by his attention lagged and he knocked off reading to think once more. If a case can be made out that Leo Runcible is responsible for the condition of our baby, he thought, then why stop with that? Why not carry out such logic to its conclusion? In a sense, Runcible *is* responsible for the fact that there will be a baby at all, that Sherry is pregnant in the first place.

He thought, If I hadn't gotten into such a fight with her that Saturday morning when I got home with the slip from the bank, we never would have gone to bed so abruptly, without contraception. Runcible, he thought, made my wife pregnant, the god damn bastard. And at that, he smiled to himself.

"Why are you smiling?" Sherry said.

I see, he thought. I see how the reasoning goes. How she makes it work. Terrific. It's possible to do anything with people, facts and events; they can be reshaped, the way I reshape wet plastic in the workshop. Form is imprinted on them, through very forceful ways.

Who really made her pregnant? he asked himself. And why? And, he thought, what does it mean? It means that she has lost out in some deep and irreversible way, that she can't get now what she wanted to get. And, he thought, I'm no longer in jeopardy from her; the constant, tireless pressure is gone. I can relax. For instance, I can stand at the window and look up the hill at Runcible's house and his wild party and not feel upset. I can read the paper with tranquility. I can come and go as I please, and she can't stop me.

And I did it, he thought. By bringing Chuck Halpin home that night. That made Runcible mad; that made him call the highway patrol on me when I got stuck in the ditch. My bringing Chuck here cost me my job at Lausch Company and got Sherry her job there; it got me started working on the skull — the whole business. He thought, It got Leo Runcible steamed up so that he made an ass out of himself, as usual; he went off the deep end and wound up financially ruined and owning a water company that will keep him ruined for the rest of his life. Let's say I got him into that water company, he said to himself. I ruined him. And *I* got Sherry pregnant; I did it all — no one else did a god damn thing except shoot off their mouths — Runcible to everybody, Sherry to me.

They talked, he decided, but I did something. I didn't just stand around gassing.

And yet, he thought, maybe Runcible will get the last word. He felt a tremor of uneasiness as he thought about the baby.

Standing near him, Sherry said, "You're as scared as I am about the baby. I can tell by the way you're sitting, and the expression on your face. But you won't admit it. Even to yourself."

Am I? he wondered. Possibly. Again he laid down his newspaper.

Runcible's revenge, he thought. His way of getting back at us. Through our child.

In his mind he had a vivid image, almost a hallucination, of the future. All the details were there; they entered his mind in a throng. God, get away! he thought.

He saw himself and Sherry.

Together they drove up the street. He had on his good wool suit, tie, the black shoes he had gotten for Christmas. Sherry was dressed-up, also; she had on earrings, a little white cap-like hat with a trailing net, powder and eyebrow pencil and mascara and her new lipstick, her fur cape and light brown suit, her high heels with metal ends, the ones that always hurt her ankles so. On her lap she held her shiny black purse, which she had never before used or even taken out of the box in which it had come. As the car moved along she stared out at the tall old-fashioned houses, saying nothing. He concentrated on the numbers, and searched for a parking place.

Between them on the seat their little boy sat with his hands on his knees. They had dressed him up, too; they had, in addition to scrubbing his neck and face and ears, combed his hair and gotten him to put on his pressed pants and polished shoes and white shirt. Over the shirt he wore his sweater. He carried with him a five-cent balsawood glider which they had picked up at the drugstore for him; of course they had had to assemble it. He had not flown it, yet. They had promised him that he could, as soon as they got where they were going. He could fly it at the school, assuming there was space. They were sure there would be . . .

"Almost there," Walt Dombrosio said.

"Yes," Sherry murmured. She shifted about and crossed her legs, smoothing down her skirt and picking at a bit of white lint.

"Light me a cigarette," he said.

Opening the glove compartment, she rummaged about. "I can't find any," she said. "I didn't bring my own. Do you have to?"

"No," he said. "Forget it." Now he had caught sight of the building, the old, unpainted, wooden three-story house that had been converted several years ago to the nursery school. The special day school. The yard had been cleared of trees and bushes and flowers — he could compare the other houses and yards in the block — and asphalt pavement had been put down. Various children's devices had been set up: a jungle gym, a revolving wheel on which the children rode, slides, seesaws, the canvas swings popular with pre-school children. A high metal Cyclone fence surrounded the yard and building.

"I dislike those metal fences," Sherry said.

"Yes," he said. "Makes it look like a prison."

"They always have that look," she said. "Even if there are roses in them. Have you ever seen anybody grow roses in them? It's like blood or something. Red roses. Paul Scarlets."

He parked the car across the street.

"Are we early?" she said. "Do we have to go right in?"

"We're on time," he said. "Don't be nervous."

"School always made me nervous," she said. "I always wanted to run away or throw up or wet my pants. Even when I was in high school." Sitting up high, she turned the rear view mirror to get a glimpse of herself, her face in particular. "Repressed rebellion, I imagine." Opening her purse she got out her lipstick.

He and the boy waited while she touched up her lips.

"Ready?" he said, finally.

"Yes," she said. She smiled briefly at him.

With the boy between them, holding onto both of them, they walked slowly across the street, very formally and silently. A few children were outside playing in the yard, and they looked up.

"Doesn't that look like fun?" Sherry said, bending to speak to their boy. "Those slides, and all those other babies. So many babies to play with."

"Not babies," Walt Dombrosio said. "Don't call them that, for christ's sake. They're children." She had for some reason picked up the habit of calling all pre-grammar school children "babies," and it irritated him.

Between them, clutching their hands, the boy began to sniffle.

"Yeah," Walt said. "This'll be fun." He squeezed his son's hand. They reached the cars parked on that side of the street, and he let go of his son's hand so that Sherry could lead him between two cars and up onto the sidewalk.

Seeing the wide old wooden steps of the building, the huge railings, the boy started to cry. But at the same time, Walt Dombrosio saw, he was excited. He was trembling, trying at the same time to see and to shrink back behind his mother.

The front door of the building had opened and a woman, smiling broadly, stepped out and held her hand down in greeting. The teacher who operated the school, Miss Thackman, coming down the steps and bending to say hello to their boy. Speaking to him the moment she saw him.

"Jimmy Dombrosio," she said, her eyes sparkling with friendliness. "I'm so glad to meet you. Do you know who I am, Jimmy? I'm Miss Thackman. I'm going to be your teacher. We're going to have lots and lots of fun." And she led him away from his parents; Walter Dombrosio felt his son's fingers loosen as he moved up the steps with Miss Thackman. Beside him, Sherry had become pale with tension. She shot a quick glance of panic at him.

"It's okay," he said to her, putting his hand against her back and gently urging her forward, up to the porch and through the door that Miss Thackman held open for them. Now they had come into a dark hallway, with doors open here and there.

An exceptional school, he thought. For the exceptional child. This heavy, middle-aged woman with her dry face, no makeup, dress wrinkled and spotted with paints and clay, this teacher, psychologist, social worker rolled into one, leaning down, smiling as she led their son along the carpeted hall to her office. Already filling him with anticipation, picturing to him in her mannish, hearty voice the games the children played, the toys they had, the exciting things they did — he felt his tension ease, a little. She had the situation so well in hand; she was so clearly a professional.

"And you'll have a table," she was saying. "All your own. And you can slop it up all you want; won't that be fun?"

The little boy was looking up at her. The slow little face, the slow reaction. So dulled, he thought. So stupid. Attempting to understand, to follow what she was saying. She has to talk more slowly, he thought with anger. Doesn't she know that? She's had others; that's the whole point. The whole reason for bringing him here and not somewhere else. This is supposed to be the place.

Beside him, Sherry said in a barely audible voice, "Among the children outside, in the yard. Did you—" Her voice ceased.

"I didn't see any," he said. "They're probably under closer supervision. Because of falls. Bodily injury. Didn't they tell us that's a problem?"

"Yes," his wife said as they entered the office. Her voice had a flat, deadened quality and her face, under her little veil, was stark. He moved a chair up for her and she seated herself in front of Miss Thackman's desk, arranging her skirt and putting her purse down carefully where she could get at it. As he also found a chair he saw her open her purse and look to see if she had her checkbook and pen; she removed her gloves, put them into her purse, and halfway drew out the checkbook. Turning her head, she said to him, "Broken arms or something. A lot of stumbling. You know."

"Well," Miss Thackman said, dropping into the old-fashioned oak swivel chair behind the desk. She reached up and led Jimmy around to her. "My," she said, still smiling; she had never ceased to smile, nor had she ever ceased keeping her eyes fixed on the boy. She had gotten him to smile back, to keep a smile as equally fixed. Walt Dombrosio thought, She has already gained control. And that has to be. That is very important.

The woman, he thought, devoted to this. Trained for this, to handle the retarded child, the special child, the malformed child. Not flinching, not showing any reaction at the sight of the heavy jaw, the ridged brows, the stooped posture, the idiotic, empty face with its timid hopefulness and anxiety . . . of course, this is not the first time; she has — what is it? — seven of them, here. Among the other children.

"Stick out your tongue," Miss Thackman was saying to their boy. "And say ahh." She waved a flat tongue depressor, and the boy after a moment obediently opened his mouth. Humming to herself, she inserted the tongue depressor and, squinting, gazed at what she saw; with her right hand she wrote notes in a ledger on the desk. What is it she's seeing? Walt Dombrosio asked himself. Not really whether his throat is red or his tongue is coated. This is a ritual that we've all gone through, but it is something different, here, in this case. It is the teeth, the jaw. That is what she's examining. The palate. Because, he thought, she wants to know what hope there is for speech therapy.

To him, Miss Thackman said, "Who did you say you had working with him? Calder?"

"Yes," Sherry said. "We've been bringing him in three times a week. For two years, now." She had lit a cigarette, but he saw her hand tremble too badly; she put the cigarette out. "To San Rafael," she said. "Calder isn't there, but his clinic is."

"Yes," Miss Thackman said. She put the tongue depressor into the wastebasket, and then, folding her hands, she said to the boy in a booming, expectant voice, "Now, James L. Dombrosio— tell me something." Very slowly and deliberately, she said, "Tell me how you feel."

The massive jaw moved. Walter Dombrosio set himself; he half-shut his eyes and stopped his breathing. Beside him his wife did the same.

The boy said, "I-I-I—" He broke off. "F-f-f-f—" he said,

294 · PHILIP K. DICK

and the sounds sputtered away; saliva dribbled, and at once Miss Thackman, with no sign of emotion, produced a Kleenex and wiped the boy's chin.

Sherry said, "He can do better when he's alone with us."

"Fine," Miss Thackman boomed. "Well, Jimmy," she said, clapping her hands to his shoulders and rising from her chair. "Do you want to go down now and meet the other children? And play?"

The boy's eyes glowed. He spluttered; no words came, only hoarse sounds, wet and muffled. But the desire was obvious. Miss Thackman, smiling, took his hand and led him carefully toward the door of the office; she did not hurry him, but let him come at his own pace.

As the boy passed in front of Walt Dombrosio, he thought to himself, There he goes. Off to be taken care of, to be given trained care. Professional care. By competent, sympathetic people. As he will be for the rest of his life, probably. It's too soon to know, he thought. We'll know — we'll all know — in a few more years.

The profile, he thought as he saw his son's jaw moving; the boy was still trying to speak. Exactly the way I produced it. The way I carved and molded and cut, down in the basement of the Hall. All that work. All the research. I got what I wanted, though; I got it perfect. Accurate, complete. Authentic.

After Miss Thackman and their son had left the room, he and Sherry sat without speaking. At last she said in a jerky, strained voice, "What are we supposed to do, I wonder? Sit? Wait?"

"I guess so," he said.

"It's almost too much for me," she said.

"We'll be going back home in a few minutes," he said.

"To see her leading him off," she said.

"I know," he said, aloud.

"What?" Sherry said, standing at the window of their living room.

At once he was out of his thoughts, his imagination; he saw her standing with her hands resting on her enormous belly, her eyebrow raised with curiosity.

"You know what?" she said. "You scare me when you sit in your chair like that — I know you don't even see me; you're not aware of me. What am I supposed to do while you read the paper and make up letters to the editor or whatever you're doing? My god." She crossed the room toward him. "You're like some eighty-year-old senile man, snoring away after dinner."

He heard her, but he paid no attention; her tone and her words did not matter to him.

"Stop looking at my big fat stomach," she said. "It makes me uneasy. I wish I had my old figure back — god, how I will be so glad when this is over and I can wear some of my clothes again."

Did I see right? he asked himself. Did I see what's ahead for us, the vengeance waiting for us in another four months? Or is it just a guilt-ridden fear on our parts? Maybe there is no Miss Thackman, he thought. There will be no special school, no Cyclone fence, no old oak desk. None of it. Our little boy will run without falling, yell like the other kids, figure out how to put together his five-cent balsawood glider and then fly it — fly the hell out of it, all day long, until we have to drag him in for dinner.

We'll see, he thought. We'll have to wait and see.

Off in a corner of the living room, away from the other guests and noise, Bob Leghorn discussed topics of importance with his real estate broker Leo Runcible.

"What I feel," Leghorn said, holding his drink but not sipping it, "is that there is no cheap source of power here. No industry will move in because look at the electricity rates. They're prohibitive. And transportation in with their products to market is out of the question. Over that mountain. They'd have to level it."

Studying the younger man, Runcible said, "You're new here. Let me bring you in on something. Sure there's cheap power here." He pointed his finger at Leghorn. "Have you turned on a water tap at your house, yet? Have you noticed what comes out?"

"Sure," Leghorn said. "Good clean water."

"There's plenty of good clean water," Runcible said. "That's power, basic cheap power. The historic source of power for the entire civilized world, for centuries. Don't worry about power in this area."

Leghorn said, "Somebody told me you own the water company."

"This is true," Runcible said.

"How'd you ever happen to buy into a water company? Is it a paying proposition?"

Runcible said nothing.

"I suppose it pays in the summer," Leghorn said. "Not in the winter, when it rains. I think though you're mistaken when you regard water in terms of power. Of course, I don't know a hell of a lot about it directly, but I think because you own a water company you maybe tend to be biased. If water is to be a source of power it has to be used as a source of electrical power. Nobody uses water directly any more; that was in the old days when they had water wheels, like in the old water-powered mills." He laughed. "No, not unless somebody builds a dam, one of those hydroelectric plants out here. And they're not much likely to do that."

"Excuse me," Runcible said. He got to his feet and moved away; he joined another group, leaving Leghorn by himself.

"What is this, Leo?" a male guest asked, pointing to a black, plate-shaped metal object on the wall. "Not a French World War One helmet, is it?"

"No," Runcible said. Going over, he lifted the helmet down. "This is from the time of Oliver Cromwell," he said. "Don't you see the round head? Try it on." He handed it to the man, who placed it gingerly on his head. Guests gathered to comment.

"How much is it worth?" a woman guest asked.

"About two hundred bucks," Runcible said. "Not much."

A guest said, "Leo, why don't you sell it and put the dough into your water company?"

They all laughed, then, Runcible in particular. He grinned, stuck his hands in his pockets, nodded to them. "That's no joke," he said. But his goodhumored tone said that it was a joke, and a good one. "You know what I'm thinking of doing?" he said. "I'm thinking of offering a share of stock in the Carquinez Water Improvement Company, free, to everyone who buys a house from Runcible Realty."

"Better yet," a guest said. "Offer a house free to everyone who buys a share in the water company."

At that Runcible laughed so hard that he had to excuse himself; he left the living room and went into the kitchen.

There, he found his wife and Mrs. Leghorn.

Martha Leghorn, standing up, said to him, "Mr. Runcible, your wife was just telling me how you put all your money and property and everything you owned, and how you mortgaged yourself up to the hilt, to improve the water supply, here. She tells me you've gone into debt for years to come."

Runcible said, "How about a drink."

"No, thanks," Mrs. Leghorn said. "My husband is very strict. He doesn't like me to drink."

Turning to Janet, Runcible said, "You already have yours, I see." He watched her as she filled her glass from the great jug. "Be careful," he said, as she let the glass slip slightly; the colorless liquid spilled down from her wrist, onto the tabletop.

Janet said to him, her eyes shining, "Leo, if these people knew how great you are. How you saved them. Why don't they recognize it?" She gazed at him helplessly, barely able to hold onto her glass; it seemed to him as if she were about to pitch forward onto her face, and he took a step toward her. Mrs. Leghorn had re-seated herself at the table. She watched silently.

"That reminds me of a joke," Leo Runcible said, taking hold of his wife's hand and unfastening her fingers from the stem of her glass. He placed the glass on the table, far back from the edge. To Mrs. Leghorn he said, "I hope you don't find that your friends consider this too far to drive, Mrs. Leghorn. Your Bay Area friends."

"Some come out," Mrs. Leghorn said.

"For those who've never been out here before," Runcible said, "it must be quite an experience, our ocean and beaches and seafood and the Ridge. The wild animals. The unspoiled land."

"Yes," Mrs. Leghorn said. "They're usually quite impressed. It's really lovely out here. I was so pleased when my husband was transferred here from Hayward."

"The smog is a literal murderer," Runcible said. "In those overcrowded cities. Car exhausts and factory smoke. This is like a paradise, just on that account alone."

He fixed himself a fresh drink. His wife was still watching him with that moronic, witless look; he had become so used to it that it did not even bother him any more. At least she was still on her feet. Christmas time always cheered her up; it had always been a big day in her childhood, she had told him.

Raising his glass to Mrs. Leghorn, Runcible said, "Well, happy Chanukah."

"What is that?" she said.

"Didn't you know this is Chanukah? It falls on Christmas day this year for the first time in a century. The Jewish holiday."

"Oh, I see," she said. "Are you and your wife Jewish?"

"I am," Runcible said.

"Are there very many Jewish people in this area?" Mrs. Leghorn asked.

"No," Runcible said. "Most of the land belongs to the big dairy ranchers, and except for one or two of them they don't have a religion; all they have is a desire to keep taxes down and as little improvement in this area as is possible."

Pulling back a chair he seated himself across from her, with the idea of telling her about the ranchers. He intended to give her the full story. Not only was she not stewed, like most of the others, but she seemed intelligent and interested. And she was new to the area. He always gave new people the background; it was part of his job.

"Are these things so important?" she interrupted, almost at once. He had barely gotten started. "I mean, is this what people here take seriously? All this about school bonds and road improvement and—" She gestured. "Isn't there anything really significant going on?"

"Like what?" he said.

Mrs. Leghorn said, "Little theater groups, or a dance group? You told us this was a vital growing area; I thought there'd be something cultural. I mean, I'm stuck here all day long." She gazed at him and Janet with distress. "Doesn't anyone even play bridge up here?"

"Of course," Janet said, smiling. "And there's a creative dance group up at Point Reyes Station, just up the highway." Seating herself between him and Mrs. Leghorn, she began to ramble on; he excused himself and left the kitchen.

Going into the bathroom he put his glass down on the edge of the washbowl and then he relieved himself. Strange, he thought. That every few hours a man has to go and unbutton his pants and pour out a stream of waste fluid that has collected inside him. If you hadn't seen it you wouldn't believe it. He buttoned his pants back up, washed his hands, and, with his glass, left the bathroom.

Maybe that's all man is to God, he thought. What that stream is to me. No matter what we do — it isn't important.

He went into his study and shut the door. For a time he sat at his desk, smoking a Christmas cigar that someone had brought him. But then he noticed the half-finished letter still in the typewriter. It was to the bank at Petaluma requesting refinancing on his house. He had tried to get them on the phone with no luck. So here this letter was. He asked for a conference about it, at the very least. He told them candidly that he could not meet the present payments. The letter was dated December 12th, and he had not yet finished and sent it.

The bastards will say no, he said to himself. He got to his feet and moved away from the desk, so that he did not have to look at the letter. That's the trouble with living in the country. Everyone knows the state of your finances; you can't keep it secret. And there's nothing more destructive to credit, he thought, than having your finances an open book.

The god damn banks, he thought. When you get low or you're overdrawn or you try to swing a loan, they tell everyone. Within half an hour it's to all the big people in the area, everyone you're trying to do any business with. You go to meet a man about buying or selling some land, and he knows exactly how much you have to back you up. What kind of hand is that? he asked himself. How can you play from that kind of position? And then my god damn wife. On top of that.

While he was meditating about that, the door to the study opened. There stood Michael Wharton. "Merry Christmas, Leo," he said at once. "Am I bothering you? Janet said you were in here."

Not speaking directly to him, Runcible said, "What did she do, put all you guys on the guest list?"

"You shouldn't still be sore," Wharton said. "You can't be sore forever, can you?" He seemed nervous and embarrassed.

Runcible said, "Sure I can. I don't advertise in that crummy little newspaper and I take any sick animal I have up to Point Reyes, and if there was another school I'd send my son there."

After a pause Wharton said self-consciously, "This is a good time of year to give up grudges."

"Christmas, shmishmas," Runcible said. "Listen, Christmas is a venture by a bunch of fink shopkeepers to do more business."

Wharton said, "Somebody told me you sold all that land you had, on the Ridge."

"That's right," Runcible said.

"Wasn't that what you were holding to sub-divide later on?" He shrugged.

Wharton said, "How much did it cost?"

"Did what cost?"

"Everything. Buying the water company. Fixing it up."

"Who knows," Runcible said.

"And you say Christmas, shmishmas," Wharton said.

"Sure I do," Runcible said. "Listen, He was a good Jewish boy but He didn't know when to quit." He didn't know when the quitting was best, he said to himself. He went on too long, and look where it got Him. "Listen," he said, "do you think God gives a shit about us and what happens to us?"

Wharton said, "Well, my own personal opinion is that religion is a past issue. A dead issue."

"Just what I'd expect from a goy," Runcible said. "No faith. You ought to read that new Herman Wouk book about what God is to him. It would do you good. Here." Going to the bookcase he reached up and took the heavy volume down. "I'm not finished with it," he said, taking out his marker. "But you need it more than I do. If you're going to mold the minds of youth, you ought to have some principles. Something to live by." He held the book out to Wharton, until at last the grammar school teacher accepted it.

"Did any of the big ranchers ever come in?" Wharton said.

"Sure."

"Who?"

With reluctance, he said, "Oh, I don't know. Some. I forget."

There was silence.

"I wonder," Wharton said finally, "what it would be like for you, now. If they had come in."

"Listen," Runcible said. "Who needs them?"

"You knew they wouldn't come in," Wharton said. "From the start. You know how their minds work; all they care about is keeping taxes down, saving a little money."

"They're good people," Runcible said.

"They could have underwritten the cost of the water company," Wharton said, "and never even missed it. Never even have known."

"Man proposes," Runcible said. "God disposes."

"Is there anything I can do?" Wharton said awkwardly.

"You have thirty-five thousand in cash?"

"No."

"Merry Christmas," Runcible said.

Wharton said, "You did a really great thing, rebuilding the water supply. Even if that business about the chupper jaw is ninety percent the superstition of rustic back-country farm people, there's still all those virus infections and colds that—"

"Listen," Runcible said. "If you don't have the money, go home. Will you? Okay?"

Wharton lingered. "Strange," he said. "You'd put everything you have into that water company; you'd bankrupt yourself, lose all your land and assets for the good of the community — and yet, after doing a thing like that you'd still carry on your grudge against me and Sheriff Christen and Faulk and god knows who else. You must not be speaking to half the people in this community. I can't make you out, Leo."

"I'm a man of principle," Runcible said. He walked to the door of the study and opened it. "And one of my principles is that I only invite people I like to my house." As long as it is my house, he thought to himself. As long as I can keep it mine. After that, you can all come in. "Wait until the Petaluma Bank takes this place," he said. "Then you guys can come over and sit down on the sofa all you want. Meanwhile," he said, ushering Wharton out of his study, "as Sam Goldwyn says, 'Include me out.'"

Seeing the two of them, Janet came forward. "I knew you two would get together," she said, smiling at her husband.

Runcible said, "Pour this person a glass of cooking sherry and then send him home." He added, "A small glass."

Her expression showed that she thought he was kidding; that it was a friendly joke.

"I mean it," he said to her.

Now she saw that he did mean it. Her smile dwindled away; she darted a glance of confusion at Wharton, then back at her husband.

"I'm going," Wharton said. "Good night, Janet. Leo."

Runcible said nothing. Presently Wharton made his way off, among the people; the front door opened and shut, and he had gone.

"Anybody else on your guest list?" Runcible said. "What about Walt Dombrosio?"

Faltering, she said, "No, of course not. I didn't invite him, Leo. I mean Wharton. Or Dombrosio."

"Okay," he said. He walked back to where Bob Leghorn sat; he took a seat opposite him and said, "How's it going, Leghorn?"

"Fine, thanks," Leghorn said.

Leaning back, making himself comfortable, Leo Runcible said, "Let me know if there's anything I can do for you." He pointed to the table of hors d'oeuvres over in the corner, the cheese and ham and chicken and dip, the various kinds of crackers. "Don't forget to pitch in," he said. "Make yourself at home. Don't hold back."

And, getting up himself, he walked over to see what he would like. At the hors d'oeuvres table he began helping himself to some of everything. It was his own house, and he made himself at home; he followed his own advice and did not hold back.